DRAYKON

THE DRAYKON SERIES: 1

CHARLOTTE E. ENGLISH

PROLOGUE

On one cool afternoon when the rain fell in gentle, glittering droplets and the ground underfoot was spongy with moisture, nine-year-old Llandry Sanfaer walked with her mother beneath the trees far to the south of the Glinnery forests. They were gathering mushrooms, diminutive little fungi with stems fat with juice and caps painted with colour. Llandry crowed with delight each time she found a new mushroom ring, picking the fattest or the most colourful specimens with nimble fingers. Their baskets were growing heavy with gathered produce when Ynara began to speak of returning home.

'Not yet, Mamma, just a little bit longer!' Llandry loved these excursions, loved the hours they spent in close companionship, just her and Mamma. She gazed up into her mother's face with her most hopeful smile, and of course Mamma relented.

'All right, little love, but don't pick too many more mushrooms, or we'll never be able to carry them home.' Llandry promised and was off once more, her small form a whirlwind of activity.

Then a faint melody reached her ears and she came to an abrupt stop, her keen eyes searching the mossy slopes for the source.

'Ma, what's that sound?'

'What sound, love?' Llandry looked up to find nothing but incomprehension in Mamma's face. She frowned and dismissed

1

the thought, dancing onward once more.

There; again, a hint of music. Not a sound at all, in fact, more of a feeling of spiralling harmony, drawing her onward through the vast, pale trunks dotted like serene guardians over the meadow. In the shade of a particularly broad-capped glissenwol tree was a glade encircled by tall, variegated fungi. The mosses that carpeted the circle of ground were not of the customary colour. Instead of the deep blue that matched the eventide sky, these were lavender touched with green. Golden sunlight drenched the clearing, bright and glittering in spite of the glissenwol cap that rose above. And the drifting motes of light that filled the air of Glinnery were thickly clustered here, twinkling far more brightly than their paler cousins, sparking with energy and laced with colour. Llandry stood, mesmerised by this scene. She was distantly aware of her mother's voice calling her name, but she was unable to answer.

The thin sound of an animal in distress reached her sensitive ears. Something moved in the centre of the glittering circle: she saw a flash of grey, heard the faint wail of unhappiness repeated.

Mamma had caught up with her. Llandry was aware of her footsteps approaching, then halting a short distance behind her. She could imagine her mother's reaction to this place; she must be filled with wonder and delight, just as Llandry had been. She was surprised, then, to hear a note of horror creep into Ynara's voice as she called.

'Llandry! Llandry, stop there. Don't move, love.' The footsteps approached, and Mamma's arms closed around her. To her dismay and confusion, she was lifted and carried backwards.

'No! Mamma, there's an animal, don't you hear it? It's hurt.' The movements of the mysterious creature had ceased, but now Llandry saw it again: a small body, long and thin, with sleek, pale grey fur. She struggled out of her mother's arms and ran forward.

When she stepped into the circle, she felt the golden light bathing her skin as if it was a physical thing, like water. The effect was beautiful, soothing and warm, but not wholly pleasant, for a feeling of tension hung heavy in the air and Llandry's skin prickled with unease. For a moment she forgot about the sleek-furred creature, but another squeak of distress drew her eyes downward into the centre of the strange lavender-hued moss.

The animal stood on short, shaking legs, its pointed face

lifted to the winds as it keened in despair. It was so small, so obviously feeble, that Llandry quickly realised it must be a baby. A baby without its mother. She picked it up, carefully cradling it against her chest.

She turned to show it to Mamma, but Mamma was gone, hidden behind a curtain of light that had fallen between her and the familiar glissenwol forests of home. It was like a wall of rain, cold and shimmering pale; she could see nothing beyond it.

'Mamma?' Fear stole her voice and the word emerged as a whisper. She screamed her mother's name and heard an answering call, thin and distant as if Ynara stood on a hilltop far away.

Llandry ran towards the curtain and tried to pass, but it was like walking through treacle; a strong pressure beat upon her limbs and her face, threatening to smother her. She fell back, sobbing.

Then the curtain rippled and pulsed, as if struggling against something. Ynara broke through the wall, her face pale and her eyes sparking with anger and fear. She picked Llandry up and marched back through. The sensation of suffocation was the same as before, and it grew worse as Ynara bore forward with Llandry in her arms. The pressure intensified until Llandry thought she must explode like rotten fruit. Then they were through the curtain. All of the strange sensations, good and bad, faded and Llandry was herself again.

Ynara did not stop. She marched onward without looking back. Llandry could feel her mother's body shaking; her arms were trembling so badly that Llandry feared she would drop her. She pressed her face against her mother's and kissed her cheek.

'Ma,' she whispered. 'I'm sorry.'

'You're safe. That's all that matters.'

'What was that place?'

'The Upper Realm.'

'What's that?'

Ynara sighed and stopped at last, easing Llandry down to the floor. She frowned in puzzlement at the little soft-furred body Llandry still held in her arms, quiet now and questing through Llandry's clothing for food.

'It's called the Dreamlands, sometimes, because it's like a dream, isn't it? It's another place, far from here, beyond the Seven Realms that make up our world. Sometimes a gate is opened and you can pass through. What we saw was a gate. The Upper Realm is beautiful beyond belief, love, but you must remember that it is dangerous.'

Llandry remembered the feelings she'd experienced as she stood in that glittering glade; the way the light had caressed her skin and the dancing motes clustered around her as if she was a friend. 'How can it be dangerous, Mamma?'

'There are dangers everywhere, love, and the Upper Realm is no different. But beyond that, there is something else. It is too beautiful a place, perhaps, too enticing; people go there, from time to time, but they very rarely return. Now, promise me you will not do such a thing again. Promise me, Llandry.' Mamma dropped to her knees to bring her face level with Llandry's. Her eyes were serious, and Llandry sensed renewed fear in the way her mother clasped her close.

'I promise, Ma.'

'Good. Now, who is your new friend?'

The creature had begun to shiver. Llandry showed it to her Mamma, who smiled in spite of herself.

'Gracious. It's an orting, love. It must have come through the gate.' She stroked the orting's round black nose and it shivered anew, this time with apparent delight.

'May I keep it?'

'We'll see. Now, are you ready to fly?'

Llandry unfurled her growing wings and flexed them. At nine, she was big enough and strong enough to fly for a few miles at a time. She smiled at her mother and nodded.

'Time to go home, then; Papa will be worried about us by now.' Mamma was wearing a coloured sash around her waist, as she often did; she removed it, and wrapped it around Llandry's torso, fashioning a sling. She smiled fondly at Llandry.

'I used to carry you this way, when you were small.' She took the orting from Llandry's arms and placed it gently inside the sling, securing it with deft movements.

'Now you may carry him home. He won't fall.'

Papa was not at home when they arrived, but his measured step was soon heard climbing the stair that wound around the trunk of the lofty Sanfaer home. He patted Llandry's hair as he passed, and she shot up in excitement and ran after him.

'Papa, you must come and meet Sigwide!'

'Oh? School friend?'

Her face darkened at the word 'school'. 'No, Pa. He's my new pet. Look!'

The orting had been lovingly installed in his own box, padded with the best blankets from Llandry's bed. He had gone to sleep with his head under the thickest of them, his stubby tail twitching as he dreamed. Aysun Sanfaer tilted his head curiously, trying to get a look at the creature.

'Sigwide is what you've called it?'

'Yes. I chose it myself.'

'What is it?'

'Ma said it's an orting.'

He said nothing at all in response. Llandry looked up, puzzled. His face was set and his eyes glittered with some fierce emotion that looked like anger. Ynara came back into the room at that moment and went straight to her husband.

'Aysun, it's not as bad as—'

'It's an *orting*?'

'Yes—'

'Summoned?'

'No. Wild.'

Mamma drew her husband away and lowered her voice, and the conversation passed beyond Llandry's hearing. She sensed her father's anger, feeling his eyes on her as her mother spoke. She sat down next to Sigwide's box, confused and a little afraid. Her parents' voices grew louder, and she overheard snippets of conversation.

'...as stubborn as your father.' That was Mamma.

'...nothing like my father!' Papa sounded quite upset, and Llandry began to feel sick.

'The similarity is obvious. You take an idea, no matter how irrational, and refuse to be moved.'

'Because my father couldn't accept you, you persist in assuming—'

'This isn't about me! This creature is harmless and it will be good for Llan to have a companion. Why can't you see that?'

'If she wants a companion we will get her a pet. Something safer.'

Mamma snorted at that and walked away a few steps. When she turned back to Pa, she spoke too quietly for Llandry to hear any more. Llandry could only sit near Sigwide's box, crouched and miserable, and wait.

At length her parents' conversation was over. Papa approached and knelt down before her with a sigh.

'Llandry. Your mother's already received a promise from you, but I need you to promise me as well. If you ever see anything like that again, you must keep away from it. Understand?'

He was stern but no longer furious. Llandry was so relieved she would have promised anything at all. She nodded her head solemnly.

'I need you to understand why, Llandry. It's dangerous. You could be drawn away from us, and you wouldn't be able to come back very easily. We might not be able to find you. And the creatures you would meet there are not all as harmless as this one.' He frowned at the tiny grey body curled up in the box. Llandry bit her trembling lip, suddenly anxious.

'Papa! I may keep him, mayn't I?'

'I would rather you didn't, but yes. He must be trained, though. I'll get a summoner to come to the house tomorrow.'

Llandry beamed, expressing her gratitude with an enveloping hug. He patted her head a little awkwardly, then swung her up onto his wingless back.

'Let the little beast sleep.'

1

The stone polishing machine rattled its last and the barrel stopped spinning, its cycle complete. Opening it up, Llandry slipped a deft hand inside and extracted a few of the gems. They lay in the palm of her hand, glittering darkly indigo under the light-globes that hovered over her head. Smooth and perfect, they were quite ready for use.

She never cut the istore stones. It seemed wrong, somehow, to break these perfect jewels into pieces, so she merely gave them a day or two in the polisher to bring up the brilliancy of the surface. It was a pleasing test of her ingenuity as a jeweller to find ways to set them as they were.

She selected one of the smaller pieces, tucking the rest away in the top drawer of her work table. A setting was already prepared for this one, a large, handsome ring designed for a man to wear. Wrought from silver, her favourite metal, she had lightly engraved it with a pattern of tiny stars. This motif echoed the tiny points of light that winked in the depths of the stone.

In fact, Llandry had named it for the stars. She had discovered the gem by accident, walking one day under the glissenwol trees with Sigwide darting ahead. Thoughts lost in daydreams, she had drifted away from their usual route. Her reverie had been suddenly interrupted by the sensation of falling as she tumbled down a hole hidden beneath the bracken. The hard earthen walls of the underground grotto sparkled ferociously in the thin light beaming down from above. The gems fell easily into her hands when she touched them, shining like shards of night fallen from the skies. She had taken to calling them "istore", after the Old Glinnish word for star.

Not that she was particularly familiar with the night sky. The permanent sun of the Dayland Realms hid the stars from her sight, and the moon only occasionally appeared as a pale and feeble disc in the heavens. Therein lay the nature of her fascination, perhaps. Llandry picked up her lapidary tools and bent over the ring, carefully and skilfully working the gem into its setting. Intent on her task, she barely noticed the faint scratching of Sigwide's feet on the wooden floor as he wandered in. She distantly sensed an air of speculation about him as he paused before the table, haunches bunched to jump. But no: he knew better than to disturb her when she was working. He pattered off again, finding the blanketed basket she left him on the other side of the room.

'Just a few more minutes, Siggy,' she murmured without looking up. He grumbled in reply, sending her a plaintive series of impressions: hunger, emptiness, imminent starvation. She stifled a laugh.

'In theory, Sig, you are a wild animal. A feral beast, part of brutal, brilliant nature. You could go forth and forage for your own food. In theory.'

Sigwide ignored her. His claws scrabbled on the wicker as he turned in his basket, curling up with an offended air.

'All right, fine. Food.' She put down her tools and wrapped up the ring and the precious gem in soft cloth, unwilling to leave them lying abandoned on the table. Sigwide jumped joyfully out of his basket and wove his thin grey body around her feet, beating her to the door. She stepped over him with the nimbleness of long practice, chuckling.

Sigwide's favourite food was a complex, carefully balanced mixture of dried bilberries, fresh rosehips, assorted nuts and a scattering of pungent mushrooms. He was completely spoiled, dining like a king on this rather expensive mixture every day, but she didn't begrudge him his luxuries. He had been her faithful companion — her only reliable friend, other than her parents — for the last eleven years. He ought to be slowing down now that age was catching up with him, but so far he had never lost his inexhaustible energy.

Llandry leaned against the kitchen table, watching him eat. She tried to keep her thoughts focused on Sigwide, but as usual her mind betrayed her. Tendrils of nerves snaked through her belly and began to grip, clutching hard. She hadn't wanted to stop working because as long as she was fully occupied, she was safe from apprehension. Now, though, her treacherous thoughts turned to tomorrow. *Tomorrow.*

It had been her mother's idea to take the istore jewellery to the market. Ynara thought it would be popular. Doubtless she was right; the istore never failed to interest and attract those who saw it. Short of the money to cover the rent on her small, but pleasant tree, Llandry had allowed herself to be persuaded about the market; after all, it was preferable to having to ask her parents for help.

She had begun to regret it immediately. She was to have her own stall at the next Darklands market, which was held every full moon in Glour. It was a popular event attracting thousands of shoppers, which of course was why it was so suitable a venue for her glorious new jewellery. That fact also made it a prospect of pure terror for Llandry. Thousands of people pushing and shoving and jostling each other, staring at her jewellery, her stall, her face. She would have to talk to some of them. Talk, comfortably and persuasively, to a succession of complete strangers. The only saving grace about this hideous prospect was the opportunity to stand for a while under the stars and the light of the full moon. It was not nearly enough to balance out her fear.

Feeling the tell-tale tingling sensation beginning to creep up her arms, Llandry tried to pull back her thoughts. She walked about the room briskly, swinging her arms. It was no use. Within minutes her fingers had cramped and curled with tension and her whole body was tingling uncomfortably. Soon afterwards she began to shake uncontrollably, hyperventilating, growing dizzy and faint. She sat down with her head between her knees, trying to breathe deeply. Sigwide abandoned his repast and trotted over to her, thrusting his nose against her legs.

'I'll b-be fine, Sig. Just... give me a moment.' At length the dizziness faded and her shaking eased. She stood up carefully, stretched and shook her befogged head. Her face was wet with tears; these attacks always left her feeling intolerably shamed and humbled. She patted her face dry on her sleeve, then picked up

Sigwide. It comforted her to have him close for a time afterwards, the warmth of his little body soothing the vestiges of her fear.

'Why did I agree to this, Siggy?' She sighed. Hidden in her top kitchen cupboard rested a bottle of dark brown glass, containing a rather repulsive mixture her mother had purchased from one of Glinnery's foremost herbalists. It tasted revolting, but it was effective. She took a small measure of the stuff, welcoming the feeling of lassitude that gradually swept over her afterwards. She would just have to keep herself dosed up on it until the market was over.

Furthermore, her mother had offered to accompany her. Llandry had refused, wanting to prove — to herself, more than anyone else — that she could manage it alone. Now she felt differently. Dosed or not, she knew she would be suffering more of these attacks on the morrow. She was going to need her mother's help. She slid her feet into her boots, lacing them up tightly, and placed Sigwide into the carry-case she slung over her hip. Locking her tree, she launched herself into the air, letting her strong wings carry her in the direction of her parents' residence.

'Oh, love. It's nothing to be ashamed of.' Llandry stood in the circle of her mother's arms, inhaling her familiar, comforting scent. Ynara held her for some time, rocking her gently the way she had done since her daughter was a small girl. Then she seated her firmly at the table and plied her with food. Somehow her mamma always seemed to have Llandry's favourites on hand: fragrant white alberry tea with a pinch of freyshur spice, a bowl of creamed mushroom soup and a plate of tiny berry cakes appeared before Llandry in quick succession. She didn't feel inclined to eat, but she forced down a few spoonfuls of the soup, unwilling to disappoint her mother. As always, the food began to make her feel better and she ate with a little more enthusiasm.

Ynara sat down opposite her and took a cake, breaking it into small pieces and eating them elegantly with her fingers. She watched Llandry affectionately, her expression soft. 'You know, Pa would come as well, if we asked him.'

Llandry shook her head. 'Bad enough that I have to drag you

along, Ma. Pa's busy.' Pa, an engineer and inventor from Irbel, was always busy. He was remarkably good at his job and was high up in Glinnery's well-regulated guild of Irbellian expatriate engineers. Llandry's parents had always lived comfortably, even after Ynara had given up her position as an Enchanter to join the somewhat less well-paid Council of Elders.

Ynara wrinkled her delicate nose and smiled. Even such an inelegant gesture did nothing to dampen her remarkable beauty. She did very little to encourage it: her tumbling black hair was often a little disordered, and she often wandered absent-mindedly about in clothes dotted with the stains left by her regular adventures in cooking. None of it mattered a bit. Llandry often felt something of a crow beside her magnetic mother, though this was a feeling she ruthlessly stifled whenever it threatened to emerge.

'Just you and I, then, love. It'll be like the old days. Do you remember when we used to visit the Darklands Market when you were a child?'

Of course Llandry remembered. Shy even then, the bustling market had unnerved her, but she had clung to her mother's hand and felt reassured. Ynara used to go regularly in search of some of the rarer ingredients she used to create her edible delicacies. There were several fruits, grasses and mushrooms that would only grow under the endless night of the Darklands, and all of them were abundantly available at the Darklands Market. Mamma would buy new gems for Llandry's collection each time they went, and return home laden with packets of unidentifiable objects for Aysun. Llandry had always enjoyed this quality time alone with her mother. She smiled, now, trying to weld that idea into her mind in place of her extreme trepidation.

'Thanks, Ma,' she said at last. 'I'd better go and finish up that ring. It's the last piece for tomorrow.'

Ynara kissed her cheek and gave her a brief hug. 'I'll be with you early in the morning, love. I'll bring breakfast.'

Llandry made herself smile again and waved, trying to suppress the forlorn feeling she always suffered whenever she flew away from her mother's house.

2

Her carriage may be the best that money could buy, but Lady Evastany Glostrum was still lamentably cold. The chill seeped through the plush upholstery inside the vehicle, nimbly evaded the best attempts of the fitted glass windows to keep it out, and assaulted Eva's pale and shrinking flesh in spite of her heavy fur wrap. It was really too detestably cold to step beyond the door of her handsome and thoroughly comfortable house, but today's errand was too important to be missed. She was on her way to see her tailor.

Naturally she had wardrobes full of delightfully sumptuous gowns, but this was different. Something of an emergency, in fact. In a week she was to give a ball at her own house, at which she would be announcing her engagement. Such a momentous event in Glour society called for very careful treatment indeed. Eva knew she would be subjected to the closest scrutiny. The gossips and the reporters would be there in approximately equal measures, ready to tear apart every aspect of her appearance, her house, her entertaining. Most of all, they would be examining her behaviour towards her fiance. The speculation had been running high for weeks — would the elusive Lady Glostrum finally fall to matrimony? — and she had allowed for a rumour to leak out about the purpose of the ball. It was imperative that she was looking at her best.

That being the case, it was of course inevitable that the gown she had had made for the day had been ruined. One of her maids had managed to stain it with furniture polish while cleaning Eva's dressing room. She hadn't scolded the girl — the maid had been devastated enough — but nonetheless this created an unwelcome problem. As High Summoner, Eva was in the middle of interviewing candidates for two high-ranked positions within the Summoner organisation. She didn't really have the time for any more complications.

Her carriage came to a stop and Eva drew back the curtain that covered the freezing glass window. Her coachman opened the door for her and she stepped out with a smile, pulling her wrap as close around her shoulders as possible. She stepped quickly into the tailor's shop, shuddering with cold. Baynson was in the back, but he came running quickly enough when she rang the bell.

'Good morning, Mr. Baynson. I'm afraid there's been a small incident regarding the gown I purchased last week, and I'll be needing another. Before the ball.' She didn't smile. Baynson wasn't the type to appreciate it. He regarded her with an air of grave disapproval as she delivered this piece of bad news, his thin eyebrows careening up his face towards his nearly bald head.

'You'll forgive my saying so, your ladyship, but summoner or not, you ought to keep them animals away from your wardrobe. Ten to one something'd happen to your finery sooner or later.'

'Sage advice, Mr. Baynson, but in this case the culprit was one of my maids. Not her fault; these things do happen. Naturally I will pay you a considerable bonus if you are able to make me a replacement in time.'

Baynson tutted and tossed his head, muttering unflattering observations under his breath. Eva waited. The man was rude, uncouth and unpleasant but he was the best tailor in Glour City.

'I'll get it done,' he conceded at last. 'It'll take a lot extra, though. I'll have to pull my girls off a couple of other orders.'

'Fine.' Eva untied her purse from her waist and opened it. She had to count quite a large number of coins into Bayson's hands before he was satisfied, but this was to be expected with him.

'Same as before, I take it?'

She thought for a moment. 'Yes, but perhaps you could drop the neckline just a little. On the last one it was practically demure.'

Baynson tutted some more. 'Don't want to make a spectacle of yourself, your ladyship. A low neckline's the province of a woman who's not fit for polite company.'

Eva laughed. 'On the contrary, making a spectacle of myself is precisely my intention. I'm no debutante at her first season. On me, "demure" would look unforgivably coy.'

Baynson grunted. 'Reckon you could get away with it, praps,' he conceded, eyeing her figure in a manner devoid of all but dry professional interest.

'I'm certain of it. If there is an advantage to being barely shy of forty, it is that I am a mature woman quite able to carry off a hint or two of the provocative. And I'm quite determined to, while I still have the figure for it.'

'Forty, ma'am? You don't look a day over thirty-two.'

'That is my official age, Mr. Baynson, naturally, but I trust you not to give me away.'

Baynson flicked his hands at her in a shooing gesture. 'Very well, get thee gone. I've a deal of work to do. Come back in four days. It'll be ready.'

Eva smiled warmly. 'Thank you, Mr. Baynson. I can always rely on you.'

Later, Eva sat dejectedly in the large wing-back chair in her office, her feet tucked under her skirts and her hands thrust into her shawl. Was it *completely* impossible to keep warm in this cursed chill? Interviewing was one of her least favourite duties: she had gone through six applicants in the last three hours and none of them had been suitable. She now awaited the seventh, wondering whether she could get away with pulling her chair a little closer to the heating pipes.

A knock came at the door before she could put this plan into action, and her seventh interviewee appeared. This one was a woman she didn't recognise, apparently a little older than Eva herself. She wore plain, unaffected clothing and an air of cool capability that seemed promising. The previous six had been mostly men, mostly young, and mostly cocky. They had also mostly tried to flirt with her. Eva looked on this with the stern eye of decided disapproval. There was no place for flirtation when she was at work.

14

'Oona Temble,' the woman introduced herself. 'I'm from the Summoner Guild in Orstwych.' She didn't curtsey, or even bow: instead she approached the desk and offered Eva her hand. Eva shook it. It may have been a departure from protocol, but she rather liked Oona's straightforward manner.

'Sit down, Ms. Temble,' Eva said. 'Thank you for coming all this way to talk to me. I'd like to be able to offer you some cayluch, but my last interviewee seems to have been something of an addict.' She tapped the cold cayluch pot sitting on her desk, which rang emptily.

'That's quite all right, Lady Glostrum. I'm not thirsty.' Oona sat down in the chair Eva indicated. Her hair was short, rather against the prevailing fashions, and threaded with grey. The unpretentious style suited her strong face.

'You'll be aware that the position is a new creation. When new summoners come out of the Academy, they're still woefully ill-informed about the reality of a summoner's work. We're in desperate need of someone to take them in hand and give them a bit more practical education in animal acquisition and training. I'm looking for somebody to head up this proposed department.'

Oona nodded. 'Your notion was it, Lady Glostrum?'

'Yes, I believe it was.'

Oona raised her brows sceptically. 'I see.'

'Does that surprise you, Ms. Temble?'

'Somewhat,' said Oona blandly. 'You don't strike a person as made for practical measures, if you'll forgive my mentioning it.'

'Excellent. Plain-speaking is exactly what I need for this role.'

Oona lifted her brows again.

'Ah, you expected to find a pampered and temperamental noblewoman, good for nothing but the ornamental and essentially incapable of useful activity. Well, that's understandable if you read the papers. Let's just agree that appearances can be deceiving and leave it at that, hm?' She stood up, smiling down at Oona's eminently capable face wreathed in an expression of mild surprise. 'I'd like you to begin in two days, Ms. Temble. Your first task will be to choose your department members. I've budgeted for up to five to begin with. You'll inform me if that's insufficient.'

Oona pulled herself together. 'Thank you, Lady Glostrum. I'd best make my preparations.' She smiled then, unexpectedly.

'I've a feeling it may be interesting working with you.'

Eva chuckled. 'Let's hope so, indeed.'

Eva had a desk at home as well. She had resisted getting one for a long time after her appointment to the role of High Summoner, preferring to keep her professional and private lives separate. But at last she had capitulated. She was too often obliged to carry paperwork home with her, and she needed somewhere to keep it. At least she could keep her study as warm as she liked.

Her agenda was becoming complicated. Her working hours for the next few days would be occupied with introducing Oona to her new role and setting up the department. She anticipated some extra hours at the Summoners' Hall, a prospect which sank her spirits. No power in the Darklands could keep that place even remotely warm.

On top of that, there were still preparations outstanding for the ball. Fortunately the Darklands Market was scheduled for the morrow. Eva knew she could send servants to do her shopping for her, and certainly she would take some of them along as her assistants. She liked to visit herself, though. The Market always had an air of jovial confusion which delighted her, and its sheer variety of wares was no less enthralling. She planned to go in search of some rare curios and delicacies for the ball. She wondered, briefly, whether to take her fiance with her, but she decided against it. There was more than enough speculation circulating already.

Eva worked until her fingers grew cramped from holding her pen and her eyes refused to focus. At last she retired to bed. As she sank gratefully under her blankets, appreciating the warmth of the stone hot water bottles that warmed the layers, it occurred to her that she would not have this space to herself for much longer. In a little over a moon, she would be bound to share her free time, her personal space and her body with one man for the rest of her life. As if in defiance of this thought, Eva positioned herself in the middle of the bed and stretched her limbs out as far as they would go. She smiled. At least she could enjoy the vestiges of her freedom in the meantime.

3

Llandry stood on the edge of the Darklands Market, watching the surging crowds of Daylanders and Darklanders who gathered to admire and purchase its myriad wares. Held on the southern edge of Glour, its position within the Seven Realms was nearly central, and it attracted visitors from most of the realms. She saw many Glour citizens browsing the stalls, dressed in full gowns or tailored coats, their hair typically dark brown or black. Many small, slender Glinnish folk were present, honey-skinned and winged like herself. She saw a group of Orstwych Sorcerers, their draping robes painted in every imaginable colour. Nimdrens filled the air with their musical tongue, their chatter mingling oddly with the precise, clipped speech of Irbellian shoppers. Llandry regarded them all uneasily, hiding herself within the folds of her dark blue cloak.

Every single one of these people represented a threat. She knew that if any of them spoke to her, she would freeze and stammer, unable to string sentences together under the pressure of their expectant gaze. And yet, she was here as a vendor. It was her job to be communicative.

How she wished she had her mother's easy way with strangers. Nothing ever fazed Mamma. She had all the confidence that Llandry had never known; she conducted herself in company with a combination of easy friendliness and quiet, firm dignity that enchanted people. Llandry loved her with a

17

fierce pride and loyalty, but she could not help suffering envy. How she wished she could learn that skill. As it was, she had reached the age of twenty without developing so much as a shred of it.

She gathered her courage and stepped into the throng. Threading her way carefully through the crowds, she clutched her cloak close to herself as if it could protect her from their glances, their curiosity, their words. Her stall was near the outer edge of the market — she had chosen a location near to the relatively open spaces of the Glour woodlands, in case she should feel the need to escape. Her lips quirked involuntarily at the thought. As if she should feel the need? It would be a miracle if she survived more than an hour of this nightmarish experience without disintegrating.

The market was always held during the natural night hours, and the moon shone full overhead. But the skies held a scattering of thick clouds, stunting the progress of the moon's gentle light. To correct this, the market organisers had set floating light-globes drifting low overhead, illuminating the stalls with a cool white glow. The effect was gentle to Llandry's eyes, just sufficient to see by; but she noticed that many of the Darklanders wore spectacles with dark lenses in them, as if the light conditions hurt their eyes. She'd kept the lights on her own stall to a minimum in response. As a result, she could barely see the expression of anxiety on her mother's face as she stood guarding the stall.

'Mamma? Is something wrong?'

'Goodness, no. No, love, nothing's wrong. I was wondering if *you* are all right.' She smiled, but Llandry could still see the shadow of concern in her face. She sighed inwardly. If her social inadequacies were a source of pain to her, they were a still greater source of anxiety to her parents. The thought added guilt to Llandry's troubled mixture of feelings about herself. She hid it behind a smile and hugged Ynara.

'It's kind of you, Mamma, but I'm really all right. I have to learn, don't I?'

Ynara shrugged slightly, bending to assist as Llandry began to unpack her boxes. They worked quickly, and soon her table was covered with Llandry's jewellery. Gems in rich colours sparkled and winked in the light, polished metals gleaming with a cooler sheen. The best went in the centre, her prize pieces:

pendants, rings and circlets of pale silver set with her precious istore stones. They seemed to swallow the silvery light and throw it back out, gleaming pale and twinkling under the moonlight. Truly they displayed to their best under the night time conditions.

As a new vendor, Llandry had expected — nay, hoped — to go largely unnoticed at her first market. To her extreme surprise (and terror) she soon found that her wares were attracting considerable attention. Most of those who passed her stall stopped to admire her work, and many bought. They exclaimed over the richness of the colours, the intricacy of her metalwork, and most of all they pored over the istore stones.

'I've never seen anything like this before. Where did it come from?'

'By the Lowers, there's a sight. Like night itself caught in the metal. Remarkable.'

'What's this dark one, the one with the silvery sheen? What's it called? Istore? Never heard of it! Where does it come from?'

Llandry wanted desperately to answer all of these questions, but when she tried her lips trembled and she felt a constriction in her throat. It was all she could do to force a few words out. She was frowned at, less in irritation than in puzzlement at her odd silence. Words circled dizzyingly through her thoughts, words she would never be able to articulate. She hovered on the edge of panic, only the soothing warmth of her tonic keeping her largely under her own control. *This was a very bad idea. Why did I allow myself to be persuaded?*

Still, those whose questions went unanswered still bought, and Ynara's conversation satisfied the more persistent ones. The moon still shone high in the sky when Llandry's wares were almost gone. And still a stream of market-goers visited her stall, asking about the stones they'd seen their friends wearing. The word *istore* was repeated, over and over. Llandry's head swam. She brought more and more pieces out of her boxes until they were almost empty, and at last she found herself with only one of the istore items left: a silver ring set with a large oval of the dark, beautiful gem.

There was a little bustle as she brought it out, a stirring and a muttering among the crowds around her table. She looked up to find a tall, richly dressed woman in front of her, a native of Glour judging by her pale hair and dark blue, slanting eyes. Her clothes, her bearing, her manner all revealed her to be of considerable wealth and probably of high standing. Llandry inclined her head and the woman returned the gesture, smiling.

'Elder Sanfaer. I may have expected to see you in front of a stall, but not, I confess, behind one.' Llandry stiffened, but the woman's face betrayed no malice. Rather, she seemed amused. Ynara laughed, taking no offence at all.

'Lady Glostrum, what a pleasure. I am assisting my daughter.'

The lady's gaze flicked back to Llandry, studying her quite intently. 'So this is Llandry. You've spoken so highly of her.'

'Never highly enough, I assure you.'

'I've been hearing the buzz about a certain night-coloured gem. Your work, is it, Miss Sanfaer?' She pierced Llandry with a direct, uncompromising gaze. There was no getting out of giving a response.

'Yes, Lady Glostrum.'

Is that the best you can do? Pathetic.

'Very, very impressive. I don't say that merely because I know your mother.'

Llandry swallowed, trying to dislodge the lump that occupied her throat. 'Thank you.'

'Tell me about... this one.' She reached out a slender hand and picked up the istore ring, the very last one. Llandry sensed a renewed tension in the crowds around her as they watched her movements, listening for the response.

Don't panic; just talk to her. Llandry focused on Lady Glostrum's face, pleasant enough in expression and bare of judgement.

'Istore. I mean, that's what I call it. The stone.'

'I see. I have never seen it before, and I am quite an experienced collector of jewels. Who do you buy it from?'

'I — I don't buy it. I collect it myself, from — from —'

'Oh? Is it local?'

Llandry nodded. 'There is a cave, not far from — near to where I live. It's in the walls.'

Lady Glostrum nodded thoughtfully. 'If I were you, I would keep the location quite a secret, Llandry. I think this will prove to be very valuable.' She opened the elegant reticule she wore on her wrist and withdrew a handful of coins. Handing them to Llandry, she turned to the admiration of her new ring, sliding it onto one of her long white fingers.

'There. That is quite my favourite purchase of this moon's market.' She smiled at Llandry, then looked at Ynara.

'Why don't you visit me sometime soon, Ynara? Bring your daughter. I'd love to visit you, of course, but the light of Glinnery would probably kill me.'

Ynara chuckled. 'We'd love to visit, Eva. Soon, certainly.'

Lady Glostrum nodded and left the stall, leaving a quick, gracious smile as she turned away. Llandry let out a long breath, feeling weak and drained.

'That's enough, Ma. I can't bear any more.' She quickly packed away the few items that remained, ignoring the mutters of those still trying to shop. 'Who was that, exactly?'

'Eva Glostrum. High Summoner in Glour. She's a friend, though I haven't seen her for a few years.'

'I sometimes think you know everyone, Ma.'

'I meet most of them through the Council.'

'I suppose you would.'

21

4

Images flickered across the bulletin board in the centre of Glour City, headlines repeating themselves on a rotating schedule. Eva Glostrum browsed through to the society pages, seeking her own name. She didn't have to search long: the story was the first to flash up onto the board.

> *This Author has often remarked on the inability of any Gentleman to capture the lasting interest of the celebrated Lady Glostrum. The High Summoner's independent status is to come to an end at last, however, as it has just been confirmed that she is to wed Lord Vale on the eleventh of the Seventh Moon of the year! Lord Vale also revealed his intention to resign as Chief Investigator immediately after the wedding. Speculation is rife as to who will take over the coveted role...*

The article was accompanied by portraits of the couple. Eyde's was respectable enough, but Eva winced when she caught sight of hers. It was not particularly flattering. Her hair was a little disordered and shadows smudged the pale skin beneath her eyes. When had that image been taken? She hadn't noticed anybody with an image-capture in the last day or two. The bulletin team was getting very good. If only they had used an image from last night's ball, she would have been rather happier with the report.

The article had a great deal more to say about the matter, not resisting a comment or two about Lady Glostrum's 'reputation' and the suitability of the match. Eva smiled to herself. Yes, it was a highly suitable match; she had made sure of that.

'What an unusual picture.' Eva's friend Meesa Wrobsley stood at her shoulder, studying the board with the closest attention. 'Wherever did they get that?'

Eva shrugged one slim shoulder carelessly. 'Probably somebody caught me on my way home the night before last. I was a little tired.'

'More importantly, you were disordered. I'm sure there's at least one hair out of place in that picture. Maybe more.'

Eva gave a mock shudder. 'I know. Unthinkable. I'll have to make up for this lapse somehow.'

'Don't get too much more perfect, I beg you. An occasional lapse in you is comforting for the rest of us.'

'Perfect? Nonsense. I just like things to be in their proper places, that's all.'

'I know it well. That's why I'm surprised you let that pretty ring out of your sight. Its proper place was firmly on your finger, I thought.'

Eva glanced down at her slender white hand, bare of jewellery. 'It had to be resized. It kept sliding off my finger.'

'But you lost the ring anyway.'

'How could I know that the jeweller would be robbed?' Eva turned and began to walk slowly back towards the carriage that awaited her nearby. The theft of her ring had disheartened her more than she was prepared to admit. More than that, it troubled her. She had left the ring with the jeweller overnight, and by the time the Night Cloak lifted at moonrise, the ring was gone. The jeweller, poor man, knew himself to be the obvious suspect, but the sight of his broken windows and disordered shop convinced Eva that he told the truth: someone had broken in during the darkest hours with the specific purpose of finding that one item. How had anybody known that it was there? The notion that someone had been watching her actions was disturbing.

'Isn't she a friend of yours, the maker?'

'Her mother is.'

'Well, maybe you can get a new one made.'

'I'm not sure I want one.'

Meesa blinked at her, her mouth dropping open in surprise. 'Don't want an istore ring? Everyone wants an istore ring, including you. I hardly saw it off your finger until yesterday.'

'Yes, but now it's an official trend I can't possibly have anything more to do with it.'

Meesa rolled her eyes. 'True; nobody ever caught you following a trend.'

'Setting them, maybe.'

'Well, set a trend for something new then. I'm getting an istore piece of my own, and I don't want everyone to think I was just copying you.'

'What? I didn't know you were even interested.'

'Of course I am. It's far too beautiful to be ignored. Numinar ordered it for me. It's an anniversary gift.'

Eva found herself with nothing to say. She felt a vague sense of foreboding that puzzled her. A few days ago she might have sincerely congratulated her friend on the acquisition of a prized piece, but now she was changing her mind. Barely a week had passed since the Sanfaers had turned up at the Darklands Market with their unusual bejewelled wares, but enthusiasm for the strange gem had circulated with astonishing speed. Everybody wanted an istore piece. A popular fashion paper had rushed through a special article about the jewellery and its enigmatic maker, doubling its readership virtually overnight. Eva had been interviewed three times in as many days for the society pages, finding herself the subject of some unusual interest for being among the first to acquire an istore item. With each new article she received a fresh storm of requests to borrow or offers of purchase. Demand had risen so high that the prices had swiftly doubled, then quadrupled as the Sanfaer girl fought to keep up.

And now it seemed some had taken to theft in their pursuit of this new status symbol. In light of all of this, Eva could not feel entirely pleased about her friend's anniversary gift.

'Just be careful with it, Meesa.'

'No worries there. I shan't take it off my finger.'

In the coach, Meesa sank back against the comfortably cushioned seats, smiling. She loved Eva's coach almost more than Eva did herself.

'You know, I can hardly believe what's become of you.'

Eva glanced round, surprised. 'What? You speak as though I've become some kind of delinquent.'

Meesa grinned. 'Stopped being, more like. At school you were the rebel, always breaking the rules and pushing your luck. Now look at you. A model peer, a member of the government, and now you decide to get married. And just like that, you'll turn your favourite lover into your husband and become the perfect married woman. No doubt with a perfect brood of children on the way in due course.' Meesa wrinkled her nose. 'I can't decide if you're still the same Eva under all that perfect conformity.'

Eva rolled her eyes. 'Wisdom comes with age, or something. I was stupid when I was at school. It took me some time to understand why the rules are there, that's all.'

'And somehow, two decades later, this translates into a sudden urge to get married and reproduce.'

'Oh, stop probing.'

'Sorry, can't help it. I'm curious. I still can't believe you're actually going ahead with it.'

Eva sighed. 'I was fifteen when I inherited my father's title. He spent his whole life working towards it, and then he died within a year of being appointed to the peerage. And me? I was just throwing it all away.'

'I thought you didn't even like your father.'

'I didn't, but that's not the point.'

'It isn't?'

'A peerage is more important than my personal feelings for my father. Anyway, I feel like maybe my mother would've been disappointed in me.'

'You didn't even know your mother. I suppose this is your idea of explaining, but it isn't making any more sense.'

Eva shrugged. 'I tried. It makes sense to me, anyway.'

'Fine. I just hope you won't regret it. I'm pretty sure it isn't really... you.'

Eva turned her head and stared out of the window. She wouldn't dream of admitting that she had doubts, but Meesa knew her well. These, however, were unproductive thoughts. Her decision was made, for clear, rational reasons, and she wouldn't be dissuaded from it now.

Eva's coachman dropped Meesa off at the house she shared with her husband, and Eva rode the distance to her own house in solitary silence. Her thoughts wandered away from her own concerns and returned to the curious stone. She remembered Llandry's face, so like her mother's, completely guileless as she answered Eva's questions. It was hard to believe that such a thing merely lay in a cave in Glinnery, for anybody to stumble over, and yet nobody had; even now, it seemed that Llandry alone knew of its location. She knew that Llandry had been implored to give interviews; for days the papers had been printing hearsay about Llandry Sanfaer along with regretful statements about her lack of availability. She hoped the girl had the sense to keep her head down, but she feared for her. Something about Llandry had struck her as a little odd, even a little bit fey. She'd performed her role as if she viewed the market and her customers from a great distance, her mind elsewhere. Did she realise what had become of her presence at the Market? Any second appearance must be highly inadvisable. The girl would be mobbed.

The coach was moving at a steady pace, just passing a mail station. Eva called for a halt and went inside, assuaging her unease by dispatching a note to Ynara. She watched the pale-winged bird fly away into the night, her note forming a neat ring around its leg. She remembered her own words to Llandry at the market: *If I were you, I would keep the location quite a secret. I think this will prove to be very valuable.* Apparently Llandry had followed her advice. Had she been right to suggest it? No doubt the profits were princely by now, but Llandry would not be left in sole possession of the gem for long.

Eyde was waiting for her when she arrived home. He greeted her with delight, enfolding her in an embrace. She submitted to it for a few moments before pulling away, gently but firmly. She allowed him to kiss her, briefly, then busied herself pouring a drink for him.

'Is the announcement up?'

She blinked at him, confused. 'What?'

'Of our engagement.'

'Oh. Yes. It's all over the bulletin.'

He nodded. 'The boys'll know about it by now, then.' The 'boys' were his team of investigators; almost all men, because the job could be a dangerous one. Women didn't often sign up. Eva had met very few of them, but those she encountered impressed her with their earnest manner and intensity of focus. On the other hand, they did tend to seem horrifyingly young. It made her feel old.

She realised she hadn't answered him. She gave him a distracted smile as she donned a silk shawl, wrapping the fabric closely around herself. She curled up in her favourite chair, conscious of his eyes on her.

'Any news on the robbery at the jewellers?'

'I'm afraid not. I've got a couple of people working on it, though. We'll get your ring back.'

'I'm not that worried about the ring, Eyde.'

'No? You seemed very attached to it.'

'I shouldn't have been. It's not healthy to be so fascinated by a stone.'

He frowned at her quizzically. 'What's brought on this change of heart?'

'Don't you think it's odd, how people are behaving over it?'

He chuckled. 'No more so than any other trend. Remember when you wore that gown with one shoulder missing? I don't think any seamstress in Glour got a proper night's sleep for a whole moon afterwards.'

She laughed. 'And that's hardly the only time it's happened. Perhaps you're right.'

'Of course I am. What happened to that gown, by the way? I liked it.'

'Oh, I have it somewhere.'

'You should wear it again. Maybe at our wedding.'

'That would be far too cruel. Those poor tailors need time to recover.'

'Maybe a new gown, then, in a similar style. In blue. I like you in blue.'

She tugged her shawl closer around herself with a sharp movement, feeling unaccountably irritable. 'It's too soon to be thinking about the wedding.'

'It's barely a moon away. We ought to begin planning it soon.'

'Only a moon? No, surely not.' She frowned, silently counting the days. He was right. A sigh escaped her at the prospect, and she avoided his eyes.

'Eva, darling.'

Obliged to look up, she arranged her features into a cool expression.

'Are you quite sure about this?'

'This?'

'The wedding. Marrying me.'

'You have asked me that already, Eyde.'

'Yes, but still, you don't seem...' He floundered, groping for the right word.

'I don't seem what? In love?'

Her bluntness made him blink. 'I— yes. I suppose that's what I intended to say.'

'We've discussed this.'

He sat down opposite her, running a large hand through his close-cropped grey hair. 'Why did you ask me to marry you?'

'I believe I explained that at the time.'

'Tell me again.'

'It makes sense. You are of a similar social standing; of a suitable age for me; we have known each other for long enough to have a comfortable friendship. A partnership between us is likely to be beneficial.'

He looked at her sadly. 'Beneficial? Sense? Friendship? Eva. That cannot be all that you expect from a marriage.'

'Why should anybody expect more?'

'You've heard of love, I presume.'

Her lips twisted. 'I've heard of it. I've also heard of a few other things that don't exist.'

'Love doesn't exist?'

'Not in the way people describe.'

'If you believe that, why marry at all?'

'It's time.'

'I see. And these are your reasons for choosing me.'

She sighed, growing impatient. 'Why wait until after the announcement to question me about this? It's going to be awkward to change your mind now.'

'Oh, I've no intention of changing my mind. I've drawn the greatest prize in Glour, you realise.'

'Only you wish it was different.'

'No.' He paused, thinking. 'No. But I might hope you'll come to think differently in time.'

She looked at the ceiling. 'If anyone can change my mind I daresay it will be you.'

He didn't answer for a while. When she looked back at him, he gave her a tiny, tenuous smile. 'Maybe.'

He stood up suddenly, breaking the tension. He smiled down

at her. 'I ought to be going. Oh, how's my shortig coming along?'

'Well. He's almost ready.'

'I hope he's getting on well with that gwaystrel of yours. They might be working together someday.'

'Rikbeek bites.'

'Surely Rikbeek doesn't bite everyone.'

'Everyone and everything. Your hound is not exempt from the biting, I'm afraid.'

'Ah well. He's too small to do much damage.'

Eva inspected her scarred hands. 'Not for lack of trying.'

Vale chuckled. 'How long before the dog finishes training?'

'Half a moon, maybe? Certainly no more.'

He nodded, then swallowed, jangling his hands nervously in his pockets. 'Kiss me before I go.'

She grinned, amused. 'Don't say it as if I'll bite you for asking.' She rose, letting the shawl drop onto the chair. 'After all, we agreed on the merits of kissing a long time ago.'

He eyed the expanse of shoulder and bosom revealed in the absence of the shawl. 'True, but a few things have changed since then.'

She slid her arms around his neck, smiling. 'Some things haven't changed.'

Eva felt the anxiety drain out of him under the kiss, replaced by a new kind of tension. He drew her close, stroking her bare shoulders. She grinned.

'Do you really have to go this very moment?'

'Not at this exact moment, perhaps, no.'

5

The letterbox rattled loudly as letters began to tumble into Llandry's hallway. The sound was intrusive, a metallic clatter that frayed her nerves as she tried to work. She braced herself, knowing that the disturbance would take some time. She was receiving more and more mail every day, ever since the Market. Orders for jewellery came in so fast she couldn't fill them all. She hated having to raise prices — it made her feel greedy — but it was the only way to reduce the clamour. Even so, she was working at a ferocious speed day and night trying to keep up. The craze for her jewellery was completely astonishing, but she knew it wouldn't last.

The letters that bothered her more were the solicitations from other jewellers, enquiring after her supply. She'd considered writing back with the full details, until she recalled Lady Glostrum's advice. Her mother's friend was perfectly right: a true businesswoman knew better than to give away the source of her success. She'd refused the requests — politely, of course — though more recently she'd taken to ignoring them. It seemed as though every jeweller in the Seven Realms was petitioning her for information.

The letterbox shrieked again, loudly, as something large was forced through it. The sound shattered her concentration and she quickly placed down her tools before she could damage the ring she was working on. She padded through to her tiny hallway, Sigwide at her heels. If she answered the door she could accept all the mail in one go and silence that abominable racket. Stepping over the small mountain of paper on the floor, she unlocked the door and opened it.

A young man stood on the ledge, struggling with a sack of mail. His arms were full of envelopes, some of which threatened to spill over and sail away to the floor far below. She stepped forward, extending her arms.

'I'm so sorry. Let me take those.'

The boy looked harassed. He muttered a thanks as she relieved him of his burden, then glanced around nervously.

'I wouldn't hang about, miss. Get back inside, quick.'

She lifted her brows. 'Why?'

'Um, because—'

'Miss Sanfaer!' A woman's voice broke in as a slight figure swooped down from the skies, landing so swiftly that she almost knocked the mail boy off the ledge. She held up an image-capture and light flashed in Llandry's astonished face. 'Miss Sanfaer, I'm from the Herald here in Waeverleyne. Our readers are anxious to hear more about your remarkable jewellery. What can you tell us about the istore?'

Llandry was too amazed to speak. She stared as more figures appeared behind the reporter, many carrying image-captures and notepads. They hovered in the air around Llandry's front door, and more flashes of light assaulted her eyes. More figures appeared on the staircase below, wingless men and women from the other Dayland realms and even one brave (or desperate) man from Glour, his nocturnal eyes completely enclosed inside black-lensed goggles.

Stunned, Llandry felt panic racing through her as this swarm of people converged upon her. The mail boy saved her, shoving her gracelessly back into her house and slamming the door behind her. The stacks of mail fell from Llandry's numb arms as she fumbled with the key.

A knocking sounded at one of the windows. She darted through her house, breathless and shaking, slamming each window shut and barring the shutters. Only when each possible entry into her house was firmly closed did she slow down. She slumped to the floor, fighting with herself for every breath of air. She felt ready to asphyxiate. Stumbling through to her kitchen, she found her cordial and took a long swallow, her hands trembling so badly she almost dropped the bottle.

It took her an hour to calm down, an hour that she spent curled up on her kitchen floor with Sigwide in her arms. The orting was alarmed, too; her latent summoner senses caught his fear, but she was too thoroughly disturbed herself to do more than hold him close and wait until they both felt soothed. At length her breathing eased and she felt stable enough to brew tea without shattering her teapot and cups. She rose to her feet a little shakily, tucking Sigwide into the carry sling she always wore around her waist. He would be happier kept close.

The letters were more of the same. She perused a selection of them as she sipped her tea, choosing several at random. There were forty letters today, half of them containing orders for jewellery together with money in several currencies. Many of them had vastly overpaid her, even though her prices were already (so it seemed to her) extremely high. She laid a cool hand against her hot forehead, her thoughts buzzing. She had fifteen orders already outstanding, so that made thirty-five, and she had only enough istore left to fill approximately ten of them. But with that swarm of bodies outside her house, how could she possibly reach her cave without being accosted, questioned, petitioned, detained, or possibly worse?

She thought briefly about giving the whole thing up. It was a tempting thought, but would it bring the desired results? Would the letters stop coming? Would the pushy petitioners stop crowding her doorway? Doubtful. It was too late for that.

Besides, if she was honest with herself, the prospect of giving up her istore was painful. No matter how much trouble it brought her, she still felt soothed when she held a nugget of that stone in her hands. Wearing it made her feel stronger in some way, calmer, more in control of herself. She lost some of that feeling of dislocation, that sense she always carried of being out of place and out of sync with the rest of the world. Spending her days working with it, running it through her fingers, polishing its beauty and setting it into a succession of equally beauteous items made her satisfied, proud, happy. She couldn't imagine just abandoning it.

Her supply of raw gems ran out three days later, but the crush of bodies outside her house had not diminished. She'd stopped going anywhere near the door, not even to collect the mail that continued to pour through her letterbox. Every time she approached the front of her house she could hear them talking, sometimes shouting, banging on her door. She stayed near the back of the house.

But now she had ten completed items to mail, twenty-five more to make (not counting those orders that were probably lying, unopened, in her hallway) and no more istore. She would have to find a way to leave her house undetected.

She waited until the late hours of the Eventide, a time when most people across the city of Waeverleyne were asleep (usually including herself). Creeping to the front of her house, she found that everything was blissfully quiet. She packed her tools and her packages in a pack slung low on her back beneath her wings. Then, eschewing her front door, she slipped out of her kitchen window and climbed onto the roof.

Waeverleyne lay in the soft, low eventide light that was artificially created by Glinnery's sorcerers. That meant it was night time beyond the Dayland enchantments, a time when Daylanders were not usually roaming abroad. On the other hand, the muted light was more favourable for the Darklanders. She would still have to be careful. She took to the skies, angling up and up until she was flying just beneath the vast, spreading caps of Glinnery's signature glissenwol trees. She reached the nearest mail station without encountering anybody, and slid her collection of small packages into the secure box one by one. Then she was away once more, aiming this time for the outskirts of Glinnery and her cave in the ground. Nothing reached her eyes or ears save the usual soft sounds of eventide, and she finally began to relax.

Then three figures appeared in the air before her, cutting her off. She stopped, startled. Her wings beat slowly, holding her aloft as she studied the three. Two men and a woman, all clearly citizens of Glinnery, though the features and clothing of one suggested some Nimdren blood. They smiled pleasantly enough at her, but their intention to detain her was clear. She said nothing, waiting. The woman spoke first.

'I sent you a letter.'

'So did I.' That was the Nimdren.

'You never answered.'

'So we thought we'd ask you in person.'

The third man approached, looking her over. His eyes lingered on the belt at her waist, the bag hanging from her shoulders. 'On your way there now, are you? They said you only come out of your house for more istore. That's true, isn't it? We've been waiting for days.' He spoke lightly, trying to smile, but there was an intensity about him that unnerved Llandry. She shook her head, mute.

'We're going with you. That's probably easier for everyone, isn't it? No doubt you're too busy to write letters.'

Llandry shook her head again, searching futilely for her voice. The man frowned, and all three fluttered closer to her.

'We understand you want to keep it for yourself. Who wouldn't? But don't you think that's selfish? We do.'

She angled her wings, retreating a little further backwards with each slow beat. They followed her, inexorable.

'All right, you're not going there now. That's fine. Why don't you just tell us where to find it?'

Llandry blinked, one word circling around her mind. 'Selfish?'

'That's right. Don't you want anyone else to benefit from it?'

Guilt worked at her, eroding her certainty. Maybe they were right. Should she have ignored the letters? Was she behaving like a good businesswoman, or was she being greedy?

She opened her mouth, intending to tell them everything. Perhaps they sensed her weakening, for all three of them descended on her, circling her eagerly. Their proximity, their urgency, silenced her again and all she could think about was escape.

She dropped, flying hard. She heard them behind her, calling out to her as she wove through the tree trunks, trying futilely to lose them. They dogged her all the way to the balcony of her home. The doors were locked and barred from the inside, she remembered with chagrin. She darted around the building, threw herself back through her kitchen window and slammed it closed. Knocking came from different parts of her house in succession, signalling that her pursuers were seeking a way in. She stood frozen, gasping for breath, terrified. What did they mean to do if they did get in? There had been an air of desperation about them, as though they strove to act rationally but something spurred them relentlessly on. What was it about her pretty istore stone that created such fervour?

Exhausted from her eventide activities, Llandry slept late the next morning. She rose to find her parents seated in her living room, though the atmosphere was strained. Her mother looked up as Llandry entered. She was unusually pale, her face drawn and her eyes hard.

'Ma, Pa...' Llandry stopped in the doorway, unwilling to approach her livid parents. 'How did you get in?'

'You mean past the hordes of intruders swarming around your house?' said Ynara icily. 'I sent them away, of course. I could have done so earlier, had it occurred to you to contact us.'

Llandry winced. Her mother only spoke so formally when she was truly angry. 'I'm sorry, Ma. I didn't want to worry you.' She felt suddenly silly. It certainly hadn't occurred to her that her mother might be able to get rid of them.

Ynara snorted. 'Did it occur to you that you might be in danger of worse than having your picture taken?'

'They were just reporters, Ma.' Llandry risked a glance at her father. His face was closed, unreadable.

'You're sure of that, are you?' Ynara slammed her book down onto the table and stood, advancing on Llandry. 'Yesterday I received a note from Eva Glostrum. You remember her from the Market, I'm sure. She tells me her istore ring was stolen. It was sent to a jeweller's, apparently, for some small adjustment, and lifted overnight. Just that ring.' Ynara lifted her brows and gave Llandry that stare, the one that expressed her extreme disappointment. It never failed to reduce Llandry to a miserable bundle of apologies.

'Furthermore,' continued Ynara, 'My jewel box is missing. Naturally my beautiful istore bracelet is missing with it. What that means, I'm sure you'll gather, is that somebody has entered our house in the last couple of days and walked off with my jewellery. Nothing else, you understand. Only *the jewellery*. The implications of that are obvious enough. We came at once.' Llandry squirmed under her relentless stare. 'I don't know how you've avoided a break-in here, Llan, but remarkably you seem to be in one piece.'

The use of her nickname suggested her mother was beginning to relent. Llandry drew in a breath, her eyes blurring. Ynara was rarely angry, but she was truly terrifying when her ire was properly aroused.

'I'm sorry, Mamma,' she managed around the lump in her throat. 'I'm okay, really.'

'Nice job with the barricades,' Aysun put in. She smiled lopsidedly, glancing at the furniture she'd piled against the large window when she'd returned last eve.

'Thanks, Pa.'

Ynara sighed and embraced her. Llandry clung to her, weak with relief.

'Nobody's hurt you, have they?' her mother asked, fiercely. Llandry shook her head.

'Fine, well. Your "friends" are in custody overnight. They'll be released tomorrow. They'll be facing prosecution if they bother you again. Meanwhile, Llan, I want you to come home for a while. We need you under our eye, where we can keep an eye on you.'

Llandry stiffened. 'But, Ma, my house. I'm happy here. I can manage.'

Ynara cast a meaningful glance at the shuttered window and its leaning barricade of furniture. 'I'm sure you can.'

'It worked, didn't it?'

'Please, Llan. If anything happens to you...' Ynara didn't need to finish the sentence. Llandry knew that her parents wouldn't sleep unless they knew she was well. Sometimes the intense love they had for her could be stifling. She suppressed a sigh and nodded her head.

'All right, Ma. I need today to clear up a few things, then I'll come home tomorrow.'

Ynara hesitated, then nodded. 'Then I'm requesting a guard for you for tonight. Just to make sure.' Ynara steered Llandry to a seat and pressed a cup of tea into her hands, stroking her hair.

'Llan, you have to give this up.' Her father, hitherto uninvolved, now fixed her with a stern stare. 'This is out of control. Your safety is more important than your career.'

Llandry winced inwardly. He was right, too much so for her to argue with him. Truthfully she'd begun to drown under the weight of her sudden success; she wouldn't much regret being freed of the burden.

Except in one particular. Her istore was gone, entirely so. She'd used up the last pieces, fully expecting that she would soon be retrieving more. Not a single stone was left for her to keep.

That part was intolerable.

'I agree, Pa,' she said aloud. 'I'll make an announcement — no doubt there's a reporter or two still milling around somewhere — and the boards can pick it up. I suppose all those letters can simply be returned.'

Ynara narrowed her eyes, suspicious. Llandry kept her face carefully blank. If she could satisfy her mother and father with her easy capitulation on this point, perhaps they wouldn't think to extract any inconvenient promises from her. Such as a ban on visiting her precious cave.

'All right, love. Thank you,' Ynara said at last. 'I'll take the message for you later.'

Llandry thought fast. Her parents would certainly stay until the guards were in place around her house. Nothing less would satisfy them. Nor would she have any opportunity to slip out to her cave after her return to her mother's house. It would have to be this eventide: now that the swarm of reporters was gone, she would only have to evade the guards. She knew her house better than they would: slipping out would be easy. It would be a quick journey, straight to the cave and straight back, collecting a mere few small stones. As long as she had one of her precious gems to hold and carry about with her, that would be enough.

6

Eva stood in the conservatory of her home on Glour's prestigious Fifth Circle, carefully dripping nara-fruit juice onto a bed of parchment strips. From beneath a neat nest of twigs emerged a questing nose, tiny, black and twitching with eager interest. She opened her thoughts to the creature, showing it images of food, and juice, and warmth. Parchment rustled as the mouse emerged, promptly sinking its small, sharp teeth into her finger. She allowed it to draw her blood along with the juice, smiling at its enthusiasm. This one would make a fine culinary assistant to an artisan chef.

She nudged the mouse back into its parchment nest and withdrew her hand. It had built itself a home in the corner of her conservatory, settling close to the glass where the silver moonlight came through particularly strongly. The mouse seemed happy, but it would be time to move it soon.

First, though, she had a bird ready to depart the nest. Just now it was hanging upside down from the roof of the conservatory; a curious posture for a bird, but then, it was called a bird only because nobody knew how else to categorise it. She coaxed it down, drawing it to her with a mixture of command and entreaty. She took the role of its mother in the bird's mind, a being to be both trusted and obeyed. The bird soared gracefully downwards, settling on Eva's shoulder, gripping her with talons that clenched and unclenched restlessly. Eva winced as those surprisingly sharp claws pierced her skin. She objected still more when it began to peck at her ear, insistent and wholly oblivious to her pain.

'I suppose that is a mark of affection, is it?' She stroked the bird's soft feathers, careful to avoid the webby membrane of its wings. She slipped her hand into a thick leather glove and held up her hand. The bird walked obligingly onto the glove, smoothing its indigo feathers nonchalantly.

She'd taken to calling the little dringle-bird Skritch, a charitable interpretation of the effect its pacing had on the flesh of her shoulders. She was rather glad he was now ready to be delivered to his new companion-master, a herbalist living a few circles away.

She had spent the day inspecting the vast kennels the summoners kept outside the city. It was a ritual she observed every moon, even though it was years since she'd found anything to object to in the kennel masters' handling of the animals. Breeding season was approaching, and this year there was a good chance of a few new shortig pups. The species was notoriously hard to breed, and almost equally hard to track down in their native habitats in the Lower Realms. Their impressive tracking abilities made them in high demand with Vale's men, however, and he'd begged her to up the numbers available this year. Tricky, but she was certainly up to the challenge.

She was still attired in her kennel clothes, plain cottons layered against the chill in the air. She wrapped a heavy wool cloak around herself, allowing Rikbeek, her gwaystrel, to tuck himself into the folds. He availed himself of an opportunity to bite her en route, which she ignored. It was an old custom. She left the house, keeping her thoughts bent on the dringle-bird pacing up and down her glove.

It maintained its station obediently as she made her way through the streets beyond her house. Glour City was built in a series of rings, widening steadily from the nucleus of the city out to the broadest streets on the outermost edges. The innermost circles were the most prestigious: the first through to the fourth were reserved for city government offices and the manor homes — palaces, really — of its richest and most prominent inhabitants. Eva's position on the Fifth placed her among the second rank of citizens. She could have moved into the third or fourth circle years ago, taking her place among the other peers and government officials of the realm, but she liked the house she'd inherited. It made her feel a little bit closer to the father she'd lost, and the mother she'd barely known at all.

Her destination was the house of her friend Meesa's husband, Numinar Wrobsley. A prominent and skilled herbalist, he lived on Circle Twelve in the heart of the trades quarter. Instead of situating his dwelling on the edges of the forest, as any reasonable potion maker might do, he had brought the forest to his home. The building was stacked atop tall stilts, which wasn't that unusual in Glour; many citizens liked to raise their houses a little closer to the firmament. Wrobsley's house was easily twice the height of even the tallest of the residential buildings elsewhere in the city. He had a garden spread atop the roof and he spent hours and hours up there, carefully tending the rare plants he'd had imported from the Lower Realms. He swore that the proximity to the pale moonlight kept his plants stronger and healthier than their sicklier cousins elsewhere in the city. It was as reasonable an explanation as any for his particularly potent concoctions.

Eva found him in his rooftop garden as usual, bent over pots of seedlings. He was cursing their lack of progress with an enviable fluidity, impatiently pushing his escaping strands of hair back behind his ears as they repeatedly fell forward. She noticed he was wearing mismatched colours.

'Lackadaisical monsters! Destined to grace the most delicious and marvellously effective potions in Glour and you fail to produce more than a SINGLE miserable leaf?'

She cleared her throat. He shot upright, turned and stared at her.

'Damned laziness,' he muttered darkly.

'I can assure you, I have never trained a dringle-bird faster.'

'Not you,' he said impatiently. He never did have much of a sense of humour, she reflected. He was far too intense for that. His wife, on the other hand...

'It's these absurd milkleaf sprouts. Couldn't ask for a better environment, could they? Pampered like children. Food, water, moonglow, never so much as a *hint* of strong daylight...' He stepped forward suddenly, his face brightening as he observed the glove and the pacing bird. 'Dringle-bird, you said? Is this him? It's about time. I lost an entire crop of darsury grass to the mites not two days ago.'

She drew off her glove and passed it to him. 'He'll respond to the whistle, every time.'

'Perfect, perfect.' Wrobsley eyed the bird. Skritch paced, fluffed his wings and clucked. Eva gave him the hunt signal, and Skritch took to the wing. Eva and Wrobsley watched as the dringle systematically combed the tubs of plants, snaring insects and mites with deft, quick snaps of his tiny beak. Wrobsley began to walk after it, selecting pots at random and inspecting the leaves. Eva knew there wouldn't be an insect left in sight.

He returned to her at length and nodded approvingly. 'Thank you. I know you don't train much anymore. Meesa will appreciate it.'

She smiled. 'Only for friends, yes. Glour Council seems to have other things for the High Summoner to do, for some reason. Where is Meesa?'

He turned back to his plants. 'Downstairs somewhere.'

'One more thing, Numinar, if you've a moment.' He straightened up again, eyeing her impatiently. 'I've run out of the prophylactic and I need some more, fairly quickly.'

Numinar frowned. 'I don't have much. One bottle. The rylur shortage is killing me.'

'There's a shortage?'

He led the way back down to his workroom and fell to rummaging through cupboards. 'You haven't heard? I can't get any at all at the moment.'

This was curious news. Rylur was one of the trickier plants, impossible to rear properly outside of the Lowers. That meant supply was always a problem — it had to be carefully gathered by herbalists trained in Lowers survival and excursions down there were always brief and tightly controlled. But she knew that Numinar didn't always rely on the fully legal sources.

Numinar was throwing bottles around with a carelessness that made her wince, but nothing broke. 'All sources have dried up lately. I can't get a straight answer out of anybody as to why. Something about increased dangers.'

That dovetailed with a few odd reports she'd received recently from summoners. A few of them felt that the Lowers were growing more unstable, more difficult to navigate. She hadn't taken them too seriously; it was the sort of conclusion newer summoners often reached when they found themselves out of their depth down there. But perhaps there was something in it after all.

'Here,' said Numinar at last, shoving a bottle into her hands. 'Next batch I make is yours, okay?' He was already heading back up the stairs, anxious to return to his plants.

'Thanks,' she said, belatedly. She didn't bother to say goodbye; she knew he wouldn't hear her. She made her way back down the cramped staircase to the lower floors.

There were no lights anywhere in the Wrobsley home. This was not unusual; the Night Cloak had been in place for generations across the whole of Glour and the surrounding irignol forests, and the eyes of Darklanders were accustomed to the gloom. However, silvery light-spheres mimicking moonlight were popular for indoors. Eva kept some lit in her own home, and she knew that Meesa did likewise. Perhaps she was in the garden.

Eva let herself out of the house, stepping carefully through the gardens. Meesa and Numinar both would be incensed if she crushed any of their plants. She kept to the pathways between the neatly tended rows, watching for bobbing light-globes in the darkness.

She rounded the north corner of the building. There — a silver gleam announced a sphere at low ebb, bobbing hazily a few feet from the ground. She followed the little drifting beacon, calling her friend's name.

No answer greeted her, nor sign of movement. She caught up with the globe, dousing its light by tucking it inside her cloak. She stood still, searching the darkness.

'Rikbeek,' she murmured, opening her cloak. 'Search for me.' She pictured Meesa for him, offering an image made up of movement and sound. The gwaystrel sneezed in protest, but stretched out his webby wings and took flight.

Within a few minutes she caught the faint sound of Rikbeek's signal. She walked in the direction of his call, puzzled. He was using his warning sound. How could that be?

'Stop pranking me, you little beast,' she grumbled. 'Just because you didn't want to be disturbed—'

She stopped speaking. Her nose was registering a new scent: sharp, wrong. She tensed, her heart suddenly thudding.

An inert, dark shape lay on the darker ground. She released the light-globe, its feeble glow lightening the gloom by a few shades.

42

Meesa lay among the crushed remains of blooming milkleaf plants. She was barely recognisable, her upturned face displaying long gashes running from her temple to her chin. Deep wounds latticed the flesh, blood still glistening wet and red in the low light. Her flesh was cleaved through, glimpses of pale bone visible beneath the shredded meat.

Eva clenched her jaw against a desire to retch. She knelt resolutely, searching for signs of life. Nothing.

It occurred to her that the fresh wounds indicated a very recent demise. Was Meesa's attacker still nearby? She leapt to her feet and tried to listen, both with her ears and her summoner senses. Her heart thumped wildly, rushing blood drowning other sounds, but she felt the imprint of an alien beast's mind not far away. Too close.

As Rikbeek crowed and dived, Eva caught a glimpse of movement near the ground to her right. Pale eyes gleamed coldly in the darkness. She backed away, horrified, unable to look away from those icy orbs. Seconds passed. Then the blue-lit eyes winked out, and the presence vanished. She breathed, then turned, stumbling in her haste to reach the house.

Numinar's reaction was swift. He didn't wait to ask questions; he merely tore outside, leaving Eva to follow at a slower pace. She stepped into the street and accosted the first person she met, a young man who she sent hurtling away to fetch help. Returning to the garden, she found Numinar on his knees in the mud and spilled blood. He didn't move as she approached, didn't make a single sound. She took up a station nearby, trying not to look at Meesa's poor ruined body, unwilling to disturb Numinar.

Lord Vale was quick to arrive, with his boys in tow. He marched through the garden, heedless of the plants he was crushing underfoot. Reaching Eva, he wrapped her in a brief embrace.

'Take Wrobsley inside,' he murmured. He bent to speak to Numinar, though she didn't hear what he said. Numinar blinked and stood up dazedly. He allowed himself to be led indoors. She had to guide him carefully to prevent him from falling over anything. Behind her she heard Vale barking orders to his men.

A little later, Eva sat tucked into a corner in the Wrobsley's front parlour, slumped rather inelegantly into a wing-backed chair with a blanket wrapped around her shoulders. She was still shivering with shock, and no amount of blankets could warm her chilled frame.

Numinar Wrobsley sat nearby. He hadn't spoken a word in the last half hour. Eva glanced at him from time to time, alarmed at the pasty hue of his face, the way his pale eyes stared without seeing. She could do nothing for him. They waited, together yet separated by immeasurable distance, as Vale's team conducted their investigations.

Eva finally roused herself as Meesa's body was brought in. Her stomach turned over anew at the sight of her friend's poor stricken body, her blood drying in crusted patches of rust-red. There was so much of it, staining her face, her neck, her torso. All her clothes were soaked through with it. She was laid gently on the table, her limbs arranged in as much a semblance of repose as possible. Vale drew a sheet over her ruined face, casting Eva a quick glance of sympathy.

Wrobsley's reverie was broken, too. He watched fixedly as his wife's body was laid out. Eva expected some reaction from him: tears, rage, despair. Instead he observed the proceedings almost expressionlessly, as if his ability to feel anything was temporarily suspended. It was far more terrible to watch than any explosion of grief. Eva looked away.

One of Meesa's arms had slipped from beneath the sheet. Her right hand was blood-soaked but undamaged. Eva felt tears prickling at the backs of her eyes at last, looking at that lifeless hand, those clever fingers forever stilled. She stood up, letting the blanket drop onto her chair, and gently lifted Meesa's hand. She was going to restore it to the scant dignity of the sheet covering, but she stopped, her eyes narrowing.

Last time she had seen her friend, her pretty white hands had been adorned with rings. The most prized of these, her beautiful new istore piece, had occupied the third finger of her right hand. The bloodied fingers Eva now held were bare.

She gently tucked Meesa's arm beneath the sheet, then moved around the table. Meesa's left hand was bare of jewellery as well.

Meesa's voice echoed in her thoughts. *I shan't take it off my finger.* She'd grinned as she said it, full of her usual good humour, but Eva felt sure she'd meant it. Where was the ring?

'Numinar.'

He twisted his head towards her, but he didn't seem to be

44

seeing her. She sat beside him, picking up his hands in her own, and looked full into his face.

'Numinar, this is important. Did Meesa take off her ring?'

'What?' His lips moved soundlessly; she divined the word from the shape his mouth made.

'The istore ring, the one you bought for her. Did she remove it? Did she store it somewhere?'

'She says she won't ever take it off.'

'I know, but—' Eva shook her head. She wasn't getting through to him. It was clear enough, though, that he knew nothing about the disappearance of Meesa's ring.

Vale poked his head around the door frame. 'I'd like a few words, Mr. Wrobsley, if I may.'

Eva crossed to him, shaking her head warningly. She pulled him out into the hallway, pulling the door to behind her.

'He's in deep shock,' she said. 'He's barely hearing anything I say to him. Eyde, listen.' She told him the story of Meesa's istore ring, sparing no details.

'I don't think she would have taken it off, especially not so soon,' she finished. 'I think your men should search the house, see if they can find the ring. If not, then — then it's possible her death had something to do with it.' She took a breath. 'Nobody ever found out who stole my ring, did they?'

'No. We found nothing.'

She nodded. 'Also, I — I saw something, when I found Meesa's body.'

'I was coming to ask you about that, actually. Did you see the attacker?'

'I think so. Parts of it. Thin frame, black hide, pale eyes. Not a native of the Seven — definitely a Lowers beast.'

'It's hard to be sure of that, Eva. What of Orlind?'

Eva sighed. Unlike the other six realms, Orlind was almost completely closed to outsiders. It was difficult to determine whether it was even inhabited, and Glour's libraries could offer nothing but theories and speculation about what lay behind the wall of mountains that separated it from Irbel. 'I can't answer that question. Maybe it came out of Orlind — somehow — but my belief is that it's not of the Seven.'

Vale nodded. 'I trust your instincts. Do you know what it was?'

She hesitated. 'I have... a theory. Maybe. I need to look into

45

it.'

Vale nodded. 'All right. Let me know what you find out.'

There came a violent knocking at the door, a hammering repeated with frantic urgency. Eva exchanged a look with Vale.

'Probably family,' said Vale. 'We need to keep everyone out of here for now. My boys aren't finished yet.'

'Moment. I'll get it.' Eva stepped resolutely to the door, suffering a stab of trepidation. To whom was she to break the news?

But when she opened the door, a young man in the uniform of the Investigative Office stood there, breathing hard.

'Looking for the Chief,' he gasped.

Vale strode forward. 'Bensley. What is it?'

'Another death reported, sir, on Circle Eleven. Saudran Iritan. Some kind of beast attack.'

'Right.' Vale turned to Eva, looking grim. He kissed her perfunctorily on the forehead, squeezing her arms gently. 'Go home,' he said. 'Please.'

She shook her head. 'I am staying with Numinar. He shouldn't be left alone.'

He nodded. 'Just be careful when you leave.'

'Eyde. Find out if Iritan had any taste for jewellery.' Vale gave her a quick nod of understanding, collecting up several of his men with swift orders. They left in a knot of uniforms. Eva sighed as the door shut behind them. Only two remained, charged with the removal of Meesa's body. Eva watched sadly as the silent form of her friend was taken out of the house.

She returned to Numinar. He sat where she had left him, still silent and unresponsive. She sat down beside him, took one of his hands gently in hers, and prepared to wait.

The reports reached her the next day. She had remained with Numinar throughout the moonlit hours and on, as the moon disappeared and the Night Cloak shrouded Glour. She had at last persuaded him to rest; he'd responded like a man half asleep, and needed all of her help even to find his way to bed. Her own rest must wait until she reached home.

She travelled home via public carriage, half hoping to find Vale waiting for her. Instead she found a note, addressed to her in Vale's handwriting. She could barely focus on it to read the words.

Eva,

Three deaths overnight. Iritan had an istore necklace. Alen Marstry, the third victim, had an istore circlet. Both pieces missing. Both attacked by some kind of beast. Also found three recent reports of jewellery thefts beside yours, all istore. Looking into it. See you at moonset.

Eva shivered, suddenly feeling fervently glad that her ring had merely been stolen. Her mind obligingly showed her Meesa's poor ruined face once again, reminding her of the hideous quantity of blood that stained her shredded clothing. Eva had no trouble picturing herself in that position, her own istore ring conspicuously absent from her blood-covered hand.

Stop that, she told herself sharply. She folded the note, tucking it into her sash. Firmly banishing all thought of tiredness, she left the house again, this time heading for the Bulletin Office.

Within half an hour of her arrival, a new announcement was spreading throughout the bulletin boards across the city.

All examples of the substance known as "istore" are to be turned in at the Investigative Offices immediately. Continued possession of these items is known to place the owner in EXTREME peril. Act at once.

An hour later, five dark-winged birds took to the sky, bearing urgent messages across the realms.

7

Three guards had been assigned to protect Llandry's house. They arrived in the early eventide, all youngish men in light armour with weapons strapped to their uniforms. The prospect of having to speak to these grim-faced people was enough to close Llandry's throat on the spot, but fortunately they were not much inclined to talk. They took her mother's instructions silently, taking up positions at her front door, the back door and outside the largest window. When her parents had gone she wandered the house for a time, feeling as though she was under siege.

As the strong light of day began to fade, she suffered some doubts. Her mother's fears may seem exaggerated to her, but they were not unjustified. What if someone still lay in wait for her? Were they really gone? She shouldn't be so willing to endanger herself for the sake of a gem. She hovered near her kitchen window, nibbling at a fingernail. The proximity of her guards didn't prevent her escape: if she was careful she could slip out without being seen by the man at the rear door. But should she?

What it was about the istore that drove her, she couldn't say. But nonetheless it did. Pursuit or not, she would go. Besides, tomorrow she would release the location of the cave and her part in the matter would be over. It wouldn't matter if she was followed today.

Her mind made up, she slid silently out of the window. Her

stature was a source of embarrassment to her under normal circumstances; the winged citizens of Glinnery were not typically very tall as a race, but she was particularly diminutive. Now she blessed her size, her slight figure easily fitting through the frame. She pulled herself up onto the roof and lay silently for a moment, listening. Below her stood a silent guard. He had positioned himself directly before the narrow wood-and-rope bridge that connected her dwelling with her neighbour. She watched as he took a few paces onto the bridge, looked around himself, then paced back to his original station. He hadn't seen her.

Llandry waited until a passing cloud bank cast a misty grey shadow over the forest, then she silently took to the skies. She flew low, keeping beneath the cover of the glissenwol caps, trusting to their wide trunks and blankets of draping vines to conceal her movements. There was no sign of pursuit on the ground or in the air behind her, and she relaxed. She flew south and east, making for the vicinity of the border into the Darklands. Eventually she saw the darkened skies of Glour looming ahead of her and she began her descent, landing gently in the thick mosses wet from the day's rain.

She paused, disorientated. The surroundings were familiar: clusters of entwined glissenwol formed a tangled wall stretching away to her left, crowded with an obscuring thicket of ferns and moss. The path to her cave lay behind this mass of foliage, she knew the route perfectly. But the opaque darkness of Glour loomed close, too close. It should be a dark mass on the horizon. Instead, the eventide light was abruptly cut off and plunged into shadow barely one hundred feet ahead of her. Had she flown off course? She stepped forward warily, scanning her surroundings for familiar landmarks.

She stepped softly towards the wall of twining trees, twisted easily between the glissenwol trunks, ducked to avoid the hanging vines. The path was slightly overgrown, but unmistakeable; this was the same route she had passed through many times before. Her cave lay two hundred feet ahead, through the overgrown passageway and into the grassier space beyond.

Now that passage lay under shadow.

Llandry walked forward until she stood with the tips of her red boots on the very edge of the divide. The transformation from light to darkness was abrupt: the air blurred into dusk for a mere few feet and then the solid darkness of the night took over. The moon was up, silvering the land below, but with her Daylander eyes it was a strain to see into the darkness that cloaked the forest ahead of her. She could just make out the outlines of half-grown, pale glissenwol caps shrouded in palpable darkness. Starved of light, they were already fading, their shining pale trunks turning sickly, the vibrancy draining from their crumbling caps.

Anxious, Llandry flexed her wings. Then she sat, wrapping her arms around her drawn-up knees.

'What do you make of that, Siggy?' she murmured. Sigwide stared up at her with wide, trusting eyes, his long body quivering either with tension or excitement. Llandry lifted him into her lap, stroking his short silver-grey fur soothingly.

'I don't think it's a good sign, either,' she agreed.

She could not see the entrance to her cave, which meant that the hillock beneath which it lay must now be situated some distance into the gloom. Raised as she had been under the perpetual light of Glinnery, Llandry had no night vision at all. Could she even find the way to her cave? What would she find there if she did? The spread of the Night Cloak may have quite another cause, but Llandry felt a settled dread that its expansion into the vicinity of her cave was no accident.

She ought to return home. She had other work to do; if this was a mere mistake, it was a boundary problem that would soon be resolved. But tomorrow she would be restored to her parents' house, under her mother's constant, concerned scrutiny, and there would be no further opportunity to return. If she wanted her istore, it would have to be done now. In its natural environment, the stone emitted its own light, illuminating the interior of the cave; all she had to do was find her way to the entrance. Surely she knew it well enough to find her way there blinded.

Sigwide's trembling had calmed. She gently placed him on the floor and stood up.

'Stay here, Sig.' The orting sat obediently on his haunches and blinked at her, his black nose testing the air.

Llandry tucked her long hair more firmly under her cap and checked her tools, hidden away inside her cloak. Then, resolutely, she stepped into the gloom.

Immediately the air changed. The gentle warmth of Glinnery faded, replaced by a soothing coolness. The sounds of Glinnery forest receded as thoroughly as though a thick wall divided her from the glissenwol canopy. This was no illusion, then; she truly stood in Glour territory.

She strode forward a few paces and stopped, waiting for her eyes to adjust to the darkness. She stood silently for some minutes, her sensitive ears alert. No sound broke the silence of the night. She moved ahead, stepping lightly through the crisp, dying moss that still carpeted the floor. She proceeded slowly and carefully, using her hands to warn her of obstacles. She trusted her instincts to guide her, walking in what she hoped was the accustomed direction.

A flicker of movement caught her attention. She paused, ignoring a ripple of nervousness.

It's only the dark. Darkness cannot hurt me.

She moved ahead again, lifting her chin, trying to generate a feeling of confidence. She had made it most of the way there. The cave must be within fifty feet or so of her location, if her instincts had guided her well.

But then came the sharp sound of twigs cracking underfoot — the sounds of another person, or large animal, walking some way ahead. She froze, unwilling to meet a Darklander out here, groping her way through territory that had become unfamiliar. How could she possibly explain what she was doing, a Daylander creeping through the darkness without a light? She stood perfectly still, listening hard. Her straining eyes discerned a lean shape a foot or so before her, the outline of a beast's narrow head and long, powerful legs. In the darkness she could gain no clearer impression of the creature, except that it must be large. Movement flashed perilously close to her face.

She knew instinctively that this was no native of Glour. Never had she heard of such a creature, with flesh as black as night, almost as tall at the shoulder as she was. She began to retreat, moving as fast as she dared.

A mistake. The movement incited the beast: it tensed and sprang. Its weight barrelled into her and she fell, gasping. The creature turned and lunged for her again; she rolled instinctively, but not fast enough: searing pain exploded in her arm as long claws ripped easily through her flesh. She twisted away and launched herself to her feet, then into the air. Flying in the darkness was a danger in itself: repeatedly she swerved only just in time to avoid colliding with trees that loomed suddenly out of the darkness. Behind her she could hear the creature crashing through the undergrowth, easily keeping pace with her.

Light blossomed ahead of her and she burst into Glinnery's woods, weak with relief as her eyes showed her a coherent picture once more. Flexing her wings, she began to climb higher into the skies, aiming for home.

Then a small grey shape below caught her eye. Sigwide! He was prone to wandering, but now the blessed animal still sat obediently where she'd left him, waiting patiently for her return. She cursed faintly and dived, scooping up the orting. Beating her wings hard, she fought to climb back into the skies but she wasn't fast enough: claws raked over her back, tearing through her clothes and tracing deep lines of fire across her skin. She was knocked to the ground, pain-blinded and losing strength. She had fallen on the wrong side of the divide and lay again in darkness.

Eyes flashed in the gloom, icy-pale and merciless. The beast growled. Desperate, she forced herself to her feet and threw herself into the air, trusting to her wings to catch the wind and carry her aloft. She expected any moment to feel claws in her flesh again, expected to be dragged back down to earth. But to her intense relief she rose and rose, speeding away from the border and back towards the city of Waeverleyne.

Sigwide was still cradled to her chest. He was screaming in distress, the sounds shattering the calm she tried to draw around herself. His grey fur was soaked in blood, and for a horrified second she thought he was injured. Then she realised the blood was her own; her left arm was shredded, pouring blood. The extent of the injury sent a shock of terror through her; gritting her teeth, she fought it down. If she could only keep going for another few minutes, she would reach her mother's house — or somebody who could convey her there.

But moments later dizziness engulfed her and her sight blurred. She felt herself falling. She landed hard, the impact sending waves of pain through her body. Sigwide fell from her weakened arms. She lay for a moment, half-stunned, then drew a deep breath, pulling herself carefully into a sitting position. She examined her arm.

Five long gashes ran from shoulder to elbow, deep and ugly.

Blood flowed in alarming quantity, coating her skin in sticky, warm redness. She flexed her hand gingerly, breathing deeply to ward away the faintness. Pain scorched from her shoulder to her fingertips and she gasped.

She felt the gentle touch of Sigwide's nose against her knee. The orting gazed at her with his liquid eyes wide. She stroked his fur with her good hand, and gathered him up.

'Onward, and... fast.' She spoke through gritted teeth. Sigwide stuck his nose into her ear as she moved on again, trying to hold her wounded arm immobile. She swayed as faintness again threatened to overwhelm her. Sigwide settled himself against her neck, uttering a rough, grumbling purr.

Llandry took another three steps and stopped. The world blurred and her vision clouded with fog. She swayed, and Sigwide squeaked with alarm as he tumbled out of her limp arms. She fell.

Llandry woke beneath layers of blankets in a bed that was not her own. She frowned, confused, blinking in the low light of a bedside globe. Her arm throbbed painfully when she tried to move, so she lay still.

'Llandry?' Her mother's voice, muted and filled with concern. Llandry recognised the room now: the bedchamber in her mother's tree where she had slept as a child. It still flourished with the forest's most colourful fungi, well tended in neat clay pots.

Soft footsteps sounded, then her mother's face bent over her.

'Ah — you are awake.' There was relief mingled with fear in Ynara's voice. She peeled back the covers gently. Llandry glanced down at her arm reluctantly, afraid of what she might see. The pain was so excessive, she felt as though half of her arm was missing.

It wasn't. Her arm lay inert but whole, swaddled in bandages. Clouds of blood marred the white cloth in several places, alarmingly red. Ynara's lips twisted in sympathy. Llandry felt curiously detached as she watched her flesh bleed.

'Keep still, love,' said her mother. Her face vanished from Llandry's line of sight, her footsteps rapidly receding. Llandry had no intention of moving. Was it possible for a limb to spontaneously detach itself? It felt possible. Maybe it ought to be encouraged: at least it would stop hurting.

Ynara returned, and set a steaming cup to her daughter's lips. The scent was familiar: litorn mushroom, but stronger than she'd ever tasted before. She drank, and the pain gradually began to recede.

Ynara allowed a few minutes to pass before carefully rebandaging her daughter's arm. Llandry lay quietly until it was done, her mind busy. She recalled the black claws, the ice-coloured eyes in the darkness, the sudden, searing pain in her arm...

'Where's Sigwide?' Her voice sounded strange, distant and annoyingly feeble.

'In the kitchen. I left him with a whole bucket of food, so he's quite happy.'

'Was he hurt?'

'No; he's quite well.'

Llandry relaxed slightly. 'Thanks, Ma.'

Ynara tucked the blankets carefully around Llandry's chin. She was smiling, but her eyes were anxious.

'He was curled up on your stomach when you were found. Apparently he would hardly let anyone near you.'

Llandry smiled too. 'That's my Siggy.' A thought occurred to her, distantly. It took a while to work its way to the fore. She waited patiently as her mother busied herself with collecting the discarded bandages and cup.

'Ma. Should the Night Cloak change?'

'Change how, love?'

'Spread. Swallow parts of Glinnery.'

'I've never heard of that before.'

Llandry nodded drowsily. 'Well, that's what happened.'

Ynara frowned. 'And what else, love?'

'Don't know,' she said hazily. Her mind wouldn't co-operate; she felt like she was swimming through fog. 'Something else in there. Shadowy,' she added helpfully.

'All right, love. We'll talk of it when you've rested a bit more.' She placed a kiss on Llandry's brow and moved away.

'Aren't you angry with me, Ma?'

Her mother sighed deeply. 'I ought to be. But no. I am far too relieved that you're alive.' Llandry was distantly aware of her standing on the other side of the room, smiling down at her.

54

'Get some sleep, Llan.' She left, closing the door quietly behind her.

Llandry slept.

Next time she woke, she opened her eyes to see her mother sitting in a chair nearby, reading a book. She looked up when Llandry stirred, and smiled.

'I was hoping you'd wake soon. Are you hungry?'

Llandry sat up slowly, horrified by the stiffness in her body and the pain in her arm and back. 'Not even a tiny bit hungry.'

'You must eat, Llan. You lost a lot of blood. Take some soup.' A set of dishes was arranged over Llandry's bedside table. Ynara lifted the lid of one, releasing a fragrant aroma of mushroom broth. The smell alone was enough to turn Llandry's stomach, but she took the bowl and obediently applied herself to eating. Ynara waited patiently, watching the progress of Llandry's spoon as she painfully consumed half the bowl. Then she set it aside.

'Ma?'

'Yes, love.'

'You said I was "found".'

'Yes, only just in time. You were in a bad way.'

'What happened? I remember that I fell out of the sky.'

A male voice spoke in deep, rather melodious tones: certainly not her father. 'I found you.'

Llandry stiffened, peeking over her blankets. A stranger stood in the doorway, carrying Sigwide in his arms. The orting looked offensively unconcerned at his predicament; in fact he seemed quite at home in this intruder's embrace.

'May I come in?' The man looked first at Ynara and then at Llandry.

'For a minute,' her mother said, waving him in. 'Don't tire her.'

'I'm already tired,' Llandry said, trying to focus on this new person. She received a vague impression of dark hair and paler skin than was commonly seen in Glinnery. Darklands pale. But he didn't seem to suffer in the light. He approached Llandry's bed, gently placing the orting onto the covers. She noticed he avoided her injured side.

'I arrived late yesterday,' he said, chuckling as Sigwide ducked under her blanket and burrowed determinedly down to her feet. 'I found you unconscious in the moss, with that little demon sitting guard over you. He actually bit me when I tried to pick you up.'

Llandry lay unmoving, silent with discomfort. The presence of a stranger was unwelcome at any time, and still more so when she lay, prone and injured and barely conscious. She wished her mother had not let him in, then swiftly chided herself for her ingratitude.

'We haven't met,' she managed. She felt she ought to say more, but the words didn't come.

'I'm a friend of your mother's,' he said comfortably. 'I could hardly fail to realise who you were. You could've been Ynara herself, except for the colour of your wings.'

Llandry's eyes flicked to her mother's face. It was true about the resemblance, superficially anyway: Ynara's honey-brown skin, wavy black hair and grey eyes were echoed in her daughter's colouring. But to suggest that they were virtually identical was meaningless flattery. Llandry's features may be similar to her mother's, but something about their arrangement fell far short of the perfect symmetry of Ynara's. Llandry was perfectly aware that she looked plain next to her mother: that the similarities were striking but that the differences were equally so. She glowered darkly at him, refusing to make any effort to speak. Sigwide had worked his way back up to her chest, winding himself into a tight, sleeping ball of fur, and she occupied herself with stroking his soft head.

The man either didn't notice or refused to take the hint. He continued to stare at her — probably wondering how Ynara's features could be so poorly transposed onto her daughter's face. The notion made her uncomfortable and she shrank beneath her blankets, wincing as the lacerations on her back sang with pain. Divining Llandry's thoughts, her mother touched the stranger on the shoulder.

'Dev, Llandry should sleep now.'

'Dev?' Llandry's eyes returned to the man's face, too weak to phrase the questions that bloomed in her mind. He smiled and extended a hand, then remembered her arm and dropped it again.

'Devary Kant, of Nimdre,' he said. 'We'll meet properly later, no doubt.' Her heart sank a little. Obviously he intended to stay a while. She made no move as Devary Kant nodded pleasantly to her and left the room.

'Sleep, love.' Ynara paused to brush a lock of hair away from Llandry's eyes and then left as well, closing the door quietly behind her.

8

The pale moon rose high over Glour. It was almost full today, and cast a strong silvered glow down upon the buildings of the city; but its coveted radiance could offer little comfort to the citizens of Glour. Rumours swept the city streets, whispers of black beasts with the eyes of winter stalking through the houses on silent paws. The bulletin boards continued to issue their sedate, government warnings of danger. Privately printed news sheets offered more lurid accounts of the events of the past two days. Some thoughtfully included artists' impressions of the three deceased, heavy on the blood content. The mood across Glour was tense.

Eva Glostrum sat shivering in the city library. It was a vast building, so of course it was cold. After hours of crouching miserably in her chair trying to ignore the freezing drafts, she felt like a block of ice. At her left elbow rested a stack of the dailies, all hysterically reporting a great deal of misinformation. At her right lay a leaning mountain of books hurriedly pulled from the library shelves. She had been studying throughout the darkest hours, poring over all the oldest texts on the shelves until her eyes were stinging with tiredness and her fingers coated with dust and ink. She had worked her way steadily through all the tales of the old days — days before the Summoners' Board had been formed, when creatures of all kinds had roamed the Seven Realms untamed, unrecorded and uncontrollable.

She had read of gloeremes, finruks, gludrais and the inalo, fearsome beasts long banished from the Middles. She copied drawings of the caomdir, the cluine and the ulenath, creatures occasionally sighted in the Lowers but never above. Even the gwaystrel made its appearance between the pages, once a common sight and now so rare. Some of these beasts bore similarities to the creature she had seen, enough to give her a faint flicker of hope; but none perfectly fit the features she recalled so clearly.

By moonset she was miserably frozen, appallingly tired and in a deeply poor temper. But she forced herself to keep reading. Glour needed answers to this mystery, and besides: as long as she kept her mind fixed on the task at hand, she couldn't sit and dwell, uselessly and destructively, on the events of last night. Meesa's face flickered through her thoughts hour after hour, chilling her with a new thrill of horror every time she recalled her glassy eyes and blood-soaked hair. Each time she pushed the thoughts ruthlessly away and refocused her tired mind on the texts before her.

She was avoiding the truth, of course. Legend had it that the Board of Summoners had been founded several generations ago because of one particular beast; one animal too powerful to be controlled, too independent to be mesmerised, too violent to be safely approached. It was these qualities that made them popular as companions: their strength, their impressive physique and those chilling wintry eyes were more effective deterrents than even the most ferocious of guard dogs. But they caused havoc, repeatedly evading the control of their handlers and wreaking terrific damage whenever they succeeded in freeing themselves from command. The whurthag was the first name placed on the list of forbidden summons. The penalties for bringing banned beasts through from the Lowers were harsh.

Nobody had defied the ban in living memory. There was no incentive to do so: if the summoner managed to evade the punishments imposed by the Board, then sooner or later they would fall prey to the ferocity of the whurthag. No sane summoner would risk being torn apart by their own companion. The Board of Summoners in Glour took great care to ensure that their trained summoners were stable, responsible people, and she knew that the corresponding organisations in Orstwych and Ullarn did likewise. Nobody, then, would be crazy enough to pull a whurthag through.

So she told herself. Working steadily through all the oldest Catalogues of Beasts, she left the entries for whurthag until last, certain — hoping hard — that she would find an alternative explanation, some other label to place upon the thing she'd seen at the Wrobsley house. But deep down, she knew she was fooling herself.

At length, she found she had worked through every entry in every catalogue, and she'd found nothing that struck her as sufficiently similar to her memory of the creature that had killed Meesa. She could go on fooling herself — doubting the evidence of her own eyes and ears — but she had wasted enough time. She took a long breath and turned over the pages of the oldest Catalogue of Beasts, a book that dated back to before the founding of the Board. There it was, under "W": whurthag. Several paragraphs of spidery text were scrawled adjacent to an artist's impression of the creature. She recognised it immediately.

There were the sharp angles, the night-black pelt, the eyes of frozen winter. The whurthag's claws, rendered in artistic detail, filled her with renewed horror. She recollected too well the glint of cool moonlight off those razor edges as the beast had crouched in the darkness.

She stifled her growing sense of dread, drawing several deep breaths to calm herself. She copied the pages slowly and neatly, drawing a quick, precise sketch of the whurthag as it appeared upon the page. Then she left the library, travelling rapidly to the city council chambers with the book tucked under her arm.

Eva was immediately admitted to Guardian Troste's office. The Guardian was at work, her fierce black eyes intent on the paperwork before her. She put it aside as Eva entered, her brow creasing with concern.

'Lady Glostrum. Not more bad news, I hope.'

'Terrifically bad, I'm afraid.'

Troste's lips twitched. 'By all means, break it to me gently.'

Eva placed the book on the Guardian's desk, opening it to the page she had bookmarked with a scrap of paper.

'This is what was roaming the city streets the night before last.'

The Guardian needed no explanation. She drew in a sharp

breath, and Eva noticed her hand shake slightly as she smoothed down the page.

'I won't ask if you're sure; you clearly are.'

'Unfortunately.'

Troste looked up, closing the book briskly. 'Very well. What does our High Summoner suggest?'

'It's said that there's no reliable way to battle the whurthag. Their speed defies attack: they can be killed, but only at great cost to the attacker. The best way to deal with them is to banish them back to the Lowers.'

Troste closed her eyes briefly. 'Tell me something, Eva. What's happening here? Has somebody foolishly brought a whurthag through a gate and lost control over it? Are these random attacks we're seeing? Or worse?'

'I fear worse.' Eva quickly related her theory about the ring, including Vale's reported findings. 'I fear the whurthag is — at present — under someone's control. The attacks are targeted. But if legend is to be believed, the whurthag's handler won't keep it under control for long. Then we'll start seeing those random attacks. We need to find it and dispose of it, now.'

Troste nodded. 'Fine. What do you need?'

'I've already issued a summons to the guild. I'm going to need some sorcerers to open gates. I'd appreciate an armed escort for each group: not to attack the whurthag, they mustn't do that, but to deal with its handler. If we find him or her.'

'All right. I'll get Angstrun here.'

Lord Angstrun arrived within minutes. He marched in unceremoniously, all impressive height, thunderous brow and a stare to turn the moon blue.

'Is this one of those real emergencies? Not one of the fake ones you lot like to use to keep us on our toes—'

'Yes, Darae. Sit down, please.'

Angstrun strode back to the door and stuck his head around it.

'Bring my letters in here, will you.' Troste's secretary appeared at the door with a stack of papers. She handed them to Angstrun and immediately retreated, as if Angstrun were a ferocious dog best kept at a distance. Eva chuckled inwardly. She could understand the temptation to view him that way. It was said in the city that Angstrun, the foremost sorcerer in Glour, bathed in moonglow every night and drank refined essence of starine with his breakfast. It wasn't too hard to believe.

Angstrun sat heavily in a chair opposite to Guardian Troste, nodding absently at Eva on his way past. He sat amid a growing pile of paper, tearing through his letters as Troste explained Eva's errand. His head shot up at the word *whurthag*, and he stared first at the Guardian and then at Eva.

'All right,' he said at last. 'Genuine emergency. I get it.'

'Lady Glostrum is going to need some sorcerers, Darae. Some of your best. She'll need gates opened and closed with as much efficiency as possible. Get some who don't scare easily, please.'

'Right.' Angstrun stood up, but he did not depart immediately. 'How did it get here? I mean, I've never heard of a whurthag coming through a rogue gate.'

'No,' said Eva. 'It was probably brought through deliberately.' She briefly recounted the connection between the whurthag and the istore stone. Angstrun's very black brows lifted as he listened.

'That cursed "istore" nonsense is more trouble than it's worth,' he grunted.

'That remains to be seen,' Eva replied. 'Apparently somebody thinks it's worth a great deal of trouble.'

'No time to waste, Angstrun,' the Guardian interjected. 'Sorcerers, please.'

'Er, right.' He crossed to the door, which abruptly swung open before he reached it. Troste's secretary stood timidly in the doorway, clutching a rolled message.

'For your lordship,' she said, thrusting the message at Angstrun. 'Marked urgent.' She all but ran out of the room.

'It never stops,' muttered Angstrun, unfolding the note. He read quickly, then tossed the paper at Troste.

'Another emergency for you. Hope you're in the mood for them today.'

Eva glanced enquiringly at Angstrun. He glowered at her as if it was her fault.

'Missive from Glinnery. Someone's fucked about with the Night Cloak. Has to be one of my aides; nobody else could've had the right access to it, or the right skills. Seems someone thought it'd be fun to eat parts of Glinnery.' He rolled his eyes. 'They're sending a bloody delegation. Someone remind me why I took this job.'

'Because you're good at it, Darae,' said the Guardian absently. 'This is your fire to put out, I'm afraid. But get Eva some help first.'

Angstrun left, muttering a string of words that was, fortunately, just about inaudible.

Troste finished reading the note and looked up at Eva. 'Apparently someone wandered into the Night Cloak — the part that was moved — and ran into an unidentified beast. Black, big, strange eyes.' She handed Eva the paper. 'By the sounds of it, that was either before or at about the same time that the attacks occurred in the city. But it might be a place to start.'

Eva glanced at the hasty map drawn on the paper. The location of the whurthag attack was clearly marked: southwest of the city, in territory that ought to be Daylands.

'Thank you,' Eva murmured, her quick mind already formulating a plan for the search. 'May I take this?'

'Of course.' Guardian Troste sighed, looking suddenly older. 'They always told me there'd be days like this,' she said. 'Though I think this beats all. We just need giants coming down out of the skies and my week will be perfect.'

Eva smiled wryly. 'Can't say I'm enjoying it very much myself.'

'Oh, that's right. Meesa Wrobsley was a friend, wasn't she? I'm sorry, Eva.'

Eva rose briskly to her feet, waving a hand dismissively. 'Well. To work.'

It took two hours to assemble Eva's teams of summoners. By that time, Angstrun's sorcerers had arrived — eight of them, constituting most of Glour's best. Eva sorted them into groups and sent them off, tasked with searching Glour city and the surrounding forest in sections. The whurthag had been seen in multiple locations already: in theory it could be anywhere.

Her own group consisted of another summoner, a sorcerer, and two armed city guards. Roys Alin was her summoner companion, a woman older than Eva with unshakeable nerves and a strong natural ability for beast management. Her abilities combined with Eva's should be a match for a single whurthag, or so Eva hoped. All they had to do was dominate its will long enough to send it through the gate.

The sorcerer was a younger man, very tall, with longish dark hair. Eva didn't recognise him. His features and the green colour of his eyes suggested some Orstwych blood somewhere back in his family tree. He seemed curiously relaxed given the nature of the task at hand.

'Pitren Warvel,' he introduced himself, offering Eva a courteous bow. 'It's a pleasure to meet the High Summoner.'

She inclined her head in response. 'How terribly formal. Do call me Lady Glostrum.'

She detected a faint twinkle of amusement in his eyes as he straightened up. Good.

'Of course, your ladyship. Please call me Tren.'

'Tren?'

He shrugged. 'It is a nickname as good as any.'

'Fair enough. Shall we depart? It's going to be a long day.'

Eva released Rikbeek. The gwaystrel flew up in a straight line, disappearing into the darkness. She knew he would keep pace with them, scanning their surroundings in organised circles. Gwaystrels were talented scouts; they could fly tirelessly for long distances on their webby black wings, and since they observed with sound and hearing rather than with their eyes, it was difficult to hide from them. This one was trained to warn Eva in a variety of ways if he encountered trouble.

Tren watched intently as Rikbeek disappeared into the trees. 'Is that a gwaystrel? I thought nobody could catch those things anymore.'

'Mere chance,' she said. 'I was larking about in the Lowers — unattended, of course — during my irresponsible twenties. Rikbeek all but flew into my face. He'd damaged a wing somehow. By the time he was fit to fly, we had made friends.' She paused. 'As much as is possible for that little monster.'

Tren lifted his brows. 'Nice story. I'm twenty-five, by the way.'

'Oh? Well, never mind. I'm sure you're mature for your age.'

'Tremendously.'

'Well, we'll see. Let's get to work.'

Their quota was the south-west sector of the city and forest, marked clearly on the hand-drawn map that Roys carried. Eva had deliberately kept one of the most able summoners with her, knowing that they would be entering territory where the whurthag had been recently sighted. The group mounted up on the outskirts of the city, taking to nivvenback to explore the forest. They travelled for some time in near silence, each intent on the search. Eva kept her mind on Rikbeek, scanning his thoughts from time to time and listening for his signals. None came.

Eva loved the forest at this time of year. The glostrel trees were in leaf, their pale foliage stark against the dark shapes of their trunks and branches. Interspersed with these were the black irignol trees, ever leafless, but decked with gleaming lichens. Moonlight filtered down through the branches, dappling the dark forest floor with patches of silvery light. The atmosphere was tranquil, calm; Eva found it hard to believe that something as terrifying as a whurthag may be stalking through the trees not far away.

Rikbeek's call came at last, startling her out of her appreciative reverie. It was the same sound he'd made when he had found Meesa's body. Eva reined in her nivven, motioning to the others to do the same. She dismounted, moving slowly and quietly. She followed Rikbeek's call a few paces to the south, Tren and Roys falling in behind her. The two guards circled out to the sides, keeping steadily up to pace with Eva.

Catching up with Rikbeek, she stopped. The gwaystrel circled madly high above her head, repeating his high, thin call every few seconds. Eva narrowed her eyes, scanning the undergrowth.

'There,' whispered Tren. She followed his pointing finger. Oh yes, there it was. A moving patch of inky shadow, stealthy as death, eyes gleaming pale and cold in the gloom. Eva gathered herself mentally, bearing down on the whurthag will the full force of her willpower. She had to master it before it was fully aware of them, before it gathered itself to resist. She sensed Roys joining her will to Eva's, doubling the strength of the attack. Together they seized the beast's will in an iron grip, subduing its desire to fight.

They hadn't been fast enough. The whurthag fought, straining to tear free. It loosed itself enough to strike; Roys hissed with pain as its claws raked across her legs, but she bore down all the harder, using her anger and pain to compel it to obey. Nonetheless the whurthag twisted and snarled, a sound terrible enough that Eva almost lost her grip. She could feel the thing working itself loose, twisting out of her control with slippery ease.

'Tren,' she said tightly. 'Gate.'

He complied. It was as though he tore a hole in the night; moonlight leaked through from somewhere else, chilly and too bright and etched with metallic blue. A cold wind blew through the portal, raising the hairs on Eva's arms. She gritted her teeth, bearing down ferociously on the whurthag, willing it to step in the direction of the gate.

It didn't move.

'Roys...'

Roys tightened her grip, gasping with the effort. Eva had bitten her lip; blood trickled down her chin, tasting sharp in her mouth. The whurthag bunched its muscles and tried to leap in her direction. Fighting panic — why in the Seven would anyone willingly summon such a creature?! — she fought hard, streaming images of danger and peril into the mind of the whurthag. Feeling it falter, she followed that with impressions of safety beyond the gate, the comfort of the home den. *It's probably not remotely susceptible to such things*, she thought desperately, but then the whurthag weakened, gave up the fight. Inch by inch she and Roys forced it towards Tren's gate. It stalked through, and the gate closed around it, silently swallowing the whurthag's night-black form.

Eva stood motionless for a long time, breathing hard. She felt completely drained, and still rather terrified. She'd never known a fight like that to control any beast, and she was one of the strongest of the summoners.

Roys recovered first. She blinked as if waking up, moved about stiffly. 'Tricky,' she said laconically, bending over her injured leg. The flesh was striped with scratches but they bled only sluggishly. 'It's not deep,' Roys confirmed, waving Eva away.

'You were lucky,' Eva said, remembering the ferocious sweep of the whurthag's claws. She looked at Tren. He too was looking pale and shaken. She wondered whether it was the effort of holding the gate open that had tired him out, or the strain of being far too close to an only barely restrained whurthag.

'All well?' she asked him.

He nodded, smiled wryly. 'You ladies clearly had the hard work. I'm fine.'

'Good work, ladies,' said one of the guards. 'We'd better check for its handler. We'll stay close.' Eva nodded and the two of them melted into the trees, weapons drawn.

Eva tilted her head to one side, wincing at a sharp pain in her neck. How tense she must've been. How long had the job taken? The moon was still strong overhead, but it could easily have been an hour. Eva sat carefully in the grass while the guards were gone, welcoming a chance at a brief rest before the ride home.

The search didn't take long. The guards soon returned, weapons sheathed.

'No sign of any handlers,' said the talkative one — Havely, Eva recalled. She had never caught the other guard's name, and he hadn't spoken a word throughout their journey.

No handler was chilling news. It suggested that the whurthag had already broken free of its master summoner's control. They had caught it barely in time. She shivered.

'We'd better go back and call the others in,' she said. They collected the nivvens and mounted up, all three shaky and exhausted. The ride back to Glour City was slow.

Three of the teams were already assembled when they arrived back at Summoner House. Eva frowned. They should have continued the search until the whurthag was confirmed as found — or until the search was called off. Why were they here?

'We found and banished the whurthag,' she said, dismounting with none of her usual easy grace. 'It's gone.'

'So did we,' said Alys Spirin, one of her foremost summoners.

'And so did we,' said another.

'We all did.'

Eva blinked, confused. 'What.'

'There was only supposed to be one,' said Roys.

'Apparently not,' said Alys. 'The count's up to four so far. No idea yet what the other teams have found.'

Eva's heart sank. 'All banished?'

'Yes.'

Eva nodded, her eyes threatening to close with weariness. The other summoners were in little better shape; several sat with their heads in their hands, others were actually lying on the floor.

'Any losses?'

'None,' said Alys, 'but a few injuries. Trace is in the worst shape. He's at the medical halls now.'

Eva nodded again, feeling deeply thankful. 'Right, well. If there were four, there could be any number still at large. The search isn't over.'

'There's one other thing.' One of Angstrun's sorcerers stepped forward, a man with hair as pale as Eva's own.

'Yes?'

'We found three rogue gates out in the forest.'

Tren looked round at that. 'Three rogue gates open at once?'

The sorcerer nodded, his face grim. 'Maybe more.'

'That's unheard of.'

Eva was shocked, too. Rogue gates were a problem no one had yet managed to solve; they opened and closed apparently according to their own rules. The only way to deal with them was to close them as quickly as possible when they were found. Part of Angstrun's job was to organise regular patrols of the city and forest by sorcerers who could close them up quickly and efficiently.

But they were relatively rare. Barely one rogue gate was discovered per moon. Three in one day?

She passed her hands over her face, rubbing her tired eyes. 'I can see it's going to be a long day.'

Eva and her summoners worked past moonset and well beyond, relentlessly searching the forests of Glour until they were, to all appearances, empty of further dangers. The total number of whurthags discovered rose to seven. Each one was found at a distance from the city precincts, crouched in the shadows as if awaiting something. Eva found it remarkable that they had not attacked the city again. Why were these here?

More rogue gates had been found, and closed. One further report had troubled Eva: one of her teams claimed to have found an unusual type of reptile in swampy northern Glour. With blue scales, long snout and horns, it was no species commonly seen in the marshes. It had probably come through one of the rogue gates, but Eva wondered.

When she was at last free to retire to her home, it was nearly moonset. She slept the long, deep, dreamless sleep of the exhausted, waking at last long after moonrise on the following day. She cursed when she realised the time, expecting to find a heap of messages urgently requiring her attention. In fact, there were only two: one from her second-in-command confirming that no further whurthag sightings had been recorded, and one from Vale, announcing his intention to visit around moonset.

He arrived a little early, looking almost as tired as Eva had been. She ordered dinner and had some cayluch sent in, thinking he looked in need of a hot drink. He sank into the sofa beside her, cupping his hands around the mug.

'What's the news?' Eva allowed herself to lean against his shoulder, unusually grateful for the company.

He sighed deeply. 'There've been some jewellery thefts in Orstwych, and one death. All sounds far too similar. I sent a couple of the boys out there for more details. Word is Glinnery's having some trouble, too.'

'Same kind?'

'More or less. A civilian injury, probably whurthag inflicted, but no deaths yet. I've sent enquiries about any jewellery thefts going on.'

A chilling thought occurred to Eva. 'Civilian injuries? Who?'

'I don't have any names yet.'

Eva had sent a warning to Ynara Sanfaer at her first opportunity. She hoped her friend had received the note in time to act on it. If all of this chaos was over the istore, then her daughter was in more danger than anyone. She shifted restlessly, wishing there was some way she could find out.

'Anything from Irbel? Nimdre?'

'Working on it.' He smiled tiredly at her, and she smiled back.

'Sorry.'

Vale's smiled faded. 'I saw Angstrun earlier. He's out for blood. You heard about the Night Cloak?'

'Mm. I was at the Guardian's Office when the news came. He wasn't happy.'

'I imagine not.'

'Does he know who did it?'

'Think so. He said one of his men's missing. Wants my help tracking him down.' Vale sighed. 'We'll deal with it, of course, but I don't know how. I've already sent most of my best men out picking up leads all over the Darklands, and I've called in my contacts in the Daylands too. We're a bit short-handed to be sending out man hunts.'

Eva allowed her head to rest on Vale's broad shoulder. 'I know the problem. I've got to keep teams of summoners out on patrol for the foreseeable future. They need to be in groups of at least two, preferably three, to deal with the whurthags safely. The guild's stretched thin already. And we're leeching sorcerers out of Angstrun's forces to pull the gates open.'

She felt Vale turn his head to look down at her. He slipped an arm around her waist and pulled her closer.

'I wonder if it's significant that these events are taking all of Glour's best out of the city and scattering them to the winds,' said Eva. 'I fear it must be.'

'Possible.'

'I mean, those whurthags weren't out for anyone in particular. They were just standing there.' A new idea occurred to her and she sat up slightly. 'Eyde. If we marked on a map where all the whurthags were found, I wonder if we would find a pattern.'

'I'm surprised you haven't done that already.'

She sighed. 'Sorry, Eyde. I was so tired yesterday I could barely remember my own name. I'll get to it first thing after moonrise tomorrow.'

He placed a kiss on the top of her head. 'Don't blame yourself, Eva my darling. It's been a long week for all of us.'

'Not much of an excuse, that,' she said absently. Her thoughts were busy, drawing links and mapping connections. 'Has Angstrun pulled the Night Cloak back yet?'

'No. He said there's a delegation on the way from Glinnery, and they want the changes explored before it's rectified. Seems they've got a theory they want testing.'

'Oh?'

'Something to do with the istore, unsurprisingly.'

'Mm,' said Eva. 'Not at all surprising.' She remembered the little Sanfaer girl's words back at the Darklands Market. *There is a cave, near to where I live. It's in the walls.* Eva wondered whether the Sanfaer family happened to live near the border to Glour.

Vale was silent for several minutes. She rested comfortably against him, reflecting that married life might not be so bad if it included such companionableness.

As if reading her mind, Vale looked down at her and smiled. 'I fear our marriage plans will have to wait a little, in the midst of this mess. I'm sorry for that.' She said nothing. He squeezed her waist slightly, kissing the top of her head again. 'Aren't you?'

'Yes,' she replied.

9

Llandry swung her legs out of bed and stood up, gingerly. Her legs trembled, but she didn't fall. She moved her arm carefully, gently working the muscles. Days of her mother's diligent care had considerably lessened the pain, and she felt herself to be healing. She still felt weak and shaky, but that was due to inactivity as much as injury. It was high time she left her bed.

She took a few steps, smiling when she didn't topple. Sigwide sat on his haunches, watching as she pulled a woollen shawl around her shoulders. He was overwhelmed with excitement when she moved towards the door; he raced around her feet and then darted on ahead of her, making his way unerringly to the kitchen. Obviously he'd been making himself at home while she slept.

'Ah, Siggy.' She felt a surge of affection for her friend. He had barely left her side during her confinement to her room. Whenever she had woken, she'd found him curled up on her stomach or tucked against her side, purring at any sign of life from her. If she was immobile, he would be immobile too. It was comforting to be the object of such unconditional devotion.

Her pleasant feelings evaporated as she reached the kitchen door and heard two male voices inside. The dark, gruff voice was her father's. The other was Devary Kant. She froze. She had assumed he would have left by now.

Peeking into the kitchen, she saw Devary sitting in one of the dining chairs with a large book spread across his lap. She hung back in the doorway, studying him covertly from the safety of the shadows.

He wasn't a young man precisely, but he didn't look very old either. Perhaps he was about her mother's age, just entering his forties. His skin was a little weathered, as if he travelled a great deal. He said he was from Nimdre, and his accent seemed to confirm it, but his complexion was as pale as any Darklander's. He wore his longish brown hair tied into a tail. She noticed smudges of ink on his face; as she watched he absently brushed back an errant lock of hair, transferring more coloured inks from his fingers onto his temples.

Ynara wasn't visible, but her voice could be heard speaking.

'...timing is interesting, Dev. Twenty years without a word from you, and then you turn up, all of a sudden, in the middle of an inter-realm crisis?' Devary started to say something but she cut him off. 'I don't care to hear your tales again. You can't expect me to believe this is just a social visit.'

'But it is,' said Devary. 'Wait a minute, let me explain.' He sighed and closed his book. 'I admit my arrival at this time is no accident. I was sent, yes. But when I said I was retired, I spoke the truth.' Ynara snorted derisively but he ignored her. 'My employers have refused to accept my resignation from duty. They required somebody to visit this household and discover the truth about this istore stone. I believe their motives are above board, as far as that counts for anything. If I had not accepted the assignment, they would have sent someone else — someone less sympathetic to your family. And, Ynara...' He leaned forward, his expression growing earnest. 'This *is* a social visit. I've wanted to come back, for years I've thought about it. This merely gave me a reason to overcome my fears of seeing you again. I don't know if you'll forgive me, but I want to make it up to you. I do. Just tell me. Anything I can do for you or your family, I'll do it. Anything.'

Llandry felt curiosity and discomfort in equal measures. As interesting as this was, she shouldn't be eavesdropping. She backed away from the door, meaning to return to her room and await her mother's visit, but Sigwide had grown tired of waiting for her. He ran heedlessly ahead and nudged open the door with his nose. His thoughts were full of food — as usual — and he sent her an excited image of a bowl brimming with fruits and nuts. Before she could prevent him, he had darted into the kitchen.

Devary had seemingly learned that where there was Sigwide there was generally Llandry, too. His sharp hazel eyes followed the orting's casual progress across the kitchen floor, then travelled to the doorway where she stood. He smiled, looking remarkably at ease for a man with ink all over his face.

'Hello,' he said. 'Welcome back to the living world. Your mother hoped you'd be up today.'

Llandry reflexively drew her shawl closer around herself, avoiding his gaze. She went to her father and leaned against his side, pressing her face into his shaggy blond hair. He didn't say anything, which she appreciated; he merely wrapped one muscular arm around her and gave her a squeeze.

A muffled squeak caught her attention. Sigwide stood beside his empty bowl, his small body quivering with indignation. He squeaked again as she looked at him, and she recognised the sound as his polite, apologetic interruption. She grinned in spite of herself, bending to refill his supplies. The wounds on her back pulled and she bit back a cry, bending at the knees instead. When Llandry straightened, she immediately found herself wrapped in a tight hug, her mother's distinctive scent enveloping her.

'Llandry, love. How are you feeling?' Ynara lightly investigated her wounds, turning her around to check the damage to her back. Llandry winced slightly, feeling the skin pull against the half-knit wounds.

'Quite a lot better, Ma. I've a sense I may live after all.'

She heard a chuckle from behind her. Probably Devary. She turned back into her mother's embrace, hiding her face against her shoulder.

Her father spoke. 'Llandry, you were right about the border.'

Llandry looked up quickly. 'Oh?'

Aysun cleared his throat and nodded. 'The border's moved, all down the south-east side of the forest. Some places only twenty feet or so. Others, more like eighty.'

'How? Why?'

'Hard to say,' said Aysun gruffly. 'Elders are working on it.'

'Also. I don't suppose you heard the news from Glour

74

before you went haring off to that precious cave of yours, hm?' Ynara's tone had taken on that disapproving quality that Llandry so dreaded, but she couldn't blame her mother for being annoyed.

'What news?' was all she said.

Ynara tutted. 'I didn't think so. I'm glad, though, or I'd have to have you certified as insane.' She guided Llandry to a chair and gently pressed her into it. 'That beast you saw — black, pale eyes, and so on — has been sighted in Glour, too. Not just sighted. Three people were killed, all of them former customers of yours.' She fixed Llandry with a hard stare. 'All carrying istore around, Llan, and stripped of it after they were dead. The connection is obvious. There's little doubt it all has a lot to do with that cave of yours. It's southeast of the city, isn't it, near the Glour border?'

Llandry nodded, her throat too dry to speak. Three people dead? Because of her jewellery?

Aysun grimaced. 'That's it, then. The Night Cloak was moved in order to absorb that cave into Darklands territory. No saying why, just yet, but you must stay well away from it from now on, Llan.'

'Promise, Llandry, please,' said Ynara.

'No fear of that,' said Llandry faintly. 'I've no wish to die by death claw.' She felt numb. Her injuries might be severe but she had been lucky indeed to avoid a far worse fate. Probably it was only her wings that had saved her; her chances of outrunning a beast that moved with such horrifying speed were minimal.

'Does... has anybody identified it?'

'The word "whurthag" is being thrown around,' said Ynara. 'That's what the papers are saying. Sensational stuff, scare stories, the usual. It might not be true. The bulletins haven't backed it up yet.'

Llandry nodded. The papers were mostly independent, and they reported whatever they pleased — the more sensational the better. The bulletin boards, on the other hand, operated via Irbellian technologies licensed by the Glinnery government, and their content was carefully screened. Many people waited for the bulletins to pick up a story before they would give it any credence.

She cast a questioning look at her father. As an expatriate of

Irbel and a talented engineer, Aysun was employed as a technician — among other things — with Irbel's local engineering outpost. Part of his job was to maintain and update the boards with new headlines. If a story on the so-called "whurthag" was planned to appear soon, he would know.

Guessing her question, her father shook his head. 'Haven't had any orders on that kind of news.'

'What do you know of this 'istore', Llandry?' Devary's enquiry was mild enough, but Ynara shot him a look of deep suspicion. He spread his hands. 'That the istore is important is beyond question, Ynara. It must be identified.'

Llandry disliked having his attention fixed on her. She averted her eyes, instead watching Sigwide devour his dinner. 'Not very much,' she admitted. She told him, rather hesitantly, about her cave, how she had discovered it. 'I wish I had a piece to show you. It's more or less opaque, but with a bit of translucency. Indigo coloured, shines silver. It isn't like any gem I've ever worked with before.'

'It emits light?' Devary sat tapping his fingers against his cheek, apparently in thought.

'No. Well — only in the cave. When I remove it, it stops glowing.'

'When you say it is unlike a gem, what do you mean?'

Llandry pondered the question for a moment, trying to recall the way the stones felt in her hands. 'They don't feel like gems,' she said at last. 'They aren't cold the way stones are. But I've never cut one. Somehow I didn't want to.'

'The interest they have caused is ... feverish,' said Devary. 'Do you know why?'

'Well, I...' For some reason Llandry did not wish to share her connection with the stone with this stranger. But he was right: the questions were important. 'When I wear it, or hold it, I feel different. I feel less... less anxious. Calmer, stronger even. And I feel almost like I could — could —'

'Could what, love?' asked her mother. She smiled encouragingly at Llandry, squeezing her hand.

'I don't know. I feel like I could do things I've never been able to do before. I can hear animals better. Once I could almost talk with Sigwide, in a way. His thoughts were clearer to me and mine to him. And I could sense more than before. Like hearing

76

better, but not the same.' She stopped talking, embarrassed by this long speech. A hated blush crept up her cheeks.

'Clearly it is remarkable,' observed Devary. 'If it has this same effect on others, then it is no wonder it has taken the fashionable world by storm.' He smiled at Llandry. 'Thank you for answering my questions.'

Llandry merely nodded awkwardly. She was growing tired now, her limbs heavy, and her wounds were hurting.

'Back to bed, Llandry, love,' said her mother, looking narrowly at her. 'You're tired. I'll dress your wounds again first.'

Llandry was quite ready to leave the room and escape Devary's scrutiny. She stood up, slowly, but her knees weakened halfway across the room and she almost fell. Her father and Devary both reacted; Devary was the closest and reached her first. She found herself scooped up and carried to her room. She was gently laid down on her bed, and a moment later Sigwide was placed on her pillow. She barely noticed as her mother bathed her wounds and replaced her bandages. She fell asleep with Sigwide curled against her face.

Llandry was aloft, suspended in the skies over Glinnery. She was lost in the clouds, enclosed within a dense, drifting white fog that utterly obscured her surroundings. Downwards she drifted, down and down until the fog cleared and she could see the wide caps of the glissenwol beneath. She landed gently, sinking up to her knees in a carpet of spongy moss; as she fought her way through it the clouds cleared overhead, revealing a sky tinted with lavender. The glissenwol were so tall she could barely see their caps from the ground; they gleamed with a vividness that hurt her eyes. A heady scent of alberries, nara-fruit and luminaef blooms assaulted her nose and she felt she could hardly breathe under the onslaught of that tangled aroma. She gasped for breath, tasting the blood that trickled steadily from her nose. Birdsong pelted her ears with rich notes both raucous and intensely melodic.

A streak of grey fur shot across her vision, disappearing into the waving grasses ahead. The colours were wrong, she noticed abstractedly; yellow where she expected green, blue where she expected red. She followed the grey creature, calling for Sigwide to wait, wait. Hands gripped her feet and she fell into an expanse of moss that changed its colours dizzyingly, reaching up to grasp her and pull her down into the depths...

Llandry woke slowly, fighting her way to consciousness through the clinging moss that filled her mind. She felt groggy, disorientated, as if she had slept for days. Perhaps she had. She rose determinedly, ignoring the weakness that threatened to send her spinning to the ground. She recognised the feeling of muffled abstraction: her mother had fed her herbs to keep her under. That explained the dreams.

Ynara was cooking. Whatever it was smelt wonderful, and Llandry realised she was starving.

'Ma.'

'Hello, love. Do you think you could eat something?'

'Half of a nivven, probably. Maybe all of it.'

Ynara grinned. 'Good. Just a minute, then.'

'I'd like to go home, later.'

'Home?' Ynara deliberately busied herself at the stove, not looking at Llandry.

'As in, back to my own tree.'

'Oh, but, love. I don't think you're well enough yet.'

'How long have I been asleep?'

'About two days.'

'Then I think I've slept enough.'

Ynara set a bowl of soup before her, adding a plate of fresh bread. Llandry ate readily, feeling stronger with each mouthful. Her mother drew out the chair opposite and sat, watching Llandry eat.

'Your father and I are worried about you.'

'I won't be far away, Ma.'

'Far enough.'

Llandry looked up, then wished she hadn't. Her mother's face was taut with concern, her eyes dark with real fear. Llandry winced inwardly. Ynara had never been able to have more children, though she had wanted to; giving birth to Llandry had almost killed her, and Aysun had forbidden any repeat of the experience. She knew all too well that she was all her mother would ever have.

'I could stay a day or two more.'

'We just want to make sure you're all right, love.'

'I know, Ma. Can I have the balcony? I want to get some work done.'

'Of course, love. Anything you need. Only leave it a day or

78

two, hm? Your arm needs a bit more time to heal.' Her mother's obvious relief was painful. Llandry knew her day or two would turn into many more, but she didn't have the heart to argue.

Of course, if her mother's house was as it used to be — just herself, Ynara and Aysun — she might not have wanted to.

'Is... will Devary be staying much longer?'

Ynara's head tilted, her expression becoming appraising.

'Yes, love. He offered to stay and help. I asked him to keep an eye on you if we aren't home.'

Llandry sighed, not bothering to hide it. With Devary as her guardian — jailer, even — she would have no peace at all.

'Oh, love. He's quite easy to be around, I promise. You'll soon get used to him.'

Llandry nodded numbly, not meeting her mother's eyes. How she wished she'd inherited her mother's easy sociability, that understated charm and confidence that graced her every interaction. Or, failing that, could she not have followed her father's example? He freely rejected every social nicety, concerning himself with none of them. Instead she was caught in an eternal conflict: wanting to be part of her mother's easy social world, but unable to learn how.

'You trust him to take care of me?' Her mother's words in the kitchen came back to her; her distrust for Devary had been obvious, though Llandry did not understand the cause.

'I do,' Ynara replied. 'He's... capable, Llan, and he knows what will happen to him if anything happens to you.'

'What will happen to him?'

'I expect to begin with castration and move on to flaying alive.'

Llandry grinned in spite of herself. Nobody in their right mind would thwart her mother.

Ynara came around the table and hugged her, checking her arm as she did so. 'He won't be around all the time, love. There'll be other things for him to do.'

'I'll get used to him.' Llandry spoke with a confidence she didn't really feel.

'I hope so, love, because I have to leave today. Just for a few days.'

'What? Why?'

'Duty,' Ynara sighed. 'The trouble with the Night Cloak is a

79

big issue. For generations — centuries, probably — the border between the Darklands and the Daylands has been fixed, agreed between Glour and Glinnery. In the past, disputes over that border have been... bloody. We can't let this pass without some show of investigation.'

'A "show" of investigation?'

'Well. I don't personally believe the Glour Government had anything to do with it. I know most of them. They're too sensible.' Ynara smiled briefly. 'I'm willing to believe this is a different sort of problem. But nonetheless, a delegation must be sent, and inevitably I must go with it.'

'You don't want to go.'

Ynara stroked Llandry's hair. 'I don't want to leave you, sweetheart, especially while you're ill. But I must be part of this delegation. And besides, it will give me an opportunity to investigate this cave business.'

'Ma! You're going to the cave? After you forbade me?' Fear squeezed Llandry's heart, picturing her mother attacked by lethal claws.

'Don't worry, love. There will be a proper expedition launched to examine the changes to the boundary and oversee the restoration of the border to its original position. We will have all proper protection. And I hear that the whurthags have been sent back to the Lowers.'

'Whurthags?'

Ynara looked guilty. 'I hadn't meant to mention that. Yes, there was more than one.'

'And you're still going? Is it any wonder why I'm stubborn, with a mother like you?'

Ynara laughed. 'Don't get any ideas, Llan. I still don't want you wandering caveward, under any circumstances. Just wait for me to return, please, and I promise I will tell you absolutely everything.'

Llandry slumped. 'I wish I could go with you.'

'Not with those injuries, love. You're getting better, but you'd certainly rip them open again. And I don't want to take you anywhere near that area until it's declared safe.'

'I know, I know. Are you going alone?'

'No. Your father insists on coming along. To protect me, he says.' Her lips twitched at the idea.

Llandry's stomach dropped a long way. 'You're *both* going?'

'It's only for a few days, love, as I said.'

Llandry groaned. A few *days* alone with a stranger? Her life had taken a definite turn for the worse lately.

'Can't you... can't Devary go with you and Papa stay here?'

'Do you dislike Devary so much?' Her mother sounded disappointed, which was unbearable.

'N-no, not — not dislike, exactly. I just...' She couldn't find the words to explain.

'You'll soon get to know him, love. He's ... well, he has his faults, but he's easy to get along with. Abominably loveable, in fact. I think you'll like him.'

'I'm sure you're right, Mamma.' Llandry didn't feel any conviction of truth in her words, but she spoke them anyway.

'Truthfully, love, I'm hoping you'll look after Devary a bit as well. He's wearing himself out.'

'He must be more than twice my age,' said Llandry irritably. 'He doesn't need looking after.'

'He does,' said Ynara. 'He's trying too hard.'

'What do you mean by that?'

'He's overworking himself, trying to do everything at once. Helping Aysun, helping me, trying to look after you.'

'Sounds like he's trying to make up for something.' Llandry spoke casually, but her mother's gaze grew sharp.

'Why do you say that?'

'Oh... no reason.'

Ynara narrowed her eyes, but let the allusion pass. 'I need you to do one thing for me before I leave.'

'Anything.'

'Do you recognise these names?' Ynara placed a piece of paper in front of Llandry. A long list was laid out upon it in green ink.

'Some of them,' Llandry said, scanning rapidly. 'Saudran Iritan. Alen Marstry. They were some of my customers-by-post.'

'Eva said they're looking for everyone who has — or had — some of your istore. Is this a full list?'

'I don't think so. It's too short.'

'Can you give me a list of people you've crafted for?'

'I can, Ma, but I don't know who they all were. I sold a lot at the markets.'

'I know. Just write down everyone whose names you do have. It will all help.'

'What about my Daylands customers? Has somebody told them?' Llandry felt a flicker of panic, picturing her clients cold and bloodied, their jewellery forcibly removed.

'That's the other thing I'd like you to do, love. The bulletin boards have been activated to issue warnings about the istore, so some of them will already know, but perhaps not everyone has heard yet. I'd like you to write to everyone on your list, tell them to hand in their istore pieces at the Council Halls. The guard below will see that your letters are delivered.'

Llandry twisted the list in her hands, her eyes blurring. 'All these names. Ma, I got these people robbed, killed...'

Ynara released her and moved to sit in front of her daughter, stroking her face. 'No, love, you didn't. You didn't know. You've done nothing wrong.'

Llandry blinked a few times, trying to control the prickle of tears behind her eyes. She knew firsthand the sort of pain the whurthag could inflict; she only hoped the creature's victims had died too quickly to feel much of it.

Ynara kissed her, wrapping her in a quick, fierce hug. 'I have to go, love. We are leaving in an hour. Will you promise me to take care of yourself? You and Devary?'

'Of course, Ma. And you — you be careful.'

'I'll be fine. Your father will be with me. Can you picture him permitting anything to get near me without invitation?' She smiled, and Llandry couldn't help smiling back. 'I'll be home soon, love.'

Llandry wrote letters until her fingers ached. She wrote on until her fingers formed blisters and began to bleed. Hours after the departure of her mother and father, Llandry was still curled up in the parlour writing detailed missives to each person on her list. She couldn't help including apologies, useless though they were. She felt responsible for the trouble that now threatened each of these people.

Devary arrived home sometime after sunset. He entered the parlour hesitantly, as if unsure of his welcome. Llandry tried to smile. Her muscles were so tense she feared it was more of a grimace, but it seemed to help. He smiled back.

'I'm sorry you're left with me,' he said. 'It is only for a few days.'

'It's fine.'

'If your letters are done, I could take them down for you. There is a messenger waiting.'

'Thank you.' She picked up the pile of envelopes that lay at her left elbow, handing them to him. He took them, taking care not to touch her fingers. He turned to leave.

'Devary?'

He turned back. 'Hm?'

'What would you like for supper?'

He gave a genuine smile, one which lit up his eyes with real warmth. 'Why don't I cook? I will show you something from Nimdre.'

'Thank you.' She hesitated. 'M-maybe you could show me how to make it.'

'Agreed,' he said. 'Meet me in the kitchen in ten minutes.' He left, still smiling. Llandry took a deep breath, wondering what had possessed her to suggest it. Guilt at her own lack of graciousness, probably. He meant well, after all, and he was harmless; the problem lay with her.

10

Eva placed a black pebble on the map spread across Guardian Troste's table.

'That's where the seventh was found.' She'd traced a pattern across the map in seven black pebbles, marking where each whurthag had been discovered. Commander Iver of the Glinnery delegation had already drawn the new outline of the Night Cloak, marking where it had expanded into Glinnery territory. The expansion was fairly even down much of the Glinnery-Glour border, excepting one area where the line swung sharply into the Daylands, covering an area of at least a hundred feet.

The seven black pebbles formed a neat semi-circle around it.

Elder Sanfaer leaned forward and picked up a small blue pebble. Comparing the map on the table with the one in her hand, she carefully placed the blue pebble in the centre of the circle.

'That is the location of Llandry's cave.'

Six Glour officials and five Glinnery delegates stared at the map, silent. The implication was too obvious to need naming.

'Well,' said Guardian Troste, at length. 'I think that raises more questions than it answers.'

'The University of Waeverleyne is studying the stone. Some theories have been presented, but nothing solid has yet emerged.' The speaker was one of the Glinnery Elders, an elderly man whose hair was almost white. His face was mapped with wrinkles, but his bright blue eyes were sharp, focused.

'Elder Shuly, perhaps I could exact from you an agreement to notify Glour if your scholars discover anything significant.'

The white-haired man bowed his head to Guardian Troste. 'Of course.'

Eva watched all of the Glinnery officials covertly. Four of them bore wings, neatly folded against their backs. Glinnish wings had always fascinated her; they were not feathered like a bird's but more like a combination of a gwaystrel's and a daefly's wings, thin membrane over bone and painted with colour. She had a secret envy of their power of flight.

The fifth was unwinged, his colouring and accent suggesting Irbellian heritage. Eva had learned that he was Elder Sanfaer's husband, which interested her. He had said nothing throughout the meeting, merely watching with an intense, fixed attention which might be unnerving were it directed at a particular person.

Troste looked at Professor Mayn, head of Glour's University. He sat silent as usual, tugging thoughtfully at the tip of his long nose.

'Professor, we need to get the University involved immediately. Whatever you can come up with about this so-called istore should be brought directly to me. Top priority, please.'

Mayn nodded. 'Am I going to be needed here for the rest of the meeting?'

'Not urgently. I'll see that you are summoned at once if anything comes up.'

Mayn stood up, his bald head gleaming beneath the light-globes. 'I'll begin at once, then. Excuse me.' He left quietly, closing the door behind him.

Lord Angstrun stood up as well. He had withstood the meeting with ill-concealed impatience. Now he towered over the seated officials with the air of a thundercloud about to erupt.

'For my part, I've a mess to clean up and a criminal to catch. If I may be excused?'

'Not yet,' said Troste, calmly. 'Sit down a moment, please.'

Angstrun scowled, but he obeyed.

'Altering the Night Cloak is a serious offence,' continued Troste. 'Is it yet confirmed who is responsible?'

Angstrun grimaced. 'More or less. I'm a minion down. One of my aides — one of my best, typically — has absconded without leave. Naturally this suggests a rather terrific guilt over something.' He glanced at the Glinnery delegates, sighed, and elaborated. 'I have six assistants taking care of the Night Cloak, two on duty at any given time. They maintain the Cloak, activate it at moonset, deactivate it at moonrise, repair leaks, that kind of thing. I daresay you have the same arrangement.' He glared at Laylan Westry, Glinnery's Chief Sorcerer, as if the Cloaking system was entirely her fault.

'We do,' she said, mild in the face of Angstrun's lack of manners.

'One of them has vanished. Young chap, not the sort to go to the dogs I'd have said, but you never know. He has the ability and the necessary access to move the Cloak, and his disappearance implicates him.'

Vale spoke up. Today he was looking most handsome in uniform, his Chief Investigator's badge prominently displayed on his left lapel. 'And the other five? It couldn't have been any of them?'

'Naturally it *could* have been any of them, but I don't think it was. They know what I'd do to them if I found out. Anyone with enough guts to do the deed would have wits enough to put a lot of distance between the two of us.'

'You're sure the man left voluntarily?'

'No,' said Angstrun briefly. 'That's your job.'

Vale permitted himself a small smile. 'True enough. What's the name?'

'Ed Geslin. Edwae, that is.'

'Thanks.' Vale scribbled messily in a small notebook, chewing on his lower lip as he pondered the information. It was one of the habits Eva found most endearing.

'Thank you, Lord Angstrun,' said Guardian Troste. 'I believe that's everything.'

'Fine.' Angstrun stood up. 'I'll pull back the Cloak, unless anyone has any more objections.' He glared fiercely down at the group.

'I do.' Elder Sanfaer's eyes held a hint of amusement as she looked at Angstrun, though her tone was quietly firm.

'Oh, you do?' said Angstrun, with dangerous calm. 'On what

86

grounds, pray?'

'We would like to examine that cave before we return to Glinnery, and it would be preferable to have the company of several of those gathered here. Including you, Lord Angstrun. Your collected expertise will be invaluable.'

'Approved,' put in Guardian Troste. 'The cave is clearly central to these incidents. It is high time it was properly investigated.'

Angstrun looked at the ceiling. 'Do you realise how long it takes to restore the balance of the thing after an interruption? The Cloak goes back at moonset tomorrow, and not a minute later. Better do what you need to before then.'

'That will be plenty of time,' said Elder Sanfaer, gracing Angstrun with a smile. 'Thank you.'

'In the meantime, I've some assistants to question.' He left without another word.

'Well.' Troste looked at Eva. 'High Summoner Glostrum, perhaps you'd share the progress of your efforts regarding the whurthag problem.'

It was late when the meeting finally closed. Eva took the first opportunity of speaking privately to Elder Sanfaer, catching up with her outside of the Council Hall.

'Ynara. You received my letter, I hope?'

Elder Sanfaer inclined her head in assent. 'Yes. Thank you for the warning.'

'And your daughter? Has she been harmed? I heard of civilian injuries.'

Ynara nodded again, to Eva's dismay. 'She was the first to encounter the whurthag, on her way to that cursed cave. The worst injuries were to her arm, but she is healing fast. I only wish... I wish we had understood at the time what we were dealing with.'

Eva touched her arm in sympathy. 'Just as I wish it had been possible to banish the whurthags before they started killing our citizens. It's not possible to know everything in advance, alas, much as I try.'

'Eva, I'm sorry. I should have sent condolences for your friend. I'm afraid I was too preoccupied with Llandry.'

Eva smiled sadly. 'Your daughter's safety is by far the more important consideration of the two.'

'I worry about her every minute. I've left her well guarded, but still...'

Noting the shadow of worry in Ynara's eyes, Eva felt suddenly strange. Had she followed her friend's path in life, she might by now have had her own daughter, a girl nearing adulthood. She couldn't immediately decide whether or not she regretted the lack.

Shaking off the thought, she smiled and asked, 'You'll be leaving tomorrow?'

'Yes, certainly,' said Ynara. 'As soon as we are finished at the cave.'

'Why don't you and your husband dine with me tonight? Vale will be joining us.'

Ynara smiled. 'Thank you, that would be a pleasure.'

'Lovely. My carriage will be here momentarily.'

They waited in silence for several minutes, facing the horizon where the waxing moon was slowly sinking out of sight. Eva could almost feel the waves of tension from her friend as she stood, still but restless, her fingers twined through her husband's.

'She'll be all right, Ynara,' said Eva softly. 'A woman couldn't ask for more dedicated parents.' She was thinking of her own as she spoke: her mother, who'd died so young, and her father, distant and uninvolved in her life until he too passed away. She'd been alone since her fifteenth year. It was possible that she envied Ynara's daughter, just a little, for her safe, loved existence.

'She's right,' said Aysun in his gruff, laconic way. 'Llandry's tougher than she looks, too. Takes after you.' Eva glanced over to see him kiss his wife gently. An encouraging smile sat oddly on his lined face, but the expression held the more power for that.

'I hope you're right. Both of you.' Ynara smiled, but her heart obviously wasn't in it.

Eva was out well before moonrise the next day, mustering her summoners. Angstrun's sorcerers were present in greater numbers than before, closing the several new rogue gates that had appeared overnight. By moonrise the forests west of Glour City had been thoroughly explored and declared free of dangers.

Next it was the turn of Commander Iver and his Glour colleagues to advance on the cave. A contingent of summoners and sorcerers attended them in case of off-realm perils, though Eva was not permitted to be part of this initial exploratory force. She waited with Elder Sanfaer and her husband, flanked by the University heads, Lord Angstrun and Chief Sorcerer Laylan Westry. The mood was tense: everyone remembered well the lurid pictures of the whurthags' earlier victims, obligingly spread by the daily papers.

Commander Iver returned at last, bringing some of his men with him. Eva noticed Tren was one of the three sorcerers that had gone out with the group.

'It's clear,' said Iver, reining in his nivven. 'No signs of occupation at all. Though, that cave must be pretty well hidden; we haven't found it yet.'

Ynara moved her nivven forward. 'I've detailed instructions from my daughter. I believe I can find it.'

Iver nodded, but he looked annoyed. 'It might've been helpful to have her here in person.'

Ynara's jaw tightened. 'So it might have, but I forbade it.'

Iver looked at the sky, controlling his irritation with obvious difficulty. He said nothing more, however, only turned his mount and rode away in the direction from which he'd come. Ynara followed, with her husband riding beside her. Eva touched her heels to her nivven's flanks, urging the mare to keep step with the riders ahead.

They were right on the edge of the irignol forests. Within a few minutes, the irignol and glostrel trees melted away, replaced by the towering, broad trunks of the trees known as glissenwol. Eva looked up, fascinated, noting the incredible height of the things. She could faintly discern the glissenwol caps overhead, their deep colours camouflaging them under the night time. Long, draping vines hung from the tops, swaying in the breeze, painted silver in the moonlight. She sensed a lack of health about the proud trees, a hint of sickness as though their vitality was steadily draining away the longer they remained without sunlight.

Her nivven was not enjoying the moss that covered the forest floor. The mare's hoofs sank deeply into the thick, spongy stuff, and she snorted in disdain. Eva patted the beast's neck, easing her irritation with images of the warm stable and bag of feed that were to come later.

The riders up ahead drew to a halt, and Eva reined in. She watched as Elder Sanfaer dismounted, handing the reins of her nivven to her husband. She advanced, flanked by Commander Iver and a crew of guards.

'I need a bit more light,' Eva heard Ynara say. Tren obligingly opened a hand, releasing a dancing light-globe into the air. The glow steadily brightened until it dazzled Eva, and she looked away.

'Perfect, thank you,' Ynara said.

Eva blinked, hoping her eyes would grow accustomed to the light. They did not. She stopped trying to see Ynara's actions and closed her eyes, listening for activity.

Ynara's soft sound of discovery alerted Eva to her progress. She opened her eyes carefully, grateful to note that the light-globe was gradually dimming again. Ynara and Commander Iver stood before a pair of closely-growing glissenwol trunks. The space between the trees was choked with vines and ferns, but as Eva watched Iver found a way to slip through. Then his tall frame disappeared abruptly into the ground.

Several of Iver's men went down next, followed by some of Eva's summoners, and then Tren. Ynara and Aysun waited until most of them had emerged.

'It's empty,' Iver said, shaking loose dirt from his hair. 'Completely, I'd say, but you'll know best.' He nodded at Ynara and retreated out of the way. Eva approached as Ynara and Aysun disappeared into the cave. She followed, finding an opening in the ground just big enough for her to slip into. A mud slope led down into a dirt-walled cave, barely high enough for her to stand upright. She noticed some of Iver's men had to stoop in order to remain inside.

Ynara was staring at the walls helplessly. 'I don't see any of Llandry's stone, but then I can't see enough to be sure.' She looked enquiringly at Eva.

Eva walked slowly around the cave, examining the walls closely. Nothing but packed dirt met her sensitive eyes.

'Llandry said it glows a little, down in the cave,' said Ynara. She didn't need to add anything more: no hint of a glow was visible anywhere.

Instead, the walls were pitted and marked, as if something had once lain there and had been subsequently removed. Eva noticed long channels extending deeper into the walls, casings that had probably once housed pieces of Llandry's stone. The pattern was curious: the stones had not, apparently, lain closely together, nor had they been broken free of a larger mass of the gem. The emptied channels formed a more complex pattern, one which obviously extended a long way back.

'There's nothing here,' she said, turning back to Ynara. 'It's all gone, stripped out. Excuse me,' she added. 'I think Professor Mayn ought to see this.'

Mayn was, as Eva expected, intrigued. He managed the descent with remarkable ease given his age; perhaps enthusiasm helped. He took one look at the patterning on the walls and took out a notebook. Within seconds he was sketching the outlines with hasty strokes of his pencil.

'I'd get an image-capture down here,' he murmured, 'but I doubt it'd record the detail in light like this.'

'Maybe a couple of sketch-artists should be sent over,' said Eva. 'Actually, Ynara, that will lie in your jurisdiction from tomorrow.'

'True,' Ynara replied. 'I'll make sure someone's sent out as soon as I get home.'

Elder Ilae Shuly had descended with Mayn, and seemed no less fascinated. His keen eyes swept the walls repeatedly, staring into the darkness. After a while he gave up and looked over Mayn's shoulder, watching the progress of his sketching. Eva wondered what the two men were thinking as they studied that curious array of marks. For her part, she had no notion what it might portend.

'It's a shame,' Ynara said, looking at the bare walls. 'Only, I can't help feeling relieved, too.'

Eva understood. If the gem was gone, her daughter would no longer be tempted to seek it out. Nor would there be any further pieces distributed to individuals who may, later, find themselves endangered by it.

Still, it would have been as useful as it was interesting to see it in its original state. The fact that it glowed interested Eva particularly.

'Little to be done down here, now,' Eva said at last, smiling at Ynara. 'I'm going back up. I imagine the gentlemen here will be busy for quite some time yet.' Professor Mayn and Elder Shuly didn't even seem to hear her, so intent were they on their task. She smiled wryly, nodded to Ynara, and made her way carefully back up the slope.

Tren was waiting outside the entrance.

'Hi,' he said.

'Hello, Tren.'

'Interesting, huh?'

'Oh, yes. Fascinating.'

He fell silent, looked at the floor, then back up at her, shoving his hands into his pockets. Eva cast him a quizzical look.

'Anything I can help with?'

'Oh... no. Thanks. See you later, maybe.' Tren wandered off. Eva watched him go, puzzled. He didn't look back.

The Sanfaers left promptly at moonset. Eva watched them go, feeling rather sad. She felt that Ynara could be a close friend, were it possible to see more of her. If only she could visit her in the Daylands. There were rumours of new technologies coming out of Irbel; something about spectacles with manipulated lenses had reached her ears a moon or two ago, tools that would allow a Darklander to comfortably withstand the bright lights of the Daylands. She made a mental note to look into that possibility at her first opportunity.

She found, however, that her opportunity was likely to be a long time in coming. Eyde Vale was waiting for her when she arrived home, and he lost no time in presenting her with a problem.

'I need a summoner,' he said. 'Two, preferably. If you can only spare one, it'd better be the most powerful you have.'

'What? For how long?'

He shrugged. 'As long as it takes to track down Edwae Geslin. At least a few days. He'll be a long way gone by now.'

'Why do you need a summoner for that?'

'Because there might be more whurthags. If there aren't any left now, those gates are still opening all over the forest. Maybe

92

in Orstwych, too. I'm not sending my best agent out without protection from those things.'

'Eyde, I understand the urgency, really, but I can't spare any of my best summoners. They're needed here. Protecting Glour is of paramount importance at the moment.'

'Give me a couple of lesser ones, then.'

'I can't, Eyde! It's all they can do to keep the forests clear just now. You know they've been finding more than just whurthags. Those reptiles are appearing in greater numbers, and more besides. I need them where they are.'

Vale sat down with a sigh. 'I can't compromise on this, Eva. Angstrun's pushing me to get on Geslin's case, and I concur: he's the only lead we've got. There's nowhere else to look. And I need that summoner.'

She groaned. 'It never ends at the moment, does it? I'll see what I can do.'

Vale came over to her, his broad face registering remorse. 'I'm sorry, Eva. I shouldn't press you so hard. I'm short-staffed, too; I can barely find the resources to handle this case of Angstrun's, and he insists on my best agent. Even so, Geslin's going to be a hard one to track. He's one of our strongest sorcerers, well able to hide himself from just about anything I can find to track him with.' He wrapped his arms around her, resting his chin on the top of her head. 'I only wish I'd known about this before I dispatched men all over the Darklands looking for that damned istore stuff.'

'When are you sending your agent out?'

'As soon as possible. Tomorrow, I hope. Geslin's already had a long lead.' Rikbeek, squashed between Eva and Vale, squirmed and protested.

'Better watch it,' said Eva. 'He'll bite.'

He bit. Vale cursed and released Eva, putting one large hand to his belly. A neat hole adorned his shirt.

'Evil little beast,' he muttered. 'If they weren't so damn useful I'd push for them to be banned.' A thought occurred to him, and he looked keenly at her. 'Is it true that nothing can hide from a gwaystrel?'

'I haven't had cause to test him that much, but I haven't yet found anything that could conceal itself from him. He spotted the whurthags easily.'

93

'Hm. Then I bet he could spot Geslin. I don't suppose you can lend him out to someone?'

Eva grinned. 'You're just trying to get rid of him.'

'I wouldn't be completely heartbroken to see him go.'

'Sadly, no. I don't think he'd respond to anyone else. He ignores any attempt to influence him but mine.'

'Damn.' Vale fell silent for a moment. 'Well,' he said at last, 'Get me a summoner with a shortig hound, if you can. That will help.'

'I have a shortig,' she said.

'Oh? I've never seen it.'

'You've never asked.'

'I suppose not.'

Eva thought for a moment. She couldn't pull someone off the patrol teams without upsetting the careful balance she'd arranged. Besides, none of her best summoners kept shortig hounds, and while a few were in training for Vale's department, they weren't yet ready for duty. Which would mean she'd have to take at least two of the lesser summoners out of the patrol groups. Just thinking about how to rearrange them all, with their different abilities and animal companions, threatened to give her a headache.

The only person who wasn't assigned to a regular patrol, in fact, was her.

'Eyde. Why don't I go?'

'What.'

'I'll go with your agent. My shortig and Rikbeek will go with me. We'll get the job done faster that way, I'm sure. And I won't have to make a mess of my patrol teams.'

'No,' he said flatly. 'It's dangerous. Besides, aren't you needed here? You're High Summoner.'

'Oh, really. It's an empty title half the time; you know that. My second can take care of the administrative side of things for a couple of weeks. As for its being dangerous, well. I can take care of myself.'

'You can handle a whurthag unaided, can you?'

She paused, thinking. It had been difficult, before, but then it had been a new experience. In battling the whurthag, she had learned its weaknesses, learned how to deal with it. She still wouldn't dare to try full mastery over a whurthag, but all she had to do was push it through a gate.

'Yes,' she said. 'Now that I know what to expect.'

He stared at her, obviously warring with himself. Her offer presented the perfect solution to his problems, but she knew he'd hate letting her go.

'Eva,' he said at last, 'please reconsider. Surely you can find someone else. Send your second.'

'No,' she said, firmly. 'I've made up my mind.' If she was honest with herself, there was more to her offer than Vale's convenience. She was tiring of meetings and discussions and patrols; the prospect of taking more direct action excited her. 'We'll leave tomorrow. Angstrun had better be prepared to send a good sorcerer with us.'

'Eva—'

'Do you want children?'

'What?' He stared at her, nonplussed.

'Children,' she persevered. 'Small, screaming human beings that stink and break everything you own—'

'I know what they are.' His lips twitched. 'Stop changing the subject.'

She grinned. 'Were you expecting to have some?'

'I was thinking about it.' He spoke carefully, trying to guess at her opinion. 'Why, do you?'

'I'm open to it.'

He leaned down to kiss her. 'Why don't we discuss that in a bit more detail?'

11

Llandry bent over her workbench, wielding her jeweller's tools with precision. Her father had made them for her years before, and she treasured them almost as much as she treasured her stones. Her equipment had been moved from her tree to her mother's balcony earlier in the day, and she had set to work immediately, eager to return to her trade. She'd chosen the balcony because the hazy forest light soothed her, the breezes caressing her wings as she worked.

Light-globes hovered just above her head, illuminating her delicate close-work. She drew one down to the bench, blinking until her eyes adjusted to the stronger glow. On the bench lay a piece of sapphire, its polished surface reflecting the light perfectly. Sapphire had been her favourite gem before she had discovered the istore, and she still loved its rich blue colour. She was preparing to cut the stone; it was large enough to make a fine brooch, or a centrepiece for a necklace. It kept her busy in her mother's absence.

She braced the jewel and lifted her tools, beginning to cut.

'Good morning.' That cursed deep, musical voice spoke from the doorway, aggravatingly pleasant even when he was carelessly disturbing her work. Her concentration broke, her hands slipped, and a diamond-tipped edge slammed into the stone in entirely the wrong place. She gasped, gathered the gem up like a hurt child and anxiously inspected the surface.

It hadn't cracked. She wrapped it quickly in soft cloth and replaced it in her jewel box.

'The stone doesn't crack under a sudden fright, but I might,' she said without turning around. 'Mere flesh and bone, me, susceptible to surprises.'

'I'm sorry,' he said, and he did sound contrite.

Irritation had made her uncharacteristically verbose before; now she felt discomfort creeping over her, stealing her words. She changed her mind about the stone, took it out of the box and slipped it into her pocket. It was cold, and remained so despite its proximity to her skin. The way a proper gem ought to feel.

She turned away from her bench at last, and forced herself to look him in the eye. She managed something like a smile. To her dismay he smiled back, a wide, uninhibited smile full of warmth. She felt heat coming into her face again and looked away, focusing her gaze determinedly on the floor.

'So, um. How are you?' Her words emerged almost inaudibly.

'I can't speak for the floor, but I am well enough, thank you.' His tone was lightly teasing. She looked up, startled, to catch a renewed smile just fading from his face.

She nodded vaguely, becoming too aware of that smile. She looked back at the floor, feeling awkward, and drifted to the balcony rail, seeking an excuse to avoid Devary's gaze. To her dismay he followed her, settling only a couple of feet away. Much too close... and he was looking at her again, trying to catch her eye.

'Llandry?'

'Mhm.'

'You do not like me very much. Is there something I did to offend you?'

Curse him, he actually sounded sad about it. 'Why should it matter?' she said, almost savage. 'You're here for Mamma.'

'I — well, yes, but that doesn't mean—' He broke off. She glanced at him, briefly. He looked bewildered and sorry. She dug her fingers into the balcony rail, wishing he would go away.

'I don't dislike you.'

'You behave as if you do.'

She struggled with herself helplessly. How could she possibly explain?

'I don't dislike you,' she said again.

He looked away. 'All right,' he said, after a moment.

She wanted to apologise, but she couldn't find the words. 'I just don't...'

'Don't what?'

She looked at her hands. 'I need time to get used to you.'

He didn't understand, obviously. Probably he was one of those people who easily charmed others. That smile was dangerous enough.

'Well,' he said awkwardly, 'I'll be around for a while. I hope we can get along, more or less.'

She merely nodded, tired of the effort of speech. He waited for a response for a while, then seemed to give up.

'I'll be going out again soon. After I sleep, a little.'

'All right,' she said.

He nodded and turned to leave the balcony.

'Devary? Why are you here, really?'

He stopped and looked back over his shoulder at her. 'Really? I came to see your mother.'

'I know, but...' She fumbled for words. She couldn't ask her question without admitting she had eavesdropped before.

He sighed and turned around. 'We were friends, years ago, but... things did not end well with your mother. My visit was not as it should have been, and she was right to reproach me. When I tried to see her again, she hadn't forgiven me.' He smiled slightly. 'You were only about two years old at that time. You looked like your mother, even then.'

'What happened?'

'I don't think I would like to explain in more detail. I hope you will understand that. It was all a long time ago.'

Llandry sighed inwardly, but she didn't press him. 'Has she forgiven you now?'

'I think so. I hope so.' He gave her a crooked smile and left.

Curses. She hated family secrets, but neither Devary nor her parents would discuss this one with her. Ignoring the tug of unsatisfied curiosity, Llandry restored her sapphire to the bench and took up her tools again. She had to work carefully around her injured arm: the wounds had knit firmly, but her muscles were still weak. As she worked, she became distantly aware of an odd sound.

Clack clack clack.

Turning, she observed Sigwide in his basket. Since he preferred to be near Llandry at all times, a bed had been placed for him on the balcony. Devary had done it without being asked, layering it up with blankets and even a small pillow. Sig had obviously promoted it to the position of favourite bed, for he spent a great deal of time in it.

Curled up and sleeping, normally, but now he was turning and turning, his jaws working, his sharp teeth clacking loudly on something hard.

'Sig, what are you eating?' She felt for his thoughts, but for once he wasn't sharing. Llandry crossed the balcony, crouched down, and picked him up. He squealed in protest and wriggled, but she maintained her grip.

In the centre of Sigwide's blankets rested a large stone, indigo in colour, gleaming silver when the light hit it. A surge of excitement rushed through her. Tucking Sigwide — still protesting — under one arm, she scooped up the istore stone. Holding it in her hands gave her that familiar and so welcome feeling of calm and well-being, and sharpened her senses.

'Sig, you little... *thief.*' He was fighting hard to be released and at last succeeded in squirming free of her grasp. He rushed at the stone, trying to win it back. She saw his mind clearly: he remembered taking the stone off her desk when her back was turned one day. There had been several lying in a cluster on her work bench, and she hadn't noticed the absence of one piece.

She also gathered that he felt — very strongly — that he was the rightful owner of the stone and felt hard-used at her capture of it.

'You as well, hm?' It hadn't occurred to her that the widespread covetousness over this curious gem might also extend to animals. She chuckled at his distress, calming him with a quick hug.

'A deal, Siggy. We will share this one, all right? We can take it in turns to look after it.' She replaced the stone in the centre of his bed and he immediately curled up around it, looking like the draykons of legend with his long body wound around his treasure. 'You can have it for the rest of today.' The istore was trouble, undoubtedly, but this one was an unexpected bonus, a secret gift. It would be kept hidden, a private satisfaction only to herself.

Inspired, Llandry decimated her silver supplies and applied herself to the creation of the ideal setting for the stone. She didn't want to be stuffing it into a pocket or burying it in a bag; it ought to be worn next to the skin. Working with extreme care — her arm still twinged painfully if she overdid it — she crafted a pendant and chain of pale icy-white silver. As an afterthought, she engraved the metal with stars as a tribute to her original inspiration. The pendant was constructed to grip the stone in its hollow centre, allowing the back of the istore to sit directly against her skin.

The soft notes of a skilfully-played lyre reached her ears as she worked: Devary working at his hobby. He spent some time at this every day, plucking fluid notes from the golden strings and singing in his deep voice. She could not understand the words, but the melodies were glorious by themselves. He seemed to be composing something today; the music came in snatches, gradually lengthening into a full song. His voice was compelling; she felt an agreeable shiver when he sang, like a breath of cool wind over her skin. She wanted to go into the other room and listen, but she did not dare to intrude.

A streak of grey interrupted her thoughts. Sigwide's small form shot across the balcony, moving at speed. Llandry glanced up as Sigwide, yipping, hurtled after a scrap of flickering colour that hovered dangerously close to the balcony's edge. She dropped her tools and dived in pursuit, her wings unfurling with a snap. She stretched out her hands and caught the orting just as he leaped, heedlessly, into the open air.

'Oh, Sig...' She breathed the words in tones of despair and relief, clutching him close. He jerked his head this way and that, his jaws moving oddly. He had something in his mouth.

Applying her fingers and thumb either side of his jaw, she pressed firmly. His mouth reluctantly opened, and something colourful fell to the floor.

'Sig, what have you done?' She scooped the thing up and took both creatures inside, shutting the balcony door before she released Sigwide. He retreated from her, muttering.

The thing he had caught was only a few inches long from nose to tip, fitting into the palm of her hand. It lay on its side, weakly flapping lightly furred wings of jade green and rose. Its slender body was covered in soft, pearly fur, and it sported a long, oddly curled tail and a thin snout. Its four legs scratched at her skin without inflicting any damage: apparently it lacked claws. It looked like a miniature drauk crossed with a daefly.

It lay still, finally, and she worried that it had died; but it breathed still, its furred sides heaving in panicked hyperventilation. She couldn't see any wounds.

'Just shock, then,' she murmured.

'What?'

She looked up guiltily. She'd forgotten Devary for a moment.

'Sorry. I... found something.'

'Oh?' He stood up to come and look. He had to stand quite close to see the colourful little oddity that lay in her palm.

'Curious,' he said mildly. 'Another escapee from the Uppers, by the looks of it.'

She nodded, trying to ignore his unsettling proximity.

'Sig ate it,' she said.

'He is a fearsome hunter,' he replied with a smile. 'What will you do with it? I do not think it can fly.'

'Mm.' She moved away from him, carrying the thing up to her chamber. She laid it in a nest of soft fabric in the warmest part of the room, and left it to recover. She prudently closed the door as she left, keeping Sigwide out.

She didn't realise Devary had followed her. She found him standing on the landing, hovering politely outside the door to her room. He smiled as she emerged.

'Do you think it will live?'

'Hard to say,' she replied. 'If it lives until tomorrow, it might be all right.'

'I like it,' he said. 'It is pretty. Do you know what kind of creature it is?'

'I've never seen anything like it before.'

'A pity; neither have I. Perhaps your mother will know.'

She nodded her head in agreement, wondering why he had followed her. Silence fell, and she sought for something else to say.

'I enjoyed your song.'

His brows lifted in surprise. 'I didn't realise you were listening.'

'I can hear you quite well on the balcony.'

'You like music?'

'I like yours.'

He smiled, gratified. 'You play an instrument yourself, perhaps.'

'I never learned. Unfortunately.'

'Unfortunately?'

'Well. I sometimes think it might be nice.'

'I could teach you a little, if you like.'

She thought fast. On the one hand, the prospect of spending any considerable length of time with Devary filled her with trepidation. She had survived thus far by limiting the amount of time she spent in the same room with him.

On the other hand...

She looked up at his handsome face, his hazel eyes friendly and inviting.

'Thank you,' she said. 'Why not?'

She spent the next hour seated cross-legged on the floor of the parlour, her left knee pressed against Devary's. She cradled the beautiful lyre in her lap, tentatively plucking the slender golden strings according to his direction. She blushed every time she made an error, but he didn't seem to notice. She took to the art rapidly, enjoying the sensation of the metallic strings under her deft fingers, revelling in every shimmering note she produced. Devary smiled and complimented her and taught her a short, simple song; by the end of the day she could play it quite comfortably.

Singing, however, she outright refused to do. Nothing he could say could prevail upon her to expose her singing voice to his scrutiny. In the end, she played and he sang. It seemed a perfect arrangement to her.

By the following day, Llandry had mastered her song and was rapidly learning another.

'You are a natural, I think,' said Devary. 'You must go to Nimdre someday, and learn from a real professional.'

'You aren't a professional?'

He smiled complacently. 'No, no; I am a poor hobbyist only. I play for my own pleasure, and I do not often teach.'

'Oh, I thought... then, what is your profession?'

'Ah, well. I travel a lot, and sometimes I do play to an

audience. It is not the same thing as being a true *professional*, you understand.'

Llandry didn't. He played like a master to her ears. Her fingers missed their mark as she pondered this and a wrong note sounded jarringly. Frowning down at the strings, Llandry said, 'I am doing you little credit as a student. Perhaps it's time for a break.'

'Certainly,' he replied, bowing his head. He rose and offered her a hand up. Ignoring it, she jumped lightly to her feet, thrusting the lyre at him.

'I'd like to...' An odd noise broke the peace of the house, coming from somewhere behind her. It reminded her of the sounds Sigwide made when he was angry.

'Moment,' she murmured, padding through to the balcony. 'Sig?'

Sigwide stood near the balcony rail, faced off against a beast she'd never seen before. It was five times the orting's size, scaled and clawed, with a snout that snapped warningly at Sigwide as it advanced. The orting refused to move, growling deep in his throat. He was answered with a roar as the creature charged.

She dived, grabbing Sigwide and rolling out of reach. She screamed in pain as her injured arm hit the ground, but she didn't pause; she was up in seconds, darting away, clutching her brave but foolish orting to her chest.

Devary appeared in the doorway, wielding a pair of wicked-looking daggers. Gaping in astonishment at this incongruous sight, Llandry almost lost her healthy arm to a snap of the beast's jaws. She rolled again, narrowly evading its strike. Her senses were suddenly crowded with information: she felt the beast's confusion and fear, its desperation at finding itself stranded suddenly in wholly unfamiliar territory. It had emerged through a gate, a direct escapee from the Uppers, but it wasn't here by its own desire.

Devary charged the beast, daggers ready to hack into its beautiful leaf-green hide.

'Don't kill it!' She released Sigwide and bounded to her feet, mentally reaching out to the creature. Its mind was little different from Sigwide's, its aggression a product of its fear and disorientation. Clumsily she thrust herself into its thoughts, trying to replace its notions of danger with sensations of safety.

The technique might work with Sigwide, but this beast shrugged off her interference. Recognising Devary as the greater threat, it turned on him and leaped.

'Wait, please,' Llandry gasped. Devary dropped his daggers and wrestled with the thing, holding its jaws away from his face by sheer strength of muscle.

'You might... hurry, with whatever you are doing,' he panted.

Cajoling wasn't working: the beast was too enraged. Collecting herself, Llandry matched aggression with aggression and bore down with a fierce will, forcing it to obey. To her immense relief, it gradually ceased its attempts to swallow Devary's face and slowed. She felt the shift in its mind, from viewing her as a threat to seeing her as its master.

Tentatively, Devary loosened his grip, his muscles still tense and ready to fight. When the animal didn't react he surged to his feet, collecting one of his daggers as a precaution.

'Can you open a gate?' Llandry's words were strained; the unaccustomed effort of holding the beast to her will was tiring her fast.

'Yes, it will take... a moment.'

'Faster would be better.'

'Cannot be helped,' he murmured. While he worked, Llandry turned her thoughts back to her temporary captive. She had no wish to exacerbate its terror, so she adjusted her ideas, trying to meld the force of her command with the security she'd tried to give it before. Her untrained attempts were clumsy, and she came close to losing her grip on it altogether.

The gate appeared, a ripple in the air. It grew steadily more solid, until Llandry could see the little slice of the Uppers to which it was connected. Distracting, that vision: vivid colour and golden sunlight, and a hint of a rich aroma that teased at her senses.

'Llandry?' Devary prompted.

'I... yes.' Llandry refocused, shoving the beast towards the gate. In her anxiety she had probably overdone the command: the poor creature shot forward and straight into the gate. Devary grimaced and the gate faded gradually, too slowly for Llandry's frayed mind. At last it disappeared and the balcony grew still and quiet once more.

'Quite good,' Devary said at last. His hair had come down

out of its ponytail, but other than that he looked remarkably unperturbed. Llandry was too muddled and disturbed to answer. Feeling the warning buzzing in her limbs and tightness in her chest, she bolted from the room before she could humiliate herself by suffering a bout of panic in front of her mother's friend.

12

When Eva arrived at Vale's office, she found Tren waiting.

'Mr. Warvel,' she said coolly, wondering what he was doing there.

'Lady Glostrum.' He looked up, smiling. 'What brings you here?'

'I was going to ask you the same. Surely you aren't...?'

'Aren't what?'

'Did Lord Angstrun send you? For Vale's job?'

'No,' he said slowly. 'I come here every moonrise to admire the view.' He looked at the cluttered office, covered with Vale's maps and papers.

'Oh,' she said, feeling suddenly very weary. She sat down in Vale's chair, surveying Tren as he stood near the doorway. Youthful: that was the primary impression she gathered of him. Young, and with an air of optimism that suggested a lack of experience. 'You'd better be here because you're his best.'

'I am,' he said. 'Thank you.'

She lifted her brows. 'At... what was it? Twenty-three?'

'Twenty-five. How old were you when they made you High Summoner?'

'Older than that.'

'Not by very much.'

Eva sat back, huddling into her coat. 'If you read the papers,

106

you'll know that I was the beneficiary of some revolting elitism and probably a dash of nepotism as well. What's your excuse?'

Tren laughed. 'Or you were the best candidate for the job. It depends on the point of view.'

'Oh?' She surveyed him, trying to read his expression. 'To which interpretation do you subscribe?'

'I haven't decided yet.'

The door opened, revealing Chief Investigator Vale with an armful of papers. He looked startled to find his office occupied.

'Am I late, or are you two peculiarly eager?'

Tren checked his watch. 'The latter, it appears.'

Vale looked at Tren. 'No sign of Fin, I suppose?'

'Not yet.'

Vale dropped his papers on the desk. The stack landed with a thud that shook the furniture. Eva lifted an ironic brow at him.

'I need three secretaries to keep on top of all of this,' Vale grinned. He picked up Eva's hand, his smile fading. 'There's talk of more activity from the Lowers. More gates, more beasts. I suppose it's no use asking you to reconsider?'

'None whatsoever.

He sighed. 'I didn't think so.'

'We won't be gone long, Eyde, and I don't anticipate encountering anything that Tren and I will not be able to deal with.'

He eyed her sceptically. 'You don't, hm?'

She smiled encouragingly, trying to impart some of her own sense of confidence to him. He grunted and looked away.

'Here,' he said, handing her a freshly-printed daily newspaper. The headline read: *Missing sorcerer suspected of Night Cloak crime*. A picture of Edwae Geslin was printed below: a young man with dishevelled hair, rather plain features and a hesitant smile. The overall impression Eva received was one of mildness, even blandness. She frowned.

'He doesn't look like the type.'

'He isn't.' Tren took the paper from her, reading it with a gathering frown.

'Do you know him?' said Eva.

'We're close friends,' said Tren, tossing the paper aside in disgust. 'I can't think of any reason why Ed would do such a thing.'

Vale spoke up. 'Did he tell you he was leaving?'

'No.'

'Has he said, or done, anything recently that struck you as out of character?'

Tren thought. 'He seemed anxious lately, but he's often worried about money. I didn't think it out of the ordinary.'

'Why does he worry about money?'

'His mother's a widow and he has younger siblings. He sends most of his earnings to her.'

'Good,' murmured Vale. 'Where does the mother live?'

'Orstwych.'

'Clear motive,' said a new voice. Eva glanced up, startled. The door had opened so quietly she hadn't noticed. Another man stood behind Vale, dressed for travelling. He surveyed the office expressionlessly, then softly shut the door.

'Ah, Fin,' said Vale. 'Sit down.' The man took the seat nearest to the exit, without looking at anyone.

'This is Finshay Arrerly,' said Vale. 'My agent in this business. Fin, you already know Tren. The lady is Evastany Glostrum, High Summoner.'

Finshay turned cold grey eyes on her. She returned his stare coolly, assessing him rapidly. She detected more than a hint of arrogance in his manner.

'You're sending your fiancee with us.' Finshay's voice was chill and quiet.

'She's the best person for this job,' said Vale. Eva raised her brows, surprised at his change of attitude. He'd been trying to talk her out of it ever since she suggested it.

'Oh?' said Finshay. 'A noble and a bureaucrat?'

'She's a fine working summoner,' said Vale, a hint of steel creeping into his tone. 'She's one of the strongest in Glour, and besides she's in possession of some useful tools for this task.'

'Such as?'

'A shortig hound, and a gwaystrel.'

That seemed to silence Finshay, at least for a brief time. He cast another glance at her, only slightly less contemptuous than before, and subsided.

'Sir,' said Tren, tentatively.

'Don't tell me you're going to object too, Tren.'

Tren shifted uncomfortably. 'Not exactly, sir, but I'd prefer to be excused from this mission.'

'Your reasons being what.'

'Ed's a close friend, sir. I don't feel right about tracking him down like this.'

'I'm sorry, but that's exactly why I need you to be involved. You know him better than anyone else; that knowledge may prove invaluable.' Tren opened his mouth to object but Vale cut him off. 'You know it will go much easier for Geslin if he's brought in for civilised questioning.'

Instead of what? Eva wondered uneasily. She pictured again that mild young face and shivered slightly.

Tren bowed his head, but made no further objections.

'Gentlemen,' said Vale in a steely tone. 'I can do without this quibbling. You're all involved for good reasons and the matter is non-negotiable. Work together and you'll find Geslin quickly. I suggest you make your peace with the job and get it done.'

'Of course, sir,' said Tren. Finshay nodded coldly. Eva just watched.

Vale exhaled slowly. 'Good. Fin, what were you saying about motive.'

Finshay shrugged indifferently. 'Most people will do just about anything if they're stuck for cash.' Tren looked as if he wanted to argue, but he glanced at Vale and thought better of it.

Vale nodded. 'It's a fair point. You should talk with the mother, see if she knows anything. Maybe you'll find Geslin there.'

'Doubt he'd be stupid enough to hide somewhere so obvious,' said Fin.

'Maybe, maybe not. Check it out anyway. Any other leads?'

'None,' said Fin. 'He's a bloody Master Sorcerer, isn't he? He'll be stealthed up to the eyeballs.'

'Then it's lucky you have the services of a summoner with a tracker dog and a gwaystrel,' said Vale pointedly. Fin rolled his eyes.

'Tren. Any thoughts on where your friend Geslin would go?'

Tren looked troubled. He opened his mouth and closed it again, then shook his head.

Vale looked hard at him. 'Think on it well, Tren,' he said easily, but with a cold glint in his blue eyes. 'I've no doubt you'll think of something.'

Tren nodded. He looked miserable, and Eva felt a pang of sympathy for him.

'Lady Glostrum,' said Vale, turning to her. 'Am I right in thinking that the shortig will follow the man's scent, even if he tries to disguise it?'

'As far as we know, yes,' she replied. 'The shortigs seem to be immune to the known methods of disguise there. Either that or they're clever enough to see past them.'

'Good,' said Vale. 'And the gwaystrel will see through any disguise he adopts. Between the two, you've a fair chance of catching him.'

'The gwaystrel's that good?' Finshay's question dripped scepticism.

Eva turned a cold stare on him. 'Gwaystrels aren't fooled by sorcerer stealth tricks because they don't use their eyes. They're all but blind, in fact. They recognise people by sound, smell, patterns of movement — all the things that are harder, maybe impossible, to conceal or change. Geslin can cloak himself any way he likes, but Rikbeek will be looking for the things he can't easily manipulate.'

'How will he know what to look for?'

'I was hoping Tren could help with that.'

Vale looked inquiringly at the sorcerer. Tren slouched a little further into his chair, but he nodded.

'I can build a walking image of Ed as I remember him. It'll move, sound, probably even smell like him. I can only keep it up for a couple of minutes, but hopefully that'll be enough.'

'Probably,' said Eva. 'He learns fast.'

Vale nodded approvingly. 'Fin, go dig up everything you can find on Geslin. The usual procedure, please.' Fin deigned to answer the order with a nod.

'Right, get on with it,' said Vale. 'I want you all home as soon as possible.' He was looking at Eva as he said it.

Ed Geslin's house was on the twenty-seventh circle, right on the edges of the city. It was an underground dwelling, obviously cheap lodgings. He had three rooms carved through a series of great irignol roots. They were neatly kept, and virtually bare of furniture or possessions.

110

Eva wandered through the house with her shortig hound padding along softly behind her. The little dog thrust its sizeable nose into every object it encountered. Eva hoped it was gaining enough of a scent to track Geslin.

'Do you suppose he cleaned out his house before he left?' Eva asked Tren.

'No. Or, probably not. Ed never seemed to have much need for ordinary things. His house has been like this ever since I've known him.'

'Unusual.' Eva slid open a series of drawers that were fitted into a wall. They were all empty. 'Maybe he couldn't afford much.'

'That's a possibility,' said Tren. 'The position of aide to Lord Angstrun is well-paid, but he was sending as much as he could afford to his family every moon.'

Eva stepped through a low door into a small parlour. It was furnished with nothing but a pair of chairs and a bookcase, devoid of books. Finshay was sitting comfortably on the sofa.

'Slow getting here,' he remarked.

'Sorry,' said Tren.

Finshay grunted. Ignoring Eva, he said to Tren: 'Better pick up the pace, Warvel. The trail's already days old.'

Tren looked irritated. He turned his back on Finshay without replying, and began searching through the lone cupboard in the room, opening doors and drawers. Eva joined the search, rather surprised to find that there were items remaining in this piece of furniture. She collected a well-read book, a comb and sparse items of clothing. She laid them out for the shortig, then glanced back at Tren.

'I got the impression you've worked with the Chief Investigator before,' she said. 'I thought you were part of Angstrun's crowd?'

'I am, but there's always a sorc or two attached to the Investigator's Office. That includes me, just now. I assist with investigating infractions of the sorcery laws.'

'Should've got someone else for this one,' said Finshay. 'Geslin's best friend is going to aid in his capture, is he? Vale's judgement's off.'

'Ed had nothing to do with most of it,' said Tren firmly. 'Murder, theft? He didn't do those things. I'm sure of it. He ought to be here to defend himself. Besides, the Chief Investigator is right: he must have some information.'

Fin said nothing. Tren laid out two or three more items on the floor for the shortig to sort through. Eva and the two men watched with interest as the tiny black hound cast through the assembled objects with his sensitive nose, turning each one around several times with his paws and snout.

'You do your job, Fin?' said Tren after a moment.

'Of course.'

'What did you find?'

'He went to Orstwych.'

'You're sure about that?'

'Pretty much.'

'How?'

Finshay stared back at Tren, making no reply.

'Come on, Fin,' said Tren. 'We all need as much information as possible.'

'Fine. Geslin's sent a parcel out to Orstwych just after the full moon, every moon, for the past two years. Hasn't missed a single one, until last moon. Full moon last occurred about three weeks ago, meaning Ed's parcel was due roughly two weeks ago. Why didn't he send it?'

'He had nothing to send?'

'Idiot. He didn't send anything because he was planning to go in person. Means he planned to leave ahead of time. May mean he was carrying something he didn't want to entrust to the mail.'

'That's logical enough,' conceded Tren.

'Not that we'll find him at home with mother,' continued Finshay. 'Nobody's that bloody stupid. Should be able to pick up his trail from there, though.'

'I wonder if it was just the money he was sending,' mused Eva. Finshay cast her an irritated glance. She understood: she was supposed to stick to the business of tracking, while he took care of the deduction. Her lips twitched in amusement.

The shortig sat down on its haunches at Eva's feet and gazed up at her, still and alert, its long ears forward.

'The hound's ready,' she said.

'All right, pack up,' said Fin. 'Leaving in two hours, from the east gate. Don't be late.' He strode away without looking back.

'I do believe we have a self-elected leader,' murmured Eva.

'Fin's like that,' said Tren. 'He can be difficult to work with, but he's good at what he does.'

'I daresay. Now, what of that image you spoke of?'

'Ah. Yes. Do you have the gwaystrel here?'

Eva opened her cloak to reveal Rikbeek in his usual spot, tucked into her collar.

'Interesting travel arrangements,' said Tren with a small grin. 'What does he need in order to get the 'scent', so to speak?'

'Only to observe,' she said. 'Honestly I don't know exactly what it is he does, but a few minutes' observation seems to be sufficient.'

Tren nodded briskly. 'Tell me when he's seen enough.'

He closed his eyes and stood in deep concentration for several long minutes. Then his eyes opened. Where he looked, a shape began to form, slowly solidifying into a human figure.

A young man stood with his hands in the pockets of his shabby green coat. He was laughing, apparently at a joke. He began to talk in a rather slow, considered way, shaking his mousy-brown hair out of his eyes. His mouth moved but whatever he was saying was barely audible, as if he was speaking from a long distance away.

Eva released Rikbeek, directing his attention towards the figure of Edwae Geslin. The gwaystrel flew in circles around the image, darting in and out. It emitted a stream of sounds, some of which were only just within Eva's range of hearing.

'Can you make him walk, Tren?' The sorcerer closed his eyes again, conjuring a new image; now Geslin began to stride, apparently towards Eva, though his feet made no progress on the ground. He walked in place for a few minutes as Rikbeek dived and spun. Then the gwaystrel returned to his station inside Eva's cloak and firmly snapped his wings shut around himself. Eva caught an echo of the gwaystrel's thoughts. He was thinking about food.

'Apparently he's finished,' said Eva. Tren smiled, a little wanly. He looked sadly back at the figure of Geslin, still striding on the spot. Geslin vanished. Tren stood silently for a long moment, his hands stuffed into his pockets in a gesture similar to his friend's. At length Eva felt obliged to speak.

'How long have you two been friends?'

Tren answered without looking at her. 'We trained together. We were both naturally strong sorcs, and there was competition between us at one time. But Lord Angstrun took us both as aides. We became like brothers after a while.' He looked at Eva then, but abstractedly, his thoughts obviously elsewhere. 'I don't know why he would do it,' he said at last. 'Ed didn't grow up here, but he would never betray Glour. Or Angstrun.'

Eva thought of the thunderous anger on Angstrun's face when he'd heard about the Night Cloak crime. She could well believe that no rational person would lightly betray him.

'I'm sure there was a good reason,' she said, firmly.

Tren removed his hands from his pockets, drew himself up, visibly pulled himself together. 'I need to pack,' he said, with a brief smile at Eva.

'Me too,' she said. 'See you at the east gate.'

Edwae's mother lived in Westrarc, a large town about thirty miles inside the Orstwych border. The distance was swiftly covered by the four nivvens put to Eva's carriage. The clustering irignol forests lasted almost to the easternmost border of Glour, giving way at last to expanses of smooth hills, gleaming pale under the moon. Eva shivered, feeling exposed without the customary shroud of the dense irignol, but the spread of light delighted her. It was like travelling through a sea of moonglow.

Fin did not deign to speak to anybody throughout the journey. He sat with his eyes closed and his face turned away. Tren, too, was largely silent, but in his case Eva understood it. He had probably known Ed's family before, and now here he travelled to meet them in the role of Edwae's pursuer, bound to return him to Glour for questioning and probable punishment. It was a hard task. She knew not how to help him, stranger as she was, so she was silent too. They made for a cheerless company of travellers as they arrived in Westrarc under the deep cover of Orstwych's Cloaked hours.

Westrarc was of a wholly different character to Glour. They'd passed villages and isolated dwellings on their way through the countryside, dotted through tumbling wolds sparsely littered with contorted irignol trees. Westrarc was on a much larger scale, its rounded, shapely houses built of pale stone and

114

often adorned with towers and turrets. The roads were wide and smooth, walled on either side, and the moonlight shone silver off the graceful buildings and pathways of the town. Lanterns lit the roads, clear glass baubles shining with artificial starlight that wandered lazily through the air, adhered to nothing. Some of them kept pace with the carriage, lighting the road with a muted glow until an approaching set of globes took over their wardship. Eva watched as they drifted idly away again, disappearing into the soft shadows at their backs.

The hour was too late to call upon Edwae's mother immediately, so Eva directed her coachman towards her favourite inn, one of Westrarc's finest. It was expensive and luxurious, facts which earned her more of Finshay's copious scorn, but she ignored him. Where comfort was available, she was always inclined to take advantage of it. The next day, she took care to dress in the plain, simple clothes she'd brought, eliminating all overt signs of her station.

Mrs. Geslin lived in the south quarter of Westrarc, an area lacking the splendour of the rest of the town. Its streets were narrow, buildings crowding along them without much plan or reason. Some of the streets they passed through were barely wide enough for two to walk abreast; over these the houses leaned conspiratorially, the upper storeys of opposing houses almost touching one another.

It was in one such house that the remnants of the Geslin family lived, a dwelling that was poor and shabby but nonetheless neat and clean. The Mrs. Geslin who answered the door was made to match: a woman with the form and features of only middling years, but who possessed the weary air of a woman long careworn. She looked with frightened eyes at Finshay, who did nothing to conceal his grim purpose. She looked next at Tren, who tried to smile.

'Mrs. Geslin, how are you. It's been a long time.'

'He's not here.' The woman cut Tren off and tried to close the door on him, but Finshay had inserted himself between the door and the frame. Eva heard a swift, sad sigh from Tren.

'We aren't here to hurt him, Mrs. Geslin, but we need to know where he is. Please. He'll get his fair hearing.'

Mrs. Geslin looked on him with scorn. 'Oh, he will? Them great lords in Glour don't care for the troubles of folk like us,

Pitren Warvel, and you know that. They'll destroy him. How you could lend yourself to this—' She looked on Tren with such withering contempt that Eva was shocked.

Tren's pain was clearly audible as he answered. 'It's all I can do to help him, Mrs. Geslin. I know of nothing else that wouldn't imperil us both the more in the end.' He paused, and the terrible anger in Edwae's mothers face softened slightly. 'I need to know why he did it,' continued Tren. 'Much may then be explained, and more can be done for Ed.'

Mrs. Geslin bowed her head, and at last she stepped back and opened the door wider. Eva passed inside with the others. As she stepped into the tiny hallway, neatly dusted but rather bare, she felt Mrs. Geslin's scrutiny turned upon her. Her gaze was not a friendly one.

'Sorceress,' said Mrs. Geslin, low and harsh. 'Pale-haired witch! Are you the one who led my boy astray?' Eva was astonished to see tears in the woman's eyes, her hands trembling as they twisted in the folds of her shabby old dress.

'No, I — your son and I have never met,' she said calmly. 'And I'm not in the sorcery line.'

'Why then do you pursue my son, stranger to him and his ways?'

Eva gestured to the small hound at her feet, though she kept the gwaystrel hidden in the folds of her cloak.

'I am a summoner,' she said. 'My arts aid the search.'

Mrs. Geslin turned away her face. She led them into a small parlour, shooing away three young children as she went. A fourth, slightly older child sat stubbornly in the parlour, resisting dismissal. She was a little prettier than her brother, though she had the same thin brown hair and pale face.

'Mindra,' said Mrs. Geslin, warningly. The girl sighed and sloped away. Eva was motioned to the chair that she had occupied.

'I can't offer you anything,' said Mrs. Geslin, with a fierceness that seemed to dare complaint.

'That's all right,' said Tren quickly. 'We are quite well fed.' He cleared his throat uncomfortably. 'Mrs. Geslin, am I right in thinking that Ed was sending you money every moon? Had he been doing so for a long time?'

'All he could afford,' she said sadly. 'I never wanted to be

116

taking his money, but we couldn't manage without it.' Her eyes blazed suddenly. 'I know what they're saying about my boy. You tell me. Does a man who'll give every penny he has to his family become a thief? A *murderer*?'

Tren made a placating gesture. 'I'm as certain as you are that he didn't do those things. But there's no doubt he is involved somehow. He is certainly the person who altered the agreed boundaries of the Night Cloak. It's my belief somebody put him up to that, and we need to find out who. And why.'

Mrs. Geslin nodded and sat down next to Tren. He picked up one of her hands and squeezed it encouragingly. She cast him a small, grateful smile.

'There isn't much to tell,' she began. 'But I knew something wasn't right. For two years Ed's been sending us everything he could spare, and probably more. But he knew it wasn't enough, not with me out of work and four to feed besides. He began sending more, much more. He wouldn't tell me where he got the extra money.'

She took a deep breath, her spare hand joining the one Tren held. She gripped him as if clutching a lifeline. 'He came home, a few days ago. He had money with him, more of it than ever before. He said it would be enough to keep us for several moons, while he went away. He was going travelling, he said, and for some time, though he wouldn't say where or why. I knew he must have done something that wasn't right. Then the papers came, with their pictures and their nasty tales.' She stopped, her grip tightening on Tren's fingers. She looked like she must be hurting him by now, her knuckles white with strain, but he didn't move.

'A few days ago?' said Tren, thoughtfully. 'Did he give you any idea at all where he went?'

'No,' she said. 'I tried to make him tell me. All he would say was that he had something to put right.'

Tren frowned. 'He wasn't running away from something?'

Mrs. Geslin shook her head. 'Eddie wouldn't run from a mess he'd made. He'd put it right somehow.'

'Mrs. Geslin,' said Eva. 'What did you mean by what you said to me? "Pale-haired witch"?'

'Ed met someone. Before all this happened, it would've been. He joked about it once, asking me if I'd mind him bringing

117

a witch into the family, one of them pale-haired ones. Folk say they're more powerful.' She paused, looking intently at Eva. 'Is that true?'

Eva spread her hands. 'I'm a powerful summoner but I can't say if the colour of my hair has anything to do with it. I think it's just a myth.'

Mrs. Geslin nodded. 'Ed didn't really believe it either, but he was serious about this woman. I thought maybe she had something to do with it.'

'Why?' asked Tren. 'Did he suggest that when you saw him last?'

She hesitated. 'It's just a feeling I got.'

Tren sighed. 'It's not much to go on. True white is an unusual hair colour, but not that rare. However, we'll look into it. Did he say anything else about her that might help?'

'Nothing. He said I'd find out for myself soon. But that was before.'

'Before?'

'Before he was in trouble. A few days ago he wouldn't talk of it at all.'

'Ah, well. It all helps.' He looked seriously at Mrs. Geslin. 'I'll be doing everything I can for Ed, please believe me.'

Their leave-taking from Mrs. Geslin was painful on Tren's part and impatient on Finshay's. Eva felt subdued as she left the shabby house and its weary mistress. The children clustered forlornly around their mother as she bid farewell to her son's pursuers. Eva's last glimpse of Mrs. Geslin was her face, drawn and sad, as she closed the door behind them.

Tren's obvious pain was distressing. Eva knew there was nothing she could do, but she couldn't ignore it. She touched his arm lightly, trying to get his attention as he walked in an apparent daze. He looked up quizzically.

'We'll find him,' she said. 'Everything will be well.'

'Maybe,' he said. He looked away. 'I'm trying to imagine what he might be doing. I think his mother is right: whatever he's up to, it isn't running away. Whether that's better or worse, I don't know.'

'You think he might place himself in danger?'

'Say he moved the Night Cloak. I can imagine his horror at everything that happened afterwards. It wouldn't have taken him long to realise that they were all connected. If he thought he knew something about who was behind it, would he have taken it to Vale? Could he have? He must've realised he would be blamed: that it would be hard for anyone to believe him. I fear he's gone after the perpetrator by himself.' He smiled without humour. 'I wish he had told me about it, but he wouldn't; not if it might put me in danger, too.'

The shortig at Eva's feet stopped abruptly. It cast about in the street for some minutes, watched intently by its audience of three. Then it lifted its head and yipped, taking off down a side street at speed. Eva followed the shortig at a trot, opening her cloak and shaking Rikbeek loose. He snapped at her hands grumpily, trying to fold his wings again, but she tossed him into the sky. He flew upwards and out of sight.

'Well, here we go.' Eva split her thoughts, sending part of her awareness ahead with the shortig and part upwards to follow the gwaystrel. The trail brought the company rapidly to the east gate of Westrarc, and out into the hills beyond.

13

Llandry lifted her cordial to her lips. A tremor wracked her and the bottle slipped, spilling the oily herbal concoction over her chin. She set the vessel down quickly, wiping at her face with a handkerchief. She was up to twice the usual dose, but still the attacks came. Most of her night had been spent wide awake, staring into the darkness feeling panic on the edge of her awareness, waiting for the medicine to wear off.

She didn't even know what she was afraid of. Normally the attacks came when she found herself surrounded, buried in a crowd of people. Sometimes, on her worst days, she couldn't address so much as a syllable to a stranger without succumbing to a bout of trembling and hyperventilation. It had been a lamentably common occurrence since her early teenage years.

The experience shouldn't be remarkable, then, even if the attacks did seem to be happening more frequently. But something was different. Added to the embarrassing loss of control over her own limbs, to the humiliating inability to speak or breathe, was a sensation of *struggle*, as if her mind was trying to claw its way out of her body. Or as if her body wished to invert itself. It was growing increasingly difficult to hide it from her mother, or even from Devary, who had a habit of appearing noiselessly and unexpectedly at times when she might definitely prefer to be alone.

At the moment he was downstairs, working on his new song. The familiar melody drifted up to her bedchamber, calming her a little. At least while he was playing, he wouldn't walk in on her. She was free to restore her appearance to order, remove all signs of her torturous night before she ventured down. At length she stepped out of her room, hair brushed and clothing neat, hoping she might make it to the kitchen without being stopped.

Apparently he was on the watch, for as soon as she reached the bottom of the winding stairs he set down his lyre and approached, wearing the usual smile.

'Is everything well with you? It is unusually late.'

Since when was he paying attention to her daily routine? 'I'm fine,' she said curtly, belatedly noticing that he wore a bandage wrapped around one arm. 'What happened to you?'

'There was another intruder in the night,' he replied.

'You killed it, didn't you?'

'You were not around.'

Llandry shook her head in disgust, stalking into the kitchen. To her dismay he followed, seating himself at the table while she prepared tea. She knew she ought to eat but her stomach rebelled at the notion. She filled a teapot, with very poor grace, and gave him a cup.

'Thanks,' he smiled. 'Llandry, why are you not employed as a summoner? Your ability was quite apparent yesterday.'

She scowled into her tea, refusing to look at him. 'That is private.'

'Is it? I am sorry. It is not my intention to pry.'

Llandry sighed inwardly. If he'd only pushed, it would have been much easier to continue being ungracious and rude. His habitual courtesy was disarming.

'I'm sorry. I'm just... in a poor mood. I wanted to train as a summoner, but my father forbade it.'

'Forbade?'

'Well.' She reconsidered. 'That is not the right word. He... talked me out of it.'

'That, I do not understand. The profession is highly respected in all the Seven Realms, along with sorcery. You would be guaranteed a well-paid position. Why would he discourage you?'

'Pa's never trusted the Off-Worlds. He thinks they're too

121

dangerous. If I'd insisted, he would have been terrified every time I was sent to the Uppers, and that's an important part of training.'

Devary swirled his tea in his cup, gazing thoughtfully at Llandry. 'Your father seems to be too pragmatic a man to entertain such fears.'

'Not much scares Papa, that's true.' For a moment Llandry was silent, debating how much to tell him. It was odd that her mother hadn't already shared this piece of her husband's history: perhaps she didn't wish for Devary to know.

'Why then should he distrust the Upper Realm in this way?'

'You should ask Mamma about that.'

He smiled. 'But I am asking you.'

She sighed. 'It's because of my grandfather. He was a summoner, a strong one. Pa said he became obsessed with the Uppers, kept going back, spending more time there than he should. One day he didn't come back. Pa said he wouldn't sit by and watch while his daughter got herself killed up there too.'

'Ah.' Devary said nothing more, apparently drifting off into thought.

'If you're allowed to pressure me for information, I get to ask a question too,' said Llandry.

'That is a fair trade,' said Devary gravely. 'One question.'

'You're the most civilised person I've met, next to Mamma. You have perfect manners. You're a wonderful musician and the picture of a gentleman. Why would you be carrying daggers?'

He smiled briefly. 'I suppose it is inevitable that you would ask. That, unfortunately, is a question I cannot answer.'

'Unfair.'

'It is, is it not? Perhaps I should say, I do not wish to answer it. I think you are beginning to like me, just a little, and I would not wish to destroy that.'

Llandry eyed him. 'I have come to believe you are mostly harmless, yes. It is not the same thing as liking.'

His eyes laughed at her. 'I see. It is my mistake.'

'So you have a secret that I wouldn't like?'

'More than one, I fear. Ask me another question. I remain in debt to you by one query.'

Llandry thought back to the previous day. 'I've seen sorcs work before. They can open gates in seconds. Why did it take

122

you so long?'

'An unflattering question, but a deal is a deal. I am not a very good sorcerer. Also, I am from Nimdre. It is true that I can open gates to either of the Off-Worlds, but that comes at the price of foregoing the closer bond enjoyed by those from the Daylands or Darklands. To a Darklands sorcerer, it is as simple as reaching out, and the paths through to the Lowers are at your fingertips. Or so I believe. I, however, must search before I can find the way.' He set down his cup and stood up. 'If that concludes our arrangement, I must investigate the problem of these visitors we have been receiving. You will observe that I have enclosed the house; please do not open any windows or doors while I am gone. I won't be long.' He left, opening the exterior door only a few inches and slipping carefully through. Llandry heard the key turn in the lock, and she was alone.

Trying not to feel nervous, she climbed the stairs back to her room. The winged creature she had rescued the day before seemed better today; its breathing was calmer and it lay quietly in the nest Llandry had prepared. She mixed up a solution of sugar in water and laid it nearby, hoping it would eat. Doubtless it needed sustenance. She nudged it with her thoughts, reminding it about the concept of food, and to her pleasure it stirred and dipped its snout into the dish.

'On balance, I'd prefer more intruders like you,' she told it. 'No killer teeth. No killer claws. No killer instincts. Quite undemanding, all told.' It ignored her, drinking on until the dish was dry. Then it drank down a second dish, after which it tentatively flapped its wings.

'I suppose I ought to send you back, when you're better.' It was pretty, as Devary had said, and its mind was pretty too — full of colour and sun. She wouldn't mind much if it chose to stay.

A door rattled below and she bolted towards the stairs, alarmed. Was this Devary? Her parents coming back? Another 'visitor'? She reached the kitchen to find Devary slipping back inside. He looked relieved when he saw her.

'What's happening?'

He shut the door firmly and barred it. 'Beasts are all over the city. All over the forests too, it seems. The bulletins are screaming about it. The summoners are out in force, sending

123

them back, but they are finding it hard to keep up. I had to fight my way past several just to reach the nearest board.'

'How? Why?'

'That is unknown. There are rogue gates opening, more than there should be. Nobody knows why this is occurring.'

She said no more, noticing that blood seeped from the wound on his arm. She found her mother's healing supplies in a box on the back of the door, bathed the wound and bound it up.

'If you give me the shirt, I will mend it for you.' She pointed at the tear that marred the black fabric.

'Thank you,' he said. He left, returning a few minutes later wearing a new shirt, the torn one draped over his uninjured arm. She took it from him and settled to her darning task.

'When's Mamma due back?'

'She said maybe today, or tomorrow.' He winced. 'I hope the summoners have caught up with the problem by then, or they will have to fight their way through.'

Llandry felt her stomach tighten with anxiety. *No need to worry*, she told herself. *They can handle it*. She sensed Devary thinking the same. He prowled restlessly around the kitchen, picking things up and dropping them.

'I wonder if I ought to...'

'Hm?'

'Maybe I should go out to meet them, make sure they arrive safely.'

She said nothing. She understood his impulse to help — she felt it herself — but she knew it would be exactly the opposite of her mother's wishes. After a minute, Devary sighed.

'Your mother would kill me if I left you alone,' he said. 'And she would be right to.' He smiled at her, but his smile lacked some of his usual warmth.

'I don't like being barricaded in here either,' she said, putting a few more stitches in his shirt.

'I am sure you don't,' he replied. 'I'm sorry. It isn't your fault.' He collected Ynara's teapot and filled it with water. 'Some more tea?'

Sunset came and Llandry's parents did not appear. The dusk hours dragged by slowly, Llandry and Devary both too tense to settle to anything. At last they retired to bed, though both were awake and up before sunrise. Shortly before sunset came around again, there came a pounding on the outer door. Devary leapt up and drew back the bolts, yanking the door open. Aysun stood on the other side with Ynara behind him. They both stepped hastily into the kitchen, and Devary slammed the door shut quickly behind them.

'Ma.' Llandry went to her mother, wanting to feel Ynara's arms around her. She sensed weariness and looked up searchingly into her mother's face.

'I'm all right, love, and so are you it seems, so everything is well.' Ynara kissed her forehead. 'We are in sore need of tea, though.' Llandry went immediately to the stove.

'Did you run into trouble on the way back?' said Devary.

'Some,' said Aysun. 'Seems someone's put a small army of animals between Glour City and Waeverleyne.'

'They were in the city too, yesterday,' said Devary. 'Summoners have been cleaning them out.'

Ynara looked up at that. 'Any trouble here?' Her perceptive eye shifted from the shuttered windows to her daughter's face.

'We had an intruder, yesterday,' said Devary, sitting across from Ynara at the table. He gestured with his hands, indicating the size of the beast. 'Green hide. Big teeth. Llandry banished it.'

'Banished?' Ynara looked intently at her daughter.

'Devary was going to kill it,' explained Llandry, glancing guiltily at her father. He lifted one shaggy blond eyebrow at her, but said nothing.

'A second visited us the night before last, which I was obliged to destroy,' added Devary. 'Oh, and another newcomer two days ago. Small thing, wings. Not dangerous. Llandry has been tending to it.'

'It's still alive,' she reported. 'I'm going to keep it. Unless Sig tries to swallow it again. Anyway, Ma, what's the news from Glour?'

Llandry had the sense that her mother was trying not to look at her. 'Some good, some bad.'

'Start with the good.'

'Mm, well. The Glour summoners have taken care of the whurthag problem. Also, the Night Cloak has been pulled back to its original position.'

Llandry's spirits lifted. 'Great! Then I can go to the cave soon?' She frowned. 'Maybe after the beast-army's gone.'

'The bad news,' persevered Ynara, 'is that the cave is empty.'

Llandry's frown deepened. 'Empty?'

'There's no istore left. It's all gone.'

Llandry felt suddenly cold. 'It can't be all gone. The walls were full of it.'

'Nonetheless, it's gone. I'm sorry, love. I saw it myself. There's no doubt about it. Also,' she continued, 'our new beast friends are coming through from the Lowers as well, in similar numbers. Some of them have been identified. There are at least five species so far that were previously thought to be extinct.'

'Five?' Devary echoed. 'That is an extraordinary degree of error.'

'Mm,' Ynara agreed. 'It's true that the Off-Worlds are large; there must be areas that are unexplored, and these animals have been hiding out of reach. Though why they would now be venturing into inhabited territory is another question.'

Llandry stopped listening. The stone had endangered her clients; she knew that. She'd had no intention of making any more jewellery with it, and besides, had there been any istore remaining in the cave it would have been taken by the university. So why was she upset? The prospect of its complete loss affected her deeply, almost as though she'd lost some part of herself.

She slipped a hand into the pocket of her skirt, curling her fingers around her beautiful istore pendant. She had finished it yesterday while Devary was absorbed in his music, and so far it remained a secret. At least she could keep this one piece for herself.

'Ma? Do they know who shifted the Night Cloak?'

'Yes, that's known, and he's being sought. But it seems unlikely that he was responsible for all of this chaos, no matter what some people in Glour are saying. He isn't a summoner, for a start.'

Llandry pursed her lips. The istore was remarkable, certainly, and its apparent effects were desirable, but why should anybody go to such lengths to acquire every known piece?

Ynara seemed to guess her thoughts. 'Don't worry, love. Most of the University of Glour is working on this now, and our

126

own university. That's a lot of very bright minds. And the person — the sorcerer — who changed the Cloak, well, he may have information. We will learn something soon.'

14

Eva was up to her ears in sorcery, and hating it.

Once they'd left the environs of Westrarc, Tren had been firm in the need for defences. 'No telling what's about out here,' he said cheerfully. He made Eva stand still with her eyes closed while he worked on her. She felt a Cloak settle over her like a shroud, cold and clinging and faintly damp. When he'd finished, she stood wrapped and tangled in enchantments that lay heavily upon her.

'How repulsive.' A violent shiver wracked her, and she wrapped her arms around herself, trying to warm up.

'You're welcome,' Tren smiled as he moved away.

Eva sighed. She'd been Cloaked before, years ago. It was something she'd steadfastly avoided since then. She knew it would take her hours to accustom herself to the burden of breathing and moving beneath the weight of the sorcery.

'It's quite worth it, I assure you,' said Tren over his shoulder, as if reading her thoughts. 'You're now part of the Night Cloak. Nothing's very likely to spot you unless you speak.'

'Except some of the more sensitive beasts pouring out of the Lowers these days.'

Tren shrugged. 'Nothing's perfect.'

Finshay submitted to his Cloaking without a syllable. Hours later, Eva still felt stifled, cold and burdened by the weight. She refused to complain, however; and so on they went, following the trail marked out by the shortig and with the gwaystrel ghosting on silent wings overhead. As they travelled further across Orstwych, the landscape changed again: the gentle hills ended, and trees closed in. These were different to the dark, contorted irignol that crowded the forests of Glour and western Orstwych. Her night-eyes caught hints of deep colour glinting in the moonlight, shades of blue and green and purple patterning the bark. Frondy red foliage rose above like tattered lace.

They saw nothing of whurthags, though the forests were by no means as they ought to be. Eva sensed several animal presences as they passed through the woods, traces of beasts that were obviously far from home. They were not aggressive, however, and not inclined to trouble their party. Eva left them alone.

As the moon sank out of sight and the Night Cloak rolled over the lands, Eva found herself with cause to be grateful for Tren's sorcery. The eager steps of the little hunting hound brought them through a dense thicket, choked with the deep-hued ferns and mosses that were everywhere in evidence in this part of the forest. They were deep in the midst of the thicket when Rikbeek sounded his alarm call from overhead.

The three halted, wary. Movement caught Eva's eye, and she slowly turned her head. Out of a shadowed burrow in the ground crawled a great creature, furred like a mammal but built more like the ferocious reptiles that lived on the shores of Lake Glanias in the north. An astwach, definitely a predator and decidedly unfriendly. Its movements were slow, but its head turned with alarming speed as it sought the source of Rikbeek's cry.

The three stood, immobile, as the beast emerged fully from its underground home. Eva's breath stopped. It was longer than she was tall, standing as high as her shoulder. Teeth glinted pale in the dark, and a long tail twitched with the stealthy intent of a predator. It stood, nose lifted to scent the air. Eva tried hard to remember whether the Cloak would mask scent as well as visage. She thought not.

As if reaching the same conclusion, Tren beside her began to move. She mimicked his movements, slow and measured, creeping steadily away from the beast. As they were almost past

129

the den, Eva noticed a smaller animal emerge from the burrow: unsteady on its legs and ungainly in its proportions, it was nonetheless an obvious copy of its parent.

The creature rounded on its young with a hiss, startlingly loud in the quiet of the night. Eva could not suppress a spasm of fear at the sound, full of menace and power. The smaller beast was relentlessly herded back into the den, its mother turning to follow. She heard Tren whisper, 'Run.'

And run she did, though the moment she increased her pace the forest floor seemed to suddenly bristle with twigs — dry ones that crackled loudly underfoot. Cloaked or not, there was no hiding after that.

Eva turned, already reaching out with her summoner senses. Before she could bring her will to bear upon their attacker it leapt towards her, snarling. A jump back didn't quite take her out of reach: she screamed as claws raked fire across her left hand, biting deep.

Then she was thrust aside. Finshay surged past her, daggers in his hands, and hurled himself on the beast. He fought fearlessly, his daggers flashing with astonishing speed, and within moments the astwach was in retreat. Finshay didn't stop.

'Fin,' yelled Tren. 'Let it be.'

Finshay lowered his daggers but he didn't turn, not until the astwach had retreated back into its burrow. Then he walked on for several minutes without saying a word. Eva followed, cradling her injured hand.

'An astwach, with young,' spat Finshay at last. 'Dangerous, and your *gwaystrel* betrayed us to it! No need for sorcery with friends like that.' He did not grow excitable in his anger, only colder than ever, his eyes flat and hard.

'We would have disturbed it anyway if we'd gone blundering past,' said Tren. 'It might've had one of us before we knew it was there. Rikbeek's warning was timely.'

'*Rikbeek,*' said Finshay viciously, as if the mere fact of granting the gwaystrel a name offended him personally. 'The *High Summoner* is meant to be able to sense nearby beasts without companion assistance, isn't she? I didn't see that happening.'

'It's a little bit harder when I'm already tracking two companion animals, one on the wing and one on the ground.' Eva spoke with chilling calm, refusing to be riled.

Finshay ignored her. 'We could have managed this assignment ourselves,' he said to Tren. 'I knew it was a mistake to have her along.'

'That's enough, Fin,' said Tren, with uncharacteristic harshness. 'Since when did you begin questioning orders? Besides, how else would you like to do it without a scent hound?'

'Could've borrowed a scent hound.'

'Without an experienced handler? Admit it, Fin, you're prejudiced.'

Fin narrowed his eyes at Tren. 'What if I am? Never known a useful noble yet. Pack of ornaments, all of them.' His eyes swept over Eva's undeniably fine figure and neatly arranged hair. She merely stared back at him coolly. He snorted, walked away. Tren shrugged apologetically, awarding her a consolatory smile.

'Don't mind him. He's good at his job.'

Eva resumed her steady pace, sending the shortig on ahead again. 'I'm not upset. What is his problem with the peers?'

'I don't know. He's always had those opinions, as long as I've known him.'

'And how long is that?'

'Hmm. Three years, thereabouts. We've worked together a few times.'

Eva nodded thoughtfully. She'd encountered resentment before from those who felt she must have bought her way into her position; who found it inconceivable that she could be any good at her role. Finshay's was particularly bitter. No doubt there was a reason for that, but she found it didn't interest her much. She dismissed the problem.

'You're hurt,' said Tren suddenly, noticing her odd way of carrying her hand.

'A bit,' she admitted. He took her fingers gently, uncurling her arm. The gash was deep, but the blood flow was already slowing.

'Um. I don't have any... Fin?' He looked around, but Finshay stalked a long way ahead, resentment evident in his stride.

'You don't happen to be carrying bandages, I suppose?' He looked at her hopefully.

She smiled ruefully and shook her head. 'I can't remember the last time I was injured. I didn't think of it.'

131

'It'll have to be my shirt, then,' he said regretfully.

'Oh no, really, it's fine...' She stopped. Tren had already tugged a clean shirt out of his bag and started ripping it up. She eyed the rather fine cloth with regret.

'I owe you a new shirt.'

'Offer accepted.' He worked with considerable care, barely hurting her at all. When he had finished, her hand was tightly bound, but an experimental flex of her fingers confirmed that she could still use it.

'Thank you. You're a useful person to have around in a minor crisis.'

'You're welcome.' He flashed her a quick smile and picked up his bag, slinging it over his shoulder. Glancing ahead, she realised Finshay was out of sight; apparently he didn't care if they were ripped to pieces by a returning astwach while he was having his moment of pique. But the shortig waited for her, sitting on its haunches about thirty feet ahead. She started walking.

'Do you mind if I ask you something a bit personal?' Tren kept pace beside her. She could feel him tugging and tweaking at the sorcerous Cloak that shrouded her, adjusting it, probably repairing it.

'Only a bit personal? That can be allowed.'

He smiled briefly. 'Why did you insist on coming?'

'I was the best person for the task.'

'Why? I don't mean to question your abilities, but you're the High Summoner.'

'You think I should have sent someone else? One of my seconds, perhaps?'

'It might have made more sense.'

'You're not sold on the gwaystrel idea, I take it.'

'Oh, no. He's a remarkable creature. But there must be *one* other summoner in Glour with a gwaystrel.'

'I'm not at all sure about that, actually. I've never heard of one.'

Tren made a noncommittal noise. She understood. He wasn't questioning her right to be along so much as taking the opportunity to sound her out.

'I lost a friend. She was the first person slain by the whurthag.'

'Ah... I'm sorry.'

'I want to make sure the culprit is caught.' She paused, feeling a tug of guilt. 'If I'm completely honest, though — and I don't see why I should be, but nonetheless — that's not the whole reason. I think I wanted to escape.'

'From?'

'I've been a member of the peerage since I was fifteen. I've been High Summoner for eleven years. I'm shortly to become a married woman, probably with a family to raise; and I decided to do that because I knew it was appropriate. A rational decision to make at my time of life. Ties and burdens and responsibilities have dogged me since before I was fully grown, and I think... I wanted to get away before I lose the chance to make choices like this. I wanted to be directly involved, instead of arranging for somebody else to be.' She grinned ruefully. 'Having Rikbeek really just gave me an excuse to push for my own way in this. Really, I can hardly blame Mr. Arrerly for being angry.'

'No,' said Tren slowly. 'We were lucky to get you. And Rikbeek's already proved to be worth his weight in gold.'

Eva smiled, surprised. 'If you happen to have Beekie's weight in gold, you're welcome to him.'

Tren laughed. 'Is he so tiresome a companion?'

Eva inspected her good hand, adorned with several small, healing bite-scars. 'He is a bit grouchy in the mornings.'

'I'm afflicted with a similar problem,' admitted Tren. 'We'd make a good pair, perhaps.'

'You're first on my list of potential buyers, then. I apologise in advance.'

'Apology accepted.'

A faint yip sounded in the night. Eva turned her thoughts towards the shortig.

'Has he found something?' Tren stared hard into the darkness, trying to make out the small black shape of the scent hound somewhere ahead.

'I don't think so,' Eva said. 'We're falling behind, though.' She increased her pace, catching up to the dog. She searched briefly overhead, finding the gwaystrel still sweeping in slow circles beneath the canopy of the trees.

They were two days and a half on foot, travelling steadily southwards through Orstwych. Their journey had taken them a long way south, aiming with alarming accuracy for the wilds of Ullarn. The prospect of crossing into that notoriously perilous territory pleased nobody. Finshay had recovered from his temper at last, though he merely returned to his usual uncommunicative state. Eva was grateful for Tren's presence: without his friendly face and light-hearted chatter, the experience of following Edwae's trail could have been excruciating. She guessed that Tren talked in order to take his mind off their task. The tactic was effective for her, too, keeping her from undue pain over Meesa's fate.

They encountered a few more Lowers beasts, including one that Eva could have sworn was on the list of extinct species. Of these, only two posed any danger, and Eva was able to master them quickly enough to banish them through the gates Tren opened. Finshay was not obliged to repeat his athletic performance with the daggers.

The moon was sinking on the third day's journey when the shortig's steady pace began to pick up. His nose lifted to the winds and he barked, a high, thin sound full of excitement. They were close to Ullarn, and the terrain was growing steadily more difficult to navigate: uneven, and choked with thorned plants. She could smell burning coal on the air.

'He's got something,' murmured Eva, running forward. She was dimly aware of Finshay behind her, alert and tense, as she caught up with the hound.

The soft earth beneath her feet was dark and wet, stained in patches of a foreboding hue. A ripple of nervousness shivered over her skin as intuition suggested to her the nature of the stain. Tren knelt, dipping his fingers into the mud.

'Blood.'

Finshay's curved and wickedly sharp daggers appeared in his hands as he stood scanning the surrounding trees. The sight gave a sense of reality to the danger, and suddenly she was alert. Her eyes swept the branches overhead, seeking Rikbeek. He was nowhere within range, but no warning call came from him.

The shortig quivered, awaiting commands. She urged him on, following as he tore ahead.

'Any way of telling if that's Edwae's blood?' Tren was beside

134

her, keeping pace, his eyes on the trees before them.

'No,' she panted. 'If there was another trail there, the shortig would ignore it. It could be anyone's.'

He didn't answer. She understood why as she felt the cursed Cloak tighten around her, shrouding her movements in increased shadow. She drew in a shocked, gasping breath as the weight of it doubled. Her legs felt leaden and she had to fight to maintain her pace.

'Sorry,' Tren gasped. 'Got to do it.'

She couldn't find the breath to respond. She forged doggedly ahead, straining to keep up with the flying pace the shortig set. He was on the chase, a fresh scent in his nostrils and his quarry nearby.

Then, abruptly, the hound stopped. He turned rapidly, questing, then his nose lifted and he paced slowly forward. He trotted in circles, confused. Then he faced Eva and sat down, tucking his tail neatly under.

'Um,' said Eva. 'That's not good.'

'Explain,' growled Finshay tersely.

'Means the scent ends here.'

The three paused, silent, alert for any sound or movement. Nothing stirred. Then soft wings brushed her cheek, and a sound, nearly inaudible, reached her ears. Rikbeek swept silently ahead, and she followed.

She knew what he'd found immediately. A wave of nausea and disorientation hit her before she'd gone five paces, and she gritted her teeth. Eva loved her profession, but she detested the necessity of occasionally utilising the gates to the Lower Realms. These tears in the fabric of the world disrupted the flow of light, sound, colour and scent around them; even the air flowed irregularly, torn from the natural channels of the winds and mingling queasily with the atmosphere beyond. As she travelled, she felt that curious and deeply unpleasant sensation so horribly familiar from her periodic excursions Below: a surging, roiling sensation, as if some force sought to rearrange the structure of her body. A gate certainly lay nearby.

She saw it then, a distortion of the patterns of tree, branch and leaf around her; a ripple in the air as if a great heat shimmered over the landscape. She stopped, holding up her hand.

'Feel that?' Her voice was barely a whisper, but her companions heard.

'Yes,' said Tren.

'What?' said Finshay.

Eva nodded to herself. Anyone with a shred of sorcerous talent could at least feel the pull of a gate, but those without were in danger of stumbling into one unawares. She drew a line in the mud at her feet.

'Mr. Arrerly,' she murmured. 'A gate lies beyond that line; don't step over it.' She expected a sharp answer from him at this order from her, but he was silent.

Rikbeek returned, hovering near the gate. Had he gone through? He abruptly banked and disappeared into the trees. A few moments later the gwaystrel's cry sounded. She followed the call to a small clearing overhung with low, frilled branches, dripping with moisture. She could see nothing untoward.

Rikbeek flew low to the ground, maintaining a position a few inches from the earthy floor. Still she could neither see nor sense anything untoward. She felt Tren's puzzlement echoing her own as he reached her side.

'He's found something?'

'Apparently.'

Tren went to his knees, suddenly intent. He rubbed a hand over the earth and tasted it.

'More blood,' he said grimly. A soft cry sounded unmistakably, as if someone smothered a whimper of pain. Tren's head shot up, alert, and Eva's eyes widened. She knelt too, and reached out to the empty air over which Rikbeek flew.

Her hands met a solid object: cloth was under her fingers, damp and ragged. A gasp, then, and the shape shifted under her fingers, flinching away from her.

Tren spoke.

'Ed?'

A momentary pause, and then a flicker, and a tall man appeared, lying prone, curled around his left side. He was shivering uncontrollably and his eyes stared alarmingly. She dimly recognised the features of Edwae Geslin, no longer fresh and youthful, now drawn and haggard. His appearance of mild friendliness had vanished beneath an air of desperation.

'Tren,' he gasped. 'You... took your time.'

136

'You should've told me,' said Tren sadly. 'You're hurt?' A dark bloodstain soaked the ragged cloak Edwae wore, and his hands were clasped tightly to his side. Tren moved to examine his wounds.

'No time for that,' gasped Edwae. 'You must stop him.'

'Who?'

'Don't know who. Made me change the Cloak... followed him here. There were....' he stopped speaking for a moment, panting hard for breath. 'Whurthag,' he managed at last. 'Beasts with him.'

'You don't know who it was?'

'Disguised.' Edwae, exhausted, let his head fall back into the mud. 'Wearing a different face...' he mumbled. 'Think he was... going for a gate.'

'There's no one else here,' Eva murmured to Tren. 'Rikbeek would've found them already.'

Tren nodded. He gently prised Ed's hands away from his side. The fabric of his clothing hung in tatters, and long, livid wounds striped his torso, seeping blood in sluggish flows.

'Whurthag wounded,' said Tren grimly.

'Tried to stop him,' said Edwae. His voice was faint and his breaths came shallow and infrequently.

'That was stupid, Ed,' said Tren, trying to sound light-hearted; but Eva heard the catch in his voice.

Edwae didn't answer. His eyes closed, and he lay with unearthly stillness. The sound of his breathing stopped.

15

The Mail Runner stood outside the grand gates of the University of Waeverleyne, nervously shifting her armful of packages. She was new on the job, started only last week; maybe that was why she'd been shafted with the task of delivering to the university. Everyone else had been more adept at dodging this duty.

She knew what it was she was carrying. The bulletins had been screaming about it for weeks: all istore to be turned in, for the owner's own safety. To be consigned to the care of Waeverleyne's scholars, who wanted it for research purposes. Well enough, but who was willing to cross Glinnery carrying such a thing these days? Remuneration had been offered, but the frightened owners of the remaining istore pieces preferred simply to be rid of them. And so, the mail. They packaged them up and sent them away, leaving the mail runners to take the risk. Her colleagues had been taking packages down to the university all week. Guards roamed the perimeters of the university grounds, a sight which alarmed her as much as it reassured her.

She shifted from foot to foot, waiting. It was early in the morning, true, but still everything seemed too quiet. She'd been told someone would be there to take the delivery. She juggled her parcels into the crook of one arm and lifted the knocker again, rapping loudly. The crisp, sharp sound split the silent morning air.

'Mail!' she yelled. A sudden realisation smote her: she was probably at the wrong door. Stepping back, she tried to identify some other entrance, a smaller, more accessible one. Soaring glissenwol trunks in rows met her eyes, many fitted with doors as well as windows. How was she to determine which was the correct door for the mail?

At last she heard footsteps approaching. The gigantic doors remained firmly closed, but a smaller door further down opened a crack. She drifted downwards, flexing her wings to control her pace of descent. The interior of the gigantic tree was dark; she could see nothing around the door save the suggestion of a figure and the gleam of an eye.

'Late,' somebody muttered.

'I'm sorry, uh, sir? It's really quite early for a delivery—'

'Hand it over.' The door opened a little wider, but she still couldn't make out anything inside the room save a patch of darkness that moved towards her. Trembling, she dropped most of the parcels at the figure's feet. The rest she placed into its hands, shuddering as her fingers touched something chill and damp.

'Pick those up,' said the voice. 'Bring them inside.' There was nothing in the tone to tell her whether she spoke to a male or a female. Warily she bent down, hands shaking as she scrambled to collect her dropped packages. Something moved in the darkness, moved fast; a beast leapt at her face and heavy jaws snapped at her neck. As pain blossomed in her throat she heard a few sharp syllables, harsh like curses, uttered in an unfamiliar language. Then her vision faded and she heard no more.

Devary Kant stepped beyond the confines of the Sanfaer house with a sense of relief. Not that he had especially minded acting guard over Llandry this past week; she was a sweet enough girl, when she managed to address more than two or three syllables to him, and the days had not passed unpleasantly. It was not in his nature to accept confinement for long, however.

Aysun was building something. He said it would replace the staircase that wound up the side of the stout trunk of the house, some contraption that couldn't be operated by the slew of beasts that still poured through from the Uppers. Devary watched for a few moments, endeavouring to make out the plan behind Aysun's busy activity. So far he had constructed some kind of metal frame that climbed into the air like a giant insect, swaying slightly in the winds. Now he appeared to be building a box. Apparently it was commonly used in Irbel, but Devary didn't remember seeing anything like it on the one visit he'd paid there, years ago. He shook his head, walking on.

He kept a wary eye out for roaming creatures as he walked along what passed for streets in Waeverleyne. The Summoners had been hard at work for the last two days, clearing the city of beasts and the rogue gates to the Uppers that were opening in ever greater numbers. They had succeeded in stemming the flow, or so it appeared, for Devary saw nothing untoward on his way through the city. He paused at the first set of bulletin boards he reached, stationing himself where he could read each of the three boards in turn.

The same headline blazed from all three.

Break-in at University of Waeverleyne
The respected University of Waeverleyne was broken into last eventide. The object of the crime was undoubtedly the coveted istore stone, for not a piece remains in the university's decimated research laboratories. Nothing else appears to have been taken. More news as we hear from our correspondents at the university.

Devary didn't wait to read the rest. He broke into a run, heading for the elegant cluster of trunks that made up the university grounds.

He encountered a group of infirmary workers on the outskirts. The body of a uniformed guard lay on the ground, bloodily wounded and evidently not breathing; several healers were working on him, quite uselessly.

'Was anyone inside?' he gasped, out of breath. One of the healers looked up, shook her head at him.

'Don't know,' she said tersely. Devary ran on, pushing his way through crowds of curious spectators. A glance upwards told him that the main doors were closed. He slipped through a small door at the rear, pushing his way through crowded reporters, police, infirmary workers, researchers and professors. To his relief, he found Elder Ilae Shuly standing in the centre of

140

the chaos, directing the clean-up effort. He looked up as Devary approached.

'Does Ynara know about this yet? I sent a messenger not long ago.'

Devary shook his head. 'That, I don't know. I heard the news from the bulletins.'

Ilae grimaced. 'They're quicker than ever.'

'I was afraid to see your name on the casualty list.' Elder Shuly, Ynara's closest friend on the Council, was famous for the hours he spent at the university, often staying well after it closed for the day.

'It should have been,' said Ilae bluntly. 'I developed one of my headaches yesterday, and left early. I was home not much after sunset. Two of my research assistants were here,' he added bleakly.

Devary winced. 'Were there any witnesses?'

'None surviving. Which was, of course, the point. There were a few more patrol guards on the other side of the university grounds, but they saw nothing.'

'And the istore?'

'Taken, down to the smallest piece.' Ilae sighed. All of his vaunted energy seemed lost; he looked every single one of his seventy-something years. 'Not that we were making any progress in the study. We lack the expertise, perhaps. I had hoped to consult with Nimdre, however; they've some specialist knowledge at the universities there. Oh — you'd know, of course,' Ilae added with a nod to Devary.

'What of Glour? They were forming a research team when Ynara left. They may be in danger of a similar raid.'

'I've already dispatched a note, but I imagine it will be too late for them to act on it. I wouldn't be surprised to hear that a similar break-in occurred somewhere in Glour City overnight. And really, I scarcely know how they would do better in protecting the stuff; nothing seems to hold against these people.'

Devary was silent. He couldn't help sharing Ilae's opinion.

'What puzzles me,' said Ilae abruptly, 'is how relentless this pursuit of the istore is turning out to be. The Council ordered a strong guard on the university, but I don't think we expected such an attack, not really. We had a mere few miserable pieces of the stone left; enough to study, not enough to be worth a great

141

deal. One would think.' He paused, frowning. 'Somebody seems determined to gather up every last piece. If the intention was to deprive us of the opportunity to study it properly, that's certainly been accomplished.' He looked up at Devary, his eyes fierce. 'It only makes me more determined. Apparently there's a secret here that someone thinks is desperately worth keeping. I will find out what it is.'

Devary made his way back to Ynara's soon afterwards. He had a suspicion in mind regarding the younger Sanfaer lady and her jewel crafting activities. It was now urgently necessary to determine whether he was correct.

Aysun was still at work on his machine when Devary arrived.

'She's upstairs,' he said. He didn't specify which lady he meant, but Devary found both at home, seated in the parlour with cups of tea.

'Has the news reached you yet?' he asked, bending to kiss Ynara lightly on the cheek.

'What news?' Ynara looked sharply at him. 'Bad or good?

'Bad,' he said. 'There is a messenger on the way from Ilae.' He recounted the tale in detail, including everything Elder Shuly had said. Ynara set down her cup and rose to her feet, brisk and business-like.

'I'd better go down there immediately.'

'Just one moment,' he said, catching at Ynara's arm. He'd been watching Llandry closely as he'd repeated Ilae's words about the istore research. Her face had remained impassive, but she'd slipped one small hand into her pocket as if checking for something.

'Llandry,' he said, very seriously. 'Did you turn all of your istore over to the university?'

She stared back at him for a long moment, expressionless, unmoved.

'No,' she said at last. 'I have one piece left.' She withdrew her hand from her pocket, revealing a pendant glittering with the indigo stone. He heard Ynara sigh.

'Oh, no, Llandry...'

The girl shrugged one shoulder. 'I couldn't part with it. I suppose it's lucky I felt that way.'

'Lucky?' Ynara's tone was dangerous.

142

'Yes,' said Llandry coolly. 'If the rest is gone, we've one piece left to work with.'

'Until that's taken, too, apparently over *your* dead body.' Ynara was working herself up into a fury. Devary stepped in quickly, taking the pendant from Llandry's hand before she had chance to react.

'I'll take care of it,' he said firmly. 'Please, don't either of you mention its existence just yet, not to anybody. Not even to Ilae, Ynara. I fear there are listening ears in too many places. I will find a safe way to tell him.'

Ynara cast him a look of pure fury, turning the same withering stare on her daughter. She stalked out of the house, allowing the door to slam roundly behind her. He heard a faint sigh from Llandry. She maintained her cool, but he sensed that she was hurt by her mother's anger.

'She's just worried about you,' he said gently. 'About us, I suppose. She is right to be.' He squeezed her hand briefly, and she mustered a smile for him.

'I'd better do something about this,' he said. 'Please keep inside for now. I know that you are sick of hearing that, but still—'

She interrupted him. 'I know, I know.' She waved him away.

By the time Llandry heard the news, everything was already settled. Devary was to go, and the stone was leaving with him. She found him in the parlour, sitting with his lyre in his lap, tuning the instrument. He gave her his smile, the nice one that made her feel comfortable.

'You're leaving? I thought you meant to stay for some time.'

'So I did,' Devary replied. 'But it is necessary. '

Llandry nodded vaguely, looking at the floor. 'Won't you be in danger?'

'It's hard to imagine how anyone could guess that I am carrying anything unusual. You have kept it secret very ably.'

'A lot of stranger things have happened lately.'

'That's true,' he conceded. 'But you must not worry.'

Llandry had nothing to say in the face of such confidence. She could only nod again. 'It's Nimdre you're heading for?'

'Yes. Draetre, specifically. There is a university there that may be able to tell us something about this stone.'

'Is that the real reason?'

Devary stopped tuning the lyre and placed it carefully down on the table. 'The "real" reason? Yes. Of course. Clearly, we are dealing with something extraordinary. There is a faculty in Draetre dedicated to, ah... esoteric studies, shall I say? I have a friend on the staff whom I intend to consult.'

'Secrets, you mean.' Llandry mulled that over. It didn't ring quite true. No doubt the University of Draetre was knowledgeable, but so was the University of Waeverleyne. She didn't really believe that Nimdre had many resources not shared by Glinnery's scholars.

'Mamma wants it out of Glinnery, doesn't she? As far away from me as possible.'

'It might be fair to say that its departure from Glinnery would be a desirable bonus.'

Llandry thought back further, remembering the conversation she had overheard between Devary and her mother. 'Did mother ask you to take the stone to Nimdre?'

He gave her a quick, penetrating glance. 'I believe it was her idea, yes.'

Llandry sighed. Ynara liked her world to be neat and uncomplicated. The istore was certainly a complication, and apparently Devary was scarcely less so. As such, away both must go.

'I'm going to bed,' she said. 'When are you leaving?'

'Not until tomorrow. I'll see you before I leave.'

She nodded curtly and quickly left the room. Expecting sleeplessness, she collected her favourite novel from the bookcase on her way past and took it upstairs with her. Curling up in bed with Sigwide on her pillow, she flicked through to the best parts. The story charted the life of a girl with extraordinary summoning abilities, who went on to become a famous High Summoner. The heroine became everything Llandry wished to be: smart, confident, powerful, popular. Her very favourite chapter was near the end, when the heroine married a prince and became a princess.

Even the wedding chapter couldn't entirely absorb her today, however. Her mind worked restlessly, refusing to be stilled or distracted, and as page after page glided away before her eyes

144

without imparting any clear idea of the plot, she finally closed the book and let it drop to the floor. Sigwide was already asleep, but he didn't wake when she gently stroked his soft fur.

The imminent departure of her last, prized piece of istore was a sad prospect, that much was a given. But she felt curiously saddened that it was Devary who would be taking it away. All her wariness of him had disappeared, and while she couldn't yet claim to be comfortable with him, she felt sure that she could be, in time. For her, that was remarkable. She had never had a real friend outside of her family.

But now it would all be over. Devary was leaving, and she had little doubt that he wouldn't be coming back, not for some time. She might never see him again. She pictured herself after tomorrow's eventide, left cooped up alone in the house while her mother sat on the Council and her father built elevators for the city. No istore to soothe her anxieties and bolster her confidence, and no Devary to keep her company and teach her to play the lyre. Her stomach twisted with misery at the thought.

Perhaps she could go along. The idea caught her imagination, and for a few minutes she indulged in the idea, picturing herself travelling with Devary, seeing Nimdre. She had rarely travelled outside of Glinnery, and then only to Irbel once as a child, or to the Darklands Market on the edge of Glour. Devary's tales of Nimdre, where the sun rose and set and the days turned regularly between light and dark, were thrilling to her.

But her mother would never agree to it, not while there was the smallest chance of her encountering another whurthag. Llandry's spirits sank again. But the idea refused to leave her, and as long as it nagged at her thoughts, she was unable to sleep.

She could try to persuade her mother. Ynara would probably forbid it, but the attempt must be made.

Maybe she could begin by persuading Devary.

Llandry was up early the next day in spite of her poor night's sleep. She waited until her mother had left the house on some errand, then she went to find Devary.

'I should go with you,' she said without preamble.

He looked at her quizzically. 'Why is that?'

She straightened her shoulders, lifting her chin. 'Because I

145

know more about the stone than anyone else. If you're taking it to be studied, I should be there.'

'Your mother wouldn't like that, I think. You could give me all the information that you have, and I'll pass it to the university at Draetre.'

'That's not the same.'

He lifted his brows. 'Oh?'

'I want to go. It's my fault that most of this has happened. I should have left those gems where I found them.'

'You couldn't have known what would happen, Llandry. It doesn't mean you should endanger yourself again trying to resolve it.'

'Didn't you say there was no particular danger?'

He sighed helplessly. 'Yes, but — that applies to me. Not necessarily to you.'

'I can't take care of myself?'

He looked gravely at her. 'In many ways, yes. If your life is endangered, I fear not.'

Llandry sat down, subdued. Devary may be unfailingly courteous, but he had a firm will too.

Either that, or he was far too afraid of her mother to risk her disapproval.

'Please take me along,' she said.

'We will ask your mother's opinion.'

Llandry turned on him a look of contempt. 'That,' she said flatly, 'is a cop-out. You know she won't hear of it.'

'With good reason.'

'I am a grown woman!' she hissed, horribly aware that she sounded anything but adult as she said it. 'My mother does not make my decisions for me.'

Devary was unmoved. 'I cannot agree to something that will worry your mother.'

Definitely afraid of Ynara. Not that Llandry could blame him, not entirely.

'What's the trouble?' Ynara herself appeared behind Devary, carrying Sigwide. She handed the bundle of fur over to Llandry, pecking her on the cheek in the process.

'I'm going with Devary to Draetre, Mamma,' Llandry said firmly, accepting a kiss from Sigwide too.

'Oh?' Ynara raised her brows at Devary, who lifted his

hands.

'Her idea,' he said. 'I have not agreed to anything.'

'I don't need you to agree,' Llandry said coolly.

'But, love, your arm...'

'It's healed.' She backed away but Ynara bore down on her, peeling back her sleeve. The flesh beneath was still ruptured, but shiny new skin was rapidly forming over the wounds.

'It's healed enough,' Llandry amended. 'I'm fit to go, Ma.'

'It is dangerous, love,' Ynara said gravely. 'Remember, we still don't know who is responsible for all of this, nor where they might be.'

'Now that the cave has been discovered — and emptied — I am no longer a target. You said yourself that the attempts to contact me stopped some days ago. I'm not afraid.'

'I think you should be.' Ynara's tone was swiftly developing that note of steel that meant she did not mean to be overruled. 'Why is it so important to you, love? Devary will take care of it.'

'It's my responsibility.'

'No! No part of your duty involves risking your own hide in pursuit of this ridiculous gem. That's what it's really about, isn't it? You can't bear to see it go. I think you need to question whether that's healthy, Llan.'

'It isn't the stone, Ma!'

Ynara gave her the cold stare.

'All right, it isn't just the stone. I'm going mad locked away in the house. I need to get out of here, stretch my wings.'

'So go to the library. I will provide a guard for you.'

'I've been to the library a hundred times. I want to go somewhere new.'

Ynara shook her head. 'No. I'm sorry, Llan, but it's unthinkable. The rogue gates are slowing down, but those beasts are still coming through, and there's no telling whether the whurthags are truly gone. This is not the time to be taking sight-seeing expeditions.' Llandry opened her mouth to speak, but her mother cut her off. 'No further arguments. When this is all over, your father and I will take you to Nimdre, if you wish. In the meantime, you'll stay here. I don't want to bury my only child.' She stalked out of the room, forestalling Llandry's response.

Llandry was silent, smarting with a mixture of frustration, disappointment and humiliation. To be lectured and controlled

147

like a child, in front of Devary! She pushed back her chair, intending to leave, but he startled her by laying a hand briefly over hers.

'Your mother loves you more than anything, Llandry. I only wish she had the same concerns for my safety.'

Llandry snorted. 'You want to be kept behind locked doors all your life?'

'She is right, at least for the present. Now is not the time for sight-seeing.' He released her hand and stood up. 'I must pack. But, Llandry, perhaps you will come and see me when you make your projected visit to Nimdre? I will be glad to see you.' She couldn't tell if he was sincere, but his smile was warm.

'Thanks,' she said. She couldn't find anything else to say. After a moment, he left.

The day passed sluggishly. Too crushed to settle to any productive task, Llandry drifted aimlessly about the house, observing the preparations from a distance. Ynara had arranged for an armed escort for Devary, along with a summoner-sorcerer team to accompany him as far as the Nimdre border. She watched dully as Devary talked with her mother, always in corners and in undertones so she couldn't hear what was said. At last, when it was time for him to leave, her heart rebelled. She couldn't sit at home, safe and protected, while Devary risked himself over the stone. And she couldn't sit at home, cherished but stifled, while Devary took his part in the tale unfolding around the istore.

Slipping silently up to her room, she packed a small bag. A change of clothes, a blanket, and two bottles of her tonic went in. She was trembling already, but this time with excitement mixed with the dread of defying her mother. It didn't feel the same as her usual attacks, but no doubt those would plague her still.

As an afterthought, she added her favourite book. If her courage failed her, she could read again the passages where her heroine achieved her greatest victories. Perhaps she would feel empowered.

She hid the bag under her bed and laid Sigwide's carry case atop the covers. Now she had only to wait. She wouldn't try to steal out of the house too soon; her mother would be on the watch. She would wait for a short time after Devary's departure, then catch up with him. She knew his projected route. If she tailed him as far as Nimdre without being discovered, when she finally revealed herself it would be too late to send her home.

Trying to ignore the excited thumping of her heart, Llandry sat down to wait.

16

'We have to get him to an infirmary.' Tren surged to his feet, his hands and clothes covered in Edwae's blood. He looked ready to run all the way back to Westrarc by himself.

'Tren.' Eva caught at his arm, restraining him lest he fly off without thought. 'Look at him. He'd never survive the trip.'

Tren looked. Poor Edwae lay inert save for the pained heaving of his chest as he fought to breathe. That ragged breath had stopped, started, stopped again; his chest was laid open with the same wounds that Eva had seen on Meesa's destroyed body. Finshay had ripped a cloak to pieces and bandaged Edwae's chest, but nothing could halt the flow of blood.

'We must be miles from anywhere with a healer. We'll be lucky to move him at all without—' She stopped. She was going to say 'without killing him,' but Tren's face whitened so rapidly at the implication of it that she feared for his health.

'Sit down,' she said gently. He obeyed, numbly. Finshay was still tending to Ed, brisk, efficient and entirely without sympathy. His ministrations seemed to be helping, however. Eva watched as he unstoppered a phial and placed it to Edwae's lips, forcing him to swallow the contents. After a few minutes Ed's breathing stabilised a little, and his contorted face eased.

'What's that?' Tren asked, suspicious.

'Pain draught,' said Fin. 'Strong one.'

'How strong?'

'Strong enough to kill a healthy person. He's got about an hour.'

'*What*?' Tren knocked the phial out of Finshay's hands, leaned over to stare anxiously into Ed's greying face. 'How could you just —?' He stared at Finshay, tensed as if ready to strike him.

'Don't be an idiot,' said Finshay brutally. 'He's going to die. Even if we could get him straight to an infirmary, he couldn't be saved now. We need him able to talk, get what information we can out of him.'

'No,' whispered Tren. 'There's time, there must be more we can do for him. Something.'

'Like what?' Finshay stood up, cleaning his hands. 'Forget it, Warvel. You can do the interrogation if it's going to bother you, but get on with it. There isn't much time.' He retired to the other side of the clearing, lay down with his cloak under his head as a pillow, and to all appearances went to sleep.

Tren said nothing. He turned his face away from Finshay, his jaw clenched tight. He picked up one of Edwae's hands and gripped it hard.

'Ed?'

Edwae turned unfocused eyes on him, obviously seeing nothing. Eva fetched her notebook out of her bags and seated herself beside Tren. She handed him her water bottle.

'He might be able to speak if he drinks something,' she said quietly. Tren silently took the bottle from her and fed Ed with a thin trickle of water, patient and silent as his friend swallowed some and spilled rather more.

'Ed,' Tren tried again. 'Ed, you need to tell us what happened.' He gripped his friend's fingers as Ed tried to rise, placing a gentle hand on his chest to hold him down.

'Don't try to move,' he said softly. 'You're badly hurt.'

'So it appears,' said Edwae weakly. 'Somehow I don't feel anything.' He looked vaguely down at himself, puzzled.

'You're under a pain draught.'

Ed blinked at the bloody bandages that swathed his torso and abdomen. 'What happened,' he repeated. 'Right.' He eased his head back and closed his eyes. Tren leaned over him, repeating his name with growing urgency.

'I'm awake,' said Ed vaguely. His eyes opened again and he focused on Eva. 'New girlfriend?'

Tren chuckled. 'No. Lady Evastany Glostrum, High Summoner.'

'M'lady.' Edwae frowned at her. 'Right. Seen your picture in the papers.'

'That happens more than I'd like,' Eva said.

'Reckon it would,' Ed replied, with a ghost of a chuckle. 'Got any family?'

'Not yet.'

'You sure?'

'Quite sure, yes.'

Ed's eyes lost their focus on her face and he closed them again.

'Speaking of girlfriends, what's this I hear about yours?' Tren spoke lightly, but Eva knew he was hurt that his friend hadn't confided in him.

Ed's eyes opened. 'You heard about that.'

'We saw your mother,' Tren said gently. 'She's worried about you.'

'Ah...' Ed sighed faintly. 'You'll take care of them, Tren? They'll need you, till the girls are grown up.'

'Don't speak of that,' said Tren lightly. 'You'll be fine.'

'Tren. You seen this?' He nodded slightly down at the mess of his torso.

Tren swallowed. 'I noticed it, yes.'

'Don't talk rubbish, then. Promise me you'll make sure the girls are all right.'

'Don't worry about that. They'll have everything they need.'

Ed nodded. 'I never meant to make such a mess,' he said helplessly. 'I just... there was never enough money, the girls are growing older and they need more all the time...'

'Someone offered you money?'

'More of it than I'd make in five years. All I had to do was make a small, temporary change to the span of the Night Cloak. They promised no one would know. I think I knew Angstrun would find out, but I couldn't say no...'

Tren sighed. 'Who paid you?'

'I don't know. I only spoke to him twice, and he was always disguised, shrouded. Never saw a face, even. Think it was a male.

152

All I can say for sure.'

'Damn.'

'Can't be that many male sorcs with disguise skills on that level. Get your man there on it.' He rolled his eyes up in the vague direction of Finshay's recumbent form. 'Had a touch of accent, probably Orstwych but could've been Ullarn.'

Eva wrote quickly, recording everything Edwae said. An idea occurred to her, and she leaned slightly forwards.

'What about the pale-haired woman?'

Ed's eyes flicked towards her. 'Looks like you.'

'Me?'

'Well.' He narrowed his eyes slightly, inspecting her. 'Might just be the hair,' he conceded.

Tren frowned. 'Ed, who is she?'

'The most beautiful woman in the world,' he said.

Tren smiled sadly. 'Your mother said she was a sorceress?'

'Sorceress? No, not that.' Ed's breathing began to grow laboured again, and he winced. 'Traitoress, though. She introduced me to her... friend. The man without a face. How strong did you say that draught was?'

'Pretty damn strong.' Tren stared at his friend, alarmed. 'It hasn't even been half an hour...'

Ed was silent for several minutes, occupied with trying to get enough air. Eva and Tren could only watch, helpless. At last he rallied a little again.

'Met her at Darklands Market,' he continued. 'Thought she liked me.'

'Didn't she?'

'She sent the shrouded man to me. I'd say not.'

'Ed, what is her name?'

'Said she was called Ana. From Orstwych, she claimed. Accent wasn't right though.'

'You think she was lying.'

'Seems likely.' Ed's eyes grew sad. 'Never saw her again after the job.'

Tren shook his head. 'Why did you run, Ed? Why didn't you tell me about this before?'

'Couldn't stay around, could I? I knew they'd be looking for a scapegoat.' His breathing grew wet, stifled with blood. 'Tren, I swear. I never knew what would come of it. I never meant for anyone to be hurt.'

'I know, Ed. It's okay.'

'I met him in Orstwych after I'd done the job. Got the money. Left it with the girls. Then I followed him. He came out here, fast, sure, like he knew where to go. Turned out there's a regular gate here.' Edwae was talking fast, now, sensing that he was running out of time. 'Tried to stop him going through. Obviously I failed.'

'You said he was a sorc.'

'Right.'

'Why did he need to find a gate? Why didn't he just open one?'

'No idea. He went through it, though, with his entourage in tow.'

'Wait. There was only him? Nobody else was with him?'

'Just him.'

'He's a *sorc*, and he's dragging whurthags around with him?'

Ed gave a tiny shrug. 'He had a couple of them.'

'And they were obeying him?'

'Just about. Barely.' Ed was gasping for breath again, gritting his teeth. 'I wanted to stop him, make up for what I did. I failed.'

'We'll find him.' Tren spoke firmly, confidently. 'One way or another, we'll make sure that it ends.'

Ed sighed, his distress easing. 'Should've told you before.'

'That's true enough.'

'I'm sorry. You were always the... one the girls liked. I didn't dare tell you about Ana. I thought she'd ditch me in a second if she saw you. I was a fool.'

Tren tried to smile, but his face wouldn't obey him. A sob emerged from his throat as Ed's eyes closed again, the harsh sound of his breathing fading into silence.

They waited, but he did not rally again. Still Tren would not move, maintaining his station by his friend, still clutching those cold fingers in his own. Eva waited with him for a long time, but at last she moved quietly away, leaving Tren alone with Ed's remains.

She felt almost as much pain as he did, watching him grieve. It brought the memory of Meesa's death back to her mind with too much clarity, and she mourned anew for both her friend and his.

154

At last, Tren moved, stiffly after his long, motionless vigil. He wandered aimlessly about the clearing, dazed, his face drawn and stained with drying tears. Eva watched him silently, unable to determine how to comfort him. Finally he wandered in her direction, slumping down by her.

'Cold bastard,' he muttered, indicating Finshay. Vale's agent remained oblivious, though he was obviously awake. He was reading from a tatty volume, head propped casually on one folded arm.

Eva shrugged. 'It's his job to be, I suppose.'

Tren muttered something inaudible. He lay silent for some time, watching Eva. She returned to the perusal of her notes, tidying and arranging her comments, letting Tren pursue his own thoughts.

'Got everything?' he said at last.

She nodded. 'I believe so. I'm making copies now, for you and Mr. Arrerly.'

'How efficient.'

She smiled sadly. 'It's necessary.'

'I suppose it is.'

'Tren, I'm so sorry.'

He nodded. 'I don't know what to do, now.' His customary cheerfulness was gone; he sounded helpless and frightened. 'His mother needs to be told, Vale will want a report immediately and your notes must be handed over. But...'

'But?'

'But I don't want to do any of that. I want to take up Ed's pursuit.'

Eva shifted, feeling a sense of foreboding. 'Into the Lowers?'

'Yes.'

'Alone?'

'Yes. If necessary.'

'Tren, Ed's flight was... ill-considered. Had he had help, he might be alive now. It won't help him for you to follow his example and get yourself hurt, too.'

'He should have told me. I could have been with him; between us we might have fared better.'

'Might have.'

Tren sighed deeply. 'If we wait to go all the way back to Glour, convince Vale of the truth of Ed's story — because after

155

all he is still the main suspect — and then return with 'help', whoever Ed was chasing will be long gone. I want to take it up *now*.'

'Tren —'

'I know, it's crazy.'

She watched him warily, trying to gauge his seriousness from his expression. She couldn't read him.

'You can't go alone.'

'As far as I am concerned, I don't have a choice.'

'Have you ever been there before?'

'Once or twice, in school. Never for very long. But I can manage.'

'Tren, you can't go alone. Really. Please reconsider this idea.'

'I can't. What else do we have to go on? Even Ed couldn't tell us much. There are no other good leads. It ends here, and unless I take up Ed's pursuit, it's over now. How can I turn away from that? How many other people will die if I don't *do* something?'

Eva was silent. His words spoke to her heart, even if her mind rebelled from the idea. Thinking of Meesa, she could understand his urgency.

Nonetheless...

'Tren, please. You don't — you *can't* — understand about the Lowers if you haven't spent any real time there. Even trained, experienced summoners are at risk down there alone. Even *me*.'

'It can't be helped. I'm hardly defenceless; I'll manage somehow.'

'What are you going to do if you find him, hm? Ed's as powerful as you are and *look* what became of that!' She was growing angry, frustrated with her inability to influence him.

'I have to go.'

'You don't have to. You've a duty to report to Vale, to see that Ed's family are told—'

'Don't you see? Ed thought this was important enough to risk his life for it. He needed to do it. If I want to be the friend I ought to be, I'll finish this for him.' He stood up and began collecting his things, resolute. 'You'll see that Ed's remains are taken home to Orstwych? Tell Vale everything. Speak to the family, if you can — they'll remember you.' He paused to give her a lopsided smile. 'If you get time, send somebody after me. If I get in trouble, maybe they'll find me.'

She stood up, too. 'Tren, wait. Please. This is crazy.' She felt real fear growing, threatening to choke her. The prospect of another lively young man disappearing into the Lowers on an ill-advised pursuit of the man who casually controlled two whurthags... picturing Tren's face striped with wounds, covered in his own blood as Ed and Meesa had been, her stomach turned.

'I'm going with you.'

He stopped, shocked. 'What?'

'You heard me.' She lifted her chin and stared him down. 'Don't argue.'

'You recall everything you just said to me, I suppose.'

'With perfect clarity. The two of us will manage better than you will alone.'

'Why would you do this?'

'I've as good a reason as you,' she reminded him. 'Besides, you're right. Something ought to be done now, not in a week or two weeks or however long it takes Glour government to get organised.'

'That's not what you said a moment ago.'

'That was when you were insisting on going alone.'

'I still am!'

'No, you're not. You need my summoner skills. What are *you* going to do when you meet a whurthag face-to-face, hm?'

'Fight it, I suppose.'

'That having worked so beautifully for Edwae.'

He changed tack. 'Look, I need to know someone is taking care of Ed and his family. Finshay isn't equipped for that job.'

'Like you said, this is more important.'

He stared at her, helpless. 'Why are you so determined about this?'

'I don't want you to go alone.'

He blinked at her.

'I wouldn't want *anyone* to attempt such a thing alone, Tren! It's unthinkable.'

Finshay's voice broke in on the altercation. 'If you've made a decision, perhaps you could get on with it. Time's moving on.' He rose to his feet and approached Eva, taking the notebook out of her hands. He examined it critically, then ripped a few pages out.

'Legible. Good.' He handed the book back to her with a nod. 'I'll deal with the boy, the family, the government, the notes and all the dull stuff. You two go get yourselves killed. Have fun.' He turned his back on them, stowing the pages in his pack.

Tren snorted. 'Thanks.'

'No problem. I'll tell Vale you both sent your regards.'

Tren looked at Eva. 'Last chance to change your mind.'

'Right after you do.'

He grinned, for the first time that day. 'Onward then, comrade.'

Eva's belongings were soon gathered. Tren paused long enough to pay a final goodbye to his friend. Eva heard him whisper something, though she couldn't make out the words and she didn't try. Moments later, he joined her before the gate.

'Ready?'

Eva nodded. 'Go.'

He shouldered his bag and stepped forward. His form rippled and shivered like wind through the grass, and then he vanished.

Eva took a breath and stepped in after him. The gate closed in around her, squeezing the air in her lungs and beating hard upon her skin. Then she was through into the cool, sharp air of the Lower Realms.

17

Llandry followed Devary's party south and east through the thickly-growing, sun-warmed woodlands of Glinnery. They were angling towards the major coach road that ran between southernmost Glinnery and Nimdre. The woods had been swept by the summoners and there was little out of the ordinary to be encountered. As they wended further south, the landscape grew more open and expansive, the towering glissenwol thinning and dwindling away into lesser monoliths only twice Devary's height. Their colours changed gradually, from the blues, purples and greens of northern and eastern Glinnery into a vibrant range of reds, yellows and oranges. Llandry had travelled southwest into Irbel or east into Glour, but these sights were less familiar to her. They were beautiful, but there was something saddening about the decreasing height and grandeur of the proud glissenwol caps. It suggested a fading of strength and health.

Her journey was arduous, and for a few brief moments she had even regretted her decision to go after Devary. Travelling on the wing, she was obliged to fly high in order to avoid being spotted by Devary's airborne escort of armed guards. They, too, were hanging back, taking care not to draw undue attention to Devary. He had to look like an ordinary traveller returning to his home city, and an obvious entourage would destroy that. So Llandry had to fly so far back she could barely keep Devary in sight. The strain took its toll on her injured arm and back, and by the end of the eventide hours she was flagging badly. When Devary stopped to sleep, she settled to the ground with relief. A night spent on the ground with nothing but a blanket for comfort was a new experience: exciting, though it would probably lose its piquancy after a few repetitions. At least she had the deep mosses to lie in.

'Sig, I need you to tell me when Devary goes, all right?' If he understood her he gave no indication of it. Llandry sighed and let it go. She had to sleep; if she missed Devary's departure she would simply have to catch him up.

As she lay down and shut her eyes she felt something brush lightly against her cheek. She sat up in alarm, heart pounding. Had she been discovered? She waited for several minutes, but nobody could be seen or heard nearby. The light touch came again, amid a whirl of colour and a soft buzzing sound, and at last she identified the source: her little winged friend had followed her.

'You kept yourself well hidden,' she murmured, catching it gently in her hands. Remarkable; she hadn't expected that the creature had enough awareness of her to go to such lengths.

'Well, if you're staying, hush. I want to sleep.' She released it, soothing it with a gentle touch of her will, and the buzzing subsided. Huddling under her blankets with Sigwide's warmth to comfort her, Llandry fell asleep.

They had passed through the mountains of north-eastern Irbel and begun the descent into Nimdre before Llandry's presence was discovered. Tired and in pain, she had been steadily losing height until she was flying some way below the winged guards' altitude. She had barely noticed, and when the nearest guard shouted and circled down to her level it was too late to escape. She was recognised, of course — everybody knew her mother's face — and she found herself marched forcibly ahead to be presented to Devary.

He looked down at her with an impassive face. Llandry squirmed, suddenly ashamed of herself for her deceit.

'Don't say anything about my mother,' she begged. 'I know she won't approve. I just—'

160

Devary held up a hand. 'I don't believe I need you to explain.' His tone was quite cold, and Llandry felt terrible. She had lost his good opinion, and she would be marched straight back to Glinnery to face her mother's anger. But then Devary smiled.

'That is because I imagine I can understand. Though I must inform your mother of your whereabouts, as soon as possible.' Llandry felt a wave of relief wash over her, followed by a tremor of excitement. He wasn't going to reject her. She could stay with him after all.

Then she grimaced, feeling a twinge of renewed pain work its way down her back.

'See now, you have hurt yourself again. What would your mother say?' She stiffened, but his tone was light, teasing. She smiled back shyly.

'I'm not really hurt. Just a bit tired.'

'You have flown all the way? I'm impressed, truly. You are a woman of determination.' He looked at the guard who still held Llandry's arm. 'All is well. We will take a carriage as soon as we reach the gates.' The guard nodded and took off again, returning to his station. Devary looked back at Llandry.

'Can you walk for another few miles? We are not far from Nimdre.'

'My legs are fine. It's just my arms and back that are tired.'

He nodded. 'Excellent. I will find a room for you at the Harp, I think. Your mother used to love it.'

'Ma's been to Nimdre?' The idea shouldn't surprise her; Ynara was too knowledgeable to have spent her life confined to Glinnery.

'She used to visit quite regularly, once,' he said. 'With me.' He didn't smile that time, and Llandry sensed a touch of regret in his tone. She was polite enough to refrain from questioning him further.

'Shall we go? I don't know about you but I am starving.'

He laughed. 'What have you had to eat since we left? Very little? We had better hurry, indeed.'

Their destination was Draetre in northwestern Nimdre, a town of moderate size that proved to lie in the heart of the expansive forest. It was twilight when they arrived, a condition of light that Llandry had never seen before. In its muted serenity it reminded her of Glinnery's eventide, only it was darker, full of shadows. She didn't find it disturbing; on the contrary she was enchanted by it. Watching from the windows of their hired carriage, she was completely absorbed by the curious half-light.

Devary's home town had an air of sleepy serenity which Llandry found particularly agreeable. Buildings of wood and pale grey stone were constructed with a haphazard air, as if they were not the product of conscious design but had instead shouldered their way out of the ground, developing bulges and protrusions as necessary to contain the requirements of their inhabitants. There was a charm about this, despite the aura of confusion spawned by the peculiar buildings and crowded, circuitous streets.

The Silver Harp (its odd appearance notwithstanding) proved to be a particularly elegant establishment; so much so that it was hard to credit that money changed hands in exchange for her accommodation. She was given a room near the top of a building so peculiarly constructed that, from the outside, it appeared ready to topple. But inside, the layout of the rooms possessed an inexplicable logic and harmony that was wholly unexpected, and she found no further reason to doubt its solidity. Her room was well-lit by long, clear windows, beautifully panelled with silvery wood, and comfortably upholstered in silks and velvets. Best of all, a large tub stood in an adjoining chamber which was quickly filled with hot water for her use. She was waited upon rather than served by the patrons of the establishment, and engaged in genial conversation. She felt like an invited guest more than a paying customer.

She was quite settled, and perfectly ready to take advantage of the tub next door; but Devary inexplicably lingered after the attendants had departed. He was inspecting her room rather critically, Llandry felt.

'Your mother would expect me to get the very best for you,' he explained, frowningly examining the large panes of glass through which the soft, silvery moonlight shone.

'This is the best. I can hardly imagine how it could be better.'

He smiled. 'Perhaps so. I'll call for you tomorrow, then, and we will see the town.'

162

Llandry had every intention of exploring before that time. The peculiar twilight of Nimdre intrigued her, and she wanted to experience more of it before she slept. But Devary looked exhausted, so she merely smiled. 'Mm, well. That tub is calling to me.'

'Ah, yes. I'm looking forward to doing the same. Tomorrow, then?'

'Certainly.'

Llandry kept her bathing short, eager to investigate Draetre. When she slipped out of her room, the twilight had deepened but had yet to descend into full darkness. She wore a long cloak with the hood pulled low over her face, one that was voluminous enough to conceal her wings. She wanted no well-meaning strangers confounding her with conversation. She stepped slowly into the wide road — such as it was; it wound and turned far more than thoroughfares were wont to do in cities. Standing alone, she felt a sense of thrilling freedom. She could be anybody, here; not an awkward, shy girl more comfortable with her jewels than with her peers; nor the quiet, unassuming and largely overlooked daughter of an Elder of Waeverleyne. She could go anywhere she chose: disappear into the shadows in the folds of her cloak.

She had drunk her usual tonic, but when a crowd of Nimdren singers came into view, laughing, filling the road with chaos, Llandry's artificial lassitude wavered and her brief euphoria vanished. When some of them glanced at her, curiosity evident in their lingering gaze, anxiety returned with a crushing rush and her hands began to shake. Crowds of people, too much noise... she dug in her bag for her bottle and took another drink, breathing too quickly. For a moment she was almost overwhelmingly tempted to return to her room and wait meekly for Devary, but she suppressed the impulse. She was a grown woman: she would not waste her brief taste of freedom by hiding in her room. Drawing her hood further down over her face, she clutched her cloak closer around herself and took a deep breath. With a sweep of her long skirts, she was gone, stepping quickly into the streets.

She wandered for some time, until the serene twilight had altogether gone and the moon — half full — shone fitfully from behind a scattering of clouds. Every turn took her to some new

163

sight or curiosity. She studied buildings of the most puzzling and original architecture she'd ever seen. She sketched their most intriguing features in her notebook, wishing she could see them again in the daylight with their full colours on display. Everywhere she went she heard music, sometimes lively and uplifting, sometimes dreamily melancholy. The latter reminded her of the airs Devary had often played, and she was uncomfortably reminded that she had left him behind. Perhaps it was time to return to the Harp.

But ahead of her she could see a large square, crowded with people. Her first instinct was to retreat, and she was on the point of turning when a number of fluttering awnings caught her eye. A market, then? Finding this prospect quite irresistible, she firmly buried her fears and stepped into the crush.

She was rewarded immediately by the sight of myriad colourful wares spread out for her perusal. Her artist's eye caught and appreciated the unique style of the skilfully-wrought goods that she saw: jewellery worked in metals rich and dark, winking with exotically-coloured gems; clothing in colours and textures of extraordinary beauty; musical instruments painted and engraved; food and delicacies artistically displayed and emitting tempting aromas. She forgot the crowds around her in her absorption. Sigwide's enthusiasm echoed her own; he sat up high in his sling, nose questing, his thoughts a blur of excitement. She found a stall selling plump, glossy nuts and purchased some for him. He crunched happily on them as she wandered the market.

She chose gifts for her mother and father, and a new garment for herself: a pair of loose trousers with gathered cuffs at the ankle, billowing and romantic. They would be perfect for flying. She was in the process of choosing a gift for Devary, more hesitantly and with a crippling lack of confidence in her judgement of his tastes, when her elbow was seized.

She looked up quickly, instantly alert and alarmed. Consciousness of the swirling mass of shoppers rushed in on her again all at once, and she had to swallow a sense of panic. At her elbow stood a woman with Darklander skin. Though she was obviously not old, her hair gleamed white in the muted sheen of the light-globes. She was finely dressed, with an obvious air of wealth and ease. She smiled at Llandry in a manner far too

164

familiar for a stranger.

'A visitor from foreign parts, I'd guess,' said the woman, with an accent even thicker than Devary's. Her manner was so entirely devoid of self-consciousness or awkwardness that Llandry's own increased by comparison, and she made no response save to nod her head in a cool fashion.

'Your stature suggests Glinnery,' said the woman, making a show of looking down at Llandry as if from a long way up. Indeed, she was taller, but not so extremely so as all that. Llandry bristled slightly. 'Are all your countrymen so silent?' the woman continued. 'I had not heard it of so artistically talented a people.'

'I need to depart,' Llandry said. She turned to go, but found her elbow once again seized in a determined grip. She looked angrily down at the hand that detained her, a deceptively dainty-looking appendage well covered with glittering rings.

'A moment,' said the woman, in a tone of deeper seriousness. 'That is a most interesting piece of jewellery. Did you buy it here?'

Llandry looked down at herself, startled. She didn't remember putting any jewellery on before she left her room. A quick touch to her throat confirmed it: no bracelets jangled at her wrists, and no necklace lay against her neck.

'I'm not—' she began, but the woman was looking at Sigwide. Llandry's heart sank. The orting was shuffling in his sling, still bristling with excitement, but his enthusiasm had nothing to do with the market. His mouth was full of silver, a slender chain dangling from his teeth.

From the chain hung Llandry's ill-fated istore pendant.

Sigwide carried it with care and obvious pride, full of himself for his accomplishment. Llandry felt briefly like strangling him. When had he taken it? She instantly recalled, with horrible clarity, Sigwide's antics near the end of their journey. Bored and restless, he had taken to nosing in Devary's pack. They had both been amused as he entertained himself with various of Dev's possessions, but she hadn't dreamed that he might have been going for the pendant. Or that he could secrete it somewhere without either her or Devary noticing.

Perversely the stone shone in this near-darkness with a particular radiance Llandry had never seen before. No wonder it had attracted attention. She sighed deeply.

'Well?' The woman spoke sharply, and Llandry's eyes narrowed in irritation.

'No,' she said shortly, pulling her arm from the woman's grasp.

'Oh, then I must know where you bought it! I simply must have one the same, exactly the very same as that.' The woman's eyes lit as she stared at Sigwide and his treasure. Llandry hastily took it from him, ignoring his protests, and stuffed it into the pocket of her cloak.

'I did not buy it,' Llandry said, and then immediately regretted offering even so small a piece of information to this obstructive stranger.

'Oh? It was a gift, then, from a lover no doubt. I see that in your pretty face.' The woman laughed. *Quite, quite wrong*, thought Llandry irritably, but she had finished humouring her oppressor.

'Unless... you've an artist's eye for beauty. I could not help observing that as I watched you shopping. Perhaps you are the creator of that fine piece.'

'You were watching me?'

'Strangers do attract notice, especially when they look as though they are trying to hide.' She smiled again, a much less pleasant expression than before, and her eyes flicked over the large hood that still covered most of Llandry's face and hair. 'I will pay you a great deal to make me such a pendant,' she said then. 'In fact, I will pay you a great deal more for that very pendant that you wear. Let me take it away with me now.' She produced a little wrist-bag from somewhere and opened it, displaying its contents. It was bulging with sovereigns.

'It isn't for sale,' said Llandry. 'And I cannot make one for you.' *Which is the truth*, she reflected.

'Is there nothing you want?'

Llandry shook her head, turned her back on the woman and walked away, ignoring her attempts to detain her. She walked quickly and fast, aiming for the Harp, hoping to lose herself in the crowds of shoppers, singers and wanderers. She was aware of the woman following close behind for some time, and even once her footsteps had died away, she had the uncomfortable feeling that the woman's eyes still followed her as she hurried on, gripping her cloak close as if its dark fabric could swallow her whole.

166

18

Shattering pain gripped Eva's body as she emerged from the gate between the realms, surging brutally from her head to her feet and the tips of her fingers. She felt as though her body was trying to shake itself to pieces, prevented only by force of will. She resisted the temptation to buckle under it, drawing quick, painful breaths as she willed the assault away.

How could I have forgotten this? The pain was as bad as it had been on her first visit; time and absence had removed her resilience to it. She suffered in grim silence, enduring wave after wave of agony until finally, mercifully, it began to recede. Only then did she have leisure to notice Tren's fate.

He'd fared worse than she. He lay curled up on the ground, gripping his head in his hands as if it sought to separate itself from his body. He made no sound at all.

'Sorry,' she gasped. 'Should've remembered to warn you about this.'

'Would've been nice,' gritted Tren.

'I forgot how bad it gets.' Here came the nausea, now, always the second stage. She didn't try to speak as her stomach pitched and roiled and her limbs trembled with stress. She resisted the tide, but Tren was not so fortunate. She turned away as he compulsively emptied his stomach.

'Well,' gasped Tren at last as he pulled himself more or less

167

upright. 'That was deeply miserable.'

'You get used to it.' Eva still felt shaky and weak, but she pulled herself resolutely to her feet. 'Eventually.'

'I don't think I can walk,' said Tren.

'Proximity to the gate makes it worse,' Eva replied, gathering her skirts. 'So, walk.' She cast about, searching for her companions. The shortig she found nearby, gnawing on something it had picked up in the bushes. She set it to scout the vicinity for anything telling. There probably wasn't much chance it would find a clear trace of Edwae's erstwhile employer, but it was a possibility.

Rikbeek she could not find. Casting her senses out further, she discerned a brief flicker of his presence some distance away. Curious.

'Tren?'

'Coming.' He joined her with a groan, swaying slightly. She gripped his elbow, letting her fingers dig sharply into his flesh.

'Ow.'

'Stop complaining.' She started walking in the direction she'd sensed Rikbeek, dragging Tren forcibly with her.

'Stop. I'm stable.' He pulled his arm free of her grip, maintaining the quick pace she set without her encouragement. She gave him a brief, distracted smile, then turned her attention to the dense forest that surrounded them.

It was a mirror image of the tree cover that reigned above, at first glance, but the longer she looked, the more she observed to belie that impression. The trees were taller, much taller, swaying dreamily under the influence of a harsh, cool wind. Their contorted forms were vaguely incorporeal, tissue-thin and brittle. Tattered, lacy leaves spread in a thick blanket overhead, sumptuous with dark colours and glittering faintly in the silvery-white light of the moon that shone down on this ethereal forest.

Moons, in fact, for the enormous, pale moon that hung high overhead was echoed in a smaller moon that hovered low over the horizon. It sent a deep red light shimmering weirdly through the interlacing branches of the trees, a dark counterpart to the strong, clear moonlight above. Eva blinked, puzzled. She'd never seen a red moon here before.

Tren was staring, barely paying sufficient attention to where he was putting his feet. He was absently rubbing his arm where she'd gripped him.

'Sorry,' she said.

'Hm? Oh.' He chuckled. 'You were a bit brutal.'

'Mm, well, it's not wise to spend more time here than is strictly necessary. We need to find Ed's employer as soon as possible, and get out.'

'Why's it so inadvisable? This place is *beautiful*.'

'That's exactly why. The crossing almost crippled us both, but now look at you. You're like a child with a bowl of sweets.'

'I'm not.' He made a point of drawing himself up a little straighter, assuming a purposeful air. 'I am completely business-like.'

She smiled. 'Just be wary. There's an air of tranquillity about the Lowers that's liable to send a person's wits to sleep.'

'I can't imagine that happening to you.'

'Ha. When I first came here, I spent about seven hours lying under a tree staring at the moons. I didn't even notice the time pass. I certainly didn't notice the astwach sneaking up on me. I was lucky to escape.'

'You were here alone?'

'I know it was stupid. I was young, stupid and conceited at the time.'

'But not anymore.'

'Ouch.'

He grimaced. 'I was referring to the stupid and conceited parts.'

'Oh, I don't know. I still have a shade or two of conceit. More than that, some would say.'

'You're a little preoccupied with what people say about you.'

That gave her pause. 'Am I?'

'You've brought it up a few times.'

'Hm.' She ducked to avoid some low-hanging branches, suppressing a curse as something scratched her face.

'But you're a popular figure with the papers,' Tren continued. 'I suppose that would get to a person.'

'I suppose.'

'I've been hearing about your exploits since I was a child.'

'Really.'

'Oh, yes. The Uncatchable Lady Bachelor: rich, beautiful, intelligent, powerful, relentlessly unmarried...'

169

She cast a covert look at his face. He was carefully expressionless, no hint of sarcasm discernible. She looked away, allowing herself a small sigh. 'The papers are equally happy to report my failures, of course.'

'Were there any?'

'Naturally.'

'Like what?'

'Perhaps we could just focus on the job at hand.'

'Right, sorry. Where's the Captain?'

'Who?'

'Captain Rikbeek, Leader of Operation Edwae.'

She frowned, feeling vaguely irritable. 'Are you always so frivolous in the wake of death?'

'Haven't experienced enough deaths yet to be sure. I'll let you know.'

'Great, thanks. Rikbeek's up ahead. He's flying fast, which usually means he's on to something. Since I don't have any better ideas just now, we're following him.'

'Righto.' He actually started whistling, damn him.

'How can you be so cheerful?'

'Moping isn't something I enjoy.'

'Must you enjoy everything?'

'It's preferable to being miserable.' He smiled at her, but she didn't smile back. His smile faded.

'Do I seem heartless? I'm sorry. Actually I'm cheerful because I'm unhappy. I doubt that makes any sense.'

'No... I suppose it does.'

'I can't bear tears and distress, so I... avoid them. But I care about things.'

Remembering his despair over Edwae, she didn't doubt it, but there was no chance to reply. They had caught up to Rikbeek; the gwaystrel was whirling in confused circles overhead. Eva caught a series of scattered, muddled images from his thoughts, nothing helpful.

'Damn,' she said. 'Whatever he had, he's lost it.'

'What about the hound?'

She pointed to the inky black shape near her feet. 'Found nothing. He's been at heel since we started walking.'

'So we've got nothing.'

'Nothing but our wits.'

'Encouraging.' He glanced about, turning in a full circle. 'I see trees,' he reported.

'Indeed?'

'With a few trees mixed in.'

'Come to think of it, I noticed a few of those myself.'

'So... what now?'

'Wait for a little while.'

'Just wait?'

'You'll see.'

He shrugged and sat down, tailor-style, in the soft earth. She watched, amused, as he rebuttoned the cuffs of his jacket and smoothed his shirt, picking uselessly at a slight stain. Running his fingers through his tangled dark hair had little effect: he was still tousled, wind-blown and untidy. She thought the effect was rather attractive than otherwise, though she said nothing. She sat too, smoothing the shortig's short fur under her fingers, heedless of the fate of her plain cotton skirts.

'What's his name?'

She blinked, startled. 'Hm? Who?'

He gestured at the hound. 'You just call him 'the shortig', or maybe 'the hound.'

'True. I haven't had him for very long. Why don't you pick a name.' She was only half attending to the conversation, her senses busy tracking their surroundings. She didn't sense any threatening animals nearby, but that could change.

'How about "Puppy".'

Eva silently raised an eyebrow at him.

'Fine, not Puppy. Bartel.'

'Bartel? Is that a random choice?'

'I had a dog called Bartel when I was a child.'

She smiled. 'Bartel. I like it.'

Tren devoted himself to making "Bartel" aware of his new title, and Eva returned to her vigil. After a time the quality of the light began, gradually, to change. The silver-white moonlight lost its shadow of red, deepening instead into purple. The trees around them rippled like water and began to shimmer with a brightness that hurt Eva's night-loving eyes. She closed them briefly. When she opened them again, the landscape was transformed.

The dark, twisting trees had vanished, giving way to an

171

expanse of meadow dotted with gentle slopes and knolls clustered with bushes. Flowers littered the grasses, resplendent in shades of blue and purple and green. Some were tiny, some standing higher than Eva's head. The blanketing cover of leaves overhead had disappeared, and now the moonlight shone down on them unimpeded. The radiance was verging on too bright for Eva's eyes, but she knew her vision would grow accustomed to it in time.

Insects shimmered out of the air, descending upon the fragrant, newly-opened blossoms. Furred yellow whistworms clung to the fat stems of the taller plants, intent on feeding on the insects. Striped purple-and-grey olifers levered themselves out of their burrows, intent on feeding on the whistworms. Eva's summoner senses caught the heavy tread of a muumuk away to the west. She noted its position carefully, resolved on giving it a wide berth.

Eva inhaled deeply, enjoying the rich floral fragrance that now filled the air. The scents of the Lowers were more intense, just as the colours were more vivid, the lights richer, the shadows deeper and the air so crisp and fresh the lungs struggled to take it in. She smiled at Tren, rising to her feet. The shortig leapt to attention as she shook out her skirts. Tren didn't move.

'Tren? Time to go.'

'Sorry.' He jumped up with alacrity. 'If you spent only seven hours under that tree, I'd say that was pretty restrained of you. How many times did this happen while you were lying there?'

'I don't remember. A few. The only thing which didn't change was the tree.'

'Curious.'

'That's an understatement for this place. Look over there.' She pointed behind Tren, away to the northeast. A tower rose far in the distance, tiny to their eyes, built from a pale stone that shone under the moon. 'I'd say that's worth investigating, wouldn't you?'

'I didn't know there were buildings down here.'

'There aren't many. And I'm pretty sure that one wasn't there a moment ago.'

'What, do they just... spring out of the ground?'

'Maybe. Who knows?' She started walking, whistling to Rikbeek. 'Can you unCloak me? It isn't going to help much

172

under these conditions, and in that case I'd like to actually breathe for a while.'

'So ungrateful.' The sensation of the Cloak fading was like a heavy mantle slipping from her shoulders. She straightened physically, taking a lungful of air. A mistake; the intense, heady air of the Lowers made her giddy, and she fell to coughing.

'Thanks,' she said weakly when she recovered.

'Glad the experience was a pleasant one for you,' he replied.

Eva set a fast pace, aware of the swift passage of time in this unworld. Clouds clustered over the tower, and as they approached a warm rain began to fall. Tren sighed.

'There goes my shirt.'

'I'll get you a new one.'

'That's two shirts you owe me. Think you could arrange for an upgrade while you're at it? I've always liked those silk ones.'

'If you like.'

When they reached the base of the tower, a problem emerged.

There were no doors.

'There has to be an entrance somewhere,' Tren muttered. 'A clever hidden one, maybe, that only opens if you sing *The Ballad of Mirella Heartburn* in falsetto while juggling with a litter of kittens.'

Eva grinned. 'Feel free to start singing.' She stood back, looking up at the smooth stone walls towering above her. A single window was cut into the walls near the top, a mere gap in the stonework.

'That's the entrance.'

Tren stared up at it silently. 'You're not serious,' he said at length.

'Perfectly.'

'Do you number 'climbing like a monkey' among your list of remarkable abilities?'

'I've a better idea, actually.' She placed a hand against the smooth stonework of the tower and pinched her fingers together. The stone moved under her hand like dough, forming a step. She repeated the process below and above it until a ladder formed.

Tren stared at her helplessly. 'I give up,' he said.

'Best not to ask.' She set one foot against the lowest step and

173

began to climb. Her skirts immediately tangled around her legs, threatening to dump her to the ground. She jumped down again.

'Er, Tren. This is the part where you don't look.' Lifting the hem of her skirt, she tucked the fabric into her waistband. The fabric ballooned around her — she probably looked like a walking mushroom — but at least her legs were free.

'Er,' said Tren.

'If I fall, you're to catch me,' she ordered.

'Yours to command, m'lady,' he said, with a salute.

'I know.' She smiled briefly, setting both hands to the ladder. She began to climb, pausing periodically to create the next few steps up. Her progress was slow but steady, and at last she reached the window at the top.

It was really just an opening, square, unadorned, and too small for her to fit through. Undaunted, she slipped her feet and legs through the gap, pushing against the wall. She felt the stone stretch and bend around her as she forced herself through, sliding inelegantly onto the floor of the room beyond. She turned to see the window shrink back to its neat square shape.

Tren still stood below, staring up at her. She gestured and he began, gamely, to climb. Soon he drew level with her, panting from the effort of the journey.

'All right. How did you fit through there?'

'Easy,' she said briskly. 'Come on, faster. The light will change again soon.'

'And then what happens?'

'Then the building disappears. We might move with it to wherever it goes, or we might fall a long way into whatever turns up next. It would be better to be out of here before that happens.'

'Huh.'

Eva stood back as Tren slid through the window. He made a sound of disgust as the stonework squirmed around him, reforming itself to let him through. He stood up immediately, dusting himself off.

'That's a repulsive experience.'

'There'll probably be worse yet,' replied Eva cheerfully.

'Great,' muttered Tren.

Eva circled the room. Clutter lay everywhere, covering the surface of the table that rested in the centre of the room, lying in layers over the cabinets that were fitted against the rounded walls. The furniture was dusty, the rugs on the floor crusted with mud. Eva paused before a pair of books lying open on the table.

'It's like someone lives here,' Tren commented.

'Probably someone does,' Eva replied. She gingerly picked up one of the books, handling the worn binding and loose pages carefully. The title was inscribed in wavering silver ink on the cover.

My Recollections of the Lower Realms: An Account of a Savant's Journey Below
Andraly Winnier, Lokant.

Tren looked over her shoulder. 'Lokant?'

'Any idea what that is?'

'None whatsoever.'

'Hmm. Then you haven't heard of this book before?'

'No. And I've studied the libraries pretty thoroughly.'

She opened it again, browsing rapidly through the contents. Pages of crabbed, handwritten script were broken up with sketched images and patches of colour. She saw many of the acknowledged animal species of the Lowers catalogued, along with some beasts she didn't recognise. The author had recorded flora as well as fauna; some of the flowers of the meadow they'd passed through were there on the pages, minutely outlined in black and annotated.

'Interesting,' she murmured. Opening her bag, she withdrew her spare cloak and wrapped the book in it. She eased the bundle into the bag, buttoning the flap firmly closed over it.

'That's theft, you might be interested to know.' Tren was still standing right behind her, watching her actions quite intently. She moved away, crossing to the other side of the room.

'Well, we're on the trail of a murderer. I'd say all's fair.'

'You think this place has anything to do with the man Ed was following?'

'It's possible. See, the only reason I can think of for a sorcerer to track halfway across Orstwych to use a rogue gate is because he was going somewhere specific. Am I right in thinking you can't open a gate to a particular location in the Lowers — just to whichever part of it's closest to you at the time?'

175

'Right. If I opened a gate right here, we'd end up in the Orstwych woods a couple of miles northwest of where we came through.'

She nodded, pleased. 'I think Ed's mysterious sorcerer was heading for somewhere in this area. Naturally he found it easier to do most of the travelling Above, where the landscape's constant and it's easier to navigate. If that gate's a regular opener, it might not even be a rogue. Maybe it's more like his front door.'

'That's a thought. I don't know if it's possible to cause a 'rogue' gate to re-open itself after it's been closed, but that's because we don't keep permanent portals to the Lowers. It's not permitted. But I imagine it could be done.' She was growing to recognise that look of intent speculation on his face, his thoughts obviously whirling as he pursued the idea.

'Well, the details of *how* can be examined another time,' she suggested. 'The relevant point is the probable destination of Edwae's friend. Anywhere within about a mile of the gate would seem practical.'

'This is the only building we saw, right?'

'Yes, but don't forget that a lot of things could have been either hidden or not here when we came through. It would be wise to stay in this area through another few changes, see what comes up.'

Tren nodded. 'This place strikes me as a sorc's house, though. It's got that air about it. I wouldn't mind living here myself.'

'When we've defeated our enemy you can take over the tower. Call it another incentive.'

'Generous of you.' Tren stooped to pick something up from the floor. Standing, he showed the object to Eva.

It was a ring of wrought silver. Set into the centre was an indigo-coloured stone that shone faintly silver.

'Istore,' she breathed.

'Looks like it, yep.'

Eva's senses prickled. The atmosphere was changing, the air growing heavier. Crossing to the window, she hung out of the embrasure until she could see to the south. The purple light was fading, drifting away. Something else was taking over, a radiance that held the rippling blue-green changefulness of water.

176

She swore.

'Tren, we have to go.'

He didn't ask questions. She was out of the window immediately, descending rapidly. Tren followed. They reached ground level within moments, so fast that Eva's palms began to bleed from their contact with the stone. She ignored the pain, looking anxiously across the grass.

'We need to find something that's solid.'

'Right.' He looked around. 'How do you identify "solid" in this place?'

'You don't,' she said despairingly. It was too late; all hint of purple had gone from the skies and the flickering bluish light was growing stronger by the second. She didn't bother to run. There was no point. Instead she took hold of her precious bag, wrapping the strap around her wrist and gripping it tight.

'Keep close to me,' she said.

'What?'

'I think your shirt's about to be ruined.'

She sensed olifers fleeing back into their burrows, insects melting back into the skies. The meadows rippled powerfully, the flowers dissolving.

Then the ground gave way beneath her feet and she fell into deep water.

19

Devary arrived at Llandry's door early in the morning. Llandry had been awake for two hours, riveted by the sight of the sun rising outside her window. She longed to be outside to witness this extraordinary event, but there was no balcony, and her experience the evening before made her wary of leaving the Harp. Instead she threw the windows wide open and sat in the window seat, ignoring the chill in the air as darkness gradually melted into day.

Her pendant rested on the low table in the centre of the room. Llandry had taken it out of her cloak pocket as soon as she arrived home and bound it up in cloth and ribbon, concealing the odd lavender-tinged glow that it exuded in this strangely-lit place. She had left it out of her possession knowing that, when it came to it, she would find it hard to give it out of her own hands into Devary's — no matter how willingly offered.

He arrived looking anxious, even guilty. She opened her mouth to tell him about Sigwide's theft but he spoke first.

'Llandry, I'm so sorry — I don't know how — somehow the pendant is gone.' He spoke the last part in a rush. 'I just discovered — I came right away. Are you well? Has anything happened...?' He studied her carefully, looking her up and down as if making sure she was in one piece.

'I'm fine. Sigwide took it.' She explained briefly, leaving out the part about the white-haired woman for now. Devary's face relaxed in relief as she spoke, though he gave the orting a glance of irritation.

'That creature is a liability. I suppose to keep it safe from him, I must wear it. I don't imagine he can spirit it off my neck without alerting me.' He unwrapped the little cloth bundle and fastened the chain around his neck. He smiled at Llandry as the stone disappeared under his shirt.

'We are lucky that nothing too terrible has come of it. And now, I know I promised you that we would see the town, but first I think we must see my friend at the University. Will that be all right?'

Llandry hesitated. She ought to tell him the rest, but he seemed in a hurry to depart. Perhaps they could talk on the way. 'Quite all right,' she answered. Hastily closing the windows, she collected her cloak and donned it. Devary chuckled to see the deep hood shading her eyes, but made no comment.

A small two-wheel carriage waited at the rear of the Silver Harp, with a tall, grey-scaled nivven set into the traces. Devary assisted Llandry into the passenger seat and took up the reins himself, skilfully guiding the vehicle out into the winding streets of Draetre. As they drove, Llandry nibbled a fingernail, undecided. She knew she deserved reproach for her solitary wanderings the night before, so she was reluctant to recount her adventures. But her encounter with the white-haired woman was disturbing. He ought to know. Steeling herself, she interrupted his light-hearted conversation and told him everything. She had some hope that he would dismiss it as unimportant, but of course he didn't. Instead, he was demonstrably uneasy, questioning her minutely as to the particulars.

'Did she tell you her name, or anything about herself?'

'No. I should have thought to ask.'

'Describe her again for me.'

Llandry did so, as closely as she could. Devary frowned, and shook his head.

'Could have been anybody. Did she say why she wanted the pendant?'

'No.'

'Llandry. Did you fly?'

'No.'

'Good. I knew you would have more sense.'

'She guessed where I am from. In fact, I think she may have recognised me. She asked me if I made it. I think... some of those reporters got pictures of me, before Mamma threw them out.'

Devary was silent. At last he said, 'Well then, we had better finish our business quickly.'

Llandry warred with herself, feeling a surge of guilt at his obvious anxiety. She had followed him when she knew she shouldn't, making a burden of herself, and now she had made it worse. But it was humiliating to have to keep apologising for making her own decisions.

He drove for a while in silence. 'I sent a message to your mother last night, informing her of your whereabouts. I also told her I would not be sending you home yet, and that I would ensure that you are safe. It would be ideal if you could refrain from making that harder.'

'Fine. I won't do any more wandering.'

'I am sorry that it must be that way, but it won't last forever. Now, here we are.' He guided the little carriage down an alley, barely wide enough to admit the neat vehicle. Another left turn brought them into a courtyard, inside which a few other carriages were parked. Devary handed her down from the carriage with the utmost politeness, but something in his manner suggested she had annoyed him. Her stomach twisted with miserable anxiety at the idea, and suddenly she was all too inclined to condemn her own behaviour. The notion was frustrating. How long must she rely on others to protect her? And why was Devary's disapproval so painful?

She hid her face in her hood as they passed through a narrow door into a long, oddly winding corridor. Space opened up either side of her, large rooms glimpsed through tall archways as they proceeded rapidly into the heart of the building. She saw bookcases crowded with books and framed with chairs like supplicants before a throne; each chair bore a silent occupant, absorbed in the pages of a volume.

'Where are we?' Her voice emerged startlingly loudly in the hushed atmosphere, echoing off the cool stone walls.

'Draetre's university library.'

'It really doesn't seem large enough to have a university.'

180

'It's of an unusual kind. Here.' He held open a door for her and she passed through it, registering that Devary locked the door behind them both. She surveyed a chamber smaller than the others they had passed through. A woman sat at a table near the window, studying a large book that lay open before her. The book was evidently very old; its leather covers were tattered and decaying, and its spine was supported upon a soft cushion that lay between it and the desk.

The woman looked up as they entered. Her eyes rested first on Llandry, with a considering stare that made her quite uncomfortable. Apparently around Devary's age, she was clearly Nimdren with her curling chestnut hair and light-coloured eyes. The woman's face changed as she transferred her keen gaze to Devary. She smiled, reluctantly, as if she sought to suppress the expression but it overcame her efforts. She stood up and advanced towards Devary, and he stepped forward to meet her. Llandry noticed that he was wearing the warm smile he'd so often turned on her.

'Indren. It's been far too long.'

'So it has. Your fault for moonlighting so long in Glinnery.' The woman, Indren, smiled all the more as Devary carried her hand to his lips and kissed it lightly.

'And I see you brought one of them back with you.' Indren's eyes, a rather startling pale green, rested again on Llandry.

'Yes, quite an important one. Llandry Sanfaer, Ynara Sanfaer's daughter. You remember Ynara?'

'Yes.' The word was said without inflection, and Llandry wondered whether the recollection was a pleasant one for this stranger.

'Llandry, this is Professor Indren Druaster. She's an expert in Off-World history.'

'Off-Worlds? Both of them?'

'Does that surprise you?' Professor Druaster lifted her brows at Llandry very slightly, laughing at her.

'A little,' mumbled Llandry.

'Nimdre has chained itself to neither, you see, and therefore we may study both with equal attention. Now, what of this trinket?' Professor Druaster turned a winning smile on Devary as she resumed her seat. He sat next to her, gesturing Llandry to a chair opposite.

181

'It's no trinket.'

'Oh, I am sorry. I understood that it is an item of Ms. Sanfaer's creation?'

Llandry felt a ripple of annoyance, but the implication of the statement passed Devary by. He sat back comfortably, smiling at Llandry as he opened his travel bag.

'Certainly; it is all of her own work.'

'Ah, the famed arts of Glinnery. How I wish I had a little of your creative talent, my dear.' Llandry bristled at the familiar term. She was not fooled: Indren dripped insincerity. It would not be the first time a scholar had looked down on the arts, but nonetheless Llandry felt nettled.

Devary had found the cloth bundle. He unwrapped it carefully and placed the pendant on the table before Indren. Looking at it, Llandry felt a little soothed. Evidently it was a skilled piece of work, whatever a person's feelings as to the value of the aesthetic.

Indren studied it without touching it. She drew an eyeglass from the belt at her waist and examined the stone very closely. Llandry's eyes wandered back to Devary's face. He watched Indren's procedures with apparent absorption.

'An unusual piece.' Indren lifted her head, and Llandry found herself once again subjected to that sharp gaze. 'Where did this come from?'

Llandry was silent. After a moment Devary stepped in, recounting, briefly, the history of Llandry's gem.

'Istore,' said Indren, when he had finished. Her lips twisted in a smile that held a mocking hint. 'A romantic name. You have no idea at all, I suppose, what it is?'

'Elder Ilae Shuly recommended you as a consultant,' interrupted Devary smoothly.

'Ah, Elder Shuly,' she repeated, with obvious approval. 'There's a sharp mind.' She looked back down at the stone, turning it to the light. 'It certainly doesn't originate from the Middle Realms. If anything I'd say it was from the Uppers, but there's something —' She paused. 'There's something of the Lowers about it, too. I might be inclined to conclude it has its origins in both, were that possible.' She smiled in a small way. 'You should've come to me before, Mr. Kant.' She looked under her lashes at him, with a sort of mock severity that Llandry

182

found quite repulsive. Devary shrugged and laughed.

'I'm but a poor scholar. How could I guess it would fall under your area of expertise?'

'Well. Attend me to dinner, and I may be able to forgive you.' She smiled at him, and he gave her a half-bow in response. She looked back at Llandry and the smile faded.

'You must both come. I will tell you more about this stone tomorrow, when I have had chance to study it further.'

Llandry felt a prickle of alarm. Suspicion and dislike made her bold, and she spoke up. 'The pendant stays with Devary.'

Indren's eyebrows rose. 'Oh?' Llandry's words withered away under that mocking stare, but she met the woman's insolent gaze without flinching.

'You did bring it here to be studied, I suppose?'

Llandry inclined her head.

Indren offered her a thin, false smile. 'Very well. If the pendant must stay with Mr. Kant, then Mr. Kant must stay with me. He will be happy to stand guard over me, I am sure: just in case I should try anything inappropriate with your "istore" stone.'

Devary cast Llandry a quizzical glance, and shrugged. 'Certainly,' he said to Indren.

'Ms. Sanfaer may amuse herself in the reading rooms, I've no doubt.' Indren was now outright frosty. Llandry was not wounded: on the contrary she was happy to go.

Llandry was left to her own devices for most of the day. Devary emerged from time to time to check on her, and repeatedly invited her to rejoin them, but she steadfastly refused. She wouldn't be volunteering for any more of the Professor's obvious disdain. It was bad enough that Devary could be close to such a chilly, cruel woman.

She asked him about it during one of his lamentably brief visits to her reading nook, but he was evasive.

'We have known each other for some time. She can be difficult, but... well. I must go back, if you are comfortable.'

'Bored senseless, and therefore, duly punished for my rebellion. It's been hours. Are you making any progress at all in there?'

Devary drew up a chair and sat down, though he sat on the very edge as if he intended to leave any moment. 'Some of Indren's colleagues have joined us. The consensus is that it is not a stone, as some of your friends have suspected. The current theory under investigation is that it is in fact biological matter.'

Llandry was startled. 'As in, from an animal?'

Devary hesitated. 'Yes. Perhaps. You must understand, this is only an idea. It may be discounted any moment, and another idea brought forward. But it would not be the first time that animal parts have been employed for magical uses.' He stood up, smiling down at her. 'You will forgive the brevity of my visit, but I am needed. We are consulting the university's rarer books — they have collections from the Darklands as well as the Daylands — and the search may take days. It will go faster if I involve myself.'

'Perhaps I should help?' Llandry hesitated to say it, picturing a roomful of studious strangers with horror. Before she was halfway through her sentence, Devary was already gone.

It was growing late, and Llandry was growing very hungry, when Devary finally emerged with Professor Druaster behind him. They both looked tired, but the Professor's eyes were alight with excitement. The two of them talked in Nimdren, probably discussing the istore. Llandry could only wish she could understand.

Devary's eye fell on her belatedly, and he smiled apologetically. 'Apologies, Llandry, we are being rude. We have made much progress, but there is a great deal still to do. It is time to stop for the day, and find something to eat.'

They were to go across town for dinner, it emerged, to a popular food garden; its name, the Adriana Gardens, brought a pleased smile to Devary's face as Professor Druaster announced her plan for the evening.

'How long is it since you were there, Devary dear?' Llandry didn't miss the fact that she was now using his first name.

'Must be a year. More, even.'

'Ah! Then you missed out on the fireworks displays; stupendous, truly, and only offered for the anniversary. There are new menus — all your favourites are still available, Devary

184

dear, I put a word in the proprietress's ear about that — and the desserts are particularly fine.'

The Professor's easy chatter ran on, directed entirely at Devary. Llandry followed them out of the building and watched as Devary handed the Professor into a smart new carriage and followed her inside. Llandry, left to make her own way, was not particularly mollified by Devary's apologetic smile as he realised his oversight. She ignored him.

Professor Druaster's carriage was a handsome affair, well upholstered and finely made. Its mistress sat back upon the plush seating with a proprietorial air and a satisfied smile.

'I could hardly allow you to drive all that way in that appalling little gig of yours, Devary.'

Devary chuckled. 'It's a faithful old thing, Indren. I've had it a long time, and it's never failed me yet.'

Indren wrinkled her nose disapprovingly. 'Yes, but no doubt it *will*, Devary dear. Besides, a gentleman deserves luxury.' The smile she offered with this pronouncement sickened Llandry anew, but Devary smiled back readily enough.

Llandry turned her attention away and looked out of the window as the twilit streets rolled by. She was restored to her favourite blue cloak, the hood shading her eyes and guarding the play of expression on her face. She was not afraid of her disgust being perceived by Indren Druaster: the woman was far too absorbed by Devary. It was Devary's perception of it that she wished to avoid.

The journey was moderately long given the event, but at last the carriage rolled to a gentle stop. Devary jumped out and immediately made a point of handing Llandry down first. She shook out her clothes, shivering a little in the cool air. The building that rose before her was quite low, only one storey, with balconies clustering around the roofline. The roof itself was flat and open, verdantly decorated with lush greenery that trailed in long tendrils to the ground. Diners sat up high at low tables, bathed in the cool moonlight. Llandry could hear strains of music drifting down from above.

The same scene was repeated at the rear of the building. Indren's party was quickly led to a choice table in a shady alcove, slightly screened from the chatter and stares of the other diners. Llandry took her seat reluctantly, feeling that the evening could

185

not end soon enough.

She had expected to feel like an intruder, and so she did. Indren was just polite enough to speak in Llandry's own tongue, but she made no attempt at all to include her in conversation, talking exclusively to Devary about people, places and events relevant only to they two. At first Devary was mindful of Llandry's presence, recommending her choices from the menu, addressing remarks to her and frequently offering her a smile. She was soothed and comfortable as long as he remembered her, but as the evening went on he remembered her less and less.

They had been seated barely twenty minutes before a stranger approached the table. Her curvaceous silhouette and sinuous walk made her femininity quite clear as she swayed up to Devary. Their conversation was conducted in Devary's native language, the fluid Nimdren tongue which sounded so beautiful when he sang. Llandry didn't understand a word, but that it was an intimate conversation was clear enough. The woman flirted aggressively with him, ignoring Indren Druaster's obvious contempt and apparently failing to notice Llandry at all. Devary's manner to her was a little reserved, she was thankful to note, but still he bore with her impolite behaviour with much more grace than Llandry thought reasonable. At last the woman departed.

Several other diners visited their table over the course of the meal   most of them women — and Llandry was obliged to watch the same scene play itself out again and again. In between interruptions, Indren Druaster continued to monopolise Devary's conversation, often slipping into Nimdren. Devary glanced often at Llandry and she sensed that he wished to include her more, but he would not stir himself to interrupt Indren. Mortified, Llandry could not summon any appetite no matter how many temptingly fragrant dishes were placed before them, and at last she abandoned the struggle to let it all pass her by. She stood up, raising her hood.

'I'm going for a walk,' she said. 'It's beautiful here.' She did not wait for their response but set off immediately, aiming for the garden that lay behind the restaurant.

'Don't go too far, Llandry,' she heard Devary say behind her. She did not need to go far: merely out of sight and hearing would be enough.

Peace enveloped her as she reached a pretty grove of trees.

186

The babble of the food garden receded into near silence and the heat and bustle was replaced by coolness and a soft breeze. She sighed, turning her face up to the winds.

These terrible, bold women. All of them had trouble written across them in every particular. She felt that none of them — most especially including Professor Druaster — would be a good choice for any sort of dalliance. She couldn't decide whether Devary saw it or not. If he did, why did he tolerate their intrusive attentions?

She did not need to ask herself why they flocked to Devary. It was that damned chivalrous courtesy; his understated warmth and gentleness; certainly his handsome features and winning smile. He offered them little gestures: a kiss of the hand; a special smile; the gift of a flower; a gently solicitous question or remark. None of these things were particular in themselves, but together they amounted to a distinct appearance of special interest. They were so easily caught by it; they received a little and offered everything in return.

Simultaneously the worst and best of it was that Devary seemed entirely unconscious of the effect his manner had on the women around him. Perhaps he wasn't. Llandry would prefer to believe him unaware; the possibility that he cultivated it made him appear a wholly different person to the man she'd known in Glinnery. She was sharply reminded of her own lack of experience with people. There was no way she could decipher what Devary's behaviour meant.

Distant diamond stars twinkled through the shady, moon-silvered canopy of the trees, so very far away. She took a few deep breaths of heady twilight air, feeling gradually more refreshed. A gust of wind ruffled her hair, and the ghost of a smile crossed her face as the peace of the woods filled her and she finally began to relax.

A sudden, sharp cracking sound rent the air, emanating from behind her. Footsteps sounded, loud and close. Before she could turn, hands grabbed hard at her, bruising her flesh. She cried out as much with surprise as with pain; her twilight reverie dissolved and a surge of fear filled her. She struggled hard, kicking and shouting. A hand closed over her mouth, cutting off her protests, and she was lifted and dragged backwards.

20

Eva kicked against the dark waters that threatened to swallow her, cursing the skirts that tangled around her legs. She fought her way grimly to the surface, thrusting the bag upwards ahead of her. She broke the surface, gulping air, praying that the leather of her satchel would be sufficiently waterproof to keep the book safe. She began treading water, turning slowly in circles. Water met her eye in every direction, an unbroken horizon of green-touched blue. The shortig hound — Bartel — paddled gamely not far away, but there was no sign of Tren.

Several long moments dragged by. Fear clutched at her, punching through her composure. Could he even swim? She ducked her head below the water again, staring uselessly into the dark ocean. She couldn't see him.

At last, after an agonisingly long wait, a small explosion rent the water nearby and Tren's sodden figure appeared. He gasped for air, spluttering, spitting out water. Once his lungs were filled a stream of curses emerged, fluent and unceasing. Eva swam towards him and grabbed his shirt.

'No drowning,' she chided.

'Is it time to go home yet?' he said at last, shivering.

'Nonsense; we've hardly seen the sights.'

Tren gazed at the miles of water that surrounded them. 'All right, I've seen them. Now let's go home.'

Eva spotted a length of broken tree branch sailing by, and grabbed it. It was completely sodden with water, as if it had been submerged for days, but at least it floated.

'That's not going to be big enough,' she murmured. 'Hold this.' She thrust the bag at Tren. '*Don't* let it get wet.' Her hands free, she pulled and tugged at the length of wood until it expanded, widening. She climbed onto it, dragging the shortig with her, and lay down, exhausted.

'Pass me the bag,' she said. It landed beside her and she clutched it protectively as Tren climbed laboriously onto her makeshift raft beside her.

'I like that trick you have there,' he said. 'Why don't you show me how to do that?'

'It's not me doing it. It's just the way it works down here. Everything's more... fluid, I suppose. Malleable.'

'Think between the two of us we could mould this ocean into a beach?'

She laughed. 'Sadly there are limits to everything.'

Tren devoted himself to the task of shivering, and didn't reply.

'Should only be a couple of hours before the next change, if I remember rightly,' she said, wrapping her arms around herself. 'Then again, the meadow revolved away faster than it should have. It might only be an hour before the next change.'

'Only an hour,' Tren repeated. 'Great.'

Numinar Wrobsley's words echoed in Eva's thoughts all of a sudden. He'd said that his suppliers of rylur weren't picking any up, something about increased dangers. Instability. Perhaps this was what was meant: the cycles were whirling so fast that there was scarcely time to collect anything before one found oneself, say, drowning in a vast ocean of freezing water.

'You're making the raft shake,' said Tren. Eva realised she was shivering so violently her whole body shook in spasms. She hadn't felt so completely bone-cold in her life; it made the settled chill of the Summoners' Halls seem like summer.

'Speak for yourself,' she muttered. Turning onto her side, she wrapped her arms around herself, trying uselessly to conserve her body heat. 'You're the sorc. Can't you light a fire?'

'Light a fire without fuel, while floating on a sodden raft in the middle of the ocean. It'll burn for about three seconds.'

189

She sighed deeply. 'I suppose so.' She paused for a moment as a particularly strong shiver wracked her. 'I wonder if it's more pleasant to freeze to death than to drown?'

'You are a bundle of joy.' He inched across the raft until he lay directly behind her, his arms sliding around her waist. She found herself pulled close to him. Cold as he was, he still radiated some heat.

'Sorry about this,' he said. 'Desperate measures.'

'Don't get any ideas.'

'I don't wish to ruin your dreams, but a violently shivering woman stinking of seaweed isn't my idea of the perfect romance.'

She snorted. 'You're certainly no flatterer.'

'An hour, you said?'

'About that, yes.' She paused. 'Probably.'

'Probably.' He sighed. 'I wonder if Vale knows we're down here.'

'No. It's too soon,' she replied. 'What made you think of that?'

'Oh, just wondering if Fin made it back to Westrarc yet.'

'Thinking of Mrs. Geslin?'

'Among other things.'

She was silent for a moment, picturing the worn face of Edwae's mother, drawn with anxiety, surrounded by dependent children. She imagined Tren there, breaking the news to her, comforting her distress.

'I think you made the right choice to come here, Tren.'

'You fought pretty hard against it at the time.'

'How far would you have got by yourself, do you suppose?'

'Not far,' he admitted.

'You'd probably be drowning right now.'

'Steady. Mind the ego. I concede that you were perfectly right.'

She smiled. 'We'll visit Mrs. Geslin on our way back to the city.'

Tren sighed, pulling her a little closer. 'Who knows when that will be.'

A miserable hour passed — maybe more, it was hard to tell in the Lowers — and the watery green light remained steady. Eva was forgetting what it felt like to be warm, dry and comfortable. Her stockings stuck damply to her icy legs; her skirts were a heavy, clinging mass weighing her down. Her hair had come loose from its bindings and lay over her neck like a mantle of ice. She was grateful to Tren for trying to warm her (and himself), but it was a largely ineffectual gesture.

'I don't see this ocean miraculously disappearing,' Tren murmured against her neck.

'Doesn't mean it won't, any minute now.'

'It is not looking hopeful,' he replied. 'Let's make a deal. If it comes to it, you're to eat me for survival first. I have more meat on me.'

'Raw, is that?'

'Well, Lady Glostrum, if it's a matter of survival I expect you to make sacrifices.'

'I'll make you a counter offer. If it comes to it, I'll eat one of your arms for survival, and you may have one of mine. Which would you prefer?'

He considered for a moment. 'The left one, please. There's a shapeliness to the bicep that's very appealing.'

'Done. Meanwhile, when the light changes the very first thing we'll do is make a fire. That's a promise.'

'Great. Here's your chance.'

Eva opened her eyes. The unsteady green light was indeed fading. They waited in silence as a yellowish glow built in the skies and the ocean began to churn. Eva's makeshift raft dipped and plunged on the choppy waters, and she nearly slid off into the sea; only Tren's grip on her waist prevented her descent. She clung grimly to the edge of the raft, ignoring the bite of the wood into the tender flesh of her hands. In another moment the sea abruptly disappeared. The now bone-dry raft lay marooned atop an expanse of white sand dotted with delicate objects resembling seashells, though Eva didn't think any living creature could conceivably make a home in these highly artistic creations.

'You mentioned something about a beach?' She tried to sit up, but her frozen limbs refused to obey her. She winced as pain shot through the frigid muscles.

'So I did,' answered Tren. 'You think it has something to do with this?'

'No,' Eva replied honestly.

'Well anyway, next time I'll include a timeframe with my

191

request.'

Eva tried to push herself to her feet, her frozen muscles screaming in protest. 'You can release me now, Tren.'

'It's no good, I can't move.'

'How very defeatist of you.' She unlocked his arms from around her waist and forced herself into a sitting position, biting her lip on a cry of discomfort. Tren rose shakily to his feet and stood over her, swaying. His shirt and trousers were plastered to his body and he wore a length of seaweed in his hair. He looked so dejected, she couldn't help but laugh.

'What's funny?'

'We are,' she said, simply. 'Like a pair of half-drowned kittens. Let's make that fire.'

He extended a hand to her, pulling her up beside him. 'Your ladyship,' he said, with a half-bow that he obviously regretted. Wincing, he went to work on the raft, breaking it into pieces.

'Poor raft,' said Eva. 'It wasn't exactly a work of art, but somehow I feel responsible for its fate.'

'It's performed a noble service, and now it shall perform another.' Tren laid the sodden pieces in a circle. Then he collected driftwood and seaweed from the beach — mercifully dry — and piled these up in the centre. Finally he touched a finger to the heap and the wood caught fire. The flood of light dazzled Eva's eyes until Tren dampened the radiance, after which she sat gratefully beside the little blaze, stretching out her legs and arranging her disgusting, sodden skirts. Tren seated himself to her right, tending to the fire until he had a comfortable blaze going. Eva relished the warmth that washed over her, allowing herself a small sigh of contentment. She opened her sodden satchel, removing the book. Some of the pages had taken a little water, but it was largely in one piece. She laid it open on the sand, weighing the pages down with a couple of the colourful shells.

Bartel sat as close to the fire as he could without burning himself, panting happily. Eva was amused to see Rikbeek clinging to the dog's back, wings spread out to dry. Neither hound nor gwaystrel seemed to have any objection to the arrangement.

'Is this the part where I get to study the book?' Tren smiled hopefully.

'In a minute,' she replied. 'When it's had a chance to dry.'

'I'll hold you to that, m'lady.' Tren stretched himself out by the fire, holding the sodden fabric of his shirt away from his skin, letting the air pass through it.

'You know, I wish I'd come down here sooner. There's so much to explore. Studies should be conducted, publications written—'

'All of that's been done before,' Eva interrupted. 'There's one of them right there.' She waved a hand at the book.

'I've never seen any research material on the Lowers.'

'Obviously they aren't left on the public shelves.'

'Obviously?'

'What do you think would happen if any of this was publically talked about, documented? There'd be a stampede to see the wondrous Lowers; hundreds of people would be jumping through the rogue gates, people poorly equipped to deal with the dangers down here. Most of them would never come back.'

Tren frowned. 'People should *know*, at least. They can make those choices for themselves.'

She snorted. 'When you're a little older, you'll understand about the essential idiocy of the average human being.'

'Not that that's in any way patronising.'

She shrugged. 'Patronising or not, Glour's citizens are alive and well in the Middle Realms. Down here, most of them would perish. Or did you forget the part where I said even I tread very, very carefully in the Lowers these days?'

'Where are these mythical publications kept?'

'I can't tell you that.'

'Oh my, it's a *conspiracy*,' Tren said, delighted. 'How do you even know?'

'Because when research teams are sent down here, a couple of summoners with experience of the Lowers are always sent along.'

'And sorcerers, right?'

'Right,' she said, warily.

'Where do I sign up for that job?'

'It's more that you're signed up for it.'

'Well, I want to be.'

'You may well be anyway, once it's known you've spent time down here and survived.'

193

Tren sat up, turning his still-damp back to the fire. 'That's not the whole story, though, is it? People come down here pretty regularly. Summoners, herbalists after the plant life, and what about the tales?'

'What tales?'

'Tales of the people who go looking for gates because they feel like they *need* to be down here. The ones who're never seen again in the Seven Realms, and all that.'

'The fact that they're never seen again seems to bear out the notion that it's a bad idea, doesn't it? As for the others, well. Summoner groups are sent down by the guild to collect examples of approved companion species. That's a regular thing. Other than that, there's a huge market for rare Lowers plants and animals, and as long as that's the case there'll be people who flout the conventions and mount their own expeditions. Some of them are successful, if they know what they're doing.'

'Some of them aren't?'

'Mm. People will risk a lot for untold wealth.'

'Untold wealth? Maybe I'll join that team instead.' Abandoning his efforts to dry his shirt, he shifted until his back was turned to her and stripped it off. For a scholar and a sorcerer, he was in surprisingly good shape.

'You've gone quiet.' Tren threw her a curious look over his shoulder. To her dismay, Eva actually felt herself blush. That hadn't happened in years.

'Er, I was just thinking.' Eva busied herself with rearranging her skirts, turning so the wetter parts were nearer the fire. She absolutely wasn't staring at the play of firelight over Tren's marvellously supple back muscles. Not even a little bit. 'All this upheaval. Gates appearing and vanishing, animals going bonkers, the landscape convulsing. It seems to have started when the istore was dug up. But none of it makes any sense.'

'The timing is interesting,' Tren replied thoughtfully, 'but it doesn't follow that the discovery of the istore is directly causing all of it. Don't forget Ed's mysterious sorcerer and the white-haired witch. And there may be more. They seem to be motivated by the istore, but who knows what they've actually been *doing* all this time.'

'True. Besides dragging whurthags out of Ullarn's Lowers territory and stockpiling istore.'

194

'Maybe "Ana" just likes jewellery.'

'And the tall sorcerer-without-a-face just likes black cats with the eyes of death.'

'Right. Mystery solved. Now can we go home?'

She grinned, opening her mouth to retort, but something flickered on the edges of her perception and she caught her breath.

'Tren,' she said softly. 'There's a whurthag floating about here somewhere.'

'Floating? That's new.'

'Now would be a good time to be serious,' she said pointedly. She picked up the book and returned it to her satchel, grateful to find that the leather was nearly dry. Tren was on his feet, staring around at the sand.

'I'm not seeing any cover, are you?'

'None whatsoever,' she replied, drawing herself up. A brief word brought the shortig to heel, Rikbeek leaving the dog's back and soaring into the air. 'Tren, it's approaching fast. They, because there are two. This could be our friend coming back.'

'That's what we came here for,' said Tren grimly. He sighed deeply as he fetched his still-damp shirt and shrugged it back on.

'Yes, but I thought we agreed that staging an open fight isn't likely to be productive, even with the two of us. We need information, not a twin set of early graves. You need to hide us, fast.'

'Eva, sorcery isn't made-to-order! There are no Cloaking enchantments I can produce that will do much for us under strong moonlight—'

'You're meant to be a top sorcerer, Tren, and this is a little bit important! Make something up!' She glanced nervously about, senses on edge, tracking the progress of the two whurthag beasts as they moved inexorably closer. She couldn't physically see them yet, but it wouldn't be long.

Tren muttered something. She hoped it was something constructive. She ignored him, maintaining her vigilant posture, until he spoke again.

'How's that?'

Turning, she saw empty beach. No, not entirely; if she worked at it she could discern a faint outline, a shimmer of movement working against the drift and flow of the pale sand.

'Good. Hide the animals too, please. This is not the natural environment for a shortig and a gwaystrel.'

The dog vanished, and Rikbeek's small shape disappeared too. Looking for Tren, she suffered a moment of disorientation. She jumped when his voice spoke right beside her.

'Best to keep together,' he murmured, gripping her hand. She nodded, forgetting that he couldn't see her. They waited in tense silence, watching for the first sign of the enemy's approach.

A speck of black on the horizon appeared, growing and spreading into two distinct shapes. Whurthags. Close behind them walked a human figure, tall, shrouded in a thick cloak. He wore the hood down, revealing a head of pale hair; Eva could determine nothing more definite about his appearance. The man was walking at a diagonal angle to them, heading in the direction of the small, sickly yellow-gold moon that hovered low in the sky.

'Let's follow,' whispered Eva. She and Tren mimicked the slow, measured pace of the sorcerer, keeping him in sight while maintaining a clear distance between themselves and his two brutal companions.

'I still don't understand this,' Eva whispered. 'Edwae said he was a sorcerer. One with powerful disguise skills. And yet he's manipulating those beasts like they were puppies.'

'Hmm. Might be possible for him to have someone else cast on him, but I doubt it. Not if it was that good a job. And he stinks of sorcery.'

'Tren, I think he's a summoner as well. He has to be.'

'That isn't supposed to be possible. Couldn't a summoner bind the whurthags to him?'

'No,' she said, bluntly. 'Weaker beasts, yes. Not those.'

'That's a problem.'

'Definitely, because if I can sense those whurthags from a distance, he should be able to sense my companions too.' She halted, letting the sorcerer-summoner gain a greater lead.

'It doesn't look like he has.'

'He probably isn't trying. He isn't disguised, either. I don't suppose he's expecting to meet anyone down here.'

She broke off, staring. The man and his whurthag companions had disappeared.

'Where did they go?'

'No idea,' breathed Tren. 'Come on.' He strode towards the place they'd last seen the sorcerer. She had to half-run to keep up with his long stride. Reaching out with her summoner senses, she found nothing.

No! There was a presence, weak and irregular, moving away from them. It was coming from below ground level.

'There,' said Tren, stopping suddenly. Embedded in the white sand before them was a round door without a handle.

'He's down there,' muttered Eva. 'I can feel those beasts moving away downwards.' Tren crouched down to the door, still retaining his grip on her hand. She was obliged to join him in the sand.

'Tren, this actually makes perfect sense. I was thinking, how could you live down here with the landscape so unstable? Maybe it's possible to maintain an essential structure of some sort *beneath* ground level, where the moon doesn't shine.'

'All well and good,' replied Tren, abandoning his attempts at the door, 'But how do we proceed from here? I can't get this open. It's securely locked and warded.'

'We're running out of time to try it; the moon's changing.'

Tren swore softly. 'We're so close!'

'We've learned something very important. Unhide us, quickly. I don't want to lose you if we're dumped in another ocean.'

'Let's hope for anything but.' Tren's lanky figure abruptly appeared, dark against the shimmering sand. Glancing down, Eva was reassured to be greeted with the sight of her own hands, solid again. The rest of her soon melted into existence.

'Keep hold of me,' she instructed. He nodded, moving close and tightening his fingers around hers.

The yellow light developed overtones of red, and Eva thought for a moment that the forest was returning again. But the hue brightened and paled, until it was undeniably not red.

'Pink,' muttered Tren.

'Looks that way,' she agreed, with a small smile at Tren's dismay. The soft white sand of the beach vanished. She found herself suddenly up to her waist in tall, flourishing grasses, flanked by feathery shrubs on all sides. The night-darkened sky gained a decided rosy glow, and the heady, even cloying scents of flowers assaulted her nostrils. Soft wings brushed past her

197

face and something light and delicate settled in her hair.

'You cannot be serious.' Tren stared in complete disgust at the beautiful daefly meadow, abundantly decked with pink-and-purple flowers. The gentle buzzing of lazy insects mingled with the distant sound of bright, tinkling bells. All that was missing, Eva thought with amusement, was a fragrant, beribboned boudoir equipped with a fountain.

'Don't you like my garden?'

Eva spun around. A woman stood a few feet away, wearing several colourful daeflies like jewellery. She smiled at Eva's obvious shock, her pale face satisfied, even smug. Her hair was bright white like Eva's. There could be no doubting this woman's identity.

They had found Ana.

21

Panicked, Llandry knew she was losing the fight. Her attacker was strong, and he lifted her easily from the ground. Her arms were held fast in an iron grip and kicking proved futile. She took a breath, trying to calm her mind.

Think, she admonished herself.

She opened her wings, fast and with full force. A voice muttered a startled oath — a male voice, she noticed peripherally — and the grip on her body loosened. She struggled anew, twisting sinuously in the arms of her captor. Her diminutive size and lithe figure saved her: holding her captive became as difficult as restraining a cat. She slid out of the man's grasp and fell to the floor. She was up in an instant and aloft, her wings carrying her above the tree cover.

Llandry flew fast and hard towards the food garden, landing amid the tables of the rooftop diners. She ran for the stairs, ignoring the exclamations and protests of the customers as her spread wings and tattered, flying cloak knocked dishes and glasses asunder.

Devary stood up as she approached, his face registering alarm. 'Llandry? What happened?'

'I went to the garden over there. Someone seized me. A man.'

'Stay here.' Devary darted through the archway and ran for

the trees. Llandry was momentarily tempted to follow him, but she reconsidered: her presence had already caused trouble. Instead she resumed her seat, adjusting her dishevelled hair and clothing as best she could.

Indren Druaster was staring at her with none of her customary superiority.

'Gracious,' she said faintly. 'I admit, I thought Mr. Kant exaggerated the danger that follows this trinket around.' Llandry ignored her, sitting in silence while Devary was gone, breathing deeply to calm her shakes.

'They appear to be gone,' said Devary at last, approaching from behind her. 'But we should leave, now.'

The return journey passed in a blur, conducted at a considerably faster pace than the journey out. Llandry rested her head against the cushions and closed her eyes, trying to still the whirling of her thoughts. Her hand was taken and held, gently and tenderly; she opened her eyes and turned her head, surprised. Devary's face was filled with concern, and the smile he offered her was half-hearted.

'Poor Llandry,' he murmured.

'I'm all right,' she said, suddenly uncomfortable. He nodded and opened his mouth to speak again, but he was interrupted by the carriage slowing to a quick, jolting stop. He jumped up instantly and opened the door. Llandry saw that the vehicle had pulled up barely a few feet away from the door to the Silver Harp. Devary handed her down and ushered her into the porch.

'Wait here a moment. Pull up your hood,' he instructed in a murmur. Puzzled, she obeyed, instinctively drawing the remains of her dark cloak over her clothes. He nodded approvingly.

'I'm not leaving you here tonight; it isn't safe, even with a guard. But it must appear that you returned here.' He spoke in a low whisper, and she had to lean towards him to hear the words.

'Where am I to go?'

'I shall keep you with me. Now, back we go. Keep close to me. Under my cloak, now.' He held open the folds of his own voluminous cloak, and she tucked herself under its shadow. A few steps, cumbersome in this peculiar arrangement, and she was back inside the carriage with Devary beside her.

Devary's dwelling was only a few minutes from the Harp. Llandry was relieved to see that Indren returned the wrapped pendant to Devary before he alighted. He turned as if to address a last few words to Indren, and Llandry slipped down, back into the enveloping folds of his cloak. She had time only to address a brief word of thanks to Indren, but she received in response a far kinder smile than the lady had offered her before. Then she was through a tall archway and a door was closing behind her, blocking out the sound of the carriage drawing away.

Devary bade her remain where she was and disappeared into the house. She stood, her discomfort rising, trying uselessly to neaten her disordered hair. She heard the sounds of curtains being drawn and shutters closing, then lights twinkled into life somewhere ahead of her. In another moment Devary reappeared.

'Come inside,' he said, lightly taking her arm and guiding her to a chair. 'Here. You need a drink.' He handed her a handsome glass full of dark liquid. She sipped and tasted wine, strong and sweet.

'Thank you,' she said gratefully, relishing the gently soothing sensation generated by the contents of her glass.

'I must speak with your guard,' he said. 'They had orders to remain near throughout the evening, yet you were almost taken. I saw one of them at the Harp just now. Why are they waiting there when you were elsewhere? This alarms me.'

'All right.' She hesitated. Her near escape was vivid in her memory, and she was reluctant to be left alone. She watched anxiously as he moved about the room, collecting — to her alarm — a pair of knives and slipping them into sheaths on his belt and boots. She wanted to ask him to stay, or to take her along, but her pride objected and she remained silent.

To her mingled relief and dismay, Devary collected a third knife and handed it to her. 'Keep this close,' he said. 'I don't think you will need it: I won't be gone for long.' He smiled encouragingly and left. She sighed as she heard the door close softly behind him. The key turned in the lock, loud in the silence.

Sigwide was asleep on her feet. His weight was uncomfortable; she lifted him into her lap and wound her fingers through his fur. He was warm, sleepy and grumpy at the disturbance. He twisted three times around, sneezing, and then curled himself up. She smiled faintly, comforted by the normality

201

of his antics.

Her glass was already empty when Devary returned, and she was nearly asleep. He laughed softly at the sight of her: Sigwide had wound his way up her torso and lay with his nose pressed against her face. She was so drowsy she hadn't noticed.

She pulled herself upright, blinking. How had she become so befuddled? All tension had faded from her body, and she felt absurdly relaxed. Too much so. She squinted suspiciously at the glass, still offering a few scant sips of the wine.

'Is everything well?' Her voice emerged oddly. It might have been termed 'mildly slurred', if she could bear to admit such an undignified possibility. She coughed and struggled to rally her wits.

'Not entirely,' he said grimly. 'Our guard captain swears he spoke to me personally earlier in the day. He claims that I told him the pendant would be at the Harp all evening, and that he and his men must keep a close guard over the building. That is why they were not nearby.' He sat down and kicked off his boots. 'What angers me is that I ought to have known about this. But in order to avoid drawing attention to our errand, they have had instructions to be discreet in their attendance on us. That made it too easy for them to be diverted.'

'Do you think they're lying?'

He looked at her. 'You are wondering if they betrayed us. I wondered that, too, but I think not. I believe the Captain is sincere when he says he saw me. His dismay at your near capture was sincere.'

Llandry frowned, struggling to focus her foggy thoughts. 'Is that a sorcery thing? Making yourself look like someone else?'

'Not exactly. It is not a common ability — the illusion would have to be impossibly minute — but theoretically it could be done. Certainly for the few minutes it would require to issue instructions to the Captain. This means, of course, two things. Firstly somebody has kept us under very close surveillance. That is not surprising, as such: it has been clear from the beginning that our enemy, whoever it is, is very good at gathering information. The more disturbing question...' He tailed off, staring at nothing.

'What?'

'I do not think it would be possible to create a suitably

202

convincing illusion of me after only a day's observation. The complexity is too great. I must consider that somebody who knows me well is involved.'

Llandry immediately thought of Indren. Her manner after Llandry's attack was slightly shaken, but nothing more; she had been remarkably unruffled by it. And her eyes had gleamed with excitement whenever she spoke of the istore.

'Do you think... Indren?' Devary's face darkened and she didn't have the courage to finish the sentence.

'I don't know,' he said shortly. 'But I must be careful. And you must go back to Glinnery, first thing in the morning. I will escort you.'

She bowed her head, unwilling to object. Even if she dutifully stayed in full view of Devary and a restaurant full of people, it seemed she was still in danger. And therefore, still a burden on Devary. She would have to submit to being sent home.

'We are safe for the night, I think. Two guards remain at the Harp — I wish to maintain the illusion that you are there — but the rest are currently watching over this house. You'll want to sleep. I don't have spare rooms here, I'm afraid — I've never needed any. You may have my room for tonight.'

'Where will you sleep?'

'On the sofa.'

'Oh — no, please. I couldn't turn you out of your own room. I will be comfortable here — you see it is quite big enough for me.'

He shook his head. 'Unthinkable. Worry not! It won't be the first time I've slept on a sofa.'

She rose, reluctantly. A sudden thought occurred to her and she glanced about.

'Devary. Have you seen my creature?'

'Your creature?'

'You know. The winged one that Sigwide ate.'

'Oh. That thing.' He thought for a moment. 'I haven't seen it at all today, I think.'

Neither had she. She frowned, distressed. The thing was odd, unpredictable and uninvited, but somehow she was fond of it.

'It will turn up,' he said, smiling reassuringly. 'Come, now. It's late.'

203

It was strange, lying in a room filled with Devary's personal belongings; lying in the very bed he slept in every night. The room smelled of him. As drowsy as she had been not long since, she was now wide awake and restless.

A shaft of pale moonlight shone through the window. She rose and adjusted the heavy blue drapes, peeping surreptitiously out into the night as she did so. Was that a flicker of movement? No. All was still.

She climbed back into the bed and pulled the blankets up to her face. A faint noise sounded and she was upright again in an instant, staring around the room. There: a faint scraping sound, and footsteps. The steps stopped outside her door, briefly, and then moved on. She recognised the tread: it was Devary moving around the house, probably preparing to sleep.

She sighed deeply. Relaxation eluded her: she lay, rigid with tension and acutely uncomfortable. Silence reigned again. Was Devary still up? She threw back the covers and padded silently to the door. Doubt seized her two steps away, and she halted; then, shaking her head at herself, she opened it and stepped through.

The house was dark, but a soft light still burned somewhere. She found her way, slowly, back to the living room. There was the light, a hovering globe casting a mellow golden glow over the room. Devary sat on the sofa, still awake, though apparently in some sort of reverie. He held an untouched glass of wine in one hand.

'Llandry? Is everything all right?'

'Y-yes. Well, not quite. I can't sleep.'

He nodded. 'It's been a hard day.'

'I'm afraid,' she admitted.

'Come and sit down awhile,' he said easily, making room for her on the sofa. She advanced hesitantly, trying to smile. He tilted his head at her. 'Aren't you cold like that?'

She glanced down, horrified. He had lent her a shirt to sleep in. On her it was long enough to reach to her knees, but her legs were bare and the fabric was thin. Not only was she cold, indeed, but also barely decent.

'Oh, gracious. I forgot.'

He laughed. 'Never mind. I've a blanket somewhere.' He got up and moved away. She hugged the shirt close, wrapping her arms around herself. She realised she was shivering violently,

204

with cold and with nervousness.

'Here.' He laid a length of soft wool over her shoulders and wrapped it around her. She mumbled her thanks and tugged it close, tucking her legs up under the blanket. Her shivering did not ease.

'How did you get so cold?' He sat by her and, a little hesitantly, slid an arm over her shoulders and pulled her close. 'You shouldn't walk around in nothing but a shirt,' he chided. 'See what happens?'

She wondered if he was referring to her shivering or the fact that she was suddenly in his arms. The latter consequence was not so very terrible.

'Dev?'

'Yes?'

'Who do you think is after the istore?'

'I don't know.'

'You don't even have a theory?'

'No. I really don't. If it is as Indren said, well... anybody would want it. Many people would kill for it.'

She blinked, nonplussed. 'Why?'

'Because it may be the most valuable substance in the Seven Realms.'

'I don't understand.'

He shifted slightly, making himself more comfortable, and rearranged her against him. 'You know that each of the Seven Realms is attuned more to one than the other. You of Glinnery are Daylanders, as are Irbel and, as far as we can tell, Orlind. Glour, Orstwych and Ullarn are Darklanders of the Lowers. Only Nimdre has no allegiance: we live halfway in between, faithful neither to one nor the other.

'It's highly dangerous to spend much time in the Off-Worlds. Everyone knows that. They are too volatile, too unpredictable. A mere human is at the mercy of the caprices of those lands, barely able to defend themselves. If you keep to the Realm to which you are attuned, and keeps your visits short, you'll probably be all right.

'The stories say it wasn't always that way. Some beings freely walked all of the Realms, once upon a time. Nobody knows whether they originated in the Uppers or the Lowers or the space in between: the Middle Realm, which was once a chaos of

205

conflicting influences from both sides. Whatever their origins, they were tremendously powerful.

'According to the tales, these beings were tied in to the chaotic magics of the Off-Worlds in ways no human can emulate. They could manipulate those landscapes as they chose, mould them according to their wishes. It was once thought that carrying some element of these beasts' bodies allowed some of that ability to carry over to the wearer. You know very well how many valuable plants, minerals and animals there are to be found in both the Uppers and the Lowers, so I'm sure you can guess the rest.

'It's thought that these creatures were hunted to extinction long ago, and probably they were. There have been no new sources of this bone-matter in many centuries. But then you discover a cave filled with a strange stone. Was it a cave or a grave? Are they stones, or the bones of a long-dead denizen of the Other Realms?'

Llandry was silent, thinking. Her mind whirled. Chief among her feelings, she discovered, was dismay: if this was true, her stone would never be hers again. It was irrevocably changed; no longer a keepsake, a trinket, a beautiful piece of art, a gift. It had become powerful and strange, terrible and terrifying. It had a value much higher than her own life, or Devary's.

'Who were these beings? You implied that they were not human.'

'They have many different names. None of which you will have heard, I think, and I will not say more, because these tales are usually dismissed as bedtime stories. Most people with any academic training will tell you that it is nonsense.' He smiled. 'I, of course, am no scholar, and the university here is a little more... open-minded than most.'

'I'm not a scholar either. And I might have heard of them,' Llandry protested. He only smiled and shook his head.

'Back to bed, now. We will be leaving early in the morning. I will be nearby, making sure you are safe.'

22

Ana stood smiling at Eva in an unsettling manner. Betrayer, thief and probable murderess she might be, but she had the air of a woman welcoming friends to a garden party.

'Who are you?' Tren stepped slightly in front of Eva, concealing her view of the woman. Impatient, she pushed him aside.

'I'm the person who designed this meadow,' the woman replied. 'Glorious, isn't it? Though I can imagine it wouldn't suit your tastes, sorcerer.'

'You destroyed my friend,' Tren returned, his voice trembling with anger.

The woman frowned prettily, her forehead creasing slightly. 'I don't destroy people, sorcerer-man. People destroy themselves.'

'And you don't mind helping them along, if it suits you.'

The woman shrugged. 'If people are intent on being stupid, they'll find a way without my help. Who's the friend, out of interest?'

'Edwae Geslin, aide to Lord Angstrun.' Tren threw the words at her like a challenge, but she actually giggled.

'Ah, the sorcerer boy-child. You've the look of him about you, young man. The same ungainly air, the same youth. Green as curulays, both of you.' She looked back at Eva. 'Is this your partner? I'd think you could do better.'

'And who are you to judge?' Eva replied coldly. Tren's distress was infecting Eva's composure, but she fought to stay calm.

'I, madam, am the most powerful summoner in the Darklands just now.' She beamed at them both. 'And Griel is unmatched as a sorcerer. As a pair, we're unbeatable.' Eva's senses picked up the presence of two whurthags, and moments later the man they'd glimpsed earlier emerged from the shrubs behind Ana. He stood close, smiling genially at Tren and Eva. He was about Vale's age, somewhere in his fifties, vigorous and strongly-built. His pale hair gleamed in the pink-touched moonlight. When he spoke, his voice had a pleasant timbre to it, like mature honey.

'We have guests? I didn't know we were expecting anyone.'

'Gatecrashers, my dear, but etiquette obliges us to be polite.' A tea table appeared in the grass, four chairs set around it. Their hostess gestured graciously.

'Please have a seat, do. There's tea in the pot.' An elegant teapot materialised along with a set of cups, a faint scent of yasmind rising from it.

'I'm afraid we can't stay. A prior engagement.' Eva stepped away from the table, but the sorcerer was there with his tame whurthags. He smiled at her with deceptive courtesy and pulled out a chair for her.

'Do stay a while,' he said affably. 'My wife would be disappointed otherwise.' Eva sensed the whurthags ready to spring, awaiting his command. She sat, tense and wary, as Ana elegantly poured tea.

'You can call me Ana,' said the woman. 'My husband you may address as Griel. And your names?'

'Eva.'

Tren said nothing. His face was completely cold. Ana waited expectantly, then shrugged.

'Then sorcerer-man will have to do.' She smiled, eyeing their appearance. 'You two have had some adventures, if the salt-crusted condition of your clothes is any clue. Had a little sea-bathing lately?'

'Something of that sort,' returned Eva coolly.

'Not looking for us, surely?'

'Looking for whoever is responsible for the deaths of several Glour citizens,' interposed Tren. 'Which I think was you.' He turned a cold stare on Griel, who smiled back rather pleasantly.

'Me? Now, that's harsh isn't it? And over tea, too.'

'You with your whurthag pets.' Tren was not to be mollified. He ignored the cup of tea that sat before him, his hands clenched together in his lap as though he was afraid of hitting someone.

'Well, one or two things happened that I didn't intend. The boys do get away from me now and again. They're terrifically hungry, all the time.'

'*Why* would you ever even approach a whurthag, let alone try to train one?' Eva stared at Griel as at a man deranged. He beamed still more broadly, showing a perfect set of very white teeth.

'Actually, that was my lady wife's idea. She was the first person to dominate a whurthag.'

Eva transferred her gaze to Ana's face. 'Why?' she repeated.

Ana leaned forward conspiratorially. 'Haven't you ever wondered how far you can go? Whether there really are limits to what's possible? Beyond the *reasonable*, the sensible.' She gave her cat-smile and sat back. 'Everyone says it's impossible to dominate a whurthag, but I did. Everyone says it's impossible to survive long in the Lowers, but we do. People like your friend there—' she tilted her chin in Tren's direction '—so afraid of their own shadows. Wouldn't dream of breaking a rule. But *you...*' Her pale eyes glinted at Eva speculatively. 'You're different. I can sense that about you. You've pushed the boundaries, haven't you? You're independent. You follow your own way.'

'I don't get people killed just to test my own powers.'

'But you'll risk yourself. Being willing to risk more is only a small step away.'

Eva's mind whirled, a sense of dread building. What would the woman who'd voluntarily taken on a whurthag do next?

Griel looked at Tren. 'I'd like my ring back, please,' he said pleasantly. Eva watched, thinking fast, as Tren angrily threw the ring onto the table. The indigo stone glimmered in the pink light, throwing lances of colour over the tablecloth.

'Don't tell me all of this is about the istore,' she said. 'It's too simple. Too... *mundane.* What are you really after?'

Griel retrieved the ring and began to polish it. His wife rolled her eyes towards the moonlit sky, slumping despairingly in her chair.

'Really. You're still calling it by that juvenile name?'

'Fine,' said Eva frostily. 'What are you calling it?'

'I was thinking more along the lines of draykon.'

Eva's breath stopped. '*Draykon*? You are insane.'

Ana's smile grew a little unfriendly. 'Am I? I am a living contradiction of the notion that *anything* is impossible. I say *draykon* and I mean it. It's not impossible.'

'They don't exist. They never did exist. It's a myth.'

'Oh... most myths have some basis in fact. The draykon might now be the stuff of dusty graduate theses, but that doesn't mean it wasn't once as real as you and I.'

Eva saw now that Ana wore a choker set with istore, a handsome piece made from silver. She thought she recognised Llandry Sanfaer's work in the design. She couldn't see how they were connected. The word *draykon* was a throwaway term among summoner circles, a cliche. *As likely as draykons* ran the saying. She could see, with horrible clarity, how such a statement might be taken as a challenge by a woman like Ana.

But to say that they existed? Summoner legend had it that the draykon was larger than any recorded species, twenty times larger even than the muumuk. They were winged, scaled, reptilian but they breathed fire... the notion was absurd. True, there were many strange and wondrous beasts to be found in the Off-Worlds, but a flying beast bigger than a barn would have led to reports. There would've been sightings, documented accounts, research notes...

Wasn't once as real as you and I. Wasn't that what Ana had said? Eva refocused on Ana's face.

'Once?'

'Oh, they're extinct,' she said comfortably. 'At least for the moment.'

'Eva, what's a draykon?' Tren was looking from Eva to Ana to Griel, puzzled and alarmed.

'Nothing you and I would ever like to meet,' she replied.

'I'm going to make you a gift,' said Ana, smiling prettily at Eva. 'Griel, give her the ring.' Griel obliged, placing the ring in

210

front of Eva. She frowned at it. The pieces still wouldn't resolve in her wearied brain. Jewellery and gemstones; a deranged tea garden in the Lowers; a pair of impossibly powerful sorcerer-summoners and draykons; how could all these things possibly connect?

'Put it on,' said Ana, sounding like a child at a party.

'Why?'

'You'll see.'

Eva picked up the ring. It was heavy and cool in her hand, the stone polished to perfect smoothness. She slipped it on. Ana beamed, delighted.

'Soon you'll see. Now, Griel, I think we are taking this one with us.'

'Really, darling? I don't think we have a guest room prepared.'

'Oh, I'll arrange something.' To her horror, Eva realised they were talking about her.

'And the other?' Griel was looking at Tren.

'Leave it here.'

'What? No!' Tren was on his feet, moving towards Eva. He grabbed her hand — the one that wore the istore ring — and faced the insane couple. 'We stay together.'

Ana looked at him, lips pursed, and shook her head. 'I'm sorry, I just don't see a use for you. Call it an opportunity! If you can find your way back to your *friend*, perhaps I'll reconsider.'

Eva stood up calmly. 'I don't consent to this arrangement.'

'Oh, never mind,' said Ana. Eva opened her mouth to retort, but she lost her chance. The world dissolved around her with horrifying speed. There was no gradually changing light, no ripple in the weave of the world; the daefly meadow simply disintegrated. After a deeply disorientating few moments, she found herself in an enclosed room without doors or windows. The walls were bare earth, undecorated. The room was absolutely empty. Tren, Ana and Griel had disappeared; she didn't even have Rikbeek with her.

With meticulous care, Eva searched every inch of those packed earth walls, looking for an opening of some kind, even just a crack; anything she could use to work her way out. She found nothing. She didn't even have her bag with the precious book; she was completely bereft of aid or clues. She seated herself cross-legged in the centre of the strange, bare room, arranging her heavy cotton skirts over her legs. She shivered, feeling the settled, damp chill in the chamber.

Eva wrapped her arms around herself, her thoughts spinning abruptly back to the last time she'd been bone-cold and shivering. Tren had been there, to warm her as best he could. Where was he now? Ana's words suggested he'd been left behind, which was promising as far as it went, but the prospect worried her. He'd seemed so helpless in the relentless onslaught of this world. She'd barely had time to teach him anything useful. How long would he survive alone?

She pushed the thought out of her mind. There was nothing she could do about it until she freed herself.

Tiredness clouded her thoughts and weighted her limbs. When was the last time she had slept? It might even be days, though it was difficult to track the passage of time in the Lower Realms. Maybe only two days. Trying to focus on the question of escape, she found her thoughts slipping away from her like fish through a stream. All she could think was *tired. Tired and cold. Cold and tired.*

A pillow appeared before her, then a folded blanket. Eva stared at them, wondering if they were some sort of mirage. But they felt soft and real under her fingers when she picked them up. She lay down, cushioning her head on the pillow and covering herself with the blanket. The cold earth floor continued to chill her and she shivered, wishing for the soft, expensive mattress that cushioned her bed at home. Almost immediately the hard, cold surface receded and Eva lay on something thickly padded. A glance revealed a quite stylish blue striped mattress now lying between her and the floor.

A faint blue glow was coming from somewhere. Eva searched, fighting her body's attempts to sleep. Eventually she realised it was coming from her own hand. The ring pulsed softly, glittering with colours, throwing out indigo light like a night sky full of colourful stars. She blinked at it sleepily. Her own ring had never done that.

Evidently the two events were connected, but Eva's sleep-clouded mind refused to process the implications. She made a final effort to remain awake, but her body would not obey her. She slept.

Between one heartbeat and the next, Eva vanished. Ana and Griel vanished with her, and Tren found himself alone in the daefly garden. That stupid pink light taunted him, speaking of romance and tranquillity while his heart pounded with fear and his head whirled with confusion. Daeflies tried to settle on him, and he waved them impatiently away. Did he still have the animals?

A search revealed Bartel crouched beneath one of the chairs. Rikbeek was still clinging to his fur, riding the hound like a steed. The notion might have made Tren laugh if he wasn't so tense. A long search of the garden revealed nothing of use except for Eva's bag, tucked under the chair she'd recently vacated. He secured that, checking for the book. It lay within, undamaged as far as he could tell.

The animals were clearly confused by Eva's disappearance. The shortig cast about the ground in circles, probably following her scent. He kept returning to the spot she'd been standing in when she had vanished. At last the little dog sat on its haunches in front of her chair, with an air of dejection that Tren couldn't help identifying with.

'I know,' he said. 'I feel lost without her, too. We'll see what we can manage by ourselves, though, hm?' The gwaystrel had moved from Bartel's back. Glancing up, Tren glimpsed Rikbeek swooping in widening circles over his head. He knew by now some of the sounds Rikbeek produced when he found something of use. None of these were forthcoming. Eventually the gwaystrel, too, gave up the search and returned to his station on the dog's back.

Tren tried not to let himself reflect on the possible fate of his new friend now she was under the control of Ana and her peculiar husband. They were both mad, he was certain. Ana hadn't said why she wanted Eva, but she'd spoken of some kind of use or purpose. Any purpose of Ana's would doubtless be something Eva would condemn, but how could she resist the power of people whose control over their surroundings was so complete that it was the work of a moment to abduct her? Not

213

to mention those two whurthags; apparently they were under Griel's control but he had spoken of their getting away from him once in a while. Besides, if Griel was a sorcerer, how was he exerting summoner influence over them in the first place? It made no sense.

He was weary. The events of the last two days — or three? — had left him drained, physically and emotionally. He refused to let himself think of that either. For the first time, he blessed the habit for regular all-nighters that he'd developed during training. He was inured to exhaustion.

'Right,' he said out loud, rising to his feet. The only clue he could recall as to their whereabouts was the door in the sand that he and Eva had found. The only sensible course of action open to him was to find that door, one way or another. But just as he formed the resolution he noticed that the pink light was beginning to fade. He had time for a brief curse before the daefly garden dissolved around him, overtaken by the sickly green light that was building in the sky.

He grabbed Eva's bag and the dog, clutching both to his chest as he waited for the dizzying ripple across the world to resolve into solidity. When at last it did, he was standing in a jungle. Trees decked with green and blue foliage rose so high as to block out the sky, draped in hanging vines and blistering with humid heat. The ground was virtually impenetrable, bristling with spreading bushes and ferns. He groaned at the sight.

'Right,' he said again, taking a deep breath. Thinking of the shortig's sure progress across Orstwych, he set the dog down and placed Griel's book in front of him. He couldn't communicate with him the way Eva did — in fact he had no idea how she gave the dog instructions — but perhaps the clever hound would understand.

To his relief, the dog behaved as it had at Edwae's house, investigating the book with his large nose. Tren had no way of knowing whether he was picking up enough of Griel's scent to be able to track him, but he would have to trust the dog. After a few minutes the shortig sat, finished, and gave a single, high-pitched bark.

'Good,' said Tren, exhaling slowly. 'Off you go.' He took a couple of steps towards the dog, who seemed to understand. The hound began to cast for the scent, trotting in circles with his nose to the ground. Tren watched, tense. He was staking this course of action on the theory that only the surface of this world changed; beneath it the ground stayed essentially the same. He only hoped that some vestige of a scent would remain on this altered terrain.

The dog stopped, yipped, then set off at a trot. Tren followed, confused. The hound had obviously found something, but was it relevant? How did Eva ensure the dog followed the right trail? He had no choice but to follow, however; no other idea had occurred to him as a means of finding Eva. The shortig led him swiftly into the jungle, Rikbeek taking flight again from the dog's back to resume his guard duties (at least, so Tren hoped).

He fought his way through the undergrowth for some time, rapidly growing overheated. Colours swam alarmingly bright before his eyes, even in the faint moonlight that filtered through the leafy canopy. Vibrant blossoms hung down at head height, far larger than any flower had a right to be. When Tren noticed the size of the bees that fed on the nectar of those enormous blooms, he resolved on giving them a wide berth. Insects buzzed incessantly, too loudly; the amplification implied that the bees weren't the only beasts out here that were dangerously oversized.

After half an hour Tren's clothes were wet with sweat, his hands and arms were covered with scratches and he was gasping for water.

'Wait,' he called to the dog, helplessly hoping Bartel would stop. He did. Relieved, Tren stood still for a moment, breathing deeply. It occurred to him for the first time that he was very exposed in this weird, jewel-bright canopy. How could he have forgotten to Cloak himself? He shook his head at his ineptitude and wove himself a shadow-shroud. Sufficient shadows lurked beneath the trees to hide him in his little slice of night, or so he hoped. He seemed to be hoping for a great many things lately. He wondered idly how long his luck would hold.

The dog was panting, too, and starting to tire. Where could he find water? Tren glanced about, uselessly. He hadn't come across any pool or stream in the last half hour's travel.

Tren sat for a moment, thinking. He was growing concerned at the length of time they'd been travelling. Back in the sands, he and Eva had been within sight of the strange little door in the ground when the daefly garden had appeared. They'd wandered away after that, but they hadn't travelled a half-hour's distance from it. Wherever the hound was taking him, it wasn't to that door. That might mean that Griel had gone somewhere else recently and Tren was on his way there instead. Or it could mean that the dog was following some other scent entirely. Or, perhaps, that book had not belonged to Griel. The possibilities for failure were endless, and Tren felt a moment's despair.

He sighed, letting his head drop onto his knees. He thought briefly of Eva — *Lady Glostrum*, he corrected himself — trapped somewhere, maybe hurt. Remembering Griel's tall figure with his pair of whurthags at his heels, Tren suffered a surge of fear so acute that his breath stopped. What might they do to her? Did Ana's 'purpose' involve hurting or killing her? He surged to his feet. Lady Glostrum was a woman who could take care of herself, but even she had limits. He had to keep going.

Eva woke to a flood of guilt. How could she have slept while Tren was loose somewhere in the Lowers, alone? She threw off the mysterious blanket and rose to her feet, shaking her head to clear it. At least she no longer felt as if she was trying to run underwater.

She looked down at the pillow, the mattress and the blanket that had appeared according to her needs. Had she done that? The ring had stopped glowing, resting once again dull and ordinary on her finger. She narrowed her eyes at it, thinking of gloren fruits. A bowl appeared at her feet, piled high with plump, golden-skinned fruit.

That's clear enough. She worked harder, testing the limits of this new technique. She pictured the walls squared off, lined with brick and properly papered. She envisaged a floor of polished wooden boards, a ceiling of decorated plaster and a long window framed with cream-coloured curtains. She added a desk and chair, a sofa, a fireplace and a large rug in the centre of the floor. When she had finished, she was standing in a perfect replica of her parlour at home. The only thing that was missing was the door.

She added that last, then crossed to it and seized the handle. Pausing a moment for a brief, futile wish, she turned it. The door opened easily under her hand.

Eva stopped, shocked. Could it really be so easy? Collecting herself, she pulled the door open wide and stepped through. A larger room stood beyond the threshold of her new parlour, a room filled with bookcases and workspaces. Books lay everywhere, wide open, their pages grubby and occasionally torn. Eva ventured inside, reassured by its apparent emptiness. Ana and Griel, apparently, were not here.

She stopped when the dark head of a whurthag rose above the level of the table in front of her. The creature growled, paced slowly around the furniture until it stood before her. It didn't look ready to spring, more as if it was inclined to play guard. Nonetheless, Eva wisely didn't move.

Voices rang hollowly from somewhere nearby, muffled and quiet but it was almost possible to discern words. Slowly, carefully, Eva inched a little sideways, then a bit more. The whurthag kept its icy gaze locked on her, but it didn't move. With another shuffle, the voices sharpened.

'... almost ready. Two more pieces ought to finish it, or even one! That rock the girl was wearing looked big enough.' Ana was speaking in Ullarni, and for the first time in years Eva blessed those interminable government meetings. She'd learned a lot of Ullarn's complicated language out of obligation.

'It wasn't in her room, but we'll have it soon. If she hasn't hidden it, she must be wearing it, and I've arranged for pursuit if they try to leave. My men may already have it.' Griel's voice, of course. 'But, Ana, are you sure you're ready? I don't want anything to go wrong.'

'How could it go wrong? Are we not invincible, you and I?'

'No one is invincible. Take some care, Ana. This project... it has obsessed you. I think you would pursue it even if it destroyed you, and it is dangerous.'

'So am I.' Eva could imagine Ana's smile, too happy, too confident, undoubtedly insane. 'Besides, with another summoner to help us we are even more secure. All will be well.'

'What did you do with her?'

'She is in the cell, though I hope she will find her way out soon. We have work to do. You have work to do, Griel dear. Go and get the last piece! Quickly, quickly. We're very close, and we haven't much time. They'll find us soon.'

Griel made a sound of assent, but said nothing. His footsteps receded, and all was quiet once more. Eva edged carefully back to her former spot, unwilling to be caught eavesdropping. Her quick mind worked briskly, processing what she'd heard. It wasn't very informative. She still had no real idea why Ana wanted istore — what had she meant by 'big enough'? Who was the girl mentioned? And what did she mean by "they"? Surely she could not be referring to Eva herself; she and Tren had already found Ana, and been summarily dealt with.

At least an hour passed, and Ana did not appear. The whurthag did not relax its vigilance and Eva's muscles cramped, but she dared not make any big moves like sitting down. It occurred to her, briefly, to try her luck with the whurthag; perhaps she could subvert the command that kept it standing at guard and exert her influence over it instead. But a brief cast of the creature's mind quickly dampened that hope. It was relentlessly fixed on her, and it badly wanted to kill; even her light exploration of its mind nearly unbalanced the fragile control that held it at guard. And she had no sorcerer to open a gate, and nowhere to banish it to: she was already in the Lowers and had no wish to send it back through into Orstwych. So she waited.

At length the sound of approaching footsteps broke the stifling quiet, and then Ana's voice greeted her.

'Ah! Lady Glostrum. Do come in. It took you a little longer than I expected, but no matter.' Ana came through a door to Eva's right, advancing towards her with the sort of gracious smile Eva reserved for her special guests. She glanced past Eva into the room that had previously been Eva's prison.

'I love what you've done with the room. Perhaps I'll keep it like that. Cup of tea?'

'What did you do with Tren?'

Ana looked blank. 'Who? Oh, the boy! Not sure. He's out there, somewhere.' She fluttered a hand in a vaguely upward direction.

'I want him back.'

'Maybe later.'

'No: now.'

Ana didn't reply. She sat down on a pretty, cream-upholstered divan, her beautiful silken skirts fanning around her.

218

She smiled at Eva over the cup of tea she held in her dainty hands.

'Do come and sit down. You look awfully fierce standing there like that. There's tea in the pot.'

Eva felt herself beginning to grow angry. 'You were responsible for the death of my closest friend, and Tren's. Now you've left Tren out in the Lowers by himself, with the express expectation that he'll die, and you keep me here for some purpose you haven't explained. Of course I am looking *fierce*.'

Ana looked at her critically. 'That just shows you haven't had a cup of tea in a while. Here.' She set her own cup down and poured a second one for Eva. Her tea set was a perfect porcelain one, painted with daeflies.

'Have a sip,' Ana encouraged. 'You'll feel better.'

Eva controlled herself with an effort. She made her way to the divan and sat down, watching Ana warily. The tea smelled of yasmind and rosuis and tasted like summer.

'Why don't you tell me why I am here?'

'Oh! That's a matter of seizing the opportunity, really.' Ana sat back, smiling. 'The truth is, I've a feeling we may need some help. It wouldn't hurt at all to have another powerful summoner around. And you presented yourself. Perfect, no?'

'What do you want my help with?'

Ana gave her a speculative look, then rose to her feet. 'Well, darling, why don't I show you?'

23

Llandry rose early the next day after a troubled, restless night. She stepped softly through the house, fearing to find Devary still asleep on the sofa. There was no sign of him, however, and she felt a guilty flicker of relief. She sat down, tucking her legs under her. She was wearing the trousers she had bought at Draetre's night market, and she felt both freed and rather exposed in them.

A clatter from the kitchen drew her attention, and she wandered thither. Devary stood with a cup in one hand, the other thrust into the pocket of his trousers. He was tousled and sleepy, his shirt untucked and his hair unbrushed. He looked at her expressionlessly, offering no response to her shy smile.

'Good... morning,' she said, glancing at the dark world outside. 'Not that it seems like a morning.'

'It's very early, but the sun will be up soon. I'll have breakfast ready in a moment.' He offered her a steaming teapot. She poured herself a cup and sipped gratefully, finding it to be slightly spicy and fragrant. She'd barely taken two sips before an urgent pounding began at the door. Devary frowned.

'Stay here,' he murmured and left the room. She heard the front door open and hushed voices in conversation. He was gone for several minutes, and at length she drifted that way, taking her tea along with her.

Two winged Glinnery guards stood in the hallway. Their eyes flicked to Llandry as soon as she appeared. Devary looked up also, an expression of haggard alarm on his face. Llandry looked questioningly at the guards, trying to stifle the flicker of fear that began in her belly.

'Miss Sanfaer,' said one, bowing to her. 'Bad news to report. We left two of our colleagues at the Silver Harp yesterday. Their bodies have just been discovered.' He paused, his face hard. 'Your room was broken into last night. It's been ransacked; most of your possessions are destroyed, I'm afraid.'

'Whurthags, Llan,' said Devary gently. 'It cannot be long before the search is extended to this house. We are leaving immediately.'

'We're escorting you back to Waeverleyne, Miss,' said the guard. 'I've requested some reinforcements from the guardhouse here, plus a local summoner's coming along. You'll be well protected.' Llandry guessed he was anxious to regain face after a series of failures, but she appreciated his consideration for her safety.

'Thank you,' Llandry said to the guards. 'I-I'm sorry about your colleagues.'

'Not your fault, Miss,' said the captain. 'We'll await you and Mr. Kant outside.' Both men bowed to her and left.

'It is my fault,' she said sadly, to an empty hallway.

Everything moved very rapidly after that. Devary returned within minutes, hastily groomed and dressed in his travelling clothes. She stood ready by the time he arrived, her cloak donned and her few remaining possessions clutched in her small travel bag. A carriage waited outside, with a team of four nivvens in the traces. She and Devary stepped on board and the carriage immediately began to move.

Devary settled into a seat opposite her. 'I am not letting you out of my sight until you are safely back with your mother and father. Understand?'

She nodded, twisting her small hands nervously in the folds of her cloak. She watched sightlessly out of the window as the city of Draetre blurred past, trying to ignore the knot of guilt that had taken root in her belly. Every time she stepped beyond the confines of her mother's house, she generated disaster, and she was wholly sickened by it. Her gravest mistake had been in

221

wandering the streets of Draetre while Sigwide carried the istore pendant. True, she hadn't known he had taken it, but that was little excuse. He had stolen it once before. She should have been more vigilant.

Feeling the advance warnings of an imminent attack, Llandry fumbled in her bag for her tonic. Devary's eyes flicked in her direction as she drank, heedless of his observation, but he didn't enquire. She hid the bottle away again and slumped back into her seat, trying to breathe slowly. She had been mistaken in thinking she could achieve anything by her rebellious journey into Draetre. Her presence — her mistakes — had only destroyed Devary's errand and brought death to two people — and she had almost got herself captured in the process. She had nothing to offer, no skills, no special knowledge, not even sufficient strength to handle herself without disintegrating into a heap of frayed nerves. She would have to admit defeat, accept her reincarceration at home until the istore craze had died away. The thought was severely dispiriting.

It occurred to her, belatedly, that the carriage was moving at a slow pace that didn't fit at all with Devary's apparent urgency not long before. She caught his eye.

'Shouldn't we go a little faster? It could take a week to get home at this rate.'

'We don't want to attract any undue attention,' he replied. 'At the moment we are merely one of many hired carriages travelling through the city. If we were to fly along at a dramatic pace, we would make ourselves conspicuous. We will travel faster when we reach the open road.'

This explanation made sense, but Llandry's nerves would not be soothed by it. She spent a nervous hour as the carriage ambled through the town to the northern gate and finally picked up speed beyond. Their route was to take them up the Coach Road a long way north from Draetre, and then west and back southwards into Glinnery. It was less direct, but nonetheless faster than their pedestrian journey of only two days before.

They travelled all day, putting up at an inn that night. Before sunrise the next day they were back in the carriage. Devary looked as though he hadn't slept the night before; she supposed he had been keeping watch. She hadn't slept much either. They were well out on the Coach Road now, passing through the

222

densely forested hills through northern Nimdre, and the pace was much faster than the day before; so much so that Llandry forgot her misery in the sheer physical discomfort of being bounced, jolted and shaken to pieces hour after hour. She felt that it was deserved.

As they entered Glinnery the wide Coach Road ended and the route became narrow, steep and winding, wholly unsuitable for large vehicles. They were obliged to abandon the carriage in favour of forming a mounted party. One guard rode ahead, two behind, and a few more maintained their station on the wing overhead. Devary was mounted on the largest, strongest nivven, and Llandry was set behind him. She spent several more hours with her arms wrapped around his waist and her cheek resting against his back, clinging to him as they journeyed on at speed.

For a time they were able to maintain a brisk pace, but eventually the roads became so narrow and twistingly unpredictable that they had to slow down. The way became increasingly difficult after that, and their progress painstaking. At length the bright Glinnery sunlight grew muted and the softly-lit dusk hours came on. The guard riding at the head of the party reined in and held up his hand.

'I'd hoped to reach the Sanfaer house before the end of today, but we aren't going to make it.' He was obviously chagrined — and worried. 'The nivvens are exhausted. We'll have to stop here for a few hours.' He dismounted and the rest of the party followed suit. Llandry winced as she swung down to the ground, her stiff legs threatening to buckle beneath her. She was grateful for Devary's strong grip on her arm, keeping her upright.

'Miss Sanfaer, please stay with Mr. Kant. I've sent ahead for help. We should expect to see another company arriving within two, maybe three hours.'

Devary frowned. 'Is that necessary? There's been no sign of any pursuit at all. Has there?'

The Captain glanced at him, saying nothing. Llandry understood: more had occurred than had been apparent, but nobody wished to speak of it before her.

'I can bear it,' she said. 'Tell me.'

'I've had scouts aloft, combing the route behind us for signs of activity. One of them spotted a party early this morning, some

223

way behind us but riding hard. It may be nothing — only travellers.'

Devary let out a long breath. 'How long till they catch up with us?'

'At their pace, not more than five or six hours. I've men keeping an eye on them. We'll stay here only for four.'

He nodded to them and collected the reins of his nivven, drawing the beast away for rest and food. Llandry looked anxiously at Devary. She tried not to show the extent of her anxiety, but she very much feared it was written across her face.

He smiled reassuringly and squeezed her hand. 'All will be well. I'll make sure of it.'

She wished his apparent confidence was more convincing. She couldn't help a glance back at the road behind them, half-expecting to see a group of pursuers come riding up at any moment.

Devary drew her away from the road. 'It's best to rest while we can.' He took off his cloak and laid it over the grass for her. She accepted the gesture silently, laying herself down and wrapping herself in her cloak. She closed her eyes, but all she saw was riders, riding hard and relentlessly with bright weapons in their hands.

The hours passed slowly. Minutes dragged by as Llandry lay, restless and unable to sleep under these nightmarish conditions. Sigwide lay curled against her side, but for once his small form was unable to impart any comfort to her. She was conscious of Devary lying nearby, too far away to touch but she could hear him. There was nothing of the sleeper in the rhythm of his breathing, and in the whisper of grass as he frequently changed his position. He lay as unable to sleep as she. At last she sat up.

'It's time to go, surely,' she whispered.

Devary grunted. 'I hope so. I'll see to the nivvens.'

As he rose to his feet, a shout went up on the edges of their little camp, and a uniformed figure swooped down from the skies.

'Captain,' he gasped. 'The scout's missing and we've one man unaccounted for. I fear that—' He broke off, staring beyond the borders of the camp. Then he swore and grabbed the hilt of his sword, drawing it with a hiss of steel. 'Too late.'

The Captain drew his weapons grimly, shouting orders. Their clearing, so quiet before, was suddenly a whirl of activity as guards descended from the skies and more rose from the ground. Nivvens bucked and whinnied and in the commotion Llandry saw several unfamiliar figures, Nimdrens and even — oh, horror — two winged Glinnery-folk, armed with flashing weapons and pursuing the uniformed men of the Glinnery guard. She watched, aghast, as two were instantly cut down, betrayed by the suddenness of the attack.

Devary came up beside her, his knives gleaming in his hands. 'Stay behind me,' he said tersely. He chose an opponent and attacked, not recklessly but coolly and with considerable skill. His knives flashed in the low sunlight as he fought with perfect coordination. His opponent fell, but immediately two more were upon him, and he was hard pressed; one was defeated but he fell back before the second, clutching at a wound opening redly in his side. Around her the fight raged, too evenly matched: she saw another of her guards fall. She'd kept the knife Devary had given her the night before, and she drew it now, ready to go to Devary's aid.

But before she could reach him, the two winged men appeared before her. They were much taller than she, and they easily blocked her way through to Devary.

'That's the little Sanfaer,' said one, smiling at her with a horrible approximation of kindness. 'Give us the pendant, little lady, and there'll be no need for any more bloodshed.'

The pendant! She didn't have it. It rested in Devary's care, but she had no intention of revealing that fact.

'Why's it so important to you? You've killed for it!'

The second man spoke up, and in his face and manner there was a trace of regret.

'We've no desire to kill you, truly. Just give it up and we'll be gone.'

'No,' she said, backing away. She heard her name called; Devary was trying to reach her, but as she watched he was attacked anew, three men surrounding him. Desperately he turned to defend himself, unable to help her.

'No!' she said again, anguished. 'Why are you doing this?'

'Do you know what it is you're carrying?' The first man's

225

eyes were oddly alight. He took a sudden leap towards her and grabbed her arms. 'You'll never be safe while you keep the pendant. Give it up!'

She twisted, slashing with the knife. Her attacker cried out in surprise and pain and released her.

'Llandry!' The shout was desperate. Devary tackled the man who'd grabbed her, but the second was after her. She ran hard, but she was small and her stride was short. Her pursuer caught up to her easily, knocking her to the ground. She bit at the hands that tried to subdue her, and stabbed upwards with her knife. A cry of pain rang in her ears, and then she was free. She unclasped her cloak and let it fall to the ground as she unfurled her wings. Then she was aloft, soaring upwards, flying with all the speed she could muster.

She'd only intended to get above her attacker, out of reach of his weapons, but she was followed: two men opened their wings and jumped into the air after her. She heard cursing, and a hand tried to grab her feet: she kicked hard, freeing herself, but the delay had given the second man enough time to get in front of her, cutting off her escape. She twisted to the left and darted out of reach, trying to rise, but she knew it was hopeless; her attackers had begun to circle, keeping her surrounded, and they were almost as fast as she was.

Then something hit her face. Confused, she saw flashing colour as wings fluttered directly in front of her eyes. Her absent winged friend had returned, and the stupid thing was buzzing like an enraged wasp. It threw itself into the face of the nearest foe, and the man faltered. Llandry seized her chance and shot forwards, her wings pumping as she climbed higher.

She turned, preparing to circle back, but the air abruptly blurred around her, like sheet rain, and she could see nothing through it. The sky began to ripple like a heat haze and a thick mist laced with colour rushed in, swirling visibly in front of her face. Heat beat upon her, of an intensity she'd never felt before in the temperate climate of Glinnery. When a faint but strengthening melody reached her ears and the ground turned lavender beneath her, Llandry realised what was happening.

She furled her wings and dropped, but too late. The heat vanished, the mist dissolved, and Llandry fell into deep lavender moss. Towering glissenwol caps rose around her, far taller than

226

those of her home, decked with dazzling colour. Lights filled the deep blue skies, glittering like polished gems. She saw drifting coils of silvered mist, tasted honey and nectar on her tongue. Her eyes filled with tears at the extreme onslaught of beauty, and the sheer richness of the scents and tastes and sounds struck her senses like an assault. She fought for breath as she lay helplessly on the ground, dread and rapture filling her soul and pain ripping away her strength.

The smells and sounds and sensations were familiar, so familiar, even though her one and only previous visit to the Upper Realm had been eleven years ago. She had stood in the Daylit Off-World for only moments that time, but the experience had stayed with her ever since, as clear as a memory of only yesterday. Helplessly intrigued in spite of her father's strictures, Llandry had always hoped, someday, to repeat that experience; but not like this. Not while Devary remained in Glinnery, beleaguered and in danger, and it was all her fault.

Mastering herself with an effort, Llandry pulled herself to her feet, gritting her teeth against a sudden renewed rush of grinding pain. Funny, that part she did not remember from last time. Turning wildly, she searched for the gate that had brought her through. It would appear as a ripple in the air, splashes of colour out of sync with the surroundings, a sense of heat.

There; a few metres above her and to her left. She opened her wings, but as she tried to fly her back muscles screamed in agony and she fell to the ground again. Undaunted, she launched herself once more, forcing her objecting muscles to cooperate. Another minute, another effort, and she would be back through into Glinnery.

The gate pulsed and her winged friend appeared, its small body spat out with enough force to send it tumbling helplessly through the air. She caught it quickly and surged on, frantic. The tell-tale ripple in the sky was fading, the colours had disappeared, she felt no heat as she approached. A final spurt of effort availed her nothing: the way back to Devary closed forever and she was left hovering helplessly in nothing but empty air.

227

24

Working his way laboriously through a bristling set of bushes, Tren almost tripped over the shortig that sat, panting, in the midst of the undergrowth. The dog grinned up at Tren, tongue lolling, with the air of a workman reaching the end of the day's business.

'What? That's it?' Tren stood still, looking in puzzlement at the self-satisfied creature. He couldn't see any reason why the animal would consider its task finished. He hadn't found Griel, or Ana, or Eva. He didn't appear to have discovered anything.

Tren groaned. The absurd creature had probably been following the scent of one of the brightly-coloured tree beasts that Tren had repeatedly glimpsed as they journeyed. The dog hadn't been tracking Griel at all. He exhaled slowly and sat down where he stood, weary and discouraged and afraid.

Rikbeek swooped down from above, chattering. Tren frowned. He couldn't place the meaning of the gwaystrel's utterances the way Eva did, but the string of notes sounded like a warning. Tren surged to his feet, alert. His straining ears caught the sound of cracking underbrush as somebody made their way through the jungle ahead of him.

He grabbed Bartel and slipped into the bushes. Rikbeek stopped chattering and followed, settling once again on the dog's back. Tren took up a station several feet from the little clearing the dog had found. He wanted to be out of the sight of whoever was approaching, but he also wanted to observe that person himself.

After a couple of minutes, a whurthag emerged from the trees. The beast moved with the sinuous grace of an enormous feline, at ease and apparently docile. Nonetheless, the raw power in its muscled limbs sent shivers down Tren's spine. He hoped it was fully under control.

Then Griel appeared, walking a few paces behind his terrifying companion. He whistled briefly and the whurthag stopped and sat on its haunches. The sorcerer paused approximately where the shortig had been sitting moments earlier. Tren couldn't see what he did, but he did see the door that opened in the ground. Griel and his companion walked through, their figures diminishing as if they descended a staircase. Then the door closed neatly behind them.

Tren darted forward, keeping his eyes firmly fixed on the patch of ground that had apparently held a door. He knelt before it, searching with eyes and hands. He could see nothing but damp earth and the sparse fungi that struggled to grow under the heavy canopy. His fingers, however, met wood, smooth and warm and unmistakeably forming a rounded door like the one he'd seen in the sands.

Tren cursed himself for having failed to expect that. It was an advanced illusion, one bound into the darkness that held sway beneath the trees. It wouldn't have been possible under the strong moonlight that bathed the exposed white sand, but here it was a relatively simple matter to replicate the appearance of shadow-bound earth.

He didn't expect to find a handle. The door in the sands had not had one, and he couldn't find one here either. He dispelled Griel's illusion, and a neat round door materialised in the ground. Tren blinked. There was a stylised face painted into the wood, a congenially happy face composed of a mere few lines. Beneath it was an arrow pointing to the bottommost edge of the door. Tentatively, Tren pressed the spot beneath the arrow. A latch sprung and the door popped open.

He paused for a moment, sitting on his haunches. It occurred to him that he was being toyed with. Had Griel known he was there, crouched in the bushes? Had he expected that

229

Tren would discover the entrance to his home, or were the face and the arrow aimed at someone else?

No matter. He had no choice but to proceed. Checking that the shortig and Rikbeek followed, Tren descended a set of packed earth stairs into a dark underground passage. The staircase was long, leading him far under the earth. The door closed silently behind him.

Eva followed Ana through a series of rooms, each sumptuously — if somewhat fancifully — furnished. Their underground dwelling was impressively expansive, but then, why not? People who could so freely manipulate their surroundings could have anything that they wished. She was beginning to understand the importance of the so-named "istore" stone, an example of it still adorning her finger. She'd felt the surge of empowerment from the ring as she manipulated her former prison. It was more than that, though. It seemed to bring her closer to this off-world, make her a part of it. With the istore on her finger, she could see through the solidity of Ana's house. The outlines of the furniture and objects held a degree of insubstantiality; she could easily reshape them herself, move them around, alter everything as she chose. The possibilities were staggering. But this did not seem to be a preoccupation to Ana. What, then, was the mysterious purpose she spoke of?

They paused at last in a small room that looked like an antechamber to something larger. Griel walked in through a door on the opposite side of the room, a whurthag at his heels. Ana smiled and crossed to him.

'Griel, dear, look who found us!'

Griel smiled at Eva and offered her a courtly half-bow. She inclined her head frostily, refusing to be drawn by his display of manners.

'Were you successful, darling?' Ana tugged affectionately at the lapels of her husband's coat, smiling winningly at him.

'Everything went very well, yes. Here.' Griel placed something into Ana's hand. She beamed sunnily at him, holding up a silver-wrought pendant worked with a pattern of stars.

'Beautiful,' she said, then plucked the stone from the centre with the ease of picking fruit. She bounced it in her small hand, admiring the way it sparkled.

'Your timing is really excellent, dear. I was just taking our guest to see the project. Now I will be able to add this at the same time.' She kissed Griel's cheek.

'You're welcome,' he said affably. He nodded politely to Eva and turned to follow his wife as she opened the door through which he'd arrived.

But just then it clicked open and Tren appeared. His eyes were a little wild and he looked startled to walk straight into a cluster of people. He saw Eva, and for an instant relief suffused his face. But only for an instant.

'Have you seen this thing?' He ignored Ana, ignored Griel and the whurthag. He looked so aghast that her own relief at his safety quickly dissipated.

'What thing?'

'The project!' Ana clapped her hands like a child, and flung the door wide open. 'You're quite resourceful after all, boy — Tren, was it? — so you can stay. You can help Griel.' Tren's eyes had lingered on Eva's, but at that he refocused on Ana, nonplussed.

'Help with what? This is your *project*?'

'Isn't it marvellous?' Ana swept through the door, Griel trailing after her. Eva tried to smile at Tren as she moved past him, touching his hand briefly as she did so.

Then she stopped, frozen with shock. She understood, all at once, what Ana's 'project' was, and Tren's wild look was all too clearly explained.

She stood in a vast chamber, far bigger than any room she'd seen before. The ceiling stretched away and away, its precise reaches lost in shadow. Tiny light-globes bobbed everywhere, softly illuminating the skeleton of an animal so big that it barely fitted into the room. Ana and Griel had to hug the wall in order to edge around it. Tilting back her head, Eva stared at the vast rib cage that rose before her eyes, overlapped by a wing as large as the city square in Glour.

The bones resembled nothing she'd seen in biology before. They were polished and perfect, indigo in colour, and gleaming silver. Not just a faint sheen but a strong glow that pulsed as if with a heartbeat.

She swore under her breath. The istore, as it had been called,

231

was certainly no stone. It was the bones of a creature easily fifty times the size of anything she'd ever heard of.

Worse, it was more than a collection of bones. Eva could feel the energy rippling through this marvellous construction, the hint of an awareness clinging to the physical remains. It slept, but not deeply; it stirred as Eva's mind touched it, and she sensed an obstruction, or rather, an absence. A gap yawned in its skull, not large but sufficient to retard its progress. Sluggishly, sleep-fuddled and confused, the beast was trying to close that hole, generating new bone matter to complete itself. It tried and repeatedly failed, as if it needed wholeness for complete renewal.

The missing piece was exactly the size of the stone Ana had plucked from the pendant.

Dragging her thoughts back, Eva stood reeling. One word repeated in her mind, a name previously confined to legend and forgotten memory. It worked its way to her lips, relentless though she tried to stifle it.

'*Draykon?*' The word emerged cracked and breathless, but even so it echoed in the vast hall, seeming to grow larger. Every story she'd ever heard about the draykon rushed in upon her all at once: never many tales, but all horrifying when applied to the undeniable solidity of the beast that crouched on four legs before her, wings half-open as if it was about to launch into flight.

'Isn't he beautiful?' Ana's voice, full of pride and delight, floated back to her from somewhere on the other side of the beast. Eva sensed her probing ceaselessly at the ancient draykon's consciousness, nudging it, pushing it towards wakefulness.

'What are you *doing*?' gasped Eva in pure disbelief. 'You can't wake this creature up!'

'But I can! He *wants* to wake, and he likes me.'

'Likes you? You're completely insignificant to him. We all are.' Even that may be a charitable interpretation. If the stories were true, the draykon had plenty of reasons to hate humans.

'Nonsense. He knows me. He'll be grateful to me for waking him up. He already *feels* grateful.'

Eva sensed nothing like gratitude in the draykon's sluggish awareness. If anything, she felt a stirring irritation.

'You can't make a companion out of him, Ana. He's far too

232

strong, too wild. He won't submit to you.'

'Oh, now you sound exactly like Griel. Always caution, caution. If you won't help me I'll do it myself, and when my glory wakes up, you can be draykon food.'

Eva gave up. If even Griel couldn't reach Ana, nobody could. Their only chance was to retrieve the istore piece from Ana, but even that was too little, too late. The draykon was already almost complete, its consciousness too close to wakefulness; sooner or later it would succeed in its efforts to renew itself, with or without that last piece of bone. When that happened, all they could do was hope that Ana was right about her companion elect's feelings.

Because if the draykon didn't feel any kinship with the fools who had woken him up, then they were all in very deep trouble.

25

Llandry couldn't move. When she tried, the world tilted and fell and she fell with it. She suffered nausea so intense she could only lie in the damp moss and clutch her belly, waiting to vomit. The winged daefly-thing flew into her face, beating at her with its tissue-paper wings. She ignored it. The pain and nausea seemed a fitting end to the events of that day. But Devary's face rose in her mind's eye, fighting against dangerous odds, his attackers closing in around him. She pictured him bloodied and weak, wounded, even killed. The image was enough to force her to her knees, then to her feet.

The world swam before her eyes and she closed them. She felt wings against her face again.

'Stop that,' she muttered. 'I'm up.' She caught the thing carefully in her hands and opened her eyes. She could focus on it without falling: good.

'We have to go back,' she told it, firmly. 'There must be another gate nearby, or maybe one will open. There've been enough of them lately.'

The coloured thing beat against the prison of her fingers, trying to release itself. She frowned down at it.

'You need a name. I can't call you "Thing" forever.' She thought for a moment. 'You can be Prink.'

Prink sank its sharp proboscis into her thumb. She winced,

234

releasing it.

'Well, Prink, can I rely on you to help me?' Prink fluttered away from her, distracted by a passing insect. Llandry sighed. 'No. I suppose not. Come on.' She looked around. A twisted replica of the forests of Glinnery surrounded her completely. She could see nothing but towering glissenwol, draping vines and moss. At length, she picked a direction at random. Unfurling her wings, she climbed into the air, ignoring the pain of overuse in the muscles of her arms and back. She didn't care if it hurt. She could make much faster progress on the wing than on foot. She gritted her teeth and flew on.

She flew until her back was screaming with pain and her eyes were sore with staring into the misty skies, searching for the tell-tale ripple in the air that revealed the presence of a gate. She saw nothing, no sign of gathering mist or building heat that might suggest she was drawing close to a gate. Around her the glissenwol rose in unbroken ranks, so similar to her home that she began to doubt herself. Had she indeed crossed over at all? Perhaps she was merely confused. But no: no glissenwol of Glinnery grew to such impossible, regal heights, nor were they decked with such vividness of colour. The jade-green sky spiralling with lights was no figment of her imagination.

She was angling in circles around the location where she'd come through, intent on searching every inch of the forest until she found a way back. She stopped circling when she felt a distant tug, a faint pulse of energy that drew her irresistibly to her left. She'd never felt that kind of a pull before, but things were certainly different here. She followed the sensation, feeling it grow stronger as she flew.

She landed after a time and proceeded on foot. Prink fluttered ahead of her, frequently distracted by the prospect of a fat insect or two. After a few minutes she passed between two particularly majestic glissenwol forming a kind of archway over a silent clearing. Here was where the energy came from: she could feel it filling her body, pulsing in her bones. But no gate was in evidence. Just what was it?

Instinct drew her eyes to the ground. She saw a carpet of moss, blue like the forest floor at home but twinkling in a way no Glinnish moss had ever done. She knelt, ignoring the seep of moisture through the fabrics of her trousers. Running her fingers over the soft, cushiony moss, she felt the coolness of stone.

She inhaled sharply. Buried in the mosses were motes of indigo colour, shining softly silver. She tugged gently at a piece of the stuff and it came off easily in her hand.

Istore. No doubt about it.

She could feel it, a lattice of stone spreading through the ground beneath her. It felt alive, like some dormant energy struggling to awaken itself. It stirred in response to her presence, straining towards her like a flower tilting its petals towards the sun. Llandry felt instinctively that she held some kind of power over it; that if she lent it some of her own life and vibrancy, the sleeping vigour that lay dormant underground would burst forth. The pattern of energy spread so far around and beneath her that she felt engulfed by it, tiny and insignificant in comparison to its vastness.

No, not insignificant. The piece of istore in her hand pulsed in tandem with its brethren, sending waves of energy through her, sharp and invigorating. Somehow she held a link to this behemoth. It needed her.

The thought terrified her. She jumped to her feet and backed away, spreading her wings. In another moment she was in the air, hurrying to leave the clearing and its mysteries behind.

Hours later, Llandry was ready to despair. Her efforts had availed her nothing; only once had she glimpsed a gate in the distance, and by the time she had reached it it was gone. For the first time she cursed the sorcerers of Glinnery for their efficiency; if only they were not so quick to close up the gates that spiralled out of the air, she might be home by now. At last she dropped slowly to the ground, dejected. She'd flown too far, too fast, too hard, and her muscles were worn out. Perhaps she could rest, just for a little while.

She sat carefully, easing her weary muscles into something approaching a restful posture. She composed herself to sleep a little, hoping to wake refreshed and ready to resume her search. She closed her eyes, wishing she had Sigwide to curl his comforting warmth against her. What had become of him, left behind in Glinnery? She felt a stab of loss, missing him fiercely. She hadn't been without him since she was nine years old.

Llandry sighed and twisted, turning onto her side in the hopes of easing her muscles. She resented the tear that crept from beneath her closed lids, feeling it a betrayal of her dignity. A crushing wave of embarrassment, humiliation and despair filled her, and she only cried more, wiping her face futilely with her sleeve.

At last the tears slowed. It occurred to her to wonder if her enemies knew where she was, whether there would be a renewed pursuit. A flicker of fear rippled through her at the thought, and all thought of sleep receded. Sighing, she dragged herself into a sitting position.

'That's right, duck. Shouldn't think you could sleep here in all this damp. And don't you know there are beasts about?'

Llandry sprang to her feet, heart pounding. A woman stood ten feet away, grey-haired and a little on the stout side. She was wrapped in layers of coloured fabrics so bright they competed with the bejewelled glory of the foliage around her. In fact, with her rumpled features, bright smile and wispy hair, she resembled some kind of Uppers blossom herself.

'Who are you?' Despite the woman's inoffensive appearance, Llandry backed away. She would trust nobody at present.

'There now, duck, no need to be afraid o' me. A right dance you've led me, all over the dunes, like.'

'The dunes?' Llandry blinked, puzzled. Was the woman mad?

'Well, it won't look like no dunes now, will it? You're homesick.' She spoke kindly, but Llandry had no idea what she meant.

'I haven't seen any dunes,' she said tiredly. 'I've been circling the forest for hours. Do you know where to find a gate back to Glinnery?'

The woman shook her head, advancing slowly. 'I don't think that's the right idea for you just now, duckie. You're in no state to travel. Your Grandpa's out looking for you; he'll be glad you're in one piece. Come along with me, now.'

Llandry backed away again, confusion deepening into a wisp of fear. 'I don't have a Grandpa.'

'Course you do, dear. That's a silly thing to say, isn't it?'

'Who are you?' Llandry repeated, holding her ground against the woman's approach.

'I'm your step-grandmother, or what they call it. But you can call me Mags.' The woman smiled gently, full of apparent kindness. 'I'm to take you home, duckie, and not a moment too soon I'd say. You look bushed. A good meal and a proper bed's what you need.'

Bushed? Llandry supposed she meant 'tired'. 'I don't have a grandfather,' she repeated. 'Mamma's father died ten years ago, and Pa's...' She stopped. 'Pa said his father went through a gate one day and never came back. He said he was killed up here.'

Mags looked sincerely surprised. 'Well, isn't that just like men. To think of that. Years, and him hiding up here like a spider all that time. I'll be giving him a thorough scolding, you mark my words.'

Mags didn't look like she was capable of scolding anybody. 'You... live up here?'

'Going on twenty year, now. Twenty years of Middles time, that is, near as I can tell.'

'Just like that?'

'It's not too bad, duck, if you know what you're about. Course, most don't, not these days. Come along, now, it's not far to the house.' Llandry watched her, her resolve wavering. Mags had made no move to push Llandry into anything; certainly she had not tried to attack her. Then again, the very mildness of her appearance and manner could be a trick.

'How did you know I was here?'

'Your Grandpa brought you through, dear.'

Llandry's head spun. 'You were watching me?'

'Now, dear, I think you ought to lie down before you do anything else. You're looking a bit peaky.' She was close enough now to furrow her rumpled brow at Llandry's face. 'What's that, tears? Had a bad day? I've got just the thing. Nice hot food on the stove at home. You come with me, now.'

Llandry was aware of her tiredness like a physical burden, threatening to overwhelm all of her attempts to be wary. She was about to accept Mags' offer when a new voice spoke from behind her, a low, rather rough male one. She turned around so fast that she almost lost her balance.

A man was approaching through the trees, slowly, using a cane to support himself. He was aged, but the life in him shone through his bent frame and shuffling step. He stopped a few feet away from her, looking into her face intently. He didn't smile.

'Hello, Llandry, my dear. I've been wanting to meet you since you were born.'

His hair was pale grey instead of blonde, and his eyes were hazel rather than blue, but she knew him nonetheless. The shape of his face, his broad shoulders, his short nose, heavy brow and thick eyebrows were all so familiar to her. If he hadn't had the cane — if he was, perhaps, a few years younger — he would walk with the same controlled power as his son.

There was no question at all whose father he was.

'Oh,' said Llandry, faintly. Her knees trembled. On top of everything else, it was far too much. The world blurred as more tears leaked into her eyes. She closed them, welcoming the darkness.

'Mags,' said her grandfather warningly. Llandry felt Mags' plump arms catch her as she swayed, but when she opened her eyes again she saw only grey mist. She submitted gratefully as the mist closed around her and she lost consciousness.

Llandry woke up under a patched duvet in a small bedroom. She opened her eyes to see whitewashed walls, exposed wooden beams in the ceiling and rag rugs on the floor. She sat up, feeling dizzy. Mags instantly stepped into the room, as if she had been waiting for Llandry to wake.

'You feel better, duckie?' She bent to look into Llandry's face. 'Still a bit white, but you'll perk right up after some breakfast.' She left the room and returned almost immediately with a tray, setting it in front of Llandry. She had prepared some fresh bread, serving it with butter, cheese and fruit. A cup of hot milk steamed next to the plate piled full of food. Realising her hunger, Llandry ate quickly and well, feeling rapidly stronger. Mags watched with smiling approval.

'If you come down in a minute, lovie, your grandpa's waiting.' Llandry couldn't help smiling back as Mags collected the tray and departed. She climbed out of the bed, moving carefully: she still felt weak. She stood still for a moment, testing her strength, and thankfully her legs held. She was wearing a voluminous cotton nightdress that she suspected might belong to Mags. Her own clothes had been pressed and hung up to air in the wardrobe, and she dressed quickly, enjoying the feel of

239

fresh-smelling clothes next to her skin.

But as she ventured downstairs, her stomach fluttered with nerves and she knew her old shyness had come upon her again. Her grandfather sat in a wooden rocking chair near to a homey stone-built fireplace. He had a patchwork quilt over his legs — was it Mags who made all these comfortable things? — and a book lay open in his lap. He looked up as Llandry entered the large, open-plan room. Mags stood at a large stone sink washing up the breakfast things; she threw Llandry a quick, encouraging smile before turning back to her work.

Her grandfather looked up, regarding her over a pair of wire-rimmed glasses.

'Hello, Llandry,' he said in his rough voice. He still didn't smile.

'Hello,' she mumbled, almost inaudibly, busying herself with straightening her blouse. This stranger looked like her father, but his gravity and lack of warmth unnerved her. He did not feel like family. She hoped he would say something else, but he just looked at her.

'I-I don't know your name,' she said. 'Pa never said.'

'Rheas,' he replied.

'Rheas...?'

His mouth twisted. 'Ah yes. I forgot that Aysun took his wife's name. Rheas Irfan.'

Llandry nodded. He was scowling at her as though his son's actions were her fault. She hovered nervously, finally taking a chair as far away from Rheas as possible. He grinned at her mirthlessly.

'Afraid of me, are you? Timid thing. Must get that from your mother. It doesn't come from my line.'

Llandry felt a hint of annoyance. *Good*, she thought. *Annoy me and I'll stop feeling afraid of you.*

Rheas sat back, picking up his book again, but he didn't read it. He kept his gaze on Llandry.

'Don't you have questions for me?' he said at last.

Llandry did, but she didn't know how to ask them of this cold, fierce man. She looked down at her hands. 'Mags said you brought me here,' she said to her lap. 'Is that true?'

'Certainly. I didn't want my only grandchild to be slain before I got a chance to meet her.'

240

Afterwards would be all right, would it? Llandry cleared her face of all expression, steeled herself, and looked up. She felt a quiver of anxiety at Rheas's intent study of her, but she refused to look away.

'How did you know I was in danger?'

'Surely that's obvious, Llandry. You've had an irilapter following you for weeks — or did you think that was a coincidence?'

'An irilapter?'

Rheas sighed. 'Mags, where did the stupid creature go?'

'He's here, lovie. I gave him a dish of honey and he's been happy as can be.' Mags approached, her hands cupped around something winged and colourful.

'Prink?' said Llandry, in complete incomprehension.

'Prink? Is that what you called it?' Rheas was amused. He allowed Mags to place the irilapter on his lap, then waved her away. He stroked Prink's wings, very gently, and the irilapter actually began to purr.

'An old friend of mine,' said her grandfather. 'When the orting stopped speaking to me, I sent this little man to take over.'

Llandry was slightly reassured by his gentleness with Prink. Perhaps he wasn't as fierce as she'd thought.

'You were watching me through Prink?' Wait, that wasn't all. 'Through *Sigwide*?'

Rheas nodded, obviously laughing at her. 'I'm surprised your father didn't guess. Quite a huge coincidence, wasn't it, for you to happen across a helpless baby animal in the middle of a rogue portal? I was hoping to bring you through, but your mother was too fast for me. No matter: you kept the orting.'

Llandry blinked, nonplussed. She remembered that day clearly: her mother's fear, her own heartbreak at the prospect of parting with the tiny orting, and her father's trepidation. And her grandfather had meant to take her? She added that to the list of his offences, feeling a comforting buzz of anger inside that seared away her timidity.

'So... you're a summoner?'

He shrugged indifferently. 'I suppose that's the label you might put on it down there. I never cared much about these things until I came here. Spend enough time up here, it matters.

241

You pick it up.'

'How?' Llandry struggled to understand. He obviously had considerable summoning talent — more even than anyone she knew, because she'd never heard of anybody using a companion as a spy before. Yet he also controlled the gates, apparently, or was it Mags who had opened the gate that she'd fallen through?

'Think about it,' he said, watching her. 'You live up here year after year, breathing the air, drinking the water, eating the plants and the animals. It changes you.'

Llandry backtracked. 'Sigwide stopped talking to you?'

'He transferred his loyalty entirely to you,' replied Rheas. 'He wouldn't let me use his eyes anymore. I had to improvise something else. Now, it is my turn for a question or two. What in the world have you been doing, my dear, to attract so much ... *negative* attention?'

'I thought you were watching.'

Rheas grimaced. 'Irilapters are flighty. They aren't the most reliable spies. I missed a few episodes of your little drama.'

Llandry stiffened. Little? She told him the whole story, blushing as she admitted her own mistakes. When she had finished, he opened his mouth to speak but she cut him off.

'No. I have something to ask you now.' He lifted his bushy brows at her and waited. She realised she was clenching her fists in her lap, and made an effort to smooth them out.

'*Why* have you been sitting up here, watching us, interfering with our lives and never telling anyone you were alive? You didn't even tell your own son! How could you do that to your family?' She was very angry now, and she knew that it showed. She didn't care: let him see how disgusted she was with him.

Rheas's eyes glittered at her. 'Perhaps not everyone has the same value for family that you do,' he suggested. She snorted, turning her face away from him.

'Your father and I didn't get along well,' he said, more quietly. 'We fought about a lot of things, particularly about your mother. When he insisted on moving to Glinnery to marry her, I cast him off. I told him never to come home. A year or two later I left Irbel forever and settled up here.'

Llandry was too incensed to speak for several moments. 'How could you object to my mother?' she said at last, controlling her voice with an effort.

242

'I thought her a silly, flighty Glinnish woman, fit for nothing but arranging flowers and decorating her hair. Like most of the rest of them.' He said it flatly, unapologetically.

'She's nothing like that!'

'Perhaps I was wrong,' he conceded. 'Nonetheless, for your father to turn his back on his Irbellian heritage — to just up and leave for her — was unforgiveable.' He paused. 'At the time.'

Rheas's last words took some of the fury out of Llandry's anger. 'At the time?'

'I tried to go back, once,' he said. 'I regretted what I'd done. I was going to explain, maybe even apologise. But when I saw Aysun, I couldn't approach him. I knew he wouldn't welcome me. It was shortly after you were born.'

'Foolish male pride,' said Mags. Llandry realised she was standing behind her chair, listening.

Rheas cast Mags an irritated look. 'Perhaps. But she's here, isn't she? I got her out in time. So you see my 'meddling', as you term it, has not been for nothing.'

This speech puzzled Llandry, but she concluded that Mags had not approved of Rheas's spying on her.

'Thank you for rescuing me,' said Llandry, rising decisively to her feet. 'But now I must go home.'

Rheas's heavy grey brows snapped together. 'What?'

'I need to find out what has happened to my... my friend. And to Sigwide.' Rheas's brows rose at her hesitant use of the word "friend", then he frowned again, looking more fierce than ever.

'You can't go back, especially not after everything you've just told me. You must stay here, where you will be safe.'

Llandry snorted with laughter. 'Safe? Not even a full unit of guards could keep me safe. What makes you think you can do better?'

Rheas chuckled grimly. 'Glinnery guards? Flimsy pansies, not soldiers at all. I could do better than that by myself.'

Llandry looked pointedly at the cane that rested against his chair, and he scowled.

'This is my territory,' he said. 'I have complete control over it. Nobody will enter without my consent. I'll show you.' He rose slowly from his chair, leaning heavily on his cane. Mags hovered, trying to grasp his elbow to help him up, but he waved her off irritably.

'I'm fine, woman. Now, then.' He moved to the window, beckoning Llandry to follow him. She did so, unable to suppress her curiosity. What she saw outside surprised her. The glissenwol forest was gone, completely gone. The house stood instead in a pretty alpine valley, ringed with distant mountain ranges.

'How far did you bring me?' she said, her heart sinking. She must be miles and miles away from where she'd come through. How would she ever find Devary again?

'Not very far at all, in fact,' he said, glancing shrewdly at her. 'Watch.'

She watched. Nothing happened for several seconds, and then all at once plants started to erupt from the ground before the house. They grew rapidly into tall vines with thick stems, growing and growing until they were taller than the house. They put out leaves and developed thorns. Within minutes the house was surrounded by a thicket of vicious-looking vegetation, blocking out the valley. Some of them then proceeded to grow mouths and began snapping at passing flies.

'That's only the start of it,' said Rheas, his tone self-satisfied. 'So you see, you're safer up here.'

Llandry shook her head. 'And my friends? Devary? Sigwide?'

'The orting will be fine. He can take care of himself. As for your 'friend', he's a grown man, is he not? He can take care of himself, too.'

'But that wouldn't be right. He was in danger protecting *me*. It was my fault that all of it happened in the first place. And he was carrying the pendant.'

'Ah, yes. The *istore*. Do you have some of it with you? This is quite important, Llandry.'

Llandry felt in the pocket of her trousers, suddenly anxious. She had pocketed the piece she'd taken from the ground a few hours before, but had the stone fallen out when her clothes were washed? No, there it was, cool and smooth in her hand. She drew it out and handed it to Rheas. When the stone touched his skin, he gasped and almost dropped it.

'You're telling me you have no idea what this is?' He was glaring at her, brows drawn together, angry. She lifted her chin. He couldn't intimidate her anymore, not now that she knew how he had treated her parents. How he'd spoken of her mother.

244

'I think I do.' She told him about the clearing with the gems embedded in the moss. He nodded grimly.

'There are a few of those sites, scattered about.'

She looked up at him, startled. 'How do you know about them?'

'I've found many of them over the years, the same way you did. I can't help but sense them.'

She took a deep breath. He spoke slowly, portentously, and she sensed that he knew more than he had told her.

'Why do I sense them?'

He looked at her seriously. 'It would be better never to know, Llandry. Believe me.' He sat down in his rocking chair again, settling into it with a sigh. 'If you've had as much trouble over it as you say, I imagine somebody else has been making some accurate guesses about it. Possibly several somebodies.' He regarded her carefully. 'You're a summoner yourself, I think you said?'

'Yes... well, not really. I was never trained.'

'But you have the ability. Any sorcerous talent?'

'Of course not.'

He laughed softly. 'Of course not. Spoken with such conviction. You've never even tried, have you?'

'No, I...'

'Your mother is a sorcerer, yes? A strong one, I am willing to wager.'

'She hasn't practiced in years, but yes. What does this have to do with...?'

'So you've strong sorcerer heritage on your mother's side, summoner on mine. Why do you think it's hereditary? Why do only *some* people have these abilities?'

Llandry was growing impatient. 'I don't know! It doesn't matter. I'm not a sorcerer, I'm not even a trained summoner. I don't have anything to do with any of this.'

Rheas snorted. 'The ignorance is stunning.' Llandry bristled, and he raised an eyebrow at her. 'Not you personally. Well yes, you personally, but it's not your fault. Your society is ignorant. They've forgotten everything because they've lost their connection with it. Wilfully severed it, in fact. The so-called Seven Realms, so perfectly controlled and enclosed, everything relentlessly tended and deliberately designed. They've squeezed the life out of it and they don't even realise what they've lost.' His lips twisted into a sneer. 'Because they're *afraid* of it. Afraid! So they push it away, forbid travel to the Off-Worlds, limit and fiercely control anything that comes out of them. They fear the unknowable, and in the process forget almost everything they ever knew about it in the first place.' Mags was patting his hand, soothingly. She had probably heard that rant before.

'I don't understand,' said Llandry.

'You wouldn't, would you, because it's your world that I'm speaking of. You've grown up thinking everything can be neatly boxed and labelled. You're either a summoner, or a sorcerer, or neither. There are strictly prescribed options in each category, organisations to monitor useage of those talents, laws to prevent almost everything that could conceivably be achieved with the use of them, books to catalogue the two or three percent of the whole that they understand and if it isn't written in those books, it doesn't exist. In doing all this, they squandered a potent weapon and lost sight of their own identity.'

Llandry stared at him, aghast. He sounded so terribly bitter. 'But you said yourself, only a moment ago, that it's better not to know.'

'Yes,' he said heavily. 'It is, now. Because you're not equipped for it, you have no idea... It's too late to go back.' He sighed, looking very old. 'I've been watching you, my Llandry, and I fear for you. Do you realise how remarkable it is that you are essentially a capable summoner without a shred of training? Your father had no idea what he was doing when he forbade you to study. In fact, if my fears are correct, he had no idea what he was doing when he married your mother.'

'If you hadn't ostensibly got yourself killed up here, Papa probably wouldn't have forbidden it. The fault for that lies at *your* door.'

'Blame me for that if you want to,' he said testily. 'Why do you think I never went back? Your father's happier having me as a scapegoat. But no matter.' He straightened in his chair. 'I believe you're closer to those bones than you realise, Llandry. I sense them because I've been up here so long it's seeped into my skin. But you...'

She sat silently for a moment, trying to take in everything he'd told her. His convoluted statements, vague hints and portentous addendums added up to nothing comprehensible; she could barely understand what he had said.

'How do you know all of this?' she said at last.

He shrugged. 'Unimportant.'

Llandry thought of all the rogue gates that had been opening across the Seven in recent weeks, how the animal inhabitants of the Off-Worlds had been streaming through in droves. 'You think somebody is trying to bring it all back. Is that it?'

Rheas pondered her question. 'No,' he said at last. 'I don't think that is it at all. The gates, the animals, all the upheaval — it's a side effect of something else.' He sat forward. 'Think about it. When magical talents are limited to the few, that puts those few in a strong position, doesn't it? You're eligible for all manner of prestigious and well-paid positions if you're lucky enough to be a summoner, or a sorcerer.' Llandry nodded, thinking of her mother and Lady Glostrum. 'Well, and what about the hierarchy within those roles? I think someone is well aware that, these days, the summoners and sorcerers of the Seven are barely touching the tip of the iceberg. If you could tap into the rest, that would place you in a very advantageous position indeed, would it not?'

'Tap into the rest?'

'I've been seeing animals lately that I've never seen before. I'm certain some of them were extinct until recently. Somebody's been experimenting, I would say. Now, ordinarily I am all in favour of experimentation. But dragging extinct animals back out of the past is carrying it too far. It's upsetting the balance of things, causing real chaos up here. And it opens up some dangerous possibilities. You spoke of whurthags being summoned, used as *companions*. That kind of dominance isn't possible if you've spent your life cosily enclosed in the Seven; you're too distant from the source, too closed, mind and soul. But if you've lived in the Off-Worlds, really opened yourself up to them, then believe me. It's quite possible.' He frowned fiercely at her, completely intent on his train of thought, and Llandry didn't dare interrupt. 'What if you could have any animal you chose as a companion, even one that was previously extinct? Even one that's twenty times your size? How about a muumuk? How about a *draykon*?' He spoke the word softly, as in awe. 'You'd be legendary. Unbeatable. And your — *our* —

comfortable little world has no notion of what's going on. There's a world of chaos on the way and they've laid themselves wide open to it.'

'A draykon?' Llandry thought of the pattern of istore-bones beneath the ground in the little clearing she'd found, and her breath stopped. The sheer *size* of it... were such a thing to awaken, she couldn't even imagine the consequences.

Looking at her grandfather's face, she had a sudden conviction that this wasn't even the worst of it. But he said no more, and she remembered his words. *It's better not to know.*

She stood up again. 'Then I have even more reason to return to Glinnery. I can't simply sit up here and watch it all happen! What will this do to the people of the Seven?'

'You can't stop it, Llandry. It's already gone too far.' Rheas spoke low and firm, but Llandry shook her head.

'There has to be something I can do.'

'Llandry. Listen to me.' There was a new note of urgency in his tone that captured Llandry's attention. She looked at him, waiting. 'Our "friends" are understandably ambitious, but they're are out of their depth. A draykon can never be controlled; it is not like the other animals of the Off-Worlds. But it goes beyond that. Waking one of them up will set off a chain of events which I fear will involve you very personally. You mustn't leave here now.'

'I don't understand.'

He looked at her helplessly. 'I can't explain, you wouldn't have any way to understand. You wouldn't believe me. You have to trust me, Llandry.'

'Trust you? You rejected my mother, abandoned my father, and now you're trying to keep me against my will. You've given me facts without evidence and plenty of apparently baseless speculation, and you're keeping information from me. Why should I trust you?'

Rheas slumped back in his chair, defeated. 'Maybe it's meant to be,' he muttered to Mags. 'Maybe I can't stop it. Maybe I'm not meant to.'

'What?' Llandry shook her head. She didn't want to know. 'Thank you for helping me,' she said, meaning it. 'You saved my life. But I have to go.' She looked at Mags's friendly face, wearing a sad smile, and at her dejected grandfather. 'I'll come back someday,' she said. 'And I'll bring my parents.' She kissed Mags's cheek and touched her grandfather's hand, briefly. Neither of them said anything. She walked to the door, opened it, and stepped out into the valley.

26

Eva thought fast, or tried to, but her horrified mind was slow to co-operate. There were stories about the draykon, telling of their strength, their longevity, their indifference to the boundaries between the Seven Realms and the Others. It was said that they were scarcely corporeal, as changeful as the Off-Worlds themselves. Eva had no way to tell if these stories were true, but the sheer, staggering size of the skeleton before her was evidence enough of their power to change everything. She didn't want to imagine the chaos and, probably, destruction a creature like this would wreak should it be awakened. The delicate balance between the Seven Realms and the Off-Worlds would disintegrate.

She had the horrifying sense that everything was spiralling out of control. Ana was circling the skeleton with the istore piece in her hand, the pendant from which she'd extracted it lying discarded on the floor. Several possible means of detaining Ana flitted through Eva's mind, but against the success of all was Griel and his pair of whurthag pets. The sorcerer possessed a relaxed air and an unruffled, unhurried demeanour, but Eva had no doubt he was alert to her actions. He strolled around the room, hands in his pockets, watching his wife work. Each time he passed Eva he gave her a pleasant nod, as if passing an acquaintance in the street.

Ana, on the other hand, was oblivious. It didn't seem to have occurred to her that Eva might refuse to participate in her scheme. She was intent on the bones of the draykon, running her hands over those parts of it that lay within her reach. She had the air of a collector admiring her latest acquisition, weirdly overlaid with the proprietorial pride of a mother. What did she really expect to happen? Would it really bow to her will, consent to act as her companion? Eva doubted it. She had to be prevented from waking the draykon, but how? Eva's stunned mind, laced with panic, refused to offer any answers.

Tren wandered nonchalantly in Eva's direction and leaned against the wall, mimicking Griel's casual manner. He smiled at Eva, bending his head close to her ear to speak in a low murmur.

'What are we doing about this?'

Eva shook her head minutely. 'Do you have any ideas?'

'What, no plan?' Tren lifted his brows at her.

'I'm not infallible,' returned Eva, irritably. 'Ana needs to be stopped, but not forcibly or we'll have a pair of whurthags down our throats. If we can get the istore off her, even better. But, Tren, I've a horrible feeling we're too late. That thing is already half awake.'

Tren's brows lowered into a frown. 'I think there's more going on here than we realise.' Tren told her about seeing Griel in the jungle, and finding the directions on the door. 'I could swear, when I opened that door, that he winked at me,' Tren finished. 'I feel like I'm being led around by the nose. Why would he do that when he killed Ed?'

This made no sense. It sounded as though Griel had deliberately ensured that Tren discovered their underground dwelling. 'Ana spoke of your helping him,' she murmured. 'Maybe he wanted your assistance.'

'With what? I don't see what there is for another sorc to do in all this.' He paused. 'Your role is obvious enough.'

'Is it?'

'Ana's confident, but even she must realise she can't control a newly-awakened draykon by herself. Probably not even with Griel's help.'

Eva's stomach turned over. Tren was right; she was detained here for the privilege of battling wills with a confused and probably enraged creature larger than her house. Her mind reeled at the prospect.

'I don't know. I can't think.' Eva felt desperate. Her usually able mind shied away from the sheer enormity of the circumstances; the odds were stacked against every idea that occurred to her. 'I'll think of something, I promise, but I need more time. Perhaps we could distract her, somehow.'

'Somehow,' echoed Tren. 'Right.' He paused for a moment in thought, then flashing Eva a quick grin he moved away from her, heading for where Ana was crouched over one of the draykon's feet.

'So, why am I here?' he said, quite loudly.

Ana didn't look up. 'Griel,' she said briefly, her tone an obvious command. Griel sauntered over and Ana flicked her fingers in Tren's direction, absently imperious. She was running her other hand over the skeletal draykon, her eyes gleaming.

Tren was moving before Griel could reach him. Several tall ladders were set against the draykon's sides, leading to scaffolded platforms high up in the air. He scaled one of these quickly and began to walk around the beast, running his hands over it in appreciation of its smoothness.

'Oh, they come off,' said Tren, as if agreeably surprised. He plucked at the skeleton, apparently removing several pieces of stone, and then began to juggle with them. He added an offensively cheerful whistle as he wandered off.

Ana jumped up, her expression outraged. 'What? That shouldn't be possible! Don't touch anything! Get off there! *Griel!*' She looked around for her husband, but he was nowhere in sight. With an exasperated sigh, she abandoned her task and began to climb a nearby ladder.

Intrigued, Eva stepped surreptitiously closer to the draykon and examined it. Each bone was enormous, much longer than her own, but a close look revealed that many of them were laced with cracks, as though they had been pieced together from many smaller segments. She fitted her fingers around a tiny chunk of istore and pulled, then tugged harder. It wouldn't move. It felt like the stones had been embedded in granite.

Tren was bluffing, then. He might have bought her a few extra minutes to think, but no more. Could she find a way to remove some of the bones? Probing the skeleton with her summoner's senses, Eva searched for a weak point, some way to interfere with the cohesion of the skeleton. Nothing. She probed more deeply, working with the speed of desperation, but it was futile. The creature was almost complete; its building life force streamed through each bone, binding them to one another. She would have as much luck attempting to take a bone out of her own arm.

Even the suggestion of it seemed to trouble Ana, however. She reached the place where Tren had been standing moments earlier and began to run her hands anxiously over the bones, looking for gaps. She smiled when she found none.

'Griel, kill the boy,' she ordered. 'He is a liability.' She swung down from the scaffolding with the ease of long practice. Alarmed at this sudden escalation, Eva worked her way around the skeleton, obliged to keep close to the wall. She found Tren on the other side of the room with Griel not far away. The two whurthags had left Griel's heels and were stalking Tren, backing him into a corner. His casual demeanour had vanished, and a look of panic crossed his face as his back hit the wall. He was weaponless, and his sorcery was little use in this kind of fight.

Of course, her summoner skills were little use in a fight like this either. But she had to do something.

Heart pounding, Eva stepped in front of Tren. Ignoring his objections, she shoved him bodily out of the way.

'Deal with Ana,' she said tersely. She focused on the whurthags, tuning out everything else that was happening around her. The beasts approached with stealthy grace, muscles bunching and lengthening under night-black hide. She could see the pale stone of the floor through their insubstantial forms. Cold, icy-hued eyes transferred their deathly gaze from Tren to herself. Fear weakened her limbs but she held her ground, bearing down with her will. Before she'd only needed to control the beast long enough to send it through the gates that Tren opened, but now that she herself stood in the Lowers that option was no longer open to her. She would have to wrest control of them from Griel, and then retain that control. She knew that when summoners failed at this, the first person the creature turned on was usually the summoner. And now she faced two of them alone.

She took a deep breath.

The thoughts buried in the fog of the beasts's minds were a

253

chaotic swirl of sensations and urges, like those of most animals. She sensed hunger, a desire for meat, and — chillingly — a burning resentment against the one who mastered them. The whurthags resisted her efforts to influence them, snarling their objections in low growls that sent a shiver of new terror through her. She worked harder, grimly determined, and at last the slow, menacing approach stopped. The whurthags waited, the tips of their tails twitching.

Eva heard shouts, men's voices, though whether it was Tren or Griel who cried out she was unable to say. Her concentration wavered and she almost lost the tentative control she'd established. She ruthlessly thrust aside her anxiety — she couldn't help Tren any more just now — and bore down, searching their minds for the kill order they'd received from Griel.

She found their impressions of Tren, flickering images formed of his height and size in relation to their own, his scent, his way of moving. They sensed his sorcery, interpreting it as a cloud of dark, enveloping fog. They were — had been — intent on him, but Eva found no kill instinct. What she found instead was 'guard'. They had been backing him into a corner, not to kill him but merely to keep him there. Griel had encouraged them to scare him, but he had not asked them to kill him.

This was of a piece with his earlier behaviour towards Tren, though it still made little sense to her. Nonetheless, she noted the information. If Griel was working at cross purposes to his wife, perhaps she could use that.

She found her own image in their minds, a softer figure, heavily scented in a way that tormented the whurthag's sensitive noses. They saw her as a more direct threat, as though she were an equal, an animal as strong as they were. To her surprise, their image of her was also wreathed in a dense fog of sorcery, though hers was paler and flickering with light. In her case, not only was there no kill order but she detected the opposite: they had been firmly instructed *not* to hurt her.

Tren was right: she was to be kept alive in order to help subdue the draykon. Not that it was much of a reprieve: the prospect was at least as terrifying as facing down a pair of whurthags determined to kill.

The sounds of fighting intruded on Eva's mental world.

254

Instinctively she glanced up, catching a brief glimpse of Tren twisting a protesting Ana's arm behind her back. He reached for the stone she carried, but Griel grabbed him and hauled him off Ana. The sorcerer glanced Eva's way, and she sensed the tug of his mind as he sought to summon one of his whurthags. She gripped hard; the beast faltered, and held.

Surprisingly, Griel grinned at her. Then he turned his attention back to Tren, who was trying to work his way out of the other sorcerer's grip. Griel was a few inches taller than Tren and built rather bigger. When it came to a physical fight, Tren didn't stand a chance.

Anxious to help, she grimly filtered out all the distractions and refocused her will on the beasts. Sweating, she fought hard to turn their attention on Griel. If they would only distract him long enough to free Tren, there was still a chance that she or Tren could stop Ana.

But then a scream of triumph lanced into her mind like a knife, shattering her absorption. Ana's voice screamed again, shrill with euphoria, and Eva's focus disintegrated entirely. Abandoning the whurthags, she looked up to see Tren on the floor, pinned there by Griel. A bruise on his face stood testament to his struggles, but now both of them had stopped fighting. They stared up at the draykon, awed.

Eva glanced up, too, but before she could discern any detail there was a flash so bright that it seared her eyes. She covered them with both hands, feeling tears of pain and shock drenching her face. The light receded but she remained as she was for several long moments, afraid that she would open her eyes only to find herself blinded.

Somebody barrelled into her. Her eyes flew open in spite of herself, but she could see very little through the burning after-images that danced across her vision. At least she still had some semblance of vision at all. Arms wrapped around her and she realised it was Tren.

'She's done it, she's added the last piece,' Tren gasped. 'I couldn't stop her — I tried, but Griel—.'

Tren broke off as the skeleton began to pulse with an indigo glow. A feeling of unbearable energy filled the chamber, beating against her flesh, and she struggled to breathe. She could only cling to Tren, her mind numb with the knowledge that they were

255

too late.

Ana appeared, flushed with excitement. She dragged Eva and Tren apart with astonishing strength, and grabbed Eva's hands.

'*Feel it*,' she said, and planted them against the draykon's side. Eva gasped as that terrifying energy ripped through her, leaving her weak. Ana had released her hands but she couldn't pull them back; she felt welded to the creature as the bones shuddered, growing hot. Her vision was returning, but something was wrong with it: she could see straight through Ana's chamber, straight through the fabric of the world. Layered with it was a forest she recognised as Glour, irignol trees clustering in a darkened forest. Though recognisable, the Middle Realms were hazy in her vision, as if glimpsed through poor quality glass.

Her mind opened and she saw farther, her vision soaring into the Upper Realms. A landscape of glissenwol caps drenched with light and colours she'd never seen before mingled with the irignol trees, a Realm that stood distinct and separate, yet also intrinsically linked to the two 'layers' below. Her thoughts whirled, clicking through the picture and its implications. Was this how the worlds existed? Not arranged in tiers, with the Dayworlds uppermost and the Darklands beneath and the Seven Realms in between; instead the three existed *in the same place*, impossibly mingled. The draykon's presence dominated the vision, and under its growing power Eva saw the three layers drawn closer and closer together. It began to seem as though the glissenwol trees and the irignol trees and Ana's stone chamber were the same thing, the differences merely superficial.

Movement caught her attention as a slender figure faded into view. A slight female form knelt on the ground perhaps in the Uppers or perhaps in Glour, her grey wings folded over her back as she felt in the earth with deft fingers. She seemed to be only a few feet away; Eva felt that she could speak directly to the woman and she would hear. The ground glowed in the same way as the draykon bones, throwing out a strong silver light that illuminated the young woman's face. Her features were familiar...

Energy flexed under Eva's hands and the vision faded as her mind was drawn back to the draykon. The smooth, polished surfaces of the draykon's bones had vanished, along with the searing heat. Muscle, sinew and hide built under her hands with incredible speed; within minutes the skeletal structure had

256

disappeared and a vibrant, vigorously healthy draykon crouched in its place. Eva gasped for breath, torn between wonder at the beast's pure magnificence, and sheer terror at its drenching power. There wasn't the smallest chance that she and Ana could control this beast, but it was too late now to reverse Ana's deed, too late...

Griel's tall frame burst into her field of vision. He struggled with his wife, trying to wrench her away from the draykon's form. She resisted, laughing.

'Griel, we've done it! It's really alive!' Her eye fell on Eva. She was elated, beyond even her own control, but she still thought she could prevail against this beast.

'Now, Evastany! Before it is fully awake!' Eva felt her try to focus her summoner's will on the draykon, felt her try and try again as each time her will slipped off its polished mind like water over glass. She worked on, undaunted, until Griel's attempts to detach her from the beast finally broke in upon her concentration.

'Ana, this is enough. Stop now! You cannot handle this creature.' Griel picked her up and hauled her away from the draykon. She looked at him in puzzlement.

'Even you, Griel? You have been with me since the beginning. Why this, now?'

'We've overreached ourselves, we were crazy to think—' A crashing sound interrupted Griel as the stone chamber shook violently. The draykon was stirring into wakefulness, flexing its wings. Ana fought her way out of her husband's arms, biting and scratching at him. He fell back, helpless, wearing an expression of raw despair as he watched his wife run towards the draykon.

As Ana passed Eva, her hand shot out and fastened on Eva's arm in a grip of iron. Too startled to react, Eva found herself dragged bodily along as Ana raced to position herself directly underneath the draykon's head. Belatedly, Eva fought to free herself, but Ana was too viciously determined; her strong fingers dug painfully into Eva's flesh, her fingernails ripping through cloth to pierce skin. She grabbed Eva's free arm with her other hand, pinning her in place as she turned to face the draykon.

Eva sensed waves of Ana's will bear down on the beast, strong and masterful. Ana's nails bit harder into Eva's skin as she ruthlessly tightened her grip.

257

'You *will* help us,' she hissed, her face close to Eva's ear. The draykon, still weak and disoriented, had barely moved. If there was any chance that Ana's crazy plan might succeed, it would have to be now. It was like trying to dampen an inferno by stamping on it, but Eva could think of nothing better.

She joined her efforts to Ana's, reinforcing the deranged summoner's will with her own. Ana laughed delightedly, but Eva could feel the futility of it. Even combined, their willpower barely touched the powerful force of the draykon's mind. They danced in the face of destruction like flies, and were brushed aside with fitting indifference.

Ana finally seemed to realise her predicament. She began to gasp, sobbing with the effort to prevail. She was muttering something over and over under her breath: 'No, no, no, no... you're mine, you're *mine...*'

Footsteps beat behind Eva, then strong hands closed over hers, pulling them away from Ana's grip. Eva's concentration shattered and her will fractured into pieces. Ana struggled on alone as Tren half-carried Eva as far away from the draykon as possible. They fell back against the wall, both gasping for air. The draykon slowly raised its head, blinking its golden eyes, and the ceiling vanished, melting away as if it had never been. Through the new gap Eva could see a hazy pattern of glissenwol trees that wavered like water.

The beast's scaled hide shone green and blue in the white moonlight now streaming into the room. Its head moved sluggishly, its long snout opening to allow its flickering tongue to test the air. Claws as long as Eva's forearm flexed against the stone floor, grating horribly. It stretched out its long neck, rose on its haunches and let out a shattering roar.

Tren was dragging Eva towards the door, but she could barely move, so mesmerised was she by the draykon's presence. And its *mind*. It had intelligence, far more than any beast she'd encountered. Its thoughts were muddled, but only with long inaction; its mental processes were growing clearer by the second. She did not even need to reach out to it to feel its mind: it imposed its will upon everything around it with casual arrogance.

'It's not an animal,' she whispered, awed.

'What? Eva, please. We have to get away from here.' Tren

258

was pulling at her, and she knew he was right but she couldn't obey him. Not even when the fabric of the room began to ripple and shiver, similar to the Lowers' behaviour when the light began to change. But the white moon overhead remained constant. Eva felt the closeness of the other worlds, pulsing behind the flimsy fabric of the Lowers as if they sought to break through.

The draykon was nearly fully alert now, its movements growing quicker and sharper. Its attention turned to the small figure of Ana standing at its feet. It opened its mouth slightly, revealing the glitter of teeth as its body tensed, ready to strike. Eva screamed a warning, but it was futile. She couldn't possibly reach Ana in time.

She had forgotten about Griel. He emerged from the shadows, launching himself at the spot where Ana stood. Ana fell, screaming with rage, just as the draykon struck. Its powerful teeth ripped through Griel's body with appalling ease. The sorcerer didn't make a sound, just crumpled to the floor and lay still. Ana bent over him, weeping and screaming, oblivious to the renewed attention of the beast crouching over her.

It braced itself to strike at Ana, but then it stopped, distracted. The disruption in the weave of the world intensified so fast that Eva felt suddenly nauseous, sensing the fabric of the worlds fraying as though a large hole were being torn through. A figure appeared, a faint outline that grew rapidly more solid. It was the slight, winged female Eva had glimpsed walking in the Uppers. As her form solidified, Eva realised, to her complete astonishment, that she recognised the woman's black hair, grey wings and clear grey eyes.

Llandry Sanfaer.

Llandry collapsed onto the stone floor, curled up in obvious pain. She was panting, hyperventilating, her small body shaking uncontrollably. Eva rushed forward, kneeling at her side, trying with word and gesture to soothe her.

Llandry finally sat up, still shaking. She seemed so fragile, a mere wisp of a woman wracked with pain. Eva hovered over her, unsure how to help her. She realised belatedly that the stone chamber was disappearing around them, replaced with a spreading forest of glissenwol caps. The change radiated outwards from the spot where Llandry sat trembling, her eyes taking in the transformation with complete incomprehension. She was changing the Lowers in the same way Ana had done; the way Eva had done when she'd held an istore piece in her hands. But the imposition of her will over her surroundings seemed involuntary. How could she not even know what she was doing?

Then her trembling intensified once more, shaking so hard that Eva was filled with serious alarm. She gripped Llandry's delicate frame, trying to support her, talking to her soothingly. Tren knelt now on her other side, helping to steady her. His eyes met Eva's, betraying a helplessness that matched her own. Despite their efforts, Llandry collapsed back onto the stone, curling herself around her belly. Then she screamed, shockingly loud, a raw cry of absolute agony.

27

Llandry felt as though her body was turning itself inside out. The sensation mirrored the way she had felt when she had crossed into the Upper Realm, but now it was infinitely worse. It was a familiar pain; she had felt it before, with increasing frequency since she had discovered the draykon bone, but this bout was extreme; she truly felt that she might break into pieces. She lay curled around her stomach that pulsed with pain, her face wet with tears of shock. She forced her eyes open and found herself in near darkness, surrounded by figures whose faces were obscured by shadow. She closed her eyes again, squeezing them tightly shut like a child hoping it would go away if only she couldn't see it.

She tried to think back. She had left her grandfather's house a few hours ago. Finding herself still too sore to fly, she had walked instead, making her way somewhat aimlessly through Rheas's pretty alpine valley. To her confusion, the mountains had melted away before she had reached them. Glissenwol caps had crowded in upon her in their place, tall and draped with vines, just like the trees at home. This changefulness made her nervous, and she had redoubled her efforts to find a gate to take her home.

Instead of finding a gate, she had found herself back at the site of the skeleton, the one her grandfather said was a draykon.

Its bones drew her in some way that she was powerless to resist. She had replaced the piece she had taken earlier, fitting it back into the map of bones out of some compulsion she didn't understand. Then, as she crouched in the earth with her hands pressed against the bones, she'd felt energy suddenly roar into life beneath her fingers, and a mind flared abruptly into consciousness.

And that was when everything had begun to go horribly wrong.

It had begun with a sensation of tugging, as though hands grabbed at every part of her body and tried to drag her away. It had become extremely difficult to walk. Llandry fiercely resisted the tug, but then the pain hit her. Crumpling to the ground, she had had time to glimpse the world dissolving around her before her vision had darkened and she had closed her eyes.

Now, on top of everything else, she was hallucinating. A voice spoke to her, a deep female one with a refined Glour accent. Peeping through her lashes, Llandry thought she saw Lady Glostrum's face. That was not possible. She laughed weakly, trying to sit up. Dizziness engulfed her and she rapidly abandoned the endeavour. A gentle hand pressed her back to the ground.

'Don't move, Llandry. I think that would be best.'

The apparition knew her name, then. Llandry stared at the face hazily.

'Where am I?' Her words emerged weak and rather slurred. She grimaced.

'You're in the Lowers, Llandry. No, I don't know how you got here. Just lie still.'

'Are you Lady Glostrum, or am I dreaming?'

'No, I'm really here.' Llandry opened her mouth but Lady Glostrum cut her off. 'Don't ask; there isn't time to explain.'

A glitter of silver caught Llandry's eye. She turned her head painfully. On the floor a few feet away lay a pool of silver links, in the midst of which rested a round piece of wrought silver. Llandry turned her eyes away but there was a familiarity about the shape of the necklace that tugged at her. She forced herself on to her hands and knees, grimly ignoring the pain, and inched her way over to it. Before she could reach it, Lady Glostrum picked it up. She handed it to her, gently pushing her back down to the ground.

Llandry turned the silver over in her hands. It was slightly oval in shape, engraved with stars. A cavity in the centre had, she knew, once held a piece of istore. She knew because she had placed it there herself.

It was undoubtedly the same pendant that Devary had been carrying.

She hardly knew how to process this new blow. Her mind and body were ripe with so much intense pain, she could barely feel any new stab of affliction. She allowed the necklace to fall from her numb fingers, blinking eyes gone bone dry.

Llandry felt herself nudged from behind. Powerfully nudged, like being kicked by a house. The impact sent new waves of agony through her abused frame and she screamed again. Lady Glostrum's eyes widened and her face turned to ash as she stared behind Llandry.

'Tren,' she said, tightly.

'Right,' said a male voice, then a pair of strong arms were around her, trying to pick her up. Everywhere she was touched her skin *burned*, as if a brand had been applied, and she screamed anew through the rawness in her throat. The man abandoned his attempts to gather her up, mercifully taking his hands away. Llandry ceased to be aware of anything external to her own body. She was wracked by a sensation of lengthening, as though her bones were stretching through her skin. She imagined, distantly, that this must be what it felt like to be racked.

Space opened inside of her and began to expand, pushing her flesh outwards. She felt every second as though she must explode, but somehow she did not. Instead she began to feel strong, impossibly so. She opened her eyes again, and she couldn't see Lady Glostrum anymore. Everything she saw was distorted, out of proportion. She blinked, and her eyes felt strange.

She was nudged again. This time it didn't hurt. Turning, she was confronted with a huge, dark shape, a beast whose scales glittered blue and green in the moonlight. Her vision had somehow sharpened, for now she could discern colours and textures in light that, previously, had seemed near complete darkness to her.

A long snout descended into her line of sight and pushed at

her body. The gesture seemed friendly, like encouragement. Her pain finally ebbed, running off her like water, and in its place she experienced a jolt of energy. She stretched her wings and they expanded, out and out, until they encountered an obstruction.

Trees. Glissenwol caps, the same forest she had been walking through moments before, only now those stout trunks did not seem so tall. In fact the caps now hovered so close she would bump her head on them if she stretched her neck a little. The obstruction irritated her. As if in response to her unspoken command, the trees flickered and dissolved, and open air flooded in upon her. She shouted with joy, stretching her wings to their fullest extent. The wind caught under them and she was aloft, soaring into the sky with a rushing speed which terrified, then exhilarated her. Screaming in pleasure, she turned in the air like a leaf tumbling in the wind.

A terrific roar shook the air and she turned. Behind her flew the blue-scaled beast, rapidly catching up with her. He was larger than she, stronger; the gleam of his hide mesmerised her, shining gloriously with scintillating shades of blue, green and gold. She had never experienced colour in this way before: she could feel each one like a physical sensation, taste the flavours of them on the wind. She circled the creature, enthralled.

A bright flash distracted her, shining up at her from the ground. Her newly-sharp eyes caught sight of the pool of silver lying abandoned behind her, shimmering whitely under the moon. She wanted it. She flew back, covering the distance in seconds. Swooping, she caught it up in her claws. Several tiny figures gaped at her as she hurled herself back into the skies. The shape and scent and sense of their miniature forms was familiar, dragging at her memory, interrupting the wash of colour and sensation that drenched her brain. She paused, beating her wings lazily to hold herself aloft.

An image formed in her mind. A face smiled at her, pale and lit with hazel eyes. The man's brown hair fell over his shoulders. She heard music, the rippling notes of a lyre.

Another shattering roar rent the air behind her. Glittering blue scales hurtled into her line of vision, pulsing with anger. A mind invaded hers, enraged that she could turn her back on it. He was possessive, this wondrous creature; as far as he was concerned she was *his*. She found herself herded away from the

264

figures on the ground, forced up into the air. She screamed her resentment, her teeth connecting with the tough meat of a scaled flank. Then she was away, her smaller size and lighter form speeding her on ahead of the beast pursuing her. All she could think of was that pale face with the brown hair and the lyre's melancholy melody.

Devary lay in the damp grass, dreaming. Time had drifted by him at its own pace, leaving him forgotten: had he lain in the grass for mere hours, or even days? It felt like weeks. He watched insects dance in the twilit skies, absently noting his strength draining out of him in a warm, ceaseless trickle that left his clothes wet and sticky. He had an image of red in his mind, a shockingly bright, wet colour that darkened later to a crusted, rusty brown. He realised, distantly, that he was dying but the knowledge did not disturb him. He waited for sleep.

The insects were changing colour. He noticed a ghostly grey one coming towards him, throwing out silver light. Borne on expansive wings, it grew larger and larger until it filled all of his vision with scales like polished coins. It stretched out its long neck, opened its mouth and shrieked. As it plummeted towards him, Devary noticed a bright silver object clutched tightly in one of its claws. The metal dangled freely, reflecting shards of light from mirror-smooth surfaces that dazzled him. He closed his eyes as the vast shape flew over him, feeling a rush of hot wind in its wake.

He knew he was dreaming when those claws closed gently around his body and he was carried into the air, cradled carefully against gleaming silver-grey hide. The wind whipped around him, tugging insistently at his clothes and dragging at his wounds. Pain lanced through him and he cried out, shifting in the grip of pearlescent talons. His captor flew faster, driving hard into the face of a strong wind. Devary thought he saw another shape not far behind, this one shining in blue and green. He watched lazily as the creature pursued them, beating wings the size of houses.

Abruptly the flight was over. Devary's cloud-coloured dream-beast swooped to the ground and opened its talons, letting him settle into the engulfing embrace of Glinnery's thick

265

blue mosses. Its mouth opened, revealing long, pearlescent teeth; it emitted an ear-splitting shriek as it hurled itself back into the sky. Devary blinked, mistrusting his vision. The beast had vanished into the air, its pursuer disappearing along with it.

Doors were flung open and the sky filled rapidly with winged human figures, chattering in shock and excitement. Devary realised that he had been deposited at the base of Ynara's tree, and here was the lady herself, descending from the heights with her glorious dark blue wings spread wide.

'Oh, Dev,' she gasped, dropping to her knees beside him. She paled to a stark white, looking into his face with the wide eyes of fear. He wondered idly how bad his wounds were. He became aware, distantly, of a warm body clinging painfully to one of his legs. Glancing down, he saw grey fur and a stub of a tail. Ynara prised Sigwide off him, and the pressure eased on Devary's calf and shin.

Aysun came up behind her and frowned down at him. Devary tried a weak smile, but his face wouldn't work properly.

'Right,' said Aysun, slowly. 'Lucky the infirmary's not far.' Devary was suddenly surrounded by people, faces bobbing blearily at him and voices raised in a babble of indistinguishable sound. He felt himself lifted again, and pain radiated outwards from the wound in his belly.

'Dev,' said Ynara's voice from somewhere. 'Where's Llandry?'

He tried to answer, but the sky fell in on him and he dropped into darkness.

28

Nobody moved for a long time after the draykons had flown away. Ana was slumped over Griel's body, as motionless as he. Tren had the vacant look of a man whose world has suddenly inverted itself. As indeed it had. The whurthags had vanished, and a profound silence reigned in the forest that was slowly reverting back to Ana's stone-built chamber.

Eva felt stupefied. It seemed impossible to equate the day's events with anything that ought to be possible within the laws of nature and magic. No matter how hard she pushed her shocked brain, the edges refused to match up. At length she stopped trying. She stood up slowly, careful of her spinning head, and took a few deep breaths. The questions she placed to one side, to be examined later. A more pressing problem was Ana and Griel, if he was even still alive.

Ana looked up as she approached. Her face was initially blank, but when she registered Eva's identity her expression grew harsh.

'I suppose you've come to be kind to me.' She was a mess, her hands and hair stained with blood and her clothes torn. She wore it with a kind of incongruous insouciance, her air defiant rather than crippled. For the first time, Eva truly saw how dangerous she was.

'I was more inclined to arrest you.'

Ana laughed, a high-pitched sound with an edge of hysteria. 'You?'

'Mr. Warvel, actually, as the nearest representative of the Chief Investigator's Office.'

Tren came up next to her and stood looking down at the wreck of a sorceress. 'You're under arrest,' he said gravely. 'Anything to say?'

Ana snarled something inarticulate. She grabbed Griel's body, dragging it close to her own. Then she disappeared.

'Inevitable, I suppose,' Tren murmured.

'Perfectly,' agreed Eva. 'I really must learn how she does that,' she added.

'Add it to the list of mysteries.'

'There's already enough there to keep us busy for a couple of decades, I should think.'

'Then it's lucky that we're young and bursting with energy.'

Eva laughed faintly. 'Speak for yourself.'

Tren grinned lopsidedly. 'I don't think I was, even. I feel at least one hundred and fifty.' He rolled his shoulders, grimacing as joints cracked and popped. 'So... what just happened?'

'Why are you asking?'

'Because if I wasn't dreaming, a girl just appeared out of thin air, transformed into a draykon and flew away. It seemed significant.'

'I mean. Why are you asking *me*?'

Tren smiled tiredly. 'I view you as a fount of knowledge, that's why. If you're as confused as me, that's fine. You can just say that.'

'I have some theories, but I wouldn't like to hazard anything without conducting some research.'

'Admit it. You have no idea.'

Eva grimaced. 'Fine. I'm a useless scholar and I have no notion what in the world is going on.'

'Good. Well said.'

'We can work on that later. The important point is that we have two draykons on the loose. One of them was a bag of bones until today, and the other used to be a human. That's the kind of thing that ought to be reported pretty quickly.'

Searching for traces of her companions, Eva found the shortig cowering beneath a small table that was tucked into one corner of the room. Now that it was empty, the chamber seemed vaster than ever. Her footsteps rang sharply as she crossed the stone floor, the sound echoing off the bare walls. She coaxed the shortig out from his retreat, handing the small, shaking body to Tren.

'Keep a hold of him for a moment, if you will,' she murmured, her thoughts already seeking for Rikbeek. She was distantly aware of Tren's nod as he folded his arms around the little dog, stroking the fur that virtually stood on end with stress.

Rikbeek, predictably, had flown as far away as he could get. He was plastered to the wall near the ceiling, virtually insensible with fright. It took her much longer to soothe him. At last he unsealed himself from the wall and flew down, making straight for her skirts. He hid himself in the folds and refused to move. That was fine with her.

'It's a pity we've lost the book,' she said regretfully.

'Actually, it's not lost. I hid it. I'll take you to it in a moment, but we should search this place before we leave. There might be more books like that one.'

'Good thinking,' she said, flashing Tren an appreciative smile. 'Fortunate that one of us is still in possession of his mental faculties.' To her surprise Tren flushed slightly and looked away. He set off towards the far door, the one that lead back towards Eva's erstwhile prison.

The search was conducted thoroughly, but with the swiftness of weary people anxious to be gone. Many of the books Eva found were copies of common texts, duplicates of many that she herself possessed at home. She found one exception, a half-finished work entitled 'Advanced Workings of the Sorcerous Mind.' No author was listed. Eva discovered it lying open in a tiny antechamber furnished only with a desk and chair. The book lay open, surrounded by pens and pots of ink. This and its unfinished state strongly suggested to Eva that Griel was its author. She took it.

Tren had stumbled over what appeared to be Ana's library. In it were all the core texts on Summoning that Eva had been familiar with for years, along with a few she'd never heard of.

'We'd better take all of those,' Tren murmured, flicking through a small leather-bound volume. 'This one's a novel. I suppose Ana got bored sometimes.' He tossed the book back

269

onto the shelf. 'There's nothing else very interesting here.'

Eva nodded and picked up two of the unusual texts. Naturally they were enormous and staggeringly heavy. She made a pile out of them, adding Griel's book to the top of the stack, and collected them all into her arms.

'Let me,' said Tren. He was already carrying three others that looked at least as heavy, but he insisted on taking Griel's book off her and adding it to his own stack. 'I'm sure we can find a bag or something to carry them in.'

They couldn't, as it turned out. In the end Eva took off the remains of her cloak and fashioned a makeshift one. She watched with misgivings as Tren stubbornly piled all the books into it and hefted it, throwing it over his shoulder.

'It's fine,' he said as she tried to object. She rolled her eyes at this display of machismo but she let him have his way.

'Where's the other book?' she asked. He nodded his head in the direction of the draykon chamber.

'Back that way. I left it in the tunnel.'

'The tunnel?'

He nodded, setting off at a brisk pace. She followed, trying not to wince at the obvious discomfort of the bundle of books on his back. The tunnel proved to be a long corridor only just tall enough for a six-foot-something man to walk comfortably through. It was paved in stone like the rest of the house. Tren paused at the end of it, searching the darkened stonework with keen eyes. Then he dropped to his knees and slid his fingers under the edge of a protruding stone, lifting it. In a hollow beneath the stone lay her satchel and Tren's. She was relieved to find that the book was still inside, unharmed.

'How convenient a hiding place,' she observed.

'Thank you,' said Tren modestly. 'Actually I made it. I didn't have time to be precise about it or I'd have lost sight of Griel.'

Eva chuckled. 'You're an adept student. What of the door?'

Tren stood up again and tugged at the wall over his head. A door opened, illuminating a set of steps that wound upwards into the open air. She followed Tren as he climbed up them, his steps heavy with tiredness. Bartel, somewhat recovered, trotted listlessly at her heels as she emerged into a white sandy landscape.

Tren closed the door behind them. There was the arrow and

the smiling face that he'd described. 'How curious,' she said, confounded.

'I thought I was being so stealthy, following Griel like that. I'm convinced now that he knew I was there. He even found an excuse to pause briefly if I fell behind, to make sure I didn't go through the wrong door. I don't see why he didn't just kill me in the tunnel, if he was going to lure me down here.'

Eva thought fast. 'Odd, but I got the impression he didn't share his wife's fervour for her "project". He probably realised it was headed for disaster. Perhaps he hoped we could tip the scales in her favour.'

Tren shrugged. 'A rational possibility. I suppose we won't ever find out for sure.'

The light changed as he spoke, the moon turning to an unpromising shade of greenish brown. Abandoning her train of thought, Eva looked up into skies that were partially covered with fat clouds threatening rain.

'Why do I get the feeling things are about to turn unpleasant,' she muttered.

Moments later, the white sand was gone. In its place a marsh had emerged, saturated with stagnant water and stinking of decay.

'Ah, yes,' Eva sighed. 'Perfect.'

EPILOGUE

Ynara frowned down at Devary's prone form, absently smoothing the blankets over him. He had been delirious for two days, obviously hallucinating. She hadn't been able to gain a clear picture of what had happened to him and Llandry, despite her repeated questioning. He rambled incoherently about scaled beasts and wings like sails; the word 'draykon' even passed his lips at one point. Ynara thought briefly of the terrific, bestial shriek that had sent her and her husband racing down from their treetop abode to find Devary unconscious at the bottom. An unusual sound it had undoubtedly been, but Ynara did not credit Devary's ramblings. Gracious, the woods were already thick with the sorts of creatures long since banished to the pages of storybooks. Any number of strange, unidentifiable sounds resounded through the trees from the moment the sun rose through to the softest of the dusk hours. Some one or other of those had undoubtedly made that shuddering cry.

Doubt flickered through her for a moment, undermining her certainty. So many supposedly extinct or non-existent beasts had lately emerged, stepping through the gates that still opened and closed themselves with unusual frequency across the Seven Realms. If the muumuk, the whurthag and the gloereme were as real as she, why not the king of them all? Why not draykons, indeed? The thought made her heart beat hard and quick with

272

fear, and she pushed it resolutely away. She had not seen this supposed draykon, and she had been out of her house within moments of hearing that cry. Neither had any of the other bystanders present. The prospect of their simply failing to spot something so enormous was absurd. She took a deep breath, feeling better.

Devary's eyes opened. He had been sleeping peacefully for more than two hours now, and she hoped that the delirium had passed. She bent over him, adopting a reassuring smile.

'Hello, Dev,' she said quietly. 'You're looking a little better. Not so grey in the face. How do you feel?'

'Abominable.' He looked at her quite gravely, no smile tugging at his full mouth or lurking in his eyes. A premonition of disaster tugged at her, Llandry's name hovering on her lips.

'Oh?' she said lightly, smiling. 'The healers dealt very smartly with you. They said you'll be well enough to get up in a few days, if you're good.'

Devary's gaze slid away from hers. Detecting guilt foremost among the misery of his attitude, Ynara gripped his hand hard, forcing him to look back into her face.

'Dev. You must tell me. *What happened to Llandry?*'

He turned red first, then paled abruptly. 'She got away. I think.'

'You *think?*'

'I... yes. We were on our way back to you. We stopped for a few hours on the southern edge of the forest. We were attacked. Ynara, some of them were from Glinnery.'

She could have shaken him, injured or not. 'Never *mind* that, Dev. Tell me about Llandry!'

Dev hurried on, painting a horrifying picture of the fight under the glissenwol caps and Llandry's escape. Her stomach clenched with fear when he spoke of the two winged men who had followed her into the skies.

'That was the last I saw of her,' he finished. 'After that, I lost the fight. I woke up back over the border in Nimdre, with someone standing over me. Not one of the original attackers. Tall man, grey hair, obviously a sorc. Pair of whurthags at his heels.' His words were growing faint with the effort to speak, but she didn't care. She levelled her coldest stare at him and waited.

'He found the pendant and took it off me. Disappeared. All
273

of them did, left me there. I must've passed out after that.' He subsided into silence, struggling a little to breathe. Ynara felt torn between sympathy and a fierce desire to kill him herself.

'Dev, this can't be right. If you were left in Nimdre, how did you get to my tree?'

Devary repeated much of the same nonsense he'd talked in his delirium. She shook her head impatiently. 'A draykon came out of the skies and carried you back to my house? That's absurd, Dev, you must see that. What really happened?'

He looked at her helplessly. 'I swear, Ynara, every word I've spoken is the truth.'

She stood up, disgusted with him. 'Get some sleep.' She left the room without looking back.

She found Aysun bent over his work table. Since Devary's return he had been closeted in here hour after hour, working constantly at a complex device whose function she didn't begin to understand. That was all right. She had long since stopped trying to grasp the intricacies of her husband's inventions; it was enough that they satisfied and exhilarated him.

Set into the top of this contraption was a ring matching one that Llandry wore. He had given her that ring when she was five years old, and she never took it off, but neither she nor Ynara had ever realised that it was more than a trinket. Aysun had recently told her, rather tersely, that this ring was a twin to Llandry's and would be instrumental in finding her — as long as she was still wearing her own ring. Ynara hoped fervently that she hadn't lost it.

She slid her arms around his waist and hugged him from behind. He paused to pat her hands, but he didn't turn around. She realised, with a growing sense of trepidation, that something was different about him. Each time she had entered this room she had found him bent intently over his machine, working at a feverish pace. It had been frustrating him because it ought to have pinpointed Llandry's vicinity within an hour or two, but it had given him nothing. She recognised his relentless attitude as born of fear: fear that Llandry had lost her ring, fear that the machine was malfunctioning. Fear that he would fail in finding her.

Now his feverish energy had drained away. He was leaning on the table, braced on his two large hands, his head bowed. She released him and turned him gently to face her.

'Aysun?' She searched his face uncertainly. His expression was closed, unresponsive. 'Did you find her?'

'Not exactly.' He spoke with difficulty, his jaws fiercely clenched. 'I think I know why it won't show me her location.'

'Oh?' Ynara tried to keep her voice light, but it was hard. She had never seen him like this before.

'The machine cannot find her because she is no longer within its range.'

'You mean... she's dead?'

'That, or she has gone off-world.'

Ynara blanched. She knew that, to him, off-world was as good as dead. Ever since his father had stepped through to the Uppers long years ago, and never come back.

'Llandry... she wouldn't do that, Aysun. She must remember what you've always told her about the dangers up there. Perhaps the machine...' She trailed off helplessly. Aysun wouldn't want to believe it either. If he would rather believe Llandry to be off-world than that his machine was at fault, he must have sound reason.

'She may not have done so deliberately. Possibly she was taken up there by someone else.' He looked down at her. At last the iron in his face softened and he gave her a look of love. 'I'm going after her, Ynara.'

Ynara knew what a concession this was for him. He had always refused to have anything to do with the Upper Realms. He hated his wife's sorcerous abilities, and she had exercised caution in displaying them around him. She had not gone back to the Uppers after her one visit there, because it had caused him such intense fear she hadn't the heart. And he had prevented Llandry's joining the summoner guild, knowing that the profession would periodically carry her off-world. His dread of it was too wholly understandable, and her heart contracted with love at his courage.

She gripped his shirt. 'I'm going with you.'

He shook his head, gently disengaging her hands. 'Ynara. You know you can't. Glinnery is in turmoil. It needs its Council of Elders, present and active.'

'I don't care! I'll resign, someone else can take over. I want my girl.' She felt like sobbing, but she angrily blinked back the tears.

He cupped her face, kissed her gently. 'I don't want to take you up there with me. I need to know that you, at least, are safe.'

'How am I to know that *you* are safe?'

'I'll be fine.' She snorted, unable to think of a suitable reply to this piece of fatuity. He wrapped her in a tight embrace, rocking her slowly. 'What if she finds her way home? She'll need someone here to welcome her. To help her, if she's in trouble, or hurt.'

Ynara felt wretched. This was an argument that struck at her painfully, as of course he knew it would. The prospect of Llandry returning home, possibly injured, to find nothing but an empty house was devastating.

'And Devary still needs tending,' he continued.

'He can rot,' she said curtly.

Aysun tutted disapprovingly. 'You mustn't blame him. His wounds are proof enough that he did the best he could for her. You and I are really at fault; we should never have let her go.'

Tears escaped from under her tightly-shut lids. She blotted them on his shirt front.

'Make sure you come home,' she whispered fiercely. 'If I lose both of you...'

'I promise.' He pulled back enough to look seriously into her eyes, and she nodded. She knew he'd do everything in his power to keep his word.

Nonetheless, when she watched him leave a couple of hours later, she couldn't shake the feeling that her world was on its way to a disastrous end.

Eva sat alone in the private parlour of a wayside inn not far from Westrarc. Having bathed, washed her hair and dressed in clean clothes, she felt considerably improved. Now if only she could eat, she might feel more like her former self.

Her former self. For a moment, she thought longingly of the days — not very far distant — when her job as High Summoner had consisted mostly of administrative and ceremonial duties. She had been free to divide most of the rest of her time between social occasions and her lovers. Or, more recently, social events and her fiance. It all seemed such a long time ago, but in fact it had taken a shockingly brief time for her life to become a succession of disasters, afflictions, dangers, staggeringly difficult problems and fiendishly obtuse mysteries. She didn't really miss her old life — she'd felt herself slowly stagnating in her enclosed world — but this was taking excitement a little too far.

'I suppose I won't be bored,' she sighed, pushing listlessly at the freshwater fish that lay on her plate. It was quite well cooked and the sauce wasn't bad, but she couldn't force it down. The prospect of her return to Glour City weighed heavily on her mind. As soon as she returned she would have to see Numinar Wrobsley; he deserved to know the circumstances that had led to the death of his wife. She would have to alert the city to the impending draykon problem — for doubtless they had not seen the last of those creatures — and it would fall largely to her to find a way to deal with it. That would be a tale difficult to tell.

Worst of all, she would have to tell Ynara Sanfaer what had become of her daughter. This was a task that lay heavily upon her. She had no explanation to offer to Ynara, no theory at all as to how, or why, or even *what* had really happened during that chaotic hour in the Lowers. This, also, it was down to her to discover.

The door opened, interrupting her reverie. Tren stepped into the room, looking a little shy. He too was freshly scrubbed, his hair curling damply over the collar of his newly-pressed shirt.

'I hope there's plenty of food,' he said lightly, 'or I might be forced to eat one of these chairs.'

Eva turned up the corner of her mouth briefly, waving a hand at the dishes crowding the table. 'I think the innkeeper emptied the village for us. Help yourself.' She pushed her own plate away, abandoning the struggle.

'Not eating?' Tren looked at her with concern.

'I can't seem to face it,' she admitted.

Tren seated himself on her left and surveyed the table. 'Perhaps a poor choice, that's all. Why don't you try some of this white stuff? That looks harmless. Or, look, baked gloren. You could manage that.' He pushed dishes towards her, trying to tempt her, but the mixture of smells was off-putting.

'Are you going to mother me, Tren? I warn you, I am quite unmotherable.'

Tren ignored her, serving out a small piece of baked gloren

277

on a clean dish. He placed it in front of her, together with a new fork and spoon and a napkin.

'Here is the deal,' he said seriously. 'For every two forkfuls that you eat, I get to eat four. I hope you're willing to sacrifice yourself just a little, or I may starve to death before I reach Westrarc.'

'You're not heading back to the City?'

'Not yet. I'm going to see Mrs. Geslin. Start eating.'

Eva wanted to resist, but she couldn't help chuckling. 'Very well.' He smiled as she picked up the fork and took a mouthful.

'I was thinking,' she said after a moment. 'I have no explanation for Griel's control over those beasts. He was supposed to be a sorcerer, not a summoner. But it's possible that he didn't mean to kill Ed. Or Meesa. You remember he said the whurthags got away from him sometimes? Perhaps his control over them wasn't always that good.'

Tren glowered at his plate. 'That doesn't excuse it.'

'No, it doesn't. Besides, Ana was bloodthirsty enough for both of them.' She remembered Ana's casual order to kill Tren and shuddered. 'There's one thing that still puzzles me, though.'

'Only one?'

She smiled briefly. 'There are a lot of outstanding questions, yes. I'm thinking of Griel's extra abilities, though, and Ana's absurd strength as a summoner. And her disappearing act. The istore isn't explanation enough — once the draykon woke all of the bones had been restored to the skeleton, but Ana's abilities were still staggering without it. I think their enhanced abilities must be closely linked to spending time in the Off-Worlds.'

'You mean that being in the Lowers amplifies magical ability? That's already confirmed, isn't it?'

'Yes, but I think extended exposure is significant. Years ago, when I used to spend too much time down there, I could feel the change in myself. I felt progressively closer to the fabric of the realm, and I could manipulate beasts with greater skill because I felt increasingly like I was one of them. That's probably the real reason why I alone have a gwaystrel; I was the only one to break the rules that badly.'

'Ha,' said Tren. 'So much for the perfect peeress.' He set down his fork and rested his chin in his hand. 'So if the istore — the *draykon bone* — offers a similar amplification effect when

278

worn next to the skin, what does that mean?'

Eva didn't need to spell it out. The implications were clear: no other Lowers beast was known to have so powerful an effect on humans who wielded their bones or their hide. If the draykon bone was the sole exception, that suggested they were fully immersed in the Off-Worlds; born of the fabric of those Realms, part of it in a way no human could ever be. Wearing a piece of their bone was like wearing a shred of the realm itself.

'In effect, they are sorcerers too, with strong instinctive abilities. Remember how Llandry-as-draykon vanished in mid-air? She was crossing into a different realm. Perhaps the Uppers, or the Middles. She didn't need a gate.'

That triggered another recollection in Eva's thoughts. When she had touched the draykon, she had seen through the realms and grasped the truth: that they were not layered as their common names suggested but existed in the same space. She opened her mouth to share this thought with Tren, but she was interrupted by voices talking loudly in the hallway outside their parlour. One of the voices was familiar.

'I think the cavalry's here,' she said, with a small smile. The door was flung open and Vale walked into the room.

'Eva!' She found herself pulled out of her chair and roughly enfolded in an embrace. Vale began to scold and praise her by turns, apparently undecided whether she was a heroine or a villain for her reckless behaviour.

'Are you hurt? Anywhere? In any way at all?' He checked her over quite carefully, heedless of the room filling up with his men.

'I'm fine,' she said, pushing him away gently. 'I've an awful lot to tell you.'

He nodded. 'Your carriage is waiting outside.'

'Mine? How did you know I'd be here?'

'Fin told us which way you'd gone. We've been checking every inn, village and wayside tavern we've passed on the way out from Glour City.'

'What if you hadn't found me?'

'Then we were going down after you. I brought sorcs with me, summoners, people who hit things with sticks, the whole lot.'

'So this is a rescue mission.'

'Potentially. Only of course, you don't need rescuing.' He

279

seemed to remember Tren, belatedly, and looked around for him. 'Where's Warvel? I suppose he survived?'

Eva glanced around. Tren's chair was empty. 'Alive and well as of a few minutes ago. He must have slipped off somewhere.'

Tren had hidden himself so thoroughly, in fact, that he could not be found anywhere. Eva smothered her disappointment as she left the inn on the way to her carriage. The filthy clothes she'd been wearing when she emerged from the Lowers had been burned, on her request, and her few remaining possessions had been loaded up already. She had instructed that the books be placed inside the carriage itself, so she could keep an eye on them on the journey home. The air was crisp, so she had hastily purchased a new, thick woollen cloak from the landlady. It was an inelegant garment, but she welcomed the warmth as she crossed the courtyard.

Footsteps rang on the cobblestones behind her and a hand gripped hers.

'Eva, I'm sorry. I didn't realise you were — I mean — of course you would want to get home as soon as possible.'

She didn't. Actually, she was peculiarly dreading it, but she said "yes" anyway. 'Will you be in Westrarc long? I'm going to need your help convincing the Guardian that I'm not crazy.'

'I'll be a few days with Ed's mother, probably. Then I'll be coming home.' He glanced over his shoulder as Vale emerged from the inn and made his way in their direction. 'May I speak with you alone for a moment? Really briefly,' he added, seeing her hesitate.

'Of course,' she said graciously. She smiled at Vale as they passed. 'I'll join you in a moment,' she murmured, touching his hand briefly.

Tren led her back inside the inn, into the private dining room they'd shared. He stood for so long, looking at her without speaking, that she grew confused and a little impatient.

'Tren, it would be rude of me to keep the carriage waiting long.'

'Oh — yes, of course. I'm sorry.' He stared at her again. 'I just... I just wanted to ask. Will I be seeing you again?'

She frowned slightly, uncertain what he was getting at. 'Didn't we just agree on that? I hope you aren't planning to abandon me to my fate. Without your corroboration, I'll be locked up in the asylum within a week.'

'Yes, I... suppose so. But what I really meant was — was —'
He stuffed his hands into his pockets and looked at the floor.
'May I visit you? In a purely social way?'

'Oh. Well, yes, if you'd like to. You know where I live, of
course.'

He didn't. As she gave him her address he nodded solemnly,
eyes fixed on her face as if he was engraving it on the inside of
his brain. He didn't say anything else.

'I'd better go, then.'

'Yes,' said Tren. He opened his mouth to speak, hesitated,
and shut it again. 'Safe journey home,' he said with a brief smile.
Then he was gone, darting through the door as if keen to escape.

When she reached the door herself, he was nowhere in sight.
Tucking her hands into the folds of her cloak, Eva walked slowly
back out to the carriage where Vale waited to take her home.

More Stories by Charlotte E. English:

The Draykon Series:

Draykon
Lokant
Orlind
Llandry
Evastany

Seven Dreams

The Tales of Aylfenhame:

Miss Landon and Aubranael
Miss Ellerby and the Ferryman
Bessie Bell and the Goblin King
Mr. Drake and My Lady Silver

www.charlotteenglish.com

Made in the USA
Las Vegas, NV
25 June 2023